P9-CRW-870

Murder on Music Row

MURDER ON MUSIC ROW

A MUSIC INDUSTRY THRILLER

STUART DILL

JOHN F. BLAIR, PUBLISHER
Winston-Salem, North Carolina

JOHN F. BLAIR
PUBLISHER
1406 Plaza Drive
Winston-Salem, North Carolina 27103
www.blairpub.com

Library of Congress Cataloging-in-Publication Data

Dill, Stuart.
Murder on music row : a music industry thriller / by Stuart Dill.
p. cm.
ISBN 978-0-89587-565-5 (hardcover : alk. paper)—ISBN 978-0-89587-566-2 (pbk. : alk. paper)—ISBN 978-0-89587-567-9 (ebook) 1. Sound recording industry—Fiction. 2. Murder—Investigation—Fiction. 3. Nashville (Tenn.)—Fiction. I. Title.
PS3604.I456M87 2011
813'.6—dc22

2011019977

Cover design by Brooke Csuka
Interior by Angela Harwood and Debra Long Hampton

10 9 8 7 6 5 4 3 2 1

To Maral Missirian-Dill, my devoted Armenian hokijan,
in this, our twenty-fifth year of marital bliss

PRELUDE

Nashville, Tennessee
Grand Ole Opry House
Wednesday, March 9, 2011

At 9:05 in the morning, a black Ford Expedition with Tennessee plates and an Avis bumper sticker slowed to a halt in front of the guard shack on the frontage road behind the world-famous Grand Ole Opry House. The driver rolled down his window and read the name Tanner Maddox on the breastplate of the overweight rent-a-cop approaching. Security was lax.

"Good mornin', kind sir. Can I get that name, please?" Tanner said in his thick country drawl as he lifted his clipboard.

"Alex Alejandro," the man in the truck said with a distinct Mexican accent.

"Alrighty, let me see here. Oh, yeah, I got you. Says here you're Ripley's guitar tech."

"That is correct."

Tanner looked up and grinned. "Ripley must be a helluva guy to work for. I mean, as big of a superstar as he is, you can tell he's not above his raisin'—he still knows where he came from. Am I right?"

"That is correct."

"I knew it! Hardest-workin' man in show business, but that's what it takes. You can tell he doesn't take any of his success for granted. I mean, he drove up here at eight o'clock this morning. The man's already been inside working for an hour. Out late last night, up early this morning—takin' care of business. One helluva guy!" Tanner took a breath. "Now, do you know where you're goin'?"

"Yes."

"Mighty good. Okay, how 'bout I put you down there in the lower lot, just off to your right?"

"Thank you."

"No problem. No problem at all. You have yourself a great day, Mr. Alejandro. Tanner gave a toothy smile, but the driver failed to return the favor.

The man parked, opened the SUV's back hatch, and pulled out a large, triangular anvil case. Even though he had never set foot on the property, he knew every inch of its layout. He had even studied pictures of the flood of 2010—ten months earlier—that showed the Opry submerged in water chest deep from the swollen Cumberland River. During the flood, Pete Fisher, the Opry's general manager, had taken a tour of the lobby in a canoe. After $20 million worth of repairs, the state-of-the-art refurbished interior showed no water damage.

The man walked beneath the covered awning marked "Artist Entrance," gave his name to the woman at the desk inside, and followed the back hallways toward the famed Opry stage. There were no metal detectors or security cameras to worry about. Neither Tanner nor the woman at the Artist Entrance asked for a picture ID. They just needed a name that corresponded with one on their clipboards. They marked through it with their yellow highlighters, and that was the end of the background check. The name Alex Alejandro, called in by a miscellaneous Music Row insider, had found its place among the pages of working technicians, grips, runners, camera operators, assistants, and other personnel.

The man turned right at the first hallway near the newly renovated dressing rooms. Instead of going directly to the stage, where he heard plenty of commotion, he veered off to a side door leading to the floor of the concert hall. Still carrying the anvil case, he walked through the unlit side aisle of the celebrated auditorium and into the vacant front lobby. Only the eyes of the late, great Hank Williams Sr. and the legendary Bill Monroe took notice from the walls as the man climbed the stairs to the mezzanine and hid behind the front tiered retaining wall.

He peered from the darkness onto the brightly lit Opry stage, framed by the legendary barn-shaped backdrop. Bright lights bathed a circle around the center of the stage like a halo marking sacred ground. Lights hung on grids from the ceiling, the footlights were lit, and portable "green screens" on large rollers stood ready. Several movie cameras were in position. Folks rushed around in every direction while a small group gathered at center stage, talking among themselves under the glare of the spotlights. Sitting on a stool in the very center, wearing dark pants, boots, a white dress shirt, and his signature black cowboy hat, his hair dirty blond, his chiseled face showing a permanent five o'clock shadow, was the most powerful star in country music—Ripley Graham.

The man in the balcony checked his watch and then methodically opened the anvil case. Inside was a dark green, lightweight sniper-style FX-05 assault rifle. He loaded the thirty-round detachable box magazine and tightened the scope. When he looked back toward the Opry stage, he saw Ripley talking with two gentlemen—one of whom he recognized from his prep work—within the cluster of people at center stage. The marksman carefully set the firearm on the railing. He patiently looked through the scope as people zipped in and out of his sight line. His target was blocked. He waited. Then his line cleared, the red dot locked onto the target, and he fired.

Part I
Sound Effects

CHAPTER 1

SIX DAYS EARLIER

Nashville
Music Row
Thursday, March 3

Judd Nix reached for the large canister of Maxwell House coffee on the top shelf in the break room, put a filter into the industrial-sized coffeemaker, added four heaping scoops of coffee and some water, and placed the empty glass pot on the Bunn burner. Fresh coffee started brewing almost immediately.

It was a ritual Judd had actually started enjoying over the last six months. As an unpaid intern at Elite Management and the youngest person at the firm, the twenty-three-year-old wanted to make an impression as a guy willing to pay his dues to make it in the music business. Since September, when Simon Stills had given him the opportunity to work at Elite—the most prestigious personal management firm in country music—Judd had vowed to be the first person in the office and the last to leave, even when he was the only one without a salary. Not that anyone would ever say anything. He just hoped someone noticed. Besides, there were advantages to being the first to arrive. Judd knew which managers got to the firm early and came in fresh even if they had been working with clients late the night before. And he noticed which ones could not burn both ends of the candle and were ineffective until after lunch. Judd could tell which assistants were fiercely loyal to their bosses and arrived early and eager to organize the ammunition needed by their warriors. He also recognized which assistants were battle worn and couldn't care less if their warriors died on the daily battlefield.

It amazed Judd what people would say to him as they started to pour their first cup of coffee. He couldn't tell if they were simply more vulnerable before they took that initial sip or if it was human nature for them to spill their guts to someone lower on the corporate totem pole than they were. The intern was a safe ear. He knew the players but had no ability to use their words against them. Judd had become a sounding board for those who, once their day started, never were asked their opinion but only got dictated to. He would never miss the opportunity to be first in the office, to brew the coffee—and to hear the scoop from middle management before the office got distracted, manic, and guarded.

It also gave him the chance to read the daily industry news from the trade publications. As the second pot started to drip, Judd looked at the morning's *Billboard.biz Bulletin*, a daily report of entertainment news from around the globe that was sent to high-powered music executives. He had picked up a copy off the fax machine, but most of the managers in the firm got it zapped directly to their laptops, BlackBerrys, iPhones, iPads, or Droids and read it before they reached the office. Each morning before making copies for the staff, Judd read it religiously, trying to memorize names, firms, and important deals. He recognized the names of people who had called the office or were in regular correspondence with Simon and other managers at Elite. It was the best tool for him to figure out who was who—and who were the most powerful. Simon Stills was frequently quoted as the personal manager for Ripley Graham, the artist continuing a meteoric rise over North America.

Ripley Graham was on the brink of breaking records by country and pop artists in the new digital age. Following the release of his second album, *Rip Tide*, his total CD sales had now hit 10 million. Impressive, but nothing compared to his absolute dominance in the new world order of the music business—e-commerce. Ripley was now the best-selling digital artist in music history, counting more than 25 million legally purchased downloads.

And that was just the tip of the iceberg. Major record companies were trying to recover from near collapse caused by their inability to adjust to the public's demand to consume music online. The "i" generation—with its mass acceptance of iTunes, iPhones, iPods, and iPads—had broken the music industry's oligopoly and price fixing and brought it to its knees with the simple click of a mouse. The iConsumers rejected the unwanted twelve-song CD and demanded the ability to download and move music instantaneously from their laptops or tablet PCs to their iPods, so they could customize their own playlists at a price of ninety-nine cents per track.

In this environment, Ripley had emerged as the undisputed icon of online marketing—the embodiment on how music and celebrity could be branded, distributed, and monetized on the Web, a blueprint for how the music industry could save itself. Ripley had more than 28 million Facebook friends and over 7 million Twitter fans—the "Ripples" who followed his every Tweet. That was more than Justin Bieber's 6.7 million "Beliebers." Only Lady Gaga surpassed him with 8 million "little monster twitters."

With his sophomore release last year, Ripley Graham had become the Internet's most streamed artist, boasting more than 50 million songs played. *Spinner.com* placed him in its "Top 10 Most Web-Savvy 'Net-Working' Musicians" and crowned him number one in total "Net Worth." *Billboard Magazine*'s year-end edition named him Artist of the Year and printed "Ripley Believe It or Not!" on the announcement cover. In January, he made the cover of *Rolling Stone* for the second time. The issue's five-page spread was entitled, "Strapped to the Supersonic Nose Cone of Twang—America's Country Icon: Ripley Graham."

This morning's *Bulletin* had Ripley in the headlines again, announcing that this evening was opening night of his North American tour. Judd read it carefully—every word.

Billboard.biz Bulletin™

YOUR DAILY ENTERTAINMENT NEWS UPDATE
THURSDAY, MARCH 3, 2011

Ripley Graham "Rips It Up" with North American Box-Office Record

Chip Avery, Nashville

Ripley Graham continues to reach new heights at a record-breaking pace, so it's no surprise he has added another milestone to his list of accomplishments. Graham now holds the record for the most tickets sold in advance of a major concert tour in North America. Tonight, Graham kicks off his much anticipated "Rip It Up" tour in Greenville, South Carolina. Before the first hit song is sung, the tour has already generated $51 million in advance sales, the most in U.S. box-office history. With over 850,000 tickets sold to date, the 60-city tour has surpassed the box-office landmark for a multi-city tour held by Bon Jovi, Bruce Springsteen and Madonna. Michael Jackson held the advance sales record for a series of concerts at the same venue. Jackson sold out all 50 concerts slated for London's O2 Arena in 2009 by selling 190,000 tickets in two hours but tragically died less than three weeks before the first performance.

Graham's remarkable feat was underlined by Pollstar editor Gary Bongiovanni: "Ripley is now posting numbers here in the U.S. with the likes of touring titans such as the Rolling Stones and U2. He's closing in on the $100 million gross threshold without playing his first note."

Historically, the Rolling Stones still hold the number-one position in gross touring revenues. Their 2005–7 "A Bigger Bang" tour brought in an estimated $554 million worldwide. U2's current "360" tour is expected to hit $700 million by the end of 2011.

When asked why his next studio album, also entitled *Rip It Up*, was not yet released, Graham said at a recent press conference, "I hate to start the tour without the release of my third album, but I'm still looking to make some last-minute changes."

When *Bulletin* asked Galaxy Records Nashville President James Clark, Clark said, "Ripley says it's close to completion, but as a record company we never want to be heavy-handed and force a release if it could jeopardize the integrity of the creative process."

However, rumors continue on Nashville's Music Row that Graham has actually finished or nearly finished the album but is withholding his music from Galaxy Records in an effort to renegotiate his recording contract.

Rumors, Judd thought. *How strange.* He knew Simon and Ripley weren't happy with the record company, and that was the reason for the delay. He knew it, and he was just an intern. It proved once again that the most useless phrase in the music business was, "Just between me and you." No one in town could keep a secret. Everybody in Nashville either sang or talked for a living.

"Good morning, Judd."

Megan Olsen was Ripley's day-to-day manager. Her business card read, "Associate Manager/Elite Management," but the word *associate* didn't do her justice. She reported to Simon, who was Ripley's personal manager and one of the two founders of the company. Simon had several high-profile clients, but Ripley was clearly his bread and butter. Simon's role was to see the big picture—to guide and direct Ripley in all major career decisions. He built a team of professionals around Ripley to help him. Simon was that team's quarterback. He oversaw every aspect of Ripley's career and negotiated his major contracts. Megan, on the other hand, took care of the details of Ripley's day-to-day needs. She had no other client. She set Ripley's daily schedule, coordinated his travels, confirmed his tour dates, and approved his interviews. She was even known to set his wake-up calls and deliver his dry cleaning. For Megan, Ripley Graham was 24/7. Over the past four years, Simon and Megan had worked with Ripley and garnered unimaginable success.

They had the respect of the entire industry. They were a good team.

"Good morning, Megan. I didn't hear you come in."

"Just got here. Coffee ready?"

"Yep." He poured her a cup.

Judd felt sure Megan hadn't noticed, but he had been smitten with her from the moment he arrived. Megan had a subtle beauty. She had short wheat-colored hair, fair skin, thin lips, and high cheekbones. She was probably five or six years older than he was but looked like she could still be in college. Her Scandinavian lineage was detectable in her poignant blue eyes. But it was her inner strength that Judd admired even more. Megan was courteous and pleasant but held her cards close. Judd had watched closely over the past six months how she juggled the demands of her job, stayed on task, and never seemed to get rattled. She was respected but hard to read—and, as Judd had found out, even harder to get to know.

"You take it black, right?" Judd asked.

"Always."

Judd handed her the mug, hoping she'd linger for some morning conversation. He wondered if he had registered with her on any level. Megan took a sip, smiled, and thanked him—which was all he needed to get him through the rest of the day. He turned and poured a cup for himself.

Then Megan said, "Simon wanted me to tell you, with Alice now on maternity leave, you're coming off the bench until she returns."

Alice Cartwright was an office assistant assigned to Simon's desk. For the last year, everyone had known of her intention to start a family. Her due date was March 15. Yesterday had been her last day in the office, at least until July.

"Really?"

Megan picked up one of the *Bulletins* Judd had laid on the counter. She read the headlines while conversing. "Starting today. Simon spoke to Brad before leaving to see Ripley in South Carolina."

Simon had started Elite with Brad Holiday eighteen years ago. No hirings or firings occurred without their mutual consent. Judd pounded his right fist into the palm of his left hand, like a baseball hitting a catcher's mitt, and mustered a surprised but confident response: "I'm hired?"

Megan took her nose out of the *Bulletin,* looked up at Judd, and grinned. "Yeah, you're hired. They decided not to call in a temp service while Alice is out. Simon told Brad he wanted to get you off the 'intern payroll.' "

"What payroll?"

"I think that was the point. Like they say, 'Preparation meets opportunity.' Alice got pregnant and you get into the music business."

Trying not to show his excitement, Judd said, "So we'll be working together."

"Well, officially, you're assigned to Simon's desk as an assistant to him. But to some degree, yes."

"That's great!"

Megan couldn't keep from smiling. "I'm happy you think so."

An awkward pause followed as they both stared into their coffee cups.

Megan broke the silence. "Don't you have a part-time job somewhere else?"

"Yeah, I've been waiting tables downtown at Morton's three nights a week."

"Well, maybe now you can give that up."

"Yeah, maybe. Hey, whatever you and Simon need me to do, I just want you to know I'm ready to jump in and swim like Michael Phelps!"

Megan gave him a quizzical glance. His quip didn't land even a chuckle. Instead, Megan smiled politely and said, "Well, that's good to hear, I think." She thanked him again for the fresh brew and walked out of the break room toward her office.

Okay, Judd thought, *maybe I was pushing a little.* He looked down at the *Bulletin* and read the headline again. *Still, this is a fantastic start to the day.* Ripley Graham was the most successful artist in the entire world, and he had just become the aide—no, the assistant—to Ripley's personal manager. He pumped his fist in excitement and let out an animated, "Yes!"

CHAPTER 2

Greenville, South Carolina
BI-LO Center

Simon Stills, showing no outward signs of opening-night stress, leaned against the wall of the concrete corridor somewhere in the bowels of Greenville's concert and sports arena while keeping a watchful eye on the dressing-room door bearing the name of his mega-client, Ripley Graham.

Simon had always worn the role of personal manager well. As everyone rushed around him, he kept a calm, easy disposition—effortlessly advising, directing, joking, telling people no, and then smiling as if he had somehow done them a favor. Simon had an air of confidence but wasn't stiff. He was personable, grounded, and very hip. His brown hair was cut short in a stylized messy look. His standout feature was the thick mustache cascading over his entire upper lip, then moving out across his cheeks. It flirted with a handlebar upward turn but was prematurely cut short. Its density would challenge the hairy upper lips of music legend David Crosby and the *Today* show's Gene Shalit. When Simon smiled, all the recipient saw was his mustache expanding and a flash of white teeth. Simon never wore boots or a cowboy hat—just blue jeans that fit well and extremely clean sneakers. Because it was opening night, he wore his lucky Buffalo Sabers jersey.

Simon rarely, if ever, raised his voice, which was nearly unheard of in his line of work. He had no worry lines, which was also unusual, since he rarely slept. Years ago, an admiring employee had given him a small plaque that read, "Insomniac: Someone with a memory and a conscience—they both keep you up all night!" In Simon's case, it was an obvious truism.

"Simon, can you take another look at this? The box office is calling for it."

Simon looked down at a list just handed to him by Trey Michelson, better known as "Pumpkin," Ripley's tour manager. As Ripley's personal manager, Simon didn't have to attend every single concert. Over the years, he had put together one of the finest road crews in the business to execute the endless tasks required to put on a show. Pumpkin was at the helm. Now, thanks to wireless communication, Pumpkin could call in any road problem by texting or e-mailing from his BlackBerry, and Simon could respond immediately without having to be in the same state. But Pumpkin always took advantage when Simon did attend shows. And Simon would never miss an opening night.

Simon's eyes were small, clear blue, and piercing. They seemed much older than he was—windows to an ancient soul. He quickly studied the nearly one hundred names on the comp list for tonight's concert—the list of complimentary tickets given away by Ripley and Simon to VIPs, family and friends of tour members, record executives, corporate sponsors, key media, and the like. The list was always a nightmare, due to last-minute changes, unexpected requests, and limited space.

Tonight, the United States senator from South Carolina and his wife, who were cleared on the original list, had shown up with their two daughters—daughters no one in Ripley's camp knew were coming. Pumpkin had heard the conversation earlier on his two-way radio as the senator's car arrived at the secured gate off North Academy. Gate security radioed the backstage production office asking what it should do about the extra passengers not on the list. Every crew member with a two-way radio could hear the senator's driver in the background barking out the obvious: "There must be some mistake!"

Inside the production office, Pumpkin had blurted out an

exasperated, "Yeah, there is! The senator picked the wrong night to try to throw his weight around. There's the mistake." Then he took his radio from his belt and directed the gate security officer. "Gate 1, this is Pumpkin in Production." Pumpkin had a thick country accent and loved talking on the two-way. Seeing him in person made his nickname obvious. He was only five foot five and had long, straight red hair usually pulled back into a ponytail. He was as wide as he was tall and had grown up on a farm outside Hattiesburg, Mississippi. It was easy to assume he had been "Pumpkin" all his life. When he spoke, it was a mix between Rush Limbaugh and Larry the Cable Guy. "Just tell the sen-a-tor that we've got security issues, too! Hold the car at the gate until I holler back."

Simon spoke without looking up at Pumpkin. "Is this the final?"

"Oh, yeah. We're packed in. You couldn't squeeze Little Jimmy Dickens in this place."

"You can't find anything for the senator's guests?"

"No way. Fire marshal won't let us open any more seats—the handicapped sites are overflowing, and they can't watch from the side wings because of the pyro. Yeah, we've got two seats for the senator and his wife, no problem. But it looks like a double-dip night at the Dairy Queen for his girls."

Simon's eyes nearly burned a hole in the list while he thought. Then he looked up and said, "Tell the building manager that because of United States security issues, the Secret Service will not allow us to say how many are in the senator's party. Have them set up four nice cushioned folding chairs on the riser just behind our sound console in the center of the arena. There is enough space. Don't let the fire marshal tell you it can't be done, because it can. And make sure they use the real nice folding chairs—I know they have them. Then tell the senator we want him behind our console barricade because his safety is paramount. That way, he'll feel special, and no one will complain about the folding seats."

"All right," Pumpkin said hesitantly. "I'll see what I can do."

"It'll work," Simon responded in a firm but friendly tone.

Pumpkin turned and waddled down the concrete corridor toward the backstage production offices. Simon heard him speaking agitatedly into his radio as if he were on his CB talking to a host of fellow truckers: "Tell the senator to hold damn tight. It's easier to get an act through Congress than what I am about to do to get his *ass*-ets into some seats!"

Simon smiled, then tapped the shoulder of Ripley's bodyguard sitting outside the dressing-room door. "How are you doing, Jerome?"

"Fine, I guess." Jerome, one of two personal bodyguards who traveled with Ripley, looked like an out-of-work football player as he stretched his hands over his head without getting up from his chair.

"Sorry, pal, didn't mean to wake you."

Jerome chuckled. "No problem, Simon."

Simon rapped his knuckles on the door, giving it a double knock while cracking it open. "We're about forty-five minutes out, Rip." There was no reply. "Ripley," he said louder, "did you get that?"

From a back room came, "I heard you."

Simon closed the door and nodded to Jerome.

In the bathroom, just off of the large central dressing-room lounge, Ripley Graham stood alone, half-naked, talking to himself in the mirror—a ritual he performed prior to and after every concert. His hands had an ever-so-slight tremble as they held onto either side of the porcelain sink. He bent his elbows and slowly leaned in even closer to the mirror, staring. He didn't move for some time.

How odd, he thought. *So this is what it looks like to be an icon. People stare at this face all the time, blown up in photos, magazines, and posters—this close, maybe closer. They stare at this face from two inches away. They see every divot, pore, hair, and grain of skin. They are closer to this face than I am, and yet they can't hear this voice in my head. I am alone. No one else can get inside. No one can hear me right now.*

In keeping with his ritual, he took a deep breath and said out loud, "Just stay quiet."

CHAPTER 3

London, England
Kensington

Warren MacCabe's home phone rang. It was nearly eleven o'clock on a cold and dreary evening.

"Yes," MacCabe answered in his thick Scottish brogue.

"Warren, it's Tommy," the man on the other end replied in an American accent. Then, after a short pause, Tommy Strickland asked, "Are you asleep?"

"I was indeed starting to think about it," the Scotsman answered.

The distinguished chairman and CEO of Galaxy Records Worldwide, Warren MacCabe was not accustomed to being awakened after hours. And if he was, it had better be for good reason.

Tommy Strickland, president of Galaxy's North American operations and the second-most-powerful executive in the company, had flown in from New York the day before. And he certainly had reason enough for calling. In his normal secretive tone, he said, "We have a serious situation in Nashville. We must address it."

"Tonight?"

"Yes."

"Really?" MacCabe sounded surprised. "Well, then, let's talk online, on our secured site."

"I'm sorry, but we need to meet in person. Trust me. This is serious, Warren. It cannot wait until morning."

"How serious?"

Strickland hesitated, then answered, "It threatens to compromise the merger discussions. Everything could completely unravel here at the end. I suggest we meet in the privy garden in thirty minutes."

Strickland's words made MacCabe sit up in bed. "I see. Give me an hour."

CHAPTER 4

Greenville
BI-LO Center

The entire backstage area had now been cleared, as was the custom, making it ready for Ripley to walk from his dressing room to the stage without being seen. Pumpkin stood near with a small flashlight in his hand as Simon cracked the door and said, "Rip, we've got to go."

A moment later, Ripley bolted out, head down, showing no emotion. He put his black cowboy hat on and started toward the stage.

"You okay, pal?" Simon asked as Pumpkin and Nate, Ripley's other bodyguard, stepped out in front. Jerome and Simon flanked Ripley on either side as they walked. "You look a little pale."

Ripley, not looking over, said, "Just get me to the stage and I'll be fine."

"Sure," Simon said. "We were talking after sound check today about the problem with the opening stunt. We're all concerned that it never worked well at the rehearsals. So this is what we came up with. Before you step onto the launching pad under the stage, take your boots off. No one will ever notice that you're not wearing them with the cannon blast, the pyro blazing, and you being propelled into the arena. I promise."

Ripley kept walking and gave no response.

Simon continued, "Then we'll kill the lights as you free-fall to the stage and hit the safety net. When you land, two production hands will be there with your boots. They'll help you put them on and get you over to the drum platform. If we do it like that, there is no way your boots will get tangled in the net like they did today at sound check."

Ripley turned to Simon and said, "So you didn't get it worked out this afternoon, did you?"

"Yes and no. They found the smaller netting we need, but they can't get it here until tomorrow."

"Simon, I'm not talking about the damn safety net," Ripley said. "I'm talking about my career. You didn't get anywhere with the record company, did you? I bet James Clark didn't even call you back. He's probably out playing golf while we're here working our asses off. It's a disgrace to country music that he heads a Nashville label."

Simon, changing his tone, said, "Sorry. For some strange reason, my mind was on the superhuman stunt you're about to try in front of fifteen thousand screaming fans for the first time, and we don't know if it works. Actually, I spoke with Clark, and there is no movement. We are at a total impasse in trying to renegotiate your record contract. Clark said no to our request to allow you to ultimately own your recordings—the future reversion clause—and no to an increased royalty rate, and he is adamant that this record will be marketed out of Nashville, not out of New York like we've demanded. I told him that was unacceptable, and that our position remains the same—you will not turn in new music to Galaxy until all these issues are resolved. I made it clear we will continue to hold out, and that even though the music tracking sessions are done, you're not singing a note on the new album. We're boycotting."

Ripley exploded. "Who the hell does he think he is?"

Simon answered, "Well, he thinks he's the president of Galaxy Records Nashville."

"I am selling more damn records than any other human on this planet, and he still thinks I'm some backwoods country hillbilly that doesn't get the scam he's running. People have got to know, Simon. They think I'm making all this money off record sales, and the truth is the record company is stealing me blind! No other industry in America could get away with this. Where are the labor laws? They don't exist for me, Simon. I'm a prisoner being screwed by the record company, and no one's got my back. I want a new contract!"

"Ripley, look. The truth is, you have a signed, legally binding deal in place, and James Clark is not in any position to give you anything but the record-company line. He is not going to turn this over to New York and undermine his own existence. We're going to have to go above him—to Tommy Strickland in New York. Ultimately, we may have to go to Warren MacCabe himself."

Ripley wasn't really listening. "My signed deal is not industry standard anymore. The music industry is in shambles. I'm now the standard bearer. And in the meantime, Galaxy is giving Clark bonuses out the ass, like he had something to do with my success. He wasn't even with the company when I signed my record deal. Did you know he just bought a Hummer?"

"I didn't know that."

"He is so damn arrogant, man. He's just a washed-up record producer whose dad was some legendary songwriter fifty years ago. Nashville needs label presidents that understand marketing. Today, it's all about marketing. That's the difference between Nashville and New York. Nashville still thinks it's the music. New York knows it's marketing, and they have the cash to back it up. It's the marketing of the music that makes hit records. And because of that blind ignorance, Nashville keeps making record producers the presidents of labels. The president of a record company doesn't need to know how to *make* a record. The president of a record label needs to know how to *sell* a record. The last thing Nashville needs is another old record producer promoted to label head so he can drive around Music Row in his goddamn Hummer screaming, 'Look at me. I'm the man!'"

They reached the backstage landing area, from which several ramps led onto the back of the stage itself and a carpeted walkway underneath. A printed sign with an arrow pointing in the direction of the carpet read, "Launching Pad." Pumpkin, staying close but definitely not getting involved in the conversation, checked Ripley's ear monitors and the battery pack on his belt and then handed Ripley his microphone. Ripley ducked and followed Jerome's lead, walking half bent down the carpet, weaving through the metal scaffolding that held up the stage, now directly above him. Simon flanked Ripley, while Pumpkin and Nate brought up the rear. Ripley continued to talk, not at all concerned that the setting was less than ideal for an important career conversation.

"Simon, it's all about New York. James Clark is out, as far as I'm concerned."

"Ripley, the problem is that Galaxy headquarters doesn't think Nashville has a marketing problem. You're the best-selling artist in the system. Warren MacCabe in London has been quoted as saying, 'James Clark is a marketing genius.'"

"The only marketing being done is out here on this tour. Clark didn't create this. Come on Simon, you know the scam. They pay me 12 percent—12 percent! That means they take 88 percent. Hello! It's an old-school deal, Simon. And worse, before they pay 12 cents on the dollar, they charge me back for every expense they can think of, including all the recording costs. And once they recoup, they still own my record. That's like paying off the mortgage on your home, but the bank still keeps the deed. They are flat out stealing from me, and you know it!"

Just then, the house lights went out and the capacity crowd erupted in screams so loud no one could hear himself think. Pumpkin clicked on his flashlight and helped Ripley to his position on the pad that in seconds would thrust him thirty feet into the air to open the show.

Ripley grabbed Simon's shoulder and leaned toward him, yelling so he could hear. "I'm not taking my boots off—I'm planning to kick some ass!"

Simon yelled back, "Fine, it's your show!"

"I'm not talking about the show. I'm talking about Galaxy, Simon."

"Got it. I hear you, Ripley. But it's not that easy."

"Yes, it is! I want James Clark gone. I don't want him listed anywhere in the Galaxy Records company directory. Marketing genius, my ass!"

Simon leaned close so Ripley could hear him over the crowd. "You're saying you won't record your vocals until James Clark is fired?"

"If that's what you heard, then I guess that's what I said!"

"Come on, Ripley, we've been over this. We want to eventually own your records and in the meantime get a better royalty rate, especially for digital. Basically, it's a new day, and we need a new deal. That's all. It's not about getting one guy fired. It's about getting more control and making more money."

Ripley shot back, screaming over the crowd, "Let me be clear. Ripley Graham is not giving Galaxy any new music until James Clark is gone!"

The crowd was so deafening that Simon gave up on the conversation and simply mouthed his response: "Okay, okay, I hear you."

With that, Ripley gave a thumbs-up to Pumpkin, who grabbed his two-way radio and screamed, "Now!" Then Simon watched Ripley suddenly disappear as he was catapulted up through the stage. When the spotlights caught him airborne way above the arena floor, he had his boots on—and fifteen thousand fans completely lost their minds.

CHAPTER 5

London
99 Kensington High Street

Warren MacCabe entered a large gray building through the main entrance on Derry Street, even though the inscription by the door was for 99 Kensington High Street.

As the elevator door opened on the seventh floor, it revealed a marvelous rooftop restaurant. MacCabe walked past the unattended hostess stand toward the empty bar with a breathtaking view of the Royal borough of Kensington and Chelsea to a narrow stairway leading down one flight. A rather large man who looked like a rugby player in an ill-fitting suit stood guard.

As MacCabe approached the man, he asked, "Is Tommy already downstairs?"

"Yes, sir."

MacCabe descended the stairs and walked into an isolated outdoor Garden of Eden, as if all of a sudden London had vanished from the cosmos. He was surrounded by palm trees, running fountains, and multicolored tiled walkways spreading out in all directions underneath trellises of grapevines that looked as old as Europe itself. No one was in sight as he passed several live flamingos standing undisturbed in their private paradise.

In the center of the rooftop garden beside a stone statue stood a man dressed completely in black.

"Tommy," MacCabe said in his stern Scottish voice, "what is this all about?"

"We must make a change in Nashville quickly. We must force Clark out."

"What? Why would we ever do that? He *is* Nashville, as far as I'm concerned."

"We have serious pressure," the American answered.

"Have you gone mad?" MacCabe said, raising his voice. "We are now seventeen days and counting. We can't make a change in Nashville. Not right now! Not seventeen days before the vote. The Germans could walk. We just told them our original projections were off, and they took it well only because they know we have a new Ripley Graham release in the fourth quarter. We need stability in Nashville, or it will jeopardize all that we've worked for."

Tommy Strickland shot back, "And I can promise you there will be no new music from Ripley until Clark is gone. I am sure of it. How does that forecast look now?"

"Jesus Christ! You can't feed the beast now. It will only increase its appetite. We've got a merger to protect. Think about the long-term implications, Tommy. It would be a disaster!"

"Damn it, Warren. I am thinking of the merger. That's all I'm thinking about."

"What will the Germans do if Ripley makes a public statement saying his project is delayed?"

"The point is that there is no merger without a Ripley record this year, and there is no Ripley record with Clark as the Nashville president. We don't have the luxury to consider long-term implications. We have just over two weeks. Our only play is to fire Clark and keep Ripley happy."

MacCabe took a deep breath and walked toward one of the fountains. He stood there for what seemed an eternity, then walked back to

Strickland. "Are you absolutely sure Ripley will withhold the record?"

"Yes."

MacCabe took another deep breath, then asked, "Who would you have replace Clark?"

"Doug Tillman, head of marketing in New York. He is young and ambitious. Simon and Ripley like him. I'll move him to Nashville. He'll report directly to me."

"And you think this offering will be enough?"

"I'm positive."

MacCabe paused. "It's a slippery slope, Tommy. Working with artists is like trying to keep the gates closed to Jurassic Park. Those creatures are cute when they hatch out of their eggs, but they grow up, and if they escape they will eat you alive."

Strickland didn't respond.

"What do we tell the Germans?"

"Whatever we want. As long as they get a record this year, they won't care who is manning the Nashville store."

"Tommy, here is your problem. You live in New York, and you don't understand Nashville. Because I am a Scot, I have a better understanding of the South than you. The South is of Scots-Irish descent. Nashville is nothing more than a clan. Country music is not a musical genre. It's a culture, a clan. I understand the clan mentality. First of all, clans always stick together at all costs and respond only to their own kind. Secondly, a clan is suspicious toward outsiders. And third, clansmen never take kindly to rulers who are forced upon them. I'm a Scot. I know this."

Strickland's large vein running the length of his forehead bulged. He hated being talked down to by MacCabe. Trying to hide his anger, he asked, "So what are you saying?"

"I'm saying that Doug Tillman, a New York marketing executive, will never last in Nashville. That is what I'm saying."

Strickland snapped back, "Ripley likes him! He'll last long enough to get the merger through. We'll deal with any consequences later."

"From the outside, it looks easy, Tommy. But once you get inside, it becomes complicated. Doug Tillman doesn't speak their language. He doesn't understand their culture. He won't know their history."

"Damn it, Warren. We're talking about two weeks!"

"You're betting on two rather large assumptions. One, that the beast will need only one feeding. And two, that the Nashville clan will not revolt when an outside ruler is forced upon it."

"Two weeks, Warren! We must fire Clark. It will buy us the time we need."

"And how do you suggest we get rid of Clark? He knows this game, and he won't go without a fight."

"That's my job. You don't need to know the details," Strickland said in an icy tone.

"I'm the chairman of this corporation, and I sure as hell do need to know the details," MacCabe said.

"Everyone has their pressure points, their little indiscretions."

MacCabe closed his eyes. "Jesus, Tommy." Then he paused, looked at Strickland, and said, "If it has to be done, I will do it."

"I can handle it, Warren."

MacCabe snapped back, "I said *I'll* do it!"

Then MacCabe turned his back and started walking away in the direction he had come. Abruptly, he stopped and, without turning his head toward Strickland, said into the night air, "I'm not going to assume it's over. Beasts have insatiable appetites, and clans have a long history of revolting. For your sake, Tommy, let's hope I'm wrong on both accounts."

And with that, he exited the privy garden.

CHAPTER 6

The Next Day

Nashville
Elite Management
Friday, March 4
7:59 A.M.

There it was again. One line on the Elite switchboard had been ringing since Judd keyed into the office. It was not being picked up by the overnight answering service. Judd figured it must be Simon calling him early on his own extension. He sprinted down to Simon's office and picked it up.

"Simon?"

"Judd, I had a feeling you'd be in the office by eight. Is anybody else in yet?"

"No, sir. Not yet."

"Hey, how many times have I told you to lose the 'sir'?"

"Sorry, Simon. Got it."

"Thank you. So, I'm still in Greenville. I'll be back in Nashville tomorrow and in the office over the weekend to catch up."

"Got it."

"I told Megan to have all my calls sent to you. I want to bring you on board and see how you handle things while Alice is out. You can leave the heavy lifting to Megan, but I'll need you around 24/7, especially in the office to handle my calls. Are you game?"

Judd thought, *Megan is always right!* He tried to play it cool and adopt a relaxed tone. "Perfect."

"Okay, we'll talk more about it when I'm back. In the meantime, I need you to do me a favor. Where are you, exactly?"

"I'm in your office."

"Good, go to my computer."

Simon had a slick, modern glass desk supported by black metal rods with crisscross wiring and a matching work station on the side that held his computer. Judd pulled Simon's black leather executive chair up under the work station and said, "Okay, I'm at it."

"I know you're one of those young techno-savvy guys," Simon said. "You know how to forward my calls from the office phone to my cell when I'm traveling, right?"

"Sure."

"Also, sometimes I record my calls just to make sure I don't miss anything. Have you done that for me before?"

"Yes. Alice showed me."

"Really?"

"Yep," Judd answered. "You go to Tools, then Phone Log, then hit Hard Drive Recorder."

"Exactly. It records my calls, and I can pull them off my media player if I want to, just like a daily podcast. Go ahead and do that for me."

"Yes, sir. No problem."

"Who's 'sir'?"

"Uh, sorry, Simon."

"Thank you," Simon said, obviously pleased with his newest prodigy.

"No problem."

"Did you pick up my voice message from last night?"

"No. I just walked in when I heard your extension ringing."

"Yeah. I need your cell-phone number, by the way. Can you put that in my Microsoft Outlook?"

"Sure."

"Good. And go ahead and get my new voicemail messages and put them in my Tasks in Outlook so I can access them from my BlackBerry."

"Okay."

"And one more thing. I need you to set up a team conference call today. You'll need to secure the Elite conference-call extension and send everyone the access code. We need to go over some details regarding next week."

"Okay."

"This Tuesday night, we've got the gala that Galaxy Records is throwing at the Bridgestone Arena to commemorate Ripley's being named *Billboard*'s Artist of the Year. And Wednesday, he's shooting his next music video out at the Grand Ole Opry House."

"Wow, that's a schedule."

"Yeah, it is, always. And I still don't have a production book for the video shoot. I'm nervous about an early call time for Rip on Wednesday morning after the gala. He's already running on empty."

"Can you push the video back?"

"Now you're thinking like a manager! I told Rip we should push it back, since we'll have a late night the night before, but he'll have none of it. He keeps telling me he'd rather cancel the gala, which we can't do. He's in love with this video concept and is determined to knock it out on Wednesday. You know Ripley."

"What's the video about?" Judd asked.

"The treatment is on my desk. You can read it. It's a cool idea. Ripley's publicist, Janice Burns, and Megan have talked to the production company more than I have. They have all the details. So on the call this morning, it should be you, me, Janice, Megan, and Pumpkin. I especially need Janice on the line. She was here last night but took an early flight home, so she'll be in her office soon. Once you have everyone on the line, call me and patch me in."

"Sure, what time?"

"See if everybody can talk at 10:30 Central, 11:30 Eastern."

"You got it."

"Also, the most important thing: Be on the lookout for a call from Tommy Strickland. I called him in New York late last night, right after Ripley got on stage, and his service said he was in London. I left a message and told him it was urgent. He may call back anytime. It's already after lunch over there. So whatever you do, make sure you find me when he calls. Wherever I am, patch him through."

"No problem."

"And make sure the hard drive is recording all calls."

"It's on now."

"Okay, great. That's it for now. Your days of brewing coffee are coming to an end. Let's get to work."

Judd smiled and said, "The first one here still needs to brew the coffee."

"Well, it better be instant." And with that, Simon was off the line.

Judd hung up the phone, walked to the fax machine to find the *Bulletin,* and headed to the break room to start his morning ritual.

Billboard.biz Bulletin™

YOUR DAILY ENTERTAINMENT NEWS UPDATE
FRIDAY, MARCH 4, 2011

Galaxy Records Reports All-Time Low

Edward Weintraub, London

Galaxy Records announced yesterday in London that profits from its fiscal year ending March 31, 2011, will be down but not as badly as some financial experts had predicted. The new forecast by Galaxy, the third-largest record company in the world, is being buoyed by a 9.7 percent increase in digital sales, higher than expected but not high enough to ward off another year-end loss. This is the third time the company has downgraded its projections from its initial forecast.

Warren MacCabe, Chairman and CEO of Galaxy Records Worldwide, said, "This new forecast is due in large part to softer sales than expected in the U.S. during Christmas, as well as a slower economic return in the Asian market." Even with the profits warning, MacCabe went on to say the company is turning the corner and noted the significant increase in digital sales. He plans to address head on the overall decline in full-

year profits at the upcoming Board of Directors Meeting and Annual Shareholders Meeting in London.

The announcement stirred analysts to question if a merger is imminent. It has been rumored for years that German-owned Luxor Entertainment Group, the second-largest record company conglomerate, has been courting Galaxy. A Luxor/Galaxy merger would create the largest record company in the world.

Tommy Strickland, President and CEO of Galaxy North America and the man seen as the undisputed second in command, flew to London from New York to join MacCabe for the announcement. When asked about merger rumors, Strickland said, "There are absolutely no discussions in that regard. Like everyone, we are affected by an ever-changing marketplace and the world economy. The earlier projections were off the mark, but as far as the health of the company, the future of the company, we are absolutely on target."

After the announcement, the London Stock Exchange did not respond positively to the news. Galaxy's stock dropped dramatically, losing 15.5 percent on the day to reach an all-time low.

Galaxy's stock is at rock bottom? Judd thought. *How is that possible? Ripley Graham is the best-selling artist in the world, and the record company is in trouble?*

CHAPTER 7

Nashville
Elite Management
10:35 A.M.

Judd heard a beep, after which all the team members announced themselves as they joined the conference call.

"Megan."

"Pumpkin."

"Janice."

"Okay, you guys are all here," Judd said. "Let me get Simon on the line." A moment later, he was back. "Simon is now on the call with you as well."

"Let's talk about next week," Simon said.

Without further protocol, Janice began hogging the conversation. As an independent publicist for the last twenty years, she had perfected the gift of gab. Janice never missed an opportunity to expound her political point of view or to give her daily commentary on the state of country music and its most visible people, always with a healthy dose of sarcasm. To her credit, she was self-deprecating and just as hard on herself as she was on others. She considered her sense of humor to be highly evolved and commonly misinterpreted.

Others in the music industry felt sure Janice's sarcasm was a defense mechanism from years of seeing too many of her talented artists fall short, unprepared for the pitfalls of the business. Then, five years ago, Simon had invited her to see a live performance by a new artist he had recently signed. At the time, it seemed just another Music Row showcase for another dreamer who would eventually end up frustrated, angry, and jaded. Janice was already home for the evening, and a rainstorm was pounding the city. She was tired and had decided not to venture back downtown. Then she checked her voicemail and heard Simon say, "The Ripley Graham showcase is tonight at seven o'clock at Douglas Corner. He is the real deal, Janice. I'm going to put the best team in the business around him, and I want you on this project. I'm telling you, for your sake, don't miss this!" She hung up the phone, got her umbrella, and for some unknown reason drove downtown in the pouring rain. To this day, she was not sure why she had gone, but that decision changed her life.

Those who believed in Ripley now had enormous industry clout. The few connected to his career from that initial showcase had become part of a growing legend on Music Row. What had those "core four"—Simon Stills, the one credited with discovering Ripley; Trey "Pumpkin" Michelson, Ripley's first friend in Nashville and now his tour manager; Bob Weber, the retiring president of Galaxy Nashville, who, in the last signing of his career, offered Ripley a recording contract that evening, two months before James Clark took over as president of Galaxy Nashville; and Janice Burns, now the most sought-after PR agent in the industry—seen that evening that no one else noticed? How did they know in that small, dark, undistinguished Nashville club that they were watching the next musical icon? Those were the questions that gave Music Row its mystique and Nashville its nickname, "Music City USA." Answering those questions had kept Janice talking for the past five years. Now, on the conference call, she was ready to expound on the details surrounding the Galaxy gala to be held Tuesday in Ripley's honor.

"The red-carpet entrance will be set up like a regular award show," Janice said. "There will be a barricade on the street side so the fans can't get in the way, and on the other side, against the Bridgestone Arena, you will have press stations roped off all along the walkway. As the celebrities get out at the limo drop, they will file past the press stations and be pulled randomly for interviews. Hopefully, they will have only nice things to say about Ripley. Inside, a huge kabuki screen will cover the far end of the arena, and the red-carpet activity will be projected live from outside. So once the VIPs are in the arena, they will be able to watch the others still outside talking to the press on the red carpet."

"What press has confirmed?" Simon asked.

"Let's see, I've got a current list right here—E! Entertainment, CNN, Fox News, Associated Press Television, *Extra*, ABC, CBS, TV Guide Channel, CMT, GAC, VH1, *Fox & Friends*, Reuters Television, Lifetime Channel, all the local networks, photo stringers for *Parade*, *USA Today*, *In Style*, Associated Press, UPI. And I'm sure that's not all."

"It feels like the CMA Awards," Pumpkin said.

Janice was quick to add, "Well, it's an impressive list, due largely to Ripley's amazing ride but also because of who we have confirmed to attend. On the country side, it will be everybody: Reba (let's see who'll be better dressed, her or hubby Narvel), Dolly (who will be coming alone; has anyone ever seen her husband anyway?), Kenny Chesney (getting a little too much sun on the island, I guess), Rascal Flatts (they are about as country as Larry, Moe, and Curly!), Wynonna (why she asks for diet advice from Oprah, I'll never know; isn't that like asking Hank Williams Jr. to help with your drinking problem?). Let's see, who else? Vince Gill (love Vince, love Vince), Kenny Rogers (I think he's been secretly married to Dolly since the seventies), Martina McBride (too thin, that's all I'm saying), Big & Rich (but not together!), Larry the Cable Guy (whose real name is Dan, so it should be Dan the Cable Guy), Brad Paisley (I was hoping he would leave Kimberly Williams at home and bring Little Jimmy Dickens as his mini-me date). And the no responses are Shania Twain (but we can get her official impersonator, Shania Twin; I'm not joking!), Carrie Underpants, and of course George 'I Don't Do Press' Strait. And the non-country celebs and Hollywood folks are—"

Simon cut her off in midsentence. "Janice, is it possible just to give us the names at this point without any commentary?"

"Sure," Janice replied, sulking. "Uh, Sheryl Crow, Jason Alexander, Uncle Kracker, Kid Rock, Kevin Costner, Kimberly Williams, Jake Gyllenhaal, Carey Mulligan, Gwyneth Paltrow, and Garrett Hedlund."

She could give a woodpecker a headache, Judd thought.

Janice added, "And of course, there are some politicos. The RSVPs are still coming in."

"Gotcha," Simon said. "Has Galaxy given us a script for the evening?"

"They have a tentative script and schedule. Jeff Foxworthy is confirmed to host. The red carpet should be done by seven-thirty. As everyone is finding their seats inside, Foxworthy will open with some jokes and get everyone comfortable. There is a VIP table for Ripley. I think Galaxy is asking Al Gore to sit there as well. Foxworthy will introduce the former vice president, who will speak first, and then 'the Green Professor'—sorry, forgot about the colorful commentary, but let it be said for the record that he is a Democrat, so I am an equal-opportunity offender—okay, correction, 'Mr. Coulda, Woulda, Shoulda' will introduce a seven-minute video presentation that Galaxy has created. It starts with President Obama congratulating Ripley on his varied accomplishments. So, from the very top, we'll show that Republicans no longer have a monopoly on country music!"

"Janice, *please!*" Simon said. "How many times do I have to say this? You're representing Ripley Graham 24/7. I know you have strong opinions of people, but when you talk like that, it makes us all very, very uncomfortable."

After an awkward pause, Janice said, "Fine." She was obviously pissed.

"What happens after the video?" Simon asked.

Janice answered almost in a monotone, "The kabuki screen behind them will drop, revealing a wall holding twenty-five platinum single plaques, representing 25 million downloads. It's ten feet high. I haven't seen it yet, but they say it's impressive. Then James Clark will bring Ripley up to the podium."

As instructed, Janice didn't elaborate further, which created an unexpected pause in the conversation.

Judd took advantage of the break. "Hey, it may be a dumb question, but what is a kabuki screen, if I may ask?"

Pumpkin chimed in with his country twang. "It's a screen made of real light material that is usually hung from an overhead truss. You can project images on it or show lighting effects. But what's really cool is that when you drop it from the truss, it goes to the floor like a bedsheet. A lot of live shows use them to hide the stage or part of a set from the audience. You've probably seen it used in concerts when the lights go out. They hit a pyro blast, the lights come up, and boom!—there's the artist, out of nowhere. Simple trick. They just dropped the kabuki screen."

"In our case, the twenty-five platinum plaques will all of a sudden appear behind Ripley," Megan added. "It will be amazing. Janice, what happens after Ripley gets to the podium?"

"Ripley will say his thanks, and then Vince Gill—did I say I love Vince?—will come up and perform. He has pulled together an all-star band, and they will call up different stars to jam together—mainly Ripley cover tunes. That should be the highlight. And now I'm being told that Galaxy is going to film and record it all. They are telling people it's for Ripley, a personal gift, but I'm sure they're going to try to get clearances and release it in some form in the future."

Simon added, "They'll have to get our approval first, but you know how they are—do it and ask for forgiveness later. I know they've already contacted Jack Sussman and CBS, but that's another discussion." Then Simon's tone became serious. "There is still one major issue we have to address."

"What's that?" Megan asked.

"James Clark."

"He's the president of Ripley's label and the man paying the bill—next," Janice said.

"We must keep him away from Ripley the entire time. They cannot run into each other."

"What? You're joking, right?" Janice said.

"I'm dead serious."

"This party was James Clark's idea. You've got to be kidding."

"Janice, I'm not kidding. It will be a disaster if Clark brings Ripley to the podium."

"Even though Galaxy is throwing this event to honor Ripley as having the most digital sales in music history?"

"Yes. I'd suggest you have Foxworthy bring Ripley onstage. He is the MC. It would be more appropriate anyway."

"I don't get it," Janice said. "Is there some macho BS going on here between Ripley and Clark? I mean, they've just sold 25 million downloads together! And you're telling me somebody is mad at somebody?"

"I can't go into it. I'm just telling you, Janice, as Ripley's press agent, unless you want to have the biggest faux pas of your career, somehow get Ripley on and off that stage without him knowing James Clark is in the building."

"I can't believe we're upset with the record company while we're selling more records than anyone else on the planet."

"Janice, one last time, it is your job to keep James Clark away from Ripley Graham and vice versa. This goes for everyone on the call. Just so I'm perfectly clear, James Clark is not to have any access to Ripley whatsoever. I don't even want him to have a backstage pass. That's all I'm going to say."

"Clark is throwing the party for Ripley, for God's sake!"

"So don't let it become your worst nightmare."

No one dared to say a word.

Then Simon added, "Call's over."

Before Janice or anyone could say okay, Simon was off the line.

CHAPTER 8

Nashville
Music Row
11:30 A.M.

Judd stared at his computer screen, trying to act as if he didn't notice Megan walking toward his work station. She stopped. Judd took a slight upward glance. "Hello."

"Do you want to grab a quick bite to eat?"

"Wow, so I didn't totally *tank* with the Michael Phelps reference? No pun intended."

Megan smiled and shook her head. "No, not totally. But I wouldn't say it was your best line. Besides, this is strictly business."

"Do you think it's okay for both of us to be out of the office while Simon is away?"

"Let's get something fast across the street. I need to bring you up to speed on more details for next week."

"Of course!" Judd nearly took his ear off as he bolted out of his seat while his headset was still attached.

Megan chuckled at the rookie mistake. "Careful!"

Elite Management was on the top floor of Roundabout Plaza, a 205,000-square-foot, nine-story modern structure perceived by some as a cultural bridge between Music Row and the central business district of West End. The roundabout itself was two lanes of traffic at the end of Music Row encircling a ten-ton piece of artwork—*Musica*, or what the locals had nicknamed "Hillbilly Porn." *Musica* consisted of nine enormous nude dancing statues, each fifteen feet in height. Without fail, everyone circling for the first time gazed at the figures, not because they represented "the gods of the muse" but simply because it was downright shocking to see their privates so prominently displayed in the heart of the Bible Belt. Years ago, the roundabout had renovated the area, bringing in a dozen or so new cafés, bars, and coffee shops. The trendy eateries were a fresh facelift to a strip that once housed tacky tourist attractions such as the Automobile Museum, the Hound Dog hot dog stand, and other run-down traps that sold one-of-a-kind souvenirs such as Elvis Shampoo and yellow plastic Conway Twitty Birds.

Judd, unaware that Hound Dog hot dogs had once been an option, followed Megan into McGuinness Irish Pub. Megan noted it was the best place in Nashville to get authentic shepherd's pie. The hostess escorted them to a wooden booth in the back.

When the male waiter approached, Megan refused the menus and took control by saying they already knew what they wanted. "We'll have two orders of shepherd's pie, and I'll have iced tea—unsweetened, please, light on the ice, and extra lemon."

Beautiful, smart, independent—and way out of my league, Judd thought. He wasn't sure if she had a boyfriend or not. He knew someone named Mathew called her often. He also knew that patience was a virtue. He felt the waiter's stare. "Oh, right, Diet Coke for me."

A second server brought two glasses of ice water. Megan held hers up and said, "Well, you formally made it into the house of freaks and are officially one of the zookeepers. Congrats."

"Well, thank you."

"Oh, something important." Megan dug into her purse and pulled out an oversized postcard. "Since you're now on board, I need to give you this." She handed him the card.

"What is it?"

"It's an invitation to Ripley's Mardi Gras party at his home Monday night."

"Are you serious?"

"Of course. Ripley has this party every year—another excuse to spend money, I guess. He usually has about fifty people—staff and celebrity friends. The food's great, and he hires a party company that comes in and organizes some games. It is also mandatory for all team members to attend. Ripley has made that very clear over the past few years."

Judd nodded and read the invitation:

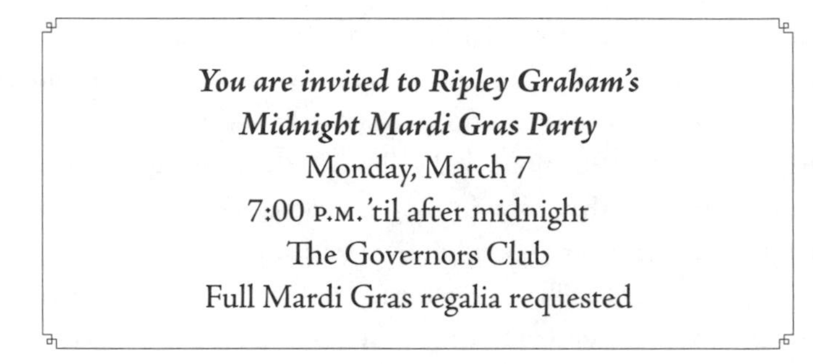

You are invited to Ripley Graham's
Midnight Mardi Gras Party
Monday, March 7
7:00 P.M. 'til after midnight
The Governors Club
Full Mardi Gras regalia requested

"I didn't realize it was Mardi Gras," Judd said.

"Mardi Gras is actually Tuesday, but Ripley likes to usher it in with a party the night before. I guess you wouldn't know the tradition unless you lived in New Orleans or Mobile, Alabama. Besides, we have the gala on Mardi Gras night."

"Mobile?"

"Mobile actually started Mardi Gras. They party all week there as well."

"I never knew that."

"Yeah. Last year, one of the games was Mardi Gras Trivia, so now I know more about Mardi Gras than your average bead-toting party girl."

"Really? Like what else?"

"Ah, now you're going to test me. Okay, let's see. Mardi Gras is French for 'Fat Tuesday.' It's a three-day indulgence, or carnival, ending the Tuesday before Ash Wednesday, the day of repentance. Basically, that means everybody pigs out on that Tuesday. Then you start fasting for Lent."

"That's impressive. And I thought it was a marketing ploy for Bourbon Street to sell more booze."

"My favorite piece of trivia: What does the word *carnival* mean in Latin?"

"A really big boat?"

Megan smiled. "Nope. *Carne vale*. It means, 'Farewell to meat or flesh.'"

"Okay, that's probably more than I needed to know. Speaking of farewell to meat, where is our shepherd's pie? I'm starving."

"Well, you asked. As I said, welcome to the house of freaks."

Then, feeling bold, Judd asked, "Since I'm the new guy, how about I drive you to Ripley's party from work?"

"I don't think so. I have to go home first. And to be honest, I always need my own car—you know, just in case Ripley wants me to run out for any reason."

"I get it. You're on Ripley duty 24/7."

"Pretty much."

That's okay. Be patient, Judd thought. "What a day! Being asked to officially work at Elite. Being invited to Ripley's house. Being able to work with Simon *and* you. Who could ask for more? I feel like I finally found my place."

"Hmm, you sound like Simon." Megan seemed surprised.

"What do you mean?"

Megan hesitated, then said, "Simon has lots of 'life theories,' and one of his more popular ones is that each of us has what he calls our 'safe place.'"

"Really? Where is that?"

"Simon will undoubtedly tell you. He always does. If you haven't noticed, Simon prides himself in taking young guns like yourself and molding them. He's done it for years. He's just as much of a mentor as a manager. You are the newest pupil in a long line of privileged interns."

"I'm starting to realize that. So help make me become a star pupil. What is a 'safe place'?"

"It's Simon's theory. He'll tell you in time."

Judd looked around for a waitress. "Seems like these folks lost the sheep, the shepherd, and his pie."

"Ouch, please stop!" Megan said. "Okay, I'll tell you, if for no other reason than to stop the hopeless jokes. Simon always says that from the moment we're born, we feel separated and insecure and start looking for our 'safe place.' Because artists are most sensitive to this separation, they are especially insecure, and it's our job to help them find their creative sanctuary, their 'safe place.'"

"Wow, that's deep."

"Simon's pretty philosophical, really. I've told him he should write a book about artist management and call it *Simon Says*."

"Well, I'm definitely learning from the best—Simon *and* you."

"Me?"

"Yes, you. Look, the two of you are guiding one of the most exciting careers in music history. As managers, you and Simon are going to be mentioned alongside the likes of Colonel Tom Parker and Brian Epstein."

Megan nearly spewed her iced tea in midsip. "Wow, okay. I know you're energized, but really, I'm not Ripley's personal manager. I'm a day-to-day manager with Elite. That's it, period. And secondly, I know Simon would be very uncomfortable hearing you make comparisons to Colonel Tom Parker and Brian Epstein. I mean, with the Beatles, Epstein practically created what we now call artist management. And Parker took 50 percent of everything Elvis Presley made. That could never happen anymore. That was a different day altogether."

"Well, I think you're being humble. You're selling yourself short. I don't think Ripley would be where he is today without the two of you."

"Judd, you're sweet. And I'm really pleased you're on the team. Everyone has noticed how hard you've worked as an intern to get a shot. But I've got to tell you that, unfortunately, now you're going to see some sides of the business that aren't very pretty. It's definitely not as glamorous as it looks. It can get ugly, sometimes really ugly. There *is* a dark side, and it's real."

"I'm not saying I know what goes on inside the business on a day-to-day basis. But I *have* been here for six months—observing, paying my dues, watching you and Simon. Let me tell you, it is impressive to an outsider looking in. You may not have discovered Ripley like Simon. And you may not officially be Ripley's personal manager. But you're working on his career every day. And it's keeping you busier than a one-armed paperhanger with an itch."

Megan laughed. "My goodness. Where do you come up with these sayings?"

Victory, Judd thought. He loved to see her smile. "All I'm saying is, one day you're going to be a fantastic artist manager in your own right with as many clients as you want."

"Oh, I'm not so sure. The more I see, the more I realize this entire line of work is way overrated."

"Really?" Judd was genuinely surprised. "Because from my perspective, you're headed for greatness. You're next in line. You're sitting in a dream position with all the opportunity in the world."

Megan looked at Judd and smiled. "Look, my job is to take care of Ripley's details. It's not rocket science. Don't kid yourself, most anyone could do what I do for an artist—handle their schedule, their mail, their travel, budgets, paperwork. You just have to be organized. By and large, it's a thankless job. Simon has the job from hell. He juggles the egos of the record-company executives, runs Ripley's team, keeps everyone focused, creates marketing strategies, sets tours, keeps his eye on the big picture, while at the same time trying to keep Ripley's dirty laundry inside the cleaners."

Stunned by her candor, Judd for once had no comeback.

The food finally arrived. Megan took a bite and groaned in delight. "Life's simple pleasures. It's worth the wait."

Judd, still a bit bewildered, answered less enthusiastically. "Saint Patty would be proud."

"The truth is, a manager and an artist are in an extremely precarious relationship," Megan said. "It's always a tightrope. Artists hire managers to give them advice and counsel, to make them rich and famous. At the same time, most artists don't want to hear what it really takes to become successful. They just want to hear what they want to hear. So what's a manager to do, become a yes-man and keep his job or tell the truth, knowing it could get him fired?"

"I'm not saying it isn't a tough gig," Judd replied. "I've seen the endless hours you and Simon put in. I've seen how Simon handles Ripley—at least to some degree. I'm sure he has to judge when to tell him things and when not to. I've heard Ripley get upset, but that's what makes an artist an artist. They're emotional people. They wear it on their sleeves. Still, at the end of the day, it looks to me that Ripley worships the ground Simon walks on."

Megan leaned in close. "Honestly, if there's one thing I've learned, it's that things are never what they seem."

Judd sat in silence, feeling a momentary lapse of gusto. But it didn't last long. He raised his glass of ice water, looked Megan in the eyes, and said, "I think you should take a minute and smell the roses. You, Megan Olsen, are helping to shape the career of one of the most successful entertainers in America ever. And it's awesome."

"Your words, not mine, but thank you just the same." After a minute, Megan added, "I live in Hillsboro Village. Come to my place after work on Monday and we'll drive over to Ripley's together. I'd hate to see the boy wonder make his entrance all alone."

Judd's expression was part exhilaration and part appreciation. He smiled his boyish grin and said, "That would be perfect."

CHAPTER 9

Nashville
Elite Management
2:10 P.M.

"Judd, it's Tommy Strickland on line three," buzzed Ellen, Elite's front-desk receptionist.

"Thanks, Ellen." Judd's gut tightened. *Okay, I can do this.* He quickly picked up the handset and punched line three. "Mr. Strickland, I'm Judd Nix, Simon's new assistant. Simon is out of town, but let me try him on his cell."

"I see. What about Megan, is she in?"

Judd noticed the slight time delay in Strickland's response. They didn't have the greatest connection. *So much for the 'Nice to have you on board' sentiment,* Judd thought. "Yes, she is. However, Simon is expecting your call. He's with Ripley Graham in South Carolina and specifically asked that I try to patch you through. Can you hold for a moment?"

Again, a slight delay. "Megan will be fine. No need to bother Simon."

"Just one second." Judd put line three on hold and quickly dialed Simon's cell phone. It rang . . . then again . . . and again. "Come on, Simon, pick up," Judd said under his breath. The ringing continued, then went to voicemail. "Simon, it's Judd. Tommy Strickland is on the line.

I've got him on hold. I'll try to keep him on the line for a minute to give you a chance to call back." He returned his attention to line three. "Mr. Strickland?"

"Yes."

"I went ahead and tried Simon, but he is not picking up. However, if you'll stay on the line one more second, I'll try him again."

"I'm actually in London, not New York, and it's getting late here."

"What time is it there, if I may ask?"

"It's eight o'clock in the evening."

Judd knew he couldn't keep Strickland on the line for long. "Well, I know Simon is anxious to speak with you. He told me he left you a message last night, or this morning—however that works."

"Yes, it was extremely late."

"So it's a six-hour time difference, then?"

"Five hours Eastern, six Central. Just connect me to Megan, please."

"If you can hold, Mr. Strickland, I'm sure this is Simon phoning in on the other line." Judd put Strickland back on hold before he could respond. He didn't have a call coming in, but he thought it would give him time to try Simon once more. Judd called Simon's cell but again got voicemail. "Damn it," Judd said. He then composed himself and hit Megan's extension. She didn't pick up either. Judd called Ellen at the front desk.

"Hey, Judd."

"Hi. I've got Mr. Strickland on hold. Simon is not picking up, and now I can't find Megan."

"Megan's on her personal call with Mathew."

What? That bit of information hit Judd like a ton of bricks. *Her personal call with Mathew? Who is this guy?* It didn't sound business related. "Okay," Judd said hesitantly, "we need to interrupt."

"Honestly, Megan is protective about interrupting this particular call."

Flustered, Judd said, "Okay, I'll deal with it." He dropped Ellen's line to pick up Strickland's, "Sorry, sir, that wasn't Simon. So sorry to keep you waiting. What number should I have Simon use to reach you in London when I speak with him?"

"Rudd, I thought you said Megan was in."

"I did. It's Judd, by the way." Judd thought Strickland would apologize and say his name correctly, but he didn't.

"Are you going to connect me with Megan, or am I going to have to call back?"

"We're tracking her down now." Judd put Strickland on hold and buzzed Megan again. This time, she answered. Greatly relieved, Judd said, "Tommy Strickland is on hold. He's been on hold for a while. I tried to get Simon twice on his cell, but I can't reach him. Strickland's been asking for you. He's on three."

"No worries. I'll take it."

"Nice guy, by the way."

Judd watched as the blinking line went solid when Megan picked up Strickland. *Real charmer*, Judd thought. He tried Simon's cell one last time but had no luck. In less than a minute, the line cleared. Megan was already off. *That was fast.*

Ten minutes later, Ellen buzzed Judd telling him Simon was on the line.

"Of course he is," Judd remarked as he picked up the phone. "You just missed him," he said to Simon.

"You're kidding! I hate this cell-phone service. It never rings in these arenas. Did he leave any numbers in London?"

"Not with me, but maybe with Megan. She spoke with him, too."

"Okay, I'll ask Megan later. We'll track him down."

"Sorry, Simon, I tried you three times. I didn't know what else to do. I kept him on the phone as long as I could."

"Don't sweat it. So what did you do, make small talk with the guy?"

"A little. I asked him, 'As the number-two guy at Galaxy, how come you've sold over 25 million Ripley singles but are still losing your ass?'"

Simon laughed out loud. "Oh, I bet that went over well. Did he discuss any economic forecasts with you?"

"No, he wasn't very warm and fuzzy. I think he's a little uptight because he can't quite figure out how to make a profit, even though he said the company's future is completely on target."

Simon laughed a little harder. "Hey, they are the kings of double-talk.

Music execs can make politicians looks like Sunday-school teachers. If he had called back sooner, maybe we could have helped him out with that little profit problem."

"That's what I was thinking. But seriously, Simon, how can that be? How can a record label with Ripley Graham be in financial trouble?"

"Well, just like every other major record company, they're trying to find a new business model. Basically, Ripley is the only supercharged artist at the moment, and he happens to be selling really well. The bad news is, no single artist—not even a Ripley Graham—can turn the battleship around in the bathtub and keep an entire multinational record company afloat by himself. A major label needs a few Ripleys around the world. Galaxy's problem is that they currently have only one giant egg in their worldwide basket. They either need to hatch fully incubated gigantic eggs—immediately, which is hard to do—or they need to create a gigantic basket that has more eggs. That's why all the merger rumors."

"But aren't we in the same boat?" Judd asked. "I mean, at Elite, we have only one gigantic egg in our basket, too."

"The difference is, management takes a bigger slice of the overall pie. We take a 15 percent commission on everything an artist generates—not just record sales, but also concert income, merchandising, TV revenues, music publishing, endorsements deals, everything. Traditionally, a record company makes money *only* from record sales. They have a thinner slice of the artist's pie. Management companies make more money on fewer clients. But in our new world order, record companies now want to change all that and get a piece of every income stream—the so-called 360 deals. So everything is changing. But it's a good lesson nonetheless. Too much power in the hands of one artist is never a good thing. Don't get me wrong, I like making the money a giant act like Ripley produces. But one giant hen can also rule the roost."

"So it's true that Galaxy's in trouble even with Ripley on the roster?"

"For a second, but this is the music business. It's like the weather on top of Mount Everest. Things develop fast out here."

"Gotcha."

"Okay, that's it for now. I'll talk to you Monday, unless you want to work this weekend on a new global recovery strategy for Galaxy Worldwide. I'll be happy to e-mail it to Tommy Strickland."

"Yeah, right. Rudd to the rescue!"

"What's that?" Simon asked.

"Nothing. I'll see you Monday."

"You got it." And with that, Simon was off the phone and racing.

CHAPTER 10

THREE DAYS LATER

Nashville
Monday, March 7
6:05 P.M.

Judd drove his Honda Accord, which was in much need of repair, south from Music Row onto Twenty-first Avenue and turned right on Blair Boulevard in Hillsboro Village. He parked in front of 2219 Blair and walked up the sidewalk to a charming English Tudor home. He checked his hair in the reflection of the front door's glass panel, rang the bell, and waited for Megan to answer.

To his great surprise, she didn't. Instead, the door was flung open, and he was looking down on a five-foot-four-inch overweight boy. No sooner had the boy opened the door than he turned and started walking back into the house. Before Judd was able to say he must have the wrong address, the boy said loudly as he walked away, "Come in, Judd. Megan is late. *Girls!*"

Judd froze momentarily as he tried to grasp what just happened. He found himself alone on the front step wondering who the boy was, if he should follow him into the house, and how exactly the boy knew his name.

Assuming Megan must be close by, Judd wandered in. He found the boy sitting on the couch while he ate Fritos and watched the Nashville Predators play a road game in Detroit on cable TV. That's when Judd knew for sure the boy had Down syndrome.

"What's your name?" Judd asked.

Without taking his eyes off the TV, the boy answered, "Mathew."

Mathew! Now it all makes sense. "Oh, so you're Mathew."

"Of course I'm Mathew. I've always been Mathew."

"Yeah, I'm sure you have. That's good. That's really, really good. So how's it going, Mathew?"

"Not good, Judd," Mathew replied without looking over.

"Not good? What's up?"

"Preds are losing."

Judd glanced at the TV. "Oh, wow, I see that. But it looks like it's early in the game. There's still time."

"There's always hope, Judd. You have to have hope."

"That's right."

Mathew was totally indifferent to Judd's presence in the house. Judd tried to start the conversation again. "So, how long have you been living here?"

Again without looking over, Mathew replied, "A long time."

Just then, Megan came down the stairs. "Hey. I'm so sorry. I got home later than I wanted."

Judd did a double take. Megan was dressed in white go-go boots, a pink miniskirt, a pink-and-white turtleneck sweater complete with colorful Mardi Gras beads, and a bright pink wig with a 1960s bob cut. He realized she wasn't messing around with the costume party. "Wow, you look fantastic!"

"Thanks." She walked over to Mathew. "What do you think?"

Mathew broke away from the Predators for the first time, looked at Megan, and smiled from ear to ear. "My sister is Katy Perry!"

"Ha!" Megan was delighted by his response. "So you guys met. That's good." Megan knelt in front of Mathew. "Do you remember that you're sleeping over at Miss Courtney's house tonight? That she wants you to finish watching the game with her?"

"Yup, hockey night at Miss Courtney's. She's making brownies."

"Exactly." She kissed him on the cheek and said, "You're the best.

Let's go. You got your things?"

"Yup." Mathew got up, put on his backpack, and started down the hall for the door.

Megan drove her 2011 Audi TT coupe on lower Broadway toward East Nashville to drop off Mathew at the home of her girlfriend Courtney Hicks. Judd was in the passenger's seat and Mathew in the back. They had a clear view of the Bridgestone Arena, where the gala would be held tomorrow night. Farther in the distance, Judd saw LP Field, home to the Tennessee Titans. Since 1999, those two structures had made Nashville a sports town. As a kid, Judd remembered watching on TV as the Titans ran the famous Music City Miracle play at the stadium during its inaugural season. With just sixteen seconds left in the game, Lorenzo Neal of the Titans caught the kickoff and handed it to Frank Wycheck, who threw the ball completely across the field to Kevin Dyson, who ran it seventy-five yards to beat the Buffalo Bills in the AFC Wild Card game. It propelled the Titans all the way to the Super Bowl.

"Mathew, are you a Titans fan as well?" Judd asked.

"Noooo. New York Jets!"

"Really? But you live in Nashville, and you love the Preds."

"Yeah, but Mark Sanchez is the greatest quarterback in the whole wide world!"

Megan leaned over. "We lived in the Bronx and in Manhattan before we moved here. We were there our whole lives until four years ago."

"Does your family still live in New York?"

Mathew blurted out, "Our mother died. We never had a father."

Megan looked in the rearview mirror. "Mathew, I think Mr. Judd was talking to me."

Surprised and embarrassed, Judd looked at Megan. "I'm so sorry."

"It's okay." Megan looked again in her mirror. "We have a nice life here, don't we, Mathew?"

"Yeah."

They had crossed the Cumberland River into East Nashville and were now apparently at Miss Courtney's house. Mathew unfastened his seatbelt while Judd opened the car door and stood to let him out.

"Don't eat too many brownies, and please don't stay up late," Megan told him.

"I won't."

"And clean up any messes, please."

"I will."

"Call me on the cell if you need anything."

"I need the Preds to win and finally go deep into the playoffs," Mathew said.

"And I hope they do," Megan replied as Mathew exited the car. The front door opened, and a young woman waved at Megan, who rolled down her window and called, "Thank you, Courtney. I'll swing by tomorrow morning!"

They headed south on I-65 toward Brentwood. *No one has it easy,* Judd thought, looking out the window. He was more impressed with Megan than ever.

Megan broke the silence. "You started in the music business here at Belmont University, right?"

"Yes and no. I actually got my degree from the University of Wisconsin last December. But when Simon interviewed me, I told him I was taking a course in the music business program at Belmont."

"You weren't?"

"I was, but I'm not anymore. When I moved here last year, I heard that the best way to break into the industry was to get an internship. And I figured the only way to do that was to go through one of the universities. So I paid to audit one class at Belmont and then signed up for a music business internship in personal management. That's how I got hooked up with Elite. I never attended the class. I was just using the school to open doors on Music Row."

"Fake it 'til you make it," Megan said. "It worked."

Truth be told, Judd didn't need Belmont to open doors on Music Row—just the door to Elite. He had dreamed about working at

Elite Management ever since he saw the Country Music Awards on TV when he was in the sixth grade. He didn't remember if it was Shania Twain when she won Entertainer of the Year or one of the other big winners who thanked their personal manager at Elite Management. But he never forgot that name—Elite Management.

Megan took the Brentwood–Concord Road exit off I-65 and passed an eight-hundred-foot tower in the middle of an open field.

"What is that?" Judd asked.

"That's the WSM radio tower. That's the tower that broadcasts the *Grand Ole Opry*. Have you been out to the Opry or backstage at the Opry House?" Megan asked.

"No, not yet. My parents and I did stay at the Opryland Hotel once when we came down on vacation. I was fifteen. I think we tried to go to the *Grand Ole Opry*, but it was sold out for the weekend."

"You should come out on Wednesday when we shoot the video there," Megan said. "You know what's amazing? I didn't know one thing about country music when I moved down here. But it doesn't take long to appreciate the heritage. Simon is the best when it comes to history. He can explain how it all began. And it really started to a large degree with the Opry."

"So it's really the longest-running radio show in the world?"

"Yeah. WSM radio went on the air with the *Grand Ole Opry* in the twenties. Country music exploded because of the invention of radio. And Nashville wouldn't be the home of country music if George D. Hay hadn't created the *WSM Barn Dance*. He nicknamed it the *Grand Ole Opry*. Early on, Mr. Hay would broadcast live from different venues in town. In the forties, he moved the show to Ryman Auditorium, its home for thirty years. It moved to the current Opry House in the seventies. President Nixon came to dedicate the building opening night. Last year was the Opry's eighty-fifth anniversary. And to this day, they have never missed a Saturday-night broadcast. Not even the flood last May could drown it out. As Simon tells it, the Opry brought the entertainers, which brought the fans, which brought the recording studios, which brought the record companies."

"So without that radio tower . . ."

"Nashville wouldn't be the home of country music," Megan said. "Look, even though CD sales are way down, country music still had something like 300 million in total album sales last year. And digital sales are growing exponentially—over 50 million. Then you add in all the ancillary income streams, like concert tickets, merchandising, cable outlets like Country Music Television and Great American Country. All in all, we're a multibillion-dollar industry. And it all started from a little radio show and a few no-name cast members."

"And today it's an empire," Judd added, "and Ripley Graham is its reigning king."

CHAPTER 11

Brentwood
The Governors Club
7:05 P.M.

Judd sat gawking at the size of the homes as they drove through Brentwood. "These are some serious cribs!" he finally said.

"I love this area. You start to see some beautiful open farmland. Ripley lives in a gated community just up here called The Governors Club. Kind of the rich-and-famous neighborhood. Carrie Underwood lives here, Joe Don Rooney of Rascal Flatts, Dolly Parton lives close, and Kerry Collins has a home here." Megan glanced at Judd. "Kerry is the Titans quarterback turned country songwriter."

"Oh, I know who Kerry Collins is," Judd said.

"As a matter of fact, Kerry and his wife were at last year's party. He'll probably be here tonight. Maybe some former Predators, some country artists, even some Hollywood stars. You never know who will show. Mel Gibson was here one year."

"By the way, maybe I should have mentioned it earlier, but obviously I don't own a costume," Judd said. "It did say Mardi Gras attire is optional, didn't it?"

He was wearing his usual jeans with a light blue button-down shirt and a dark blue pullover fleece. It worked fine with his boyish face, thin frame, and brown hair. Costumes, however, had never been an option in Judd's somewhat preppie wardrobe. He was definitely outmatched by Megan's full-blown 1960s motif.

"It actually said *requested*," Megan answered, obviously enjoying where the conversation was going. "It's a masquerade party, and people in the music industry go all out."

"So by not dressing up, I'm going to look a little out of place, like I'm new."

"I would say you are a little underdressed, yes," Megan said, smiling.

"Can I borrow some of your beads?"

Megan began to laugh. "That is so pitiful! No, you cannot borrow my beads."

"Ah, come on. No one is going to notice if you're missing a few beads. They'll be commenting on how amazing you look, but it's definitely not because of the beads."

"Flattery will get you nowhere. And besides, in New Orleans, you have to work for your beads—beg, scream, show me something."

Megan looked over and smiled. Judd stuck out his lower lip and hung his head.

"Aw, so sad." Megan pulled off about half her colorful plastic necklaces and handed them to Judd.

"Awesome! Are you sure?"

"Well, it's not going to look good for the company if the new guy is sulking at his first Ripley Mardi Gras party."

Megan slowed as she approached the enormous gated entrance to The Governors Club. The guardhouse was larger than Judd's apartment. His eyes widened as he took in the surroundings—Arnold Palmer–designed golf course, lit fountains cascading in the adjacent ponds, hilltop mansions directly in front.

A security guard approached as Megan rolled down her window.

"I'm Megan with Ripley Graham, and this is Judd Nix."

"Yes, ma'am. You're Megan Olsen, right? Let me put you in the computer. One minute, please." He turned and walked back into the guardhouse. A minute later, he reappeared and waved them in as the white gate began to open.

Megan drove straight up the hill. On the right-hand side sat Ripley's twelve-thousand-square-foot estate. It was more a fortress than a house. The walls were built of imported dry-stacked limestone. The uncommonly steep roof was of zinc and copper. The architectural design would have been much more at home in Provence than in the hilltops of Williamson County, Tennessee.

"Okay," Judd said almost in a whisper. "This is nice."

"Wait until you see the inside."

As Megan pulled around the circular drive and stopped, two young men in dark jackets hurried to open the doors.

"Ripley has his own valet guys?" Judd asked.

"They're not permanent. He hires them for special occasions. Let's go in."

Judd felt like he had walked into a Gothic church. The majestic foyer's A-frame three-story vaulted ceiling was part stone, part exposed wood beams. Lit candles were everywhere—in candelabras, on a grand centerpiece, inside wall lanterns lining the great room, where a fire roared in the oversized fireplace at one end. Judd was taken aback by the Christian relics. On the side wall was an enormous replica of Leonardo da Vinci's *Last Supper*. And if that weren't enough, underneath it on a slightly raised altar-like platform was a wooden dining table covered with a white embroidered cloth. It had thirteen wooden chairs all on one side, just like in the painting but minus the disciples. On the opposite wall hung a life-sized wooden cross.

"Is this a home or a museum?" Judd asked.

"Ripley collects early Christian relics and medieval art."

A woman appeared. "Welcome. I'm Laurie Tarbox, and I'm in charge of the games this evening."

"Hello, I'm Megan Olsen. I work in Ripley's management office."

"Yes, of course, Megan. You look adorable," Laurie said. "I love your hair!"

"Hello, I'm Judd." Judd reached out and shook Laurie's hand. "I work in the same office."

"Yes, Judd, I have you down as well. Many of the guests have already arrived. And our first game is Who's Who. If you don't have a mask, then I'll need to give you one."

"I just have beads," Judd said, realizing he definitely should have rented a costume.

"No problem. Well, you both will need masks. We have two options—the basic thin black mask, like the one Robin wore in *Batman & Robin*, or we have colorful, outlandish Mardi Gras sequined masks with peacock feathers. Which would you prefer?"

"Definitely the peacock feathers!" Megan responded.

"I'm sticking with the less-is-more approach, so the basic black works for me," Judd said.

"Excellent." Laurie handed them each their masks. "Go ahead, put them on."

Megan and Judd pulled the elastic bands over their heads and positioned the masks.

"Great. Now, I'm going to give you a piece of paper that has two rows of names. The first row has all the guests who are actually here tonight. The second row is a list of people who are not—our fictional guests."

Judd and Megan started reading the sheets immediately:

	Actual Guests	**Fictional Guests**	**Matching #**
1.	Ripley Graham	*William Shakespeare*	________
2.	Simon Still	*Bill Clinton*	________
3.	Tim McGraw	*Houdini*	________
4.	Faith Hill	*Little Orphan Annie*	________
5.	Lee Ann Womack	*The Pink Panther*	________
6.	Frank Liddell	*Helen Keller*	________
7.	Keith Urban	*Albert Einstein*	________
8.	Nicole Kidman	*Christopher Columbus*	________
9.	Tony Brown	*Willy Wonka*	________
10.	John Rich	*Monica Lewinsky*	________
11.	Stu Grimson	*Mona Lisa*	________
12.	Pam Grimson	*John Wayne*	________

	Actual Guests	Fictional Guests	Matching #
13.	Blake Shelton	*Yogi Bear*	________
14.	Miranda Lambert	*Tinker Bell*	________
15.	Kid Rock	*Winnie the Pooh*	________
16.	Dolly Parton	*Uncle Sam*	________
17.	Kerry Collins	*The Pope*	________
18.	Brooke Collins	*Winston Churchill*	________
19.	Dierks Bentley	*Alfred Hitchcock*	________
20.	Cassidy Bentley	*Robin Hood*	________
21.	Ashley Judd	*Miss Piggy*	________
22.	Dario Franchitti	*The Tin Man*	________
23.	Brad Paisley	*Thomas Jefferson*	________
24.	Kimberly Williams	*Ray Charles*	________
25.	Martina McBride	*The Incredible Hulk*	________
26.	John McBride	*Porky Pig*	________
27.	Hillary Scott	*Muhammad Ali*	________
28.	Wynonna Judd	*Lucille Ball*	________
29.	Trace Adkins	*Mark Twain*	________
30.	Rhonda Adkins	*Mother Teresa*	________
31.	Laura Bell Bundy	*Marilyn Monroe*	________
32.	Andy Davis	*Fidel Castro*	________
33.	Michelle Branch	*Walt Disney*	________
34.	Teddy Landau	*Louis Armstrong*	________
35.	Holly Williams	*Bill Gates*	________
36.	Chris Coleman	*Martin Luther King Jr.*	________
37.	Jo Dee Messina	*Julia Child*	________
38.	Chris Deffenbaugh	*Fred Astaire*	________
39.	Brad Holiday	*Scrooge*	________
40.	Sandy Holiday	*Babe Ruth*	________
41.	Megan Olsen	*Buzz Lightyear*	________
42.	Judd Nix	*Charlie Chaplin*	________

"Here's how the game works. I'm going to pin one of the names from the fictional guest list on your back without telling you which one. Then you're going to join the party and try to figure out which name

I've put on your back by asking other guests questions about who you are. But you can ask only yes and no questions. For example, if I were to pin Elvis on your back, then a good question to ask someone would be, 'Am I an entertainer?' If yes, then, 'Am I a singer?' If yes, then, 'Am I alive now?' etc., until you figure out who you are. If someone asks anything other than a yes or no question, you can't answer."

Megan said, "I've played this before. It's fun."

"Good, but we've added a twist to make it more difficult," Laurie said.

"Oh, great," Judd said, already nervous.

"While you're trying to figure out the fictional guest's name on your back, you'll see the fictional names on the backs of the other real guests. But you won't be able to tell who they really are because everyone is wearing a mask. So not only do you need to figure out who you are, you also need to match the other real guests with their fictional names as you go around asking questions to each other."

"Okay, that's harder," Megan said.

"Once you've figured out who's who, mark it down. Just match the actual guest's name to the fictional guest's name on the sheet. When everyone is finished, we'll tally the scores and take off the masks. Got it?"

"I am so over my head I can't even tell you," Judd said.

"This is going to be great," Megan said.

Laurie turned Megan around and pinned *Lucille Ball* on the back of her sweater. Then she pinned *Miss Piggy* on the back of Judd. As Megan saw which name Judd was getting, she started laughing.

"That doesn't sound good," Judd said.

"Okay, go figure out who's who," Laurie said. "The party is past this front room. Go straight ahead to the indoor pool and patio."

The indoor pool and patio looked like a spa at a five-star Las Vegas casino. The guests, all dressed in costumes, were looking at each other's backs, talking behind their masks, laughing, and marking their papers while circling the pool amid its elaborate display of rocks and waterfalls.

"Am I in Nashville or visiting some ancient Grecian bath?" Judd said out loud. "This is unbelievable!"

"Told you," Megan said.

A rather tall black-haired man wearing a toga, Mardi Gras beads, and flip-flops tapped Judd on the shoulder. He was holding hands with an attractive blonde dressed as the Statue of Liberty, complete with fake torch. The man asked, "Am I a pig?"

Judd, not ready for the question, said, "Ah, I don't know. I mean, let me look."

The man added, "Everyone is saying no. But my fiancée here, Sweet Liberty, is saying yes."

Ms. Liberty grinned while Toga Man turned his back so Judd could see his nametag: *Bill Clinton*.

Judd smiled, cocked his head, and said, "Maybe?"

Megan and Ms. Liberty laughed.

Toga Man said, "You must answer yes or no."

"Then yes, definitely. You are a pig."

The women laughed harder.

"Thank you. I'm not sure why, but thank you." Toga Man then looked at the name on Judd's back and added, "By the way, so are you!"

As they walked away, Megan said, "That's Blake Shelton and Miranda Lambert."

"Really?"

"Yep. Let's mark them down. Match Blake with Bill Clinton and Miranda with Robin Hood."

Judd looked around in amazement and said, "I've never been in the same room with so many famous people. And I can't recognize a single one of them!"

"Except one." Megan pointed to the far corner. There was Ripley—in blue jeans, white T-shirt, and black cowboy hat.

"No mask. What's up with that?" Judd asked.

"It's his party. Let's go say hi."

Judd had been around Ripley a few times now. After Judd started as an intern, Simon had let him tag along as Ripley visited some local radio stations. Then there was the "Fly Away and Win" promotion the label had orchestrated, in which fifty fans flew into Nashville and won a meet-and-greet with Ripley. Simon took Judd along for that as well. And Ripley came from time to time to see Simon in the office.

Early on, Judd was struck by Ripley's public persona—his easy, endearing way with everyday people, especially his fans. It seemed like he was the son every mother wanted, the catch every woman craved, and the best friend any cowboy could hope to find. His most noticeable public attribute was his polite nature. He had manners. Thanks to his winsome smile and athletic frame, Ripley had been called "the Brad Pitt of country."

As they got close, Ripley said, "Okay, a pink-haired female with a guy who looks like he was given some beads at the last minute. Hi, Megan. Welcome, Judd."

Megan lifted her mask. "Now, how did you know that so quickly?"

"Who else would be a go-go girl?"

Judd rested his mask on the top of his head like sunglasses. "Thanks for the invite."

"Sure."

Ripley turned back to Megan. "Hey, before I forget, I had two envelopes sent to me here at the house that I need you to FedEx back first thing in the morning. Don't let me forget to give them to you before you leave tonight."

"FedEx came to the house, not the office?" Megan seemed a bit surprised.

Ripley leaned close so no one else could hear. "This is confidential. It's a little surprise for Simon, so don't mention anything."

"Mum's the word," Megan said. After an awkward pause, she changed the subject. "So what happened to your mask?"

"I'm famous. I never take mine off."

"Nice," Megan said, smiling.

From behind, they heard a man say gruffly, "Well, here's the crew."

Judd and Megan turned and saw . . . a pirate, complete with sailor pants, striped shirt, long, curly black wig, hat, elaborate mask, and plastic shoulder parakeet.

Ripley said, "Hello, Simon."

Megan looked at Ripley again. "Man, you're good. How do you do that so fast?"

"I see through people. It's my gift."

"Okay, Ripley, let's see how good you really are," Megan said. "Who is Ms. Mother Nature over there by the first waterfall?"

They all looked over and saw a stunning woman wearing a tight green dress with embroidered flowers and a mask made of exotic tree leaves.

"That's Nicole Kidman. Who else could wear that dress?"

"He is good!" Judd said.

"Where is Dolly Parton?" Simon asked.

They all looked around.

Ripley said, "There, the construction worker."

Chuckling, Megan said, "Ms. Nine-to-Five. She's absolutely priceless."

Judd turned to Ripley, trying to score points with small talk. "So how many years have you had a Mardi Gras party?"

Ripley paused, then said with a serious look, "It's actually my Carnival party. I started it the year my old man died."

That completely killed the lighthearted atmosphere and made Judd feel like he had put his foot in his mouth.

"Sorry," he said. "I didn't mean to bring up a sad subject."

"Oh, it's not a sad subject," Ripley said. "That's why I throw this party, to celebrate carne vale. 'Farewell to flesh' and good riddance! The day of repentance has arrived."

"Okay," Judd said, feeling even more uncomfortable.

Simon rescued him. "I just came from the music room. Tony Brown and John Rich are already playing some music. I think Wynonna is going to sing. You guys should check it out. Ripley and I will be right in."

"Great," Megan said, knowing a dismissal when she heard one.

As she and Judd moved across the patio, they heard a group sing-a-long of Bonnie Raitt's "Something to Talk About" from a side room.

"That was awkward," Judd said.

"Don't worry about it."

"How was I supposed to know his dad died?"

Megan stopped and looked at Judd. Almost in a whisper, she said, "Ripley's a little different with us one on one than when he's in public. You see more of a range of emotions, that's all. And he can get a little out there sometimes. It's no big deal, really."

"What do you mean, 'out there'?"

"He's just different with us. That was what I tried to tell you at lunch on Friday. Ripley is not the same person you see in public. I don't think any of them are, that's all. Don't worry about it. It's fine."

Judd nodded. Then he turned back and saw Ripley and Simon standing off in the corner alone, having words. It was private and intense—and it was definitely not about the evening's round of Who's Who.

CHAPTER 12

THE NEXT EVENING

Nashville
Bridgestone Arena
Tuesday, March 8

The Bridgestone Arena had been transformed late in the hockey season from a state-of-the-art sports facility to a high-dollar formal evening venue complete with all the trimmings. The ice had been covered. A staging platform had been placed on one end, and around the inside of the rink were draped, candle-lit tables holding extravagant floral centerpieces and fine china. No signs of goalies, referees, or face-offs remained. The arena might appear to be the Four Seasons if not for the scoreboard hanging from the ceiling.

It was just a few minutes past seven, and Jeff Foxworthy was onstage and already had the room howling.

"Now, I'm going to be honest. It is time for us all to get together and talk about this stuff. Look at us!" Foxworthy leaned into the mic and separated his words for emphasis. "Would . . . you . . . just . . . look . . . at . . . us! We're getting out of limos, trying to walk in heels, wearing tuxedos. C'mon, y'all, *this is not natural!* Country people with money—it's just not natural. Look at Brad Paisley."

Foxworthy pointed behind him to the giant kabuki screen projecting the live action from the red carpet outside. Brad was dressed in a tuxedo jacket, black jeans, and boots and was walking hand in hand with his Hollywood wife, Kimberly Williams-Paisley.

Foxworthy continued, "Kimberly's an actress. Now, she knows how to work it, and she looks like a million bucks. But look at Brad. Tuxedo jacket with jeans—the man forgot to rent the pants!" A wave of laughter rolled through the arena. "See, that's what I'm talking about! We need to be honest here. This is not our natural state. I mean, I know country. And look at us—we're all dolled up, riding in expensive cars, smelling real good. *That ain't natural!* And check out my Blue Collar buddy, Larry the Cable Guy." Foxworthy pointed to Larry, who was talking to the media on the red carpet. "Now, Larry is so country, growing up he thought *The Dukes of Hazzard* was a documentary!"

Backstage, a saber-toothed tiger logo hung on the center of a closed door. On most nights, the logo identified the locker room of the Nashville Predators. Tonight, however, no heavily padded players were present—just Jerome and Nate, Ripley's bodyguards, hanging around in the hallway.

Inside, Ripley and Simon were back at it, having the same argument Judd had witnessed by the pool last night. Simon had wanted to discuss how they were going to handle James Clark at the gala, since Ripley refused to be seen with him. Last night's conversation had not gone well, and Simon had finally said, "Fine, let's drop it." Tonight, it wasn't going any better.

"I don't want him here!" Ripley shouted.

"Rip, c'mon. You really want me to ask security to escort the president of your label out of the building? The guy who's hosting and paying for this? That would be a pretty picture in the papers tomorrow."

"Last night, you told me he wasn't going to be here."

"Ripley, I did not. I said you wouldn't *see him*. Look, Foxworthy is almost done. There is going to be a video honoring you next. You don't have to go out early or sit at the table. We'll just hang here until Foxworthy brings you onstage and presents you with the award. Then Vince Gill is going to get up and jam. He is hoping you'll pick up the guitar and sing, too. If I were you, I'd just hang backstage until the presentation, then jam with Vince and never go out into the audience. That way, you'll never see Clark."

Onstage, Foxworthy looked to the side to get a time check. One of the producers of the event gave him the "cut it" sign.

"Well, that just about does it for me. And before we hear from tonight's honoree, I have the distinct pleasure of bringing to the podium the man who for a minute *was* the next president of the United States. Until the Supreme Court told him a little 'inconvenient truth' that the election was going to George Bush. No worries. Al decided to go ahead and write a book, make a movie, win the Nobel Peace Prize, and just take the cash. Smart man. Ladies and gentlemen, please give a warm hometown welcome to the Honorable Al Gore."

Simon heard a knock and pulled the door open. Megan, Janice, and Pumpkin walked inside.

"Mr. Renewable Resource is warming up the audience—sorry, couldn't resist—and he is going to be fast. The video is next," Janice said. "Then Foxworthy is going to bring Ripley on stage." She noticed that Simon and Ripley seemed tense. "Everything okay?"

Ripley avoided her question and asked, "So is my date just sitting by herself at the VIP table?"

Megan said, "No, I asked Judd to sit with her. I didn't know if you were going to the table first or just to the stage from here."

Ripley's longtime trophy girlfriend, Cindy Helms, was a wannabe model. In view of her stellar looks and Georgia accent, Nate had early on nicknamed her "Peaches and Cream"—because she must be so "sweet 'n juicy." She didn't know it, but from day one the entire team outside of Ripley referred to her simply as "P. C."

"Stage only," Ripley said. "I'll accept the award, stay onstage with Vince, then leave right after the jam session."

"That's fine," Megan said.

"Pumpkin, will you get Cindy backstage?" Ripley asked.

"Of course. In the meantime, I think we should get you in position on the side of the stage," Pumpkin said.

At the same time, Janice gave Simon a "what's going on?" look.

Simon didn't respond other than to say, "Let's go," as he started out the door.

Judd was sitting next to P. C. at the front table with Al Gore and other dignitaries. He didn't have much to say to her. Besides, he knew only her code name. His mind was racing. *Okay, act like you've been here before. It's just you, P. C. the supermodel, the former vice president of the United States, and the governor of Tennessee. No big deal. Kenny Rogers and Kris Kristofferson are behind us. I've got a better seat than they do. And if this airs on TV, my cell phone will never stop ringing. Keep cool, like it's just another night in show business.*

Foxworthy was back. "Tonight, we are here to celebrate Ripley Graham, who in just four years has become the fastest-selling artist in music. Twenty-five million legal downloads in four years! Think about that—the same amount of time it takes Ronnie Dunn to get his hair to stand up like that. Just four years! That's amazing! In the same span it takes Gary LeVox of Rascal Flatts to finally land on a note, Ripley sells 25 million. The same amount of time it took me to get out of the first grade—four years! As long as this introduction seems to be taking—four years! So, without further ado, I have the great privilege and honor . . ."

He stopped talking in midsentence. It was an awkward moment until everyone realized why. A nearly bald, short, and stocky man walked with great purpose directly toward him. Obviously, this was an unscripted portion of the program. Since the house lights were dimmed, no one could make out who it was. As the man approached, he signaled Foxworthy to step away from the podium to speak with him. The bald man whispered something into Foxworthy's ear, and Foxworthy nodded in agreement and simply exited the platform. The unannounced gentleman took his place, adjusted the microphone, and began to speak.

"I apologize for the interruption. For those of you who don't know me, I'm James Clark, president of Galaxy Nashville, Ripley Graham's record company."

Though no one could see it from the tables out front, those closest to the podium—including Judd—heard angry, raised voices coming from backstage.

"Before Jeff gives Ripley his award this evening, I want to say a few words. I'll keep it brief. Galaxy Records signed Ripley over four years ago, and since then, together, we've had many firsts and broken many records. The video you just saw was impressive, but it doesn't tell the entire story. It is no secret on Music Row that Ripley and I have had our disagreements. It is true that I was not yet the president of Galaxy Nashville when Ripley was signed. But I have been Ripley's label head for nearly his entire career. Because of that, I feel entitled to say a few things about his success, Nashville's success, and the success of country music. In my opinion, the success of all is based on one truth—that the *song*, not the *singer*, is king."

The room grew tense. It was becoming clear that James Clark was not at the podium to praise Ripley. And because the record company was footing the bill, no one could stop him.

Clark continued, "We are going through some difficult times in the music business. But at the end of the day, country music tells extraordinary stories about ordinary people. Don't let anybody tell you that their marketing is more important than our music. It is not. Our stories, our songs will always survive. I have worked in the country-music industry for thirty-five years. I learned the business from my father, one of country music's treasured songsmiths. Country music is an American art form that continues to weave the life stories of working people. It forges bonds stronger than any major corporation and greater than any market share. What we do on Music Row is art first, commerce second. It is the most democratic musical genre in the world because it is 'of the people, for the people, by the people.' That is where Ripley and I have always disagreed. And I say all of this as a warning. This kind of success is uncharted waters to our musical format. How can we stay true to our art form when artists like Ripley Graham and corporations like Galaxy Records are more interested in marketing and new models than in the messages in our music? I am personally more interested in honest lyrics than corporate lies."

Clark paused for a moment. "I'm sorry, but I cannot in good conscience participate in turning America's musical heartland into music with no heart. And it is for that reason that I am announcing my resignation tonight as the president of Galaxy Records Nashville."

A gasp came from the room, as if all the air in the arena had been sucked out into the Nashville sky.

Then Clark looked directly toward the head table, where Ripley was supposed to be seated. But only Al Gore, Governor Haslam, P. C., and Judd were there. "When I see that video presentation and look at Ripley Graham, I do not see any value in the future of country music. All I see is a man in country music who has no values."

He then turned to Foxworthy, who was waiting anxiously offstage. "Jeff, I'm sorry. Continue if you wish."

With that, James Clark exited the podium in the same direction from which he had come, passing directly in front of Judd's table. He glanced over but never slowed his stride. He walked down the center of the arena past the stunned guests and out the main exit.

CHAPTER 13

The Next Morning

Nashville
Music Row
Wednesday, March 9
9:45 A.M.

Music Row was so small. That had been Judd's impression of the hub of Music City over the past six months.

Because country music touched tens of millions of people every day, he assumed Music Row would be striking in terms of its physical presence—the offices, the landmarks, the studios. He also assumed it would be large and imposing in terms of the number of people working inside the industry. But in every way, things looked so much smaller than he expected. The music business in Nashville, as far as he could see, was tiny. The famed Music Row was only a couple of streets—basically Sixteenth and Seventeenth avenues. And those two one-way streets were hardly what he'd consider thoroughfares. Most of the major record companies were within walking distance of each other—not that anyone walked, but they could. And while several landmark buildings had recently been erected on Music Row, most of the daily music scene was orchestrated in small row houses—lower-middle-class homes that had been converted into office space. There were no skyscrapers. Outside of the old United Artists building and the new Roundabout Plaza, there was hardly an elevator that reached higher than five floors. It was all so . . . residential. *This is just one small town,* Judd kept thinking.

Simon accelerated his liquid-silver Jaguar XK convertible as Judd sank into the shotgun seat. Judd could count on one hand the number of times he'd ridden in expensive sports cars—Megan's Audi coupe being one. Simon's Jag was a dream machine. Trying not to be too obvious, Judd found himself gazing at the trimmed walnut dash and console. There was nothing like new leather in a luxury automobile. It smelled like money. Although Simon's upbringing had been modest, he now seemed fairly oblivious to the extravagance surrounding him. But to Judd, the smell of money made him revel in his new position. He was at the right place at the right time—and only going up!

Simon stroked his mustache with one hand and drove with the other. It was a twenty-minute ride from the Elite offices downtown on Music Row to the Gaylord Opryland Resort and Grand Ole Opry House, where Ripley was shooting his music video. Simon was more preoccupied than Judd had ever seen him. Usually, these trips around town were full of lively banter. Simon was always generous with his music-industry stories. But not today.

There was no doubt that Simon had taken Judd under his wing. It was happening exactly as Judd had hoped—find an internship, work hard, and get noticed, then pray that someone like Simon Stills hired him at an entry level. To make it, he would have to pay his dues. Music Row had a weeding-out process not just for singers but for young music-business wannabes, too. No one ever got hired from an ad in the paper, because no one on Music Row had to put ads in the paper to attract a labor force. They simply used the glut of interns available to them at all times until they found a keeper. It was the music industry's modern-day apprenticeship.

Judd had been on a high from this rite of passage until Simon's return from Ripley's opening weekend in Greenville. He knew immediately that something was different. Simon wasn't upbeat but rather introspective. Something was definitely bothering him.

Simon turned right off Sixteenth Avenue onto Demonbreun, then turned right onto the I-40 East ramp and accelerated into five lanes of traffic.

"Man, it's starting to look like L.A," Simon finally said.

"Have you ever lived in L.A.?" Judd asked, trying to kick-start a conversation.

"No, no. I was always a Buffalo dirt ball. Grew up there, went to UB—University of Buffalo. Then moved straight to Nashville to get in the music business." Simon didn't seem to want to continue the conversation. Then he totally changed the subject. "How old are you?"

"Twenty-three, soon to be twenty-four."

"You're Ripley's age."

"Exactly," Judd replied, suddenly engulfed in a sense of unworthiness.

"That's the part that always amazes me. They're growing more talented as they get younger. It's hard to believe, really. Ripley's been on every major TV show in America, hosted *Saturday Night Live*, dined at the White House, been on the cover of *Time*, sold out multiple nights in arenas all across the States, and he's only been able to legally drink beer for two years."

Then he seemed lost in his thoughts again. Knowing Simon was not in his normal mode, Judd decided to let him dictate the conversation—or lack thereof.

A few minutes later, Simon asked, "Did you remember to bring the *Bulletin*?"

"Yeah, I got it."

"What does it say about last night?"

"The gala was the headline. Want me to read it out loud?"

"Please," Simon said.

Judd picked up the paper he had laid on the dash. "'Ripley's Special Night Turns to Spectacle'—that's the headline."

He continued reading: "'An all-star cast gathered in Nashville last evening as Galaxy Records hosted a gala in Ripley Graham's honor to recognize him on being named *Billboard*'s Artist of the Year. The black-tie affair was attended by country-music celebrities, as well as rock and pop artists and politicians eager to praise Graham for his wide influence in the world of music. Among those in attendance were Reba McEntire, Vince Gill, Wynonna Judd, Rascal Flatts, former Vice President Al Gore, Sheryl Crow, Uncle Kracker and others.

"'It was billed to be a cross between an inductee entering the Rock and Roll Hall of Fame, complete with an all-star jam session, and a country-flavored comedy roast with Jeff Foxworthy hosting. However, the lighthearted scene was altered dramatically when James Clark of Galaxy Nashville took control of the podium minutes before the presentation to Graham and turned the roast into a rant. Clark chose the setting to announce his resignation as President of Galaxy Nashville and made harsh remarks toward both Graham personally and Galaxy Records, stating, "I'm sorry, but I cannot in good conscience participate in turning America's heartland music into music with no heart."'"

Judd paused to get his breath. "'Clark's announcement and critical comments about Graham, Galaxy Records and the industry as a whole upstaged the reason for the gathering. Foxworthy eased the tension by joking, "Now, that's country! See, no matter how hard we try to be fancy and highfalutin', it's just a matter of time before a good fight breaks out. Thank God. Boy, I sure feel more comfortable now!"

"'Afterward, Ripley Graham took the stage and responded with a remarkably humble and eloquent speech, claiming he had no idea this was going to happen: "I may be the most shocked person in the room at the moment, but I know for a fact that I am still the most grateful. This is a hard business, and you certainly don't break through by yourself. I am deeply saddened by James Clark's comments on the state of our industry. And par for the course, I disagree with his analysis. But I want to say publicly that I am also deeply in his debt for allowing me to chase the dream."

"'After a standing ovation for Graham, Vince Gill got up and said, "Maybe we should keep the business outside tonight and remember why we really do this for a living." Gill proceeded to rock the house with Graham and other special guests, which seemingly put out any earlier fireworks. A spokesperson for Galaxy Records in New York said by phone, "Although Clark's lack of tact in making his announcement was disconcerting, Galaxy has accepted his resignation and will announce a replacement quickly."'"

As Judd finished reading, Simon turned to him and said, "I can tell you what you need to know in order to be a real artist manager. Interested?"

Judd was surprised by the sudden candidness. *Wow,* he thought, *this is turning into a serious conversation.* "Sure," he answered.

"Well, let me first say the reason I wanted you to come on board is you remind me of myself. You have a lot to learn, of course. You can't learn it in school or by reading the trade magazines. But when I think back to when I got my first paying job in the music business, I wish someone had told me what I'm about to tell you. It's the best advice I can give you. I'm going to tell you now not because I think you will understand it, but because I think you might remember it."

"Okay." Judd wasn't sure what else to say.

"Find out what they are most afraid of—that's the trick."

"I'm sorry? Find out what who's most afraid of?"

"The artists," Simon said. "If you can figure out what artists fear the most, then you can manage them. They're all afraid. Some are afraid of success, others are afraid of failure, but they are all deeply afraid. If you don't manage their fear, it will manifest itself as hatred." Then Simon asked, "Do you know how to manage someone's fear?"

"No, I don't think so."

"Be brave enough to speak up. It's easy to say and hard to do, but you have to talk about the tough stuff and tell the truth as you see it. That's what a real manager does. And believe me, it is never easy to tell a powerful person something they don't want to hear. But ultimately, that's what we're paid to do. Here is my theory: From the moment we come out of the womb and the cord is cut, we become separated—we all innately feel it—and immediately cry out for a safe place. Creative people feel the separation to the extreme all their lives. That's what I believe. And ultimately, our purpose as managers is to provide refuge, a sanctuary for creative souls—to help artists eliminate their fears and find their safe place, their comfort zone, their purpose. Someone once said, 'An artist manager is the midwife of dreams.' But our job is not just giving birth to dreams. It's keeping our artists safe their whole lives."

Judd remembered Megan's explanation. "Okay," he said. Then he added, "What is Ripley afraid of?"

Without taking his eyes off the road, Simon replied coldly, "Himself."

The comment frightened Judd. He had never heard that tone in Simon's voice. As they rode in silence, he started thinking about Megan's comment that things "can get ugly, sometimes really ugly. There is a dark side, and it's real."

"Enough of that," Simon said. "What's your perspective on last night's fireworks?"

"What, James Clark's speech? Hey, I know I'm new, but this whole thing makes no sense to me. I mean, I certainly don't know what's going on, but to me it looks like Ripley simply makes a lot of people a lot of money. So why should anybody in his food chain complain? I mean, from where I sit, Ripley is without question the greatest thing that ever happened to Galaxy Records and James Clark. Just in the nick of time. And then Clark interrupts the program to announce to the entire country-music industry that Ripley is the Grinch that just stole Christmas? I don't get it."

"It gets complicated real fast when one guy generates that kind of money in an industry this big. Egos blur the clearest vision. Like they say, 'Egotism is the anesthetic that dulls the pain of stupidity.'" Simon paused, then added, "Let me just say it this way: When you're as big as Ripley, you become a target."

CHAPTER 14

Nashville
Grand Ole Opry House

Simon turned into the entrance of the Gaylord Opryland Resort, the largest non-casino hotel in the United States. He turned left onto a frontage road running parallel to one side of the hotel and toward the 4,440-seat Grand Ole Opry House. Simon drove past an Authorized Personnel Only sign without hesitation. He then slowed the Jag as he approached a guard shack and came to a complete stop when a security officer with a clipboard stepped out and walked toward the driver's side. The guard shack had darkly tinted glass, and when the door opened Judd saw two other guards inside and several TV monitors glowing.

The security officer leaned in as Simon lowered his window. "Hey, Simon."

"Afternoon, Tanner," Simon said.

Judd read the name Tanner Maddox on the plate pinned to the man's uniform.

"Your boy's already on the stage working. I was surprised 'cause I heard you had a big to-do last night," Tanner said.

"He's punctual. Who said artists can't keep track of time?" Simon said.

"Parking is real tight, as usual, but I got a place for you right beside Ripley's bus, next to the Artist Entrance."

"Thanks for thinking of me," Simon said.

"Well, you've got Ripley rockin' these days, Simon. I mean, *son*. He's on fire like nobody's business." Tanner looked over at Judd. "Is this feller gonna be the next big thing?"

Simon smiled. "Tanner, this is Judd Nix. He's new with our company."

"Oh, I got ya. Good for you, young man. You decided to start at the top, did ya?"

"Yes, sir, I did." Judd smiled politely back.

"Oh, yeah, I've known 'em all—managers, agents, artists. Mr. Acuff, Mr. Monroe, Miss Minnie. Course, not everybody knew 'em as well as I did, especially Miss Minnie."

Simon cut his eyes at Judd and raised his brow as if to say, *Look out, here we go.*

And indeed Tanner went on. "Oh, yeah, she was something else, Miss Minnie. Did I ever tell you about the time she organized that benefit concert for the American Heart Association a couple of years before she passed?"

"I remember the event. Yes, I believe you have actually recounted the story a couple of times, if I'm not mistaken."

"Well, I didn't tell young Judd here."

Simon shook his head and looked down at his watch.

Tanner either didn't notice or didn't care. "Yeah, Miss Minnie, Amy Grant, and of all people Robin Williams were headlining. I was working security, and Miss Minnie and Robin Williams hit it off in a big way. Backstage, they were joking and carrying on, having a big ole time. And then Robin started telling some of his jokes that would make a sailor blush. Of course, Miss Minnie laughed harder than ever. Every time Robin would come back with another off-color joke, Miss Minnie would laugh and say, 'Oh, Robin, you are *so* bad.'"

Judd laughed until he noticed Simon wasn't at all amused. He coughed to cover his awkward outburst.

Simon knew Tanner's stories all too well. "Thank you for the parking spot. Now, if you don't mind, I'm already late for my artist."

Not taking the hint, Tanner added, "Yeah, Robin loved Miss Minnie. And she really loved him, you could tell."

Simon said, "That's good stuff, hoss, but I've got to get inside."

"Okay, okay, wait just a second and I'll move a cone so you can park real close." Tanner started walking toward an orange cone guarding a coveted empty space next to a sign that read, "Artist Entrance, General Offices, Studio A."

"Next time, we won't be in such a hurry," Simon said.

Tanner looked back over his shoulder. "No problem, Simon. Good meetin' ya, Judd."

Wow, Judd thought, *Simon's got some clout.* The guard didn't even look at his clipboard once he recognized Simon and already had the prime parking spot saved.

"He's a good guy, just a little chipper," Simon told Judd as they got out of the car. "But once you know the gatekeepers, you're in."

The two stepped onto a red-brick walkway in which every other brick was imprinted with the Opry logo. The long pathway toward the Opry House was covered with a red-and-white awning and lined with decorative hanging baskets. Positioned near the entrance was a small fountain of a little girl with her hands outstretched. The sculpture had been a gift to Sarah Ophelia Colley Cannon from her beloved husband, Henry, on their twenty-fifth wedding anniversary. Later in life, Sarah Cannon—Miss Minnie Pearl—gave it to the Opry as a treasured keepsake. As Judd held the door open for Simon, he saw an imposing portrait directly in front of him—the back of Roy Acuff standing on the Opry stage, fiddle in hand, looking out beyond the footlights onto an adoring audience.

"It's hard to imagine ten months ago this place was submerged under mud and water. And look at it now. It's more beautiful than ever," Simon said proudly as he entered the sacred auditorium.

Judd walked at Simon's side as they approached the enormous wooden receptionist's station. A petite older woman was behind it, and a metro police officer stood close by.

"Can I help you?" the woman asked, head tilted down as she read a long list of names.

"Hi, Jo. I'm here to check on Ripley."

She raised her head. "Oh, Simon! Sorry. It's been so busy this morning. Seems it takes an army to shoot a music video these days."

"Indeed it does."

The elderly woman flipped through the pages in her hand until she found Simon's name. She marked it with a yellow highlighter and asked, "And who is this with you?"

"Judd Nix, ma'am."

"Judd Nix. Yes, here you are." She marked his name as well and then turned to Simon. "You know where you're going, I believe."

"I do. Nice to see you, Jo."

"You, too, and let me know if you need anything. Anything at all."

Judd followed Simon backstage. The hallways were lined with exquisitely decorated themed dressing rooms—like "Women of Country" and the "Debut Room"—each with an inlaid star on the floor in front, like the Hollywood Walk of Fame. Lining the corridor walls were large photos of Opry members, legendary and current, performing on the stage—from Jeannie Seely and Whispering Bill Anderson to Garth Brooks and Steve Wariner; from Brad Paisley and Little Jimmy Dickens to Trace Adkins and the latest inductee, Blake Shelton. Strangely, Judd noticed a wall of handsome wooden lockers like the ones found at elite country clubs. *Why on earth are there lockers in the backstage hallways of the Opry?* he thought. *I can't imagine Porter Wagoner using a locker for his rhinestones!*

Simon served up a round of facts and figures as they walked. It was like he turned docent in the hallowed halls. "The *Grand Ole Opry* plays here every Friday and Saturday night," he said. "The show is nationally syndicated to more than two hundred radio stations. It's the institution that made country music an American treasure."

"Megan was telling me some history the other night. How it started in the twenties and moved around to different venues in town early on."

"Yeah, that's right. Most people think the Ryman Auditorium was the first home of the Opry. But it actually played at the War Memorial

Building downtown first. The Opry was like early vaudeville. We still refer to Opry members as a 'cast.' This permanent home was built in 1974. Then the flood hit last May, but it's still here, $20 million later."

They reached the end of the hallway, where two open doors led to the back of the Opry stage. Directly in front were huge curtains used as backdrops that blocked any view of the stage or the house. Simon motioned Judd to follow him toward the side of the stage. That's when Judd got his first look inside the Opry House with its famed red-barn backdrop. His first impression was how bright the lights were on the stage. They were everywhere—lights hanging on grids from the ceiling, glaring footlights downstage, enormous blinding lights stage right and left. He also noticed large green screens on rollers.

A small group was gathered at center stage, talking intensely under the glare of the spotlights. The wings were dimly lit; the house floor was dark; no lights were on throughout the tiered mezzanine and balcony.

Megan suddenly appeared from the side wing. "We're having some trouble," she said to Simon.

Earlier in the office, Megan had mentioned to Judd that she was going to the video shoot to make sure there were no major issues before Ripley arrived.

"What's the problem?" Simon asked.

"The green screens. The director said it would be the easiest shoot of Ripley's career, that the screens would be placed in a few key positions around him. All he'd need to do is lip-sync to the track a few times and be done. All of the computer-generated imaging would happen in post without Ripley. But they've been debating for an hour if the green screens are in the correct positions. They've had lighting issues—the same ole 'hurry up and wait.' It's been a mess!"

"What do the green screens do?" Judd asked.

"Do you know the video concept?" Megan said.

"Yeah, I read the treatment. Ripley starts off performing a song on the Opry, current day, and then when he hits the chorus it magically turns into a live Opry show—basically a barn dance in 1939, a flashback, and Ripley is the new wonder kid."

"Exactly. Someone found a rare piece of Opry footage with no sound from the late 1930s. Ripley saw it and got this idea to shoot a video where he is actually dropped into the rare footage and plays with the early Opry troubadours. But there was not enough for an entire video, so they're creating some matching footage to emulate the original *WSM Barn Dance* by using green-screen technology. If it's done right, no one will know the real footage from the created footage. Ripley starts out current day, then steps back in time and performs with DeFord Bailey—'the Harmonica Wizard,' the Opry's first black member—and other regulars of that era. In the video, founder George D. Hay gets so excited about Ripley's performance that he sends out brand-new Opry members Roy Acuff and Bill Monroe to play along. The problem is that the green screens must be placed in exact locations where the found footage will be dropped in using computers. And for the last hour, the director has kept changing his mind as to where those exact locations are—and Ripley's about to lose it."

"I better go talk to him," Simon said.

He walked toward center stage. Ripley appeared to be zoning out on a stool. It struck Judd as odd—here was one of the most famous faces in America by himself inside the proverbial eye of a hurricane. All Judd could think was, *He looks lonely.*

Ripley spotted Simon and gave a half nod with an "I see you, but I'm not supposed to move" expression.

"Rip," Simon said, "you've got everybody in here buzzing."

"Megan said this would be done in two takes. What she didn't tell me was it would be an hour of lighting changes for each one."

Simon placed his hand on Ripley's arm. "You seem stressed."

"Just exhausted," Ripley said. "Can't get a full night's sleep."

"It's a little complicated to shoot, but it's a great concept."

"Do you have news?" Ripley asked.

"I do," Simon said. "Let's talk about it in private when you finish. I'm not going anywhere."

"Apparently, these idiots can't figure out how this works, so we might as well talk now."

Simon leaned close and lowered his voice. "Strickland called me at the office just as I was coming out here to see you."

"And?"

"The good news is, we got the guy we wanted. Doug Tillman will fill the position vacated by James Clark."

"And the bad news?"

Simon was uneasy talking in such a public setting. "He doesn't want to discuss a renegotiation or any ownership of your master recordings at any point in the future."

"Did you even argue with the man?"

Simon got a serious look on his face. "I did, but like I always say, this is a chess game. These are delicate political maneuverings. Getting Doug Tillman is a win for us. But I don't want to make another move until I know where all the players are on the board."

Ripley's voice rose. "Don't give me some stupid board-game analogy!"

Suddenly, Simon stopped caring about the video shoot and the curious bystanders. He looked right into Ripley's eyes and asked, "Have you told me everything about all of this?"

"You're the one who spoke with Strickland."

"Yes, I did, and Strickland told me that he also spoke to you opening weekend in Greenville." When Ripley didn't respond, Simon continued, "Look, I can't protect you if you're cutting deals behind my back. I can't manage you if you're trying to manage yourself. You've got to trust me. How many times are we going to have this conversation?" Still, Ripley did not respond. Then Simon leaned in and whispered, "While you were obviously trying to work out your own deal with Strickland, did he happen to mention the fact that Galaxy is about to close on its secret merger with another major record company?"

Ripley's expression went from irritation to disbelief. "It's just talk."

"Really? Maybe you should ask Strickland yourself. You two seem to be getting along rather well these days."

"It's been rumored for years. Why do you think it's real this time?"

Simon fired back, "Because that's my job. That's why you have me as your manager—to tell you things other people won't tell you, to protect you. And yes, I'm sure it's real. And it's going to be voted on next weekend."

Ripley had no comeback. Simon felt all the eyes on them. Not wanting to interrupt the exchange, everyone had frozen—except for Judd, who walked across the stage to join them.

As he approached, Judd felt the intense heat from the overhead lights. *Man, it is hot under here,* he thought.

Ripley eased off the stool. Judd wasn't expecting him to stand.

"Hello, Judd," Ripley said, clasping Judd's hand firmly.

Don't get up on my account, Judd thought. "Hi, Ripley. Sorry to interrupt." He turned to Simon. "Megan is on the phone backstage, but she said they're finally ready to start again when you guys are finished."

Simon turned to Ripley. "Okay, Rip, we're going to be back behind the monitors. Knock this thing out. And look, we can clear all this other stuff up. We'll have the rest of the afternoon to talk about it. Just put it out of your mind for a few minutes. Let's get this video done. Remember, when you're tired, smile with your eyes."

"It'll be fast, Simon, I promise," Ripley replied.

Judd turned and started to follow Simon out from under the lights. His eyes tried to adjust as they walked into the darkness of the side wing. He remembered there were lots of cables on the floor, but he couldn't see them well.

That was when he heard it—a loud, sharp explosion splintering the air. The sound originated from somewhere in the darkness of the Opry House, the echo traveling rapidly across the stage. It was so startling that Judd's entire body flinched. Then came a heavy thud. Judd heard a faint "ah" sound with a guttural, haunting reverberation. His eyes couldn't adjust fast enough. He looked back toward the stage to see if a light had exploded. As he did, he tripped over someone and landed with his full weight on his right elbow.

He came face to face with Simon, who was on the floor in a fetal position, staring right at him. Simon's eyes bulged out of their sockets as he vomited up blood. Judd smelled it immediately.

Then came another loud pop. Judd felt a sudden burning sensation engulf his left shoulder. He heard screaming. *God, I'm going to throw up, too,* he thought. He felt as if all the blood from his face were rushing down his neck, through his arms, and out from the tips of his fingers. His body began to shake. Then he heard the thud of his head falling back to the floor. But now he felt nothing. Everything went black.

CHAPTER 15

London
Kensington
Royal Garden Hotel

"Yes, Mr. Tillman, how may I assist you this afternoon?" asked the female operator at the Royal Garden Hotel in Kensington.

Doug Tillman loved her accent. Her initial words over the phone sent a message of complete competence. Immediately, he thought he'd like to have that in Nashville. He would hire a receptionist with an English accent to help rid any negative stereotype. Personally, he had always felt Southern accents in business projected an image of ignorance. If he was going to work in the South, particularly in country music, he wanted to project decisiveness—make a decision, make it quickly and accurately, and then move on. When Tommy Strickland had spoken with him confidentially about the Nashville position opening up, Strickland mentioned that the new president would need a complete staff change. His exact words were, "You will need to clear the slate. There will be too many mixed emotions and lingering loyalties to James Clark for anyone inside to stay effective." An English receptionist would be perfect.

He returned to the conversation at hand. "My message light is on."

"Yes, sir, it is indicating that you requested not to be disturbed until your appointed wake-up call, which is now in approximately ten minutes."

"Oh, okay." Tillman realized the jet lag had not fully dissipated. His body was tingling. "So what time is it now . . . here?"

"It is exactly 6:05 P.M., Mr. Tillman, and your requested wake-up call is set for 6:15 sharp. Shall I disengage the wake-up call or have it ring in ten minutes?"

"No, no, I'm awake. Thank you, miss. That's all I need."

"Very well, then. Have a lovely evening." And just like that, the pleasantly proficient voice disappeared.

Tillman thought a shower would feel nice but knew he didn't have time. He walked into the bathroom and looked at himself in the mirror. The Italian bloodline on his mother's side gave him his dark Mediterranean features. Even without much sleep, he rarely looked tired. His black curly hair never needed much attention. Other than wishing he were taller, he thought he looked pretty good for an active, health-conscious, forty-five-year-old bachelor running on virtually no sleep, having traveled overnight from New York's Kennedy Airport on American's transatlantic flight into Heathrow. After unpacking his bags and organizing his papers, he had made the mistake of lying down for a short nap—not a good idea, since the last week had been the most intense of his career.

Last Wednesday, exactly one week ago, his immediate boss, Tommy Strickland, had flown to London to meet with Galaxy chairman Warren MacCabe to prepare for the annual Board of Directors Meeting and Shareholders Meeting. As senior vice president of sales and marketing for North America, Tillman had an office in New York right across the hall from Strickland's. He had worked around the clock getting Strickland organized for his trip. Once Strickland departed, Tillman planned on taking a few vacation days to rejuvenate.

To his surprise, Strickland called from London the next evening and said he urgently needed to speak. Tillman assumed he wanted to discuss some last-minute details. However, Strickland assured him all of their prep work was in order, then asked if they could speak in the utmost confidence. Tillman reassured him they could. Strickland said he and MacCabe had decided that afternoon to make some immediate and dramatic executive-level changes prior to the meetings. Strickland said that, on the flight over, he kept thinking they needed someone in Nashville who understood marketing the way they understood it in New York. He also said he had noticed how well Ripley Graham and Tillman got along at the Galaxy Christmas party in New York last December. At dinner that night, Ripley and Tillman had talked endlessly about the differences between the New York office and the Nashville office—the pros and cons of test marketing, outsourcing radio research, and general market analysis in the music business. It was obvious to everyone that Tillman had made a strong impression on their premier artist.

Then Strickland asked Tillman if *he* would be interested in being the new president of Galaxy Nashville. Tillman would not for some time forget that feeling of utter exhilaration. Of course, he immediately expressed his interest. Strickland, clearly pleased, said several events would have to transpire quickly before he could officially offer the position. He told Tillman to fly to Nashville for a clandestine one-on-one meeting with Ripley Graham. Strickland made it clear the position was about Tillman's chemistry with Ripley. Tillman asked if Simon Stills would attend. Strickland insisted Simon would dominate the conversation and get in the way—again, it was to be not a meeting of substance but of chemistry. Strickland went on to say he had spoken with Ripley that afternoon. Ripley was in Greenville, South Carolina, preparing for his opening-night concert. Ripley confirmed he would be available the next Monday afternoon to meet secretly with Tillman at his home—but only from two to four, since he had his annual Mardi Gras party that evening. Strickland then emphasized to Tillman that he would not allow anyone to take the Nashville post without Ripley's blessing. If all went well with Ripley, they would finalize a deal memo back in New York by the end of Tuesday. Then, when Tillman signed, they would fly him to London, where on Wednesday evening Strickland would arrange an in-person audience with Warren MacCabe himself. That was the final hurdle. With MacCabe's approval, Strickland would execute the employment agreement, and Tillman would become president of Galaxy Nashville.

It had all proceeded like clockwork. Tillman knew his clandestine meeting with Ripley had gone well. He had made it clear to Ripley that he knew nothing about country music—nothing at all. But he had dedicated his career to sales and marketing, and when it came to selling music, it was all the same—pop, rock, country, or polka. It was about price, positioning, mass merchandizing, cross-promotional programs, co-ops, and general market advertising strategies. In his mind, the selling of music had never been genre specific. It was about being creative and having the funding to back it up. Ripley did not seem to care that Tillman was unversed in country music. He kept saying, "I'll make the music, you just *sell* it!" Ripley said he believed that the head of a record company should have a marketing background, not a music background, and that Nashville never seemed to understand that. Tillman had responded that, as the vice president of sales and marketing in New York for the past sixteen years, he felt sure he was the right man for the job. And as long as he was the Nashville head, Ripley would remain Galaxy's top priority.

The meeting with Ripley lasted only ninety minutes. At the end, Ripley said something that at first Tillman took as flattery. As they were saying their goodbyes, Ripley grasped his hand and said, "You're here because I specifically asked for you. I don't want you to ever forget that."

As the week passed, Tillman couldn't get that comment out of his head. Was it flattery or a veiled threat? In either case, he was certain Ripley wanted him as the new Nashville chief.

Tillman felt like fate was smiling on him. Finally, he was in the right place at the right time. Strickland must have promised Ripley there would be major changes in Nashville, and Tillman was Strickland's insurance policy to show his good faith—an insurance policy for which Galaxy was happy to pay a high premium. The base annual salary was half a million dollars. In Nashville, that would go a very long way. They expected him to replace the Nashville staff according to his own style of management and to report only to Strickland. Tillman's back-end deal, based on performance, included impressive bonus incentives including profit sharing. It was his dream ticket.

The company lawyers back in New York had made one point crystal-clear. Tillman's job security was directly and solely tied to one major objective: getting Ripley's album to the market this year.

How difficult can that be? Tillman thought. During their meeting, Ripley had assured him that his new project was all but done. Ripley said that Simon had advised him to record everything but his final vocals. There were rumors about executive changes at Galaxy, and Simon felt it would be prudent to see who exited before finishing the new recordings. It turned out to be good advice. Ripley then said, "Doug, if you accept the position, I'll get out of this holding pattern and go to work."

What a week, Tillman thought as he checked his watch. It read 1:17 p.m. He was still on Eastern Standard Time. After freshening up in the restroom, he headed out the door and down the hall toward the elevators while resetting his watch to 6:17 p.m. *Relax,* he told himself, *you've got time.* The meeting with Strickland and MacCabe was at 7:00, and he didn't want to arrive early and look anxious.

As he stepped off the elevator, Tillman contemplated the fact that this had all moved *very* fast. But he deserved it. He was a veteran of the business. He had worked tirelessly for Galaxy, been loyal to Strickland, and hit it off with Ripley. That was exactly how these things happened. For all intents and purposes, he was now the new label head for the fastest-selling artist in music history. The MacCabe meeting was just a formality. He knew Strickland and Ripley were recommending him for the position. The timing was perfect.

It all made sense. Given the unprecedented demand for a new Ripley Graham CD, Strickland wanted *him* to be the one to deliver it to the marketplace. It was simply his time, and he would make Ripley's next release the biggest in music-business history. He'd pull out all the stops. What could possibly go wrong?

CHAPTER 16

London
Kensington

As Tillman walked out through the pristine lobby of the five-star Royal Garden Hotel, he heard Bertie's Bar upstairs beginning to get rowdy. He hoped it wasn't cold outside, since he planned to walk to the Galaxy meeting, which was no more than a five-minute stroll away on Kensington High Street. Galaxy always housed its guests and visiting employees at the Royal Garden because of its luxurious accommodations and proximity to the home office. The annual Board of Directors Meeting and Shareholders Meeting were held in the Royal Garden's deluxe conference facilities on its lower level.

Although he never had an official audience with MacCabe, Tillman had been in the London office a dozen times. He loved the area of Kensington. His favorite restaurant, Cuba, was directly across the street. After a meal, he'd often walk downstairs to the Havana Club to check out its live Latin bands and take a look at the cigar list. Tonight, he thought he'd treat himself once they made his new deal official.

Outside, the air felt crisp but not bitterly cold. *Perfect,* he thought. The sounds of London were just what he needed to snap his body back into the game.

Tillman looked left at Kensington Palace and Gardens. The palace was best known as the birthplace of Queen Victoria in 1819. In modern times, Princess Diana had moved there in the 1990s and remained until her death in 1997. Locals said Princess Di often jogged around the gardens and through Hyde Park. She was someone with real power—a world figure, one of the most photographed faces on the planet. It occurred to Tillman that no one had been exploited in celebrity marketing with more success than Princess Di. She was the ultimate face in "show business"—she had looks, fame, and money and was adored by a worldwide audience. Then, in one tragic second in a tunnel in France, she was gone. Or was she? Her picture was all over London—in gift shops, on posters, on T-shirts, on postcards, in photo albums. This year, with the Royal marriage of Diana's son William to Kate Middleton, her image was being exploited even more. England's modern Cinderella story had ended in tragic Shakespearean fashion—and it sold. Tillman thought of other celebrities whose early deaths had been powerful marketing tools—Elvis, Marilyn Monroe, John Lennon, Michael Jackson.

He was now standing across the street from the historic red-brick Electric Lighting Station, the refurbished home office of Galaxy Records. It was located on a typical English side street—a mere footpath once made of cobblestone leading to Kensington Court. The Electric Lighting Station was the former universe of Colonel R. E. B. Crompton, an electrical engineer who lived and worked in the building from 1891 to 1939. Today, "Galaxy Records Worldwide Headquarters" was inscribed in gold lettering over the large onyx doors. Inside that building, Tillman planned to market the image of Ripley Graham worldwide. And it would all happen here, in Princess Diana's old neighborhood.

"Mr. Tillman, how nice to see you. How was your trip over?" asked the receptionist. Sally was an aesthetically pleasing welcome. Tillman barely remembered her from his last trip, yet she seemed excited to see him.

"Great. Uneventful, the way I like it. How have you been?"

"Fantastic, really. Thanks. I know Mr. MacCabe and Mr. Strickland are expecting you. I'll let Gwen know you are here." Sally spoke into her headset. "Gwen, Doug Tillman has arrived. . . . Sure, will do." She glanced back at Tillman. "Go right on up. Gwen will meet you at the executive level."

Tillman started up the wide staircase. As he passed the second-floor landing and looked down the corridor, it amazed him how cramped everything seemed. Cubicles filled every inch of floor space. Lining the hallways were cardboard boxes simply marked "Galaxy." Some held CDs, some were unopened, some contained rolled-up posters, and some were overflowing bins of shredded paper. It was anything but what Tillman expected from the tidy British.

At the third floor, that all changed. The glass double doors at the top of the landing reached the ceiling. Inside was a stylish suite that was part office space and part modern museum.

Gwen, a middle-aged woman with a much more conservative style than the younger employees in the building, held the door open. "Mr. Tillman, how very nice to see you. What can I get you to drink?" she asked.

"Nice to see you, too. Coffee sounds good. Black is fine."

"Certainly. They are expecting you in Mr. MacCabe's office. Go right ahead and I'll have some coffee brought in."

Tillman now stood in the atrium on the top floor of the building. The wrought-iron gridwork above supported the glass pyramid-shaped ceiling. In the daytime, sun flooded the room. Oversized urns holding ginkgo trees were evenly spaced across the Spanish terra-cotta tile floor. To the left, beyond a glass wall running the length of the atrium, was the state-of-the-art conference room. To the right, a glass-brick wall with a heavy glass door hid the offices of top executives. In the center of the atrium stood a large armillary sphere, an ancient astronomical instrument that showed the divisions of the heavens. The corporate symbol for Galaxy Records, the sphere represented humankind's unrelenting search for new stars in the universe. The plaque next to the sphere bore the inscription, "Never fear the exploration of the galaxy or the human spirit, for they are one and the same. Fear only those who see the human condition as a galaxy too vast to explore. Those who are afraid to succeed, or worse, afraid of the truth, will assuredly fail. Exploration is the father of courage and creativity. Therein lies our humanness."

It was no accident that the armillary sphere pointed in the direction of Warren MacCabe's office. Tillman pushed through the large wooden doors.

Warren MacCabe walked over from the far side of his office. A legend in the world music industry, MacCabe had been on the cutting edge of the entertainment business for his entire forty-year career. Poised and charismatic, he stood six foot two. He was fit and lean and had thinning gray hair. He dressed conservatively but always wore expensive handmade eyewear personally crafted for him by Armenian designer Alain Mikli, his signature touch in an industry that thrived on individualized trademarks. Close friends teased MacCabe for being the music industry's 007. The physical resemblance between him and Sean Connery was rather remarkable.

"How was your trip?" MacCabe asked in his thick Scottish brogue.

"Fine, thanks." Tillman had never been in MacCabe's office. As a matter of fact, he had never made it past the second floor.

The two men grasped hands as Tommy Strickland moved up from behind MacCabe.

"Tommy, good to see you," Tillman said.

Unlike MacCabe, Tommy Strickland was stoic by nature. Those who liked him said he was reserved. Those who didn't described him as cold-blooded. He never took the spotlight but always remained in the inner circle. He had a pasty complexion and bleached hair cut close to the scalp. He always wore black, usually a leather jacket, and never a tie. He had been reared in the States but never disclosed where.

"Sit down." MacCabe gestured to the seats around the antique coffee table positioned atop a finely woven Persian rug. "Tommy and I were just talking about Ripley."

As Tillman situated himself, the door opened and a young woman entered with a tray bearing a silver coffee container, three coffee cups, and a small chalice of milk. She placed them on the table in front of the three men.

"Shall I get anyone something more?" she asked softly.

"No, no, that's terrific, Heather. Thank you," MacCabe said as Heather quickly exited. "Over 25 million digital downloads sold. That is quite a feat indeed." MacCabe picked up his coffee cup and turned to Tillman. "But what scares me about these artists that sell tens of millions of records is that at some point they start thinking they can do it by themselves. Doug, do you know what the problem is with being the fastest-selling digital artist of all time?"

"Not really, no."

"How do you stay on top? If we sell 2 million copies of Ripley's next release, every Tom, Dick, and Harry will say we failed. How do you outdo yourself when you're at the top?"

"Yes, sir. I see that."

"That's why Tommy and I wanted you to come over and discuss your newly acquired position in Nashville. We need to speak on an absolutely private level at this point. Are you fine with that?"

"Of course."

"As a new president within Galaxy, you will be privy to confidential information. We are not here to discuss your position. You've got it. You're our man. We are here to discuss your agenda."

"I appreciate that, sir." Tillman was elated with the direction this was going.

"So I will get right to it," MacCabe said. "Strictly confidentially, Galaxy has a merger proposal on the table with Luxor Entertainment to create the largest record company in the world. Obviously, I have denied this in the press, but it is time for Tommy and me to bring a few of the company's top brass completely up to speed. It will be the main topic for our Board of Directors Meeting next weekend."

Just as MacCabe finished, the door opened abruptly. It was Gwen. She looked shaken.

"Mr. MacCabe, so sorry to interrupt, but you must turn on CNN International. Something terrible has happened."

"What, for God's sake?" MacCabe said.

"They just broke in with a special report, sir. Someone in Nashville tried to kill Ripley Graham."

CHAPTER 17

West Palm Beach, Florida
Kensington
Nashville

Wednesday morning at daybreak, James Clark picked up the paper in the driveway of his Nashville home. Soon afterward, he got into his Lexus LS 460 and headed straight to the airport. The cover of *The Tennessean* had a color photo of him front and center. The headline read, "Clark's Resignation Upstages Graham Gala."

He took a seven o'clock flight to Atlanta, changed planes, and then boarded a flight that landed in West Palm Beach at noon. A car service picked him up upon his arrival. With no more greeting than a nod from Clark, the chauffeur drove him east on Southern Boulevard, across the Intracoastal Waterway, north on North Ocean Boulevard, and past the Palm Beach Country Club toward Clark's palatial oceanfront getaway.

While in the car, Clark checked his cell phone. He had five new messages. The last one was ending as the car drove up to his home. Clark got out without retrieving his bags, unlocked the front door, and bolted to the living room. He turned on CNN. A second later, he was watching an aerial feed from Nashville. Below a yellow line at the bottom of the screen, he read, "LIVE—BREAKING NEWS: Grand Ole

Opry House, Nashville, TN." Clark turned up the volume.

Suzanne Malveaux anchored the CNN newsroom from Atlanta. "We are going to our affiliate, who is feeding us these live shots. Bill, what can you tell us?"

"Suzanne, all we know is that gunshots were fired about 11:15 this morning in what is now being described as an assassination attempt on the life of country-music superstar Ripley Graham."

Clark fell back onto the sofa. Under his breath, he asked, "Is he dead?"

"Metro police and SWAT teams have surrounded the building," the Nashville reporter said. "At present, no one is in custody. We do know that Ripley Graham was in the building taping a music video. We have an unconfirmed report that there are victims, though we don't know how many or their degree of injury. We have also heard Ripley Graham, though shaken, is not one of the injured. I repeat, we have been told that Ripley Graham is still in the building but unharmed. This is unconfirmed, however."

MacCabe, Strickland, and Tillman stood motionless in front of the television in MacCabe's office. Gwen watched from behind them with her hand over her mouth.

Tillman leaned closer when he saw the same CNN headline on the screen. "Holy . . ." He was so shocked he didn't finish the expletive.

"Tommy, who is in charge in Nashville since Clark is gone and Tillman is here?" MacCabe asked.

"Hal Bennett, our general manager." Strickland turned his head away from the TV for a moment, wondering what MacCabe was thinking.

"Gwen, call Hal Bennett in Nashville and Carlton Ross in New York immediately. Tell them they are on the phone with the three of us to discuss crisis management. When they are both on, connect us in here on my speaker phone, please."

"Yes, sir," Gwen said, pulling her hand away from her mouth. She quickly left.

MacCabe turned his attention back to the television.

"Bill, this is Becky Anderson in London for our CNN International audience. Do we know for sure that this was an assassination attempt on the life of Ripley Graham?"

"All early indications point to that. We know Ripley Graham was on the Grand Ole Opry stage taping a new music video. The gunshots were in the Opry House, where he was taping. Apparently, two or three people were hit, but again we have unconfirmed reports that Ripley Graham was not one of them. Becky, I'm hearing in my earpiece that metro police here in Nashville are confirming that Ripley Graham is safe and has been taken to an undisclosed secured location. We should have that feed live momentarily."

Music Row had come to a dead halt. Producers and musicians who moments ago were tracking songs in famed studios like Starstruck, Blackbird, Ocean Way, and the Sound Kitchen were all gathered in lounges and glued to TVs—as was every booking agent at William Morris Endeavor, CAA, and Paradigm, every employee at Capitol Records, Warner Music Group, Universal, and Sony, every publisher from EMI Music Publishing to Warner/Chappell Music, every personal management company from Red Light to Octagon, every entertainment law firm from Loeb & Loeb to Crownover & Blevins. Elite Management and Galaxy Records Nashville were no exceptions.

On CNN, the picture jumped from an overhead helicopter shot to a close-up of a policeman standing outdoors next to several emergency vehicles. The officer spoke loudly with a heavy Southern accent. "I'm Don Aaron of the Nashville Metro Police Department. We can confirm that at approximately 11:15 a.m., a gunman opened fire in the Grand Ole Opry House while Mr. Ripley Graham was filming a music video inside. Mr. Graham is unharmed. He has been taken to a secured area. Presently, no one has been placed in custody, and the gunman is still at large. We believe the gunman got off two, maybe three shots. There are no fatalities at present. However, three persons were injured, one of them critically. All three have been taken to Vanderbilt University

Medical Center. We can also confirm that the person critically injured is Mr. Simon Stills, Ripley Graham's personal manager. Mr. Stills was removed by helicopter and is currently undergoing emergency surgery at VUMC. We do not have the names to release of the two other victims, who sustained less serious injuries. Both of those victims also were taken via ambulance moments ago. That is all I can report at this time."

The switchboard operator at Galaxy Nashville entered the crowded conference room and said loudly, "Mr. Bennett, you have an urgent call from the home office in London. Mr. MacCabe, Mr. Strickland, and Mr. Tillman are asking that you join them on their crisis management conference call."

Gwen's voice came over the speakerphone. "Mr. MacCabe, I have Mr. Hal Bennett in Nashville and Mr. Carlton Ross in New York holding."

"Thank you, Gwen. Gentlemen, this is Warren MacCabe. I am in my office in London with Tommy Strickland and our new president of Galaxy Nashville, Doug Tillman. I am sure everyone is aware of the assassination attempt on Ripley Graham's life."

"Yes, sir."

"Yes, sir."

MacCabe continued, "We know only what we have just heard on CNN over here—that Ripley is unharmed but several others including his manager, Simon Stills, are injured. Is that correct, and do we know more?"

"Mr. MacCabe, this is Hal Bennett in Nashville. It is our understanding that the officers in charge took Ripley to Vanderbilt at his request. He is obviously very concerned about Simon Stills."

"Hal, this is Doug Tillman. Have you or anyone in the office been in contact with Ripley yet?"

"No. We tried his cell phone and got voicemail, which is not unusual. I did speak with Simon's partner at Elite Management, Brad Holiday. He was headed to Vanderbilt to check on Simon and told us Ripley was already there."

"Okay," Tillman said. "While we are all on the phone, can someone in the Nashville office try Brad Holiday again? Let's get another update—see if they know Simon's current condition and confirm for us that Ripley is not hurt."

Strickland leaned over the speakerphone. "Carlton, are you still there?"

"I am."

"We need to get a press release written from Galaxy New York. Have our staff do it, but Warren and I need to approve it. We should have quotes from Warren and Ripley."

"Got it."

"Does anyone know who writes quotes for Ripley?"

Hal Bennett answered, "Ripley's publicist, Janice Burns. We'll get it from her." After a pause, Bennett continued, "I'm hearing that we are about to have Brad Holiday from Elite Management on the phone. I'm trying the connection now. Brad?"

"Yes."

"Brad, this is Doug Tillman. I'm in London with my bosses, Tommy Strickland and Warren MacCabe. Can you hear me?"

"Yes, but please speak as loud as you can. You sound very distant."

"Are you with Ripley?"

"Close. They have him in the administration office. The police are still with him. . . . I think my cell phone is dropping out."

"What is the update on Simon?" Tillman got no reply. "Brad, Brad, are you there?" He looked up at MacCabe and Strickland. "We lost him."

The square silver plate on the wall to the right of the double doors looked like part of an emergency exit that might sound an alarm. Ripley pushed it anyway, and the doors opened quickly with a hydraulic sound. Directly above the doors was a sign that read, "VUMC Intensive Care Unit—Authorized Personnel Only." Ripley walked through with Jerome on one side and Brad Holiday on the other. Following them were two men, one in a dark suit, the other a uniformed metro police officer. The doors made a snapping sound as they fully opened, almost as if they were standing at attention while the five passed through.

The trauma unit was on the tenth floor at VUMC. The nursing station was at the center, and ICU beds circled the wing. The men reached the nursing station and stopped. A well-dressed woman approached, obviously expecting them.

"Mr. Graham, I'm Melissa Pearce with the administrative staff here at the hospital."

Ripley looked unfocused.

"We have set up a secured waiting room for you here. This is the floor where they will bring Mr. Stills after surgery. We also have a full-time media consultant on staff to handle any privacy issues and to release any statements, if needed. We've already spoken to Megan Olsen in your management office and to your PR agent, Janice Burns. I believe both Megan and Janice are on their way here now."

"What's Simon's condition?" Ripley asked.

"All we know is that he is still in surgery. We'll get word to you as soon as we have anything at all. In the meantime, the metro police have assigned Officer Mason here to stay with you."

Brad Holiday stepped into the conversation. "Excuse me, I'm with Elite Management, Ripley's management company. Simon Stills is my partner. Do you mind going ahead and showing Ripley and me to the secured waiting room? I'm concerned about his privacy, and I also need to get to a place where I can use my cell phone in private."

"Certainly."

They were being led to the room when Brad's phone rang.

"Yes, I can hear you now. Hold on one second. We're getting Ripley into a private waiting room."

Ripley asked in an irritated tone, "Is it MacCabe and Strickland again?"

"Yeah, and Doug Tillman. I think some others are on the line as well." Brad covered the phone with his hand. "How about I tell them we'll call back when we get settled?"

"No, I'll talk." Ripley took the cell phone as they entered the private waiting room and said, "The bastard missed me and hit Simon in the throat!"

"Ripley, it's Doug Tillman. So you are definitely okay?"

"Yeah, I'm fine. I mean, I'm not hurt or anything. But Simon . . . man. It was unbelievable—people running, screaming. That stuff happens in whacked-out places, but not in Nashville, not on the stage of the Grand Ole Opry. God, it was terrible. The police are saying it may have been some crazed fan trying to kill me. I mean, what the hell?" Ripley sat on the sofa and stared at the floor, visibly shaken. "So this is it, the price of fame. They say Simon may not make it. It's bad, man. I heard the bullet whiz by my head! Then Simon went down. They've got him in surgery on the second floor." Ripley's voice faded.

"Ripley, this is Warren MacCabe with Tommy Strickland."

"Yeah." Ripley sounded distracted.

Jerome opened the door, and Megan bolted into the room. Eyes filled with tears, mascara running, she immediately asked Brad who Ripley was talking to.

Ripley looked up while Megan shook her head in shock. "London," he mouthed.

"Janice is on her way," she whispered back.

Ripley nodded as MacCabe continued to talk into his ear.

"We need to go over a few important details to get us through the next twenty-four hours or so, okay?"

Ripley didn't answer.

"First of all," MacCabe said, "we are going to need to know exactly where you are for a while."

"I'm not leaving," Ripley replied.

"Good. Our people have talked to the hospital, and they are setting up a secured place for you to stay as long as you wish. I'm going to have one of our in-house security officers stay close as well. He won't bother you, but your safety is now paramount until we figure out what happened today."

"He's here already."

"Good. Also, I'm going to get Doug Tillman on a plane tonight. I want him back with you to handle the situation there and take care of anything you need. In the meantime, don't talk to anyone until Doug gets to Nashville. No press."

"I'm not planning on it."

"We will put out a press release letting everyone know you are fine and in a secured place. If you need something, ask only the security person who is with you until Doug gets there. Is that clear?" MacCabe asked.

"Whatever," Ripley answered, not used to hearing directives.

"All right, Ripley, I'm on my way back," Doug Tillman said. "I'll call you as soon as I land in Nashville."

"Yeah, man, call me." And with that, Ripley was off the line.

MacCabe looked at Strickland. Without saying a word, he communicated that Strickland was to get to work.

"Carlton, it's Tommy Strickland. Are you still there?"

"Yes."

"Get our full security to stay with Ripley. Continue to communicate directly with hospital security, the Nashville police, and the local FBI. Make sure we have constant contact with Ripley. Have the hospital keep him on the tenth floor. I don't want him off that floor without one of our escorts. He has his own security, but we must remain with him at all times. We should set up a situation room for our people on the premises. Have our office engage with the hospital's PR team to deal directly with all reporters. I do not want reporters or press briefings at Galaxy. Ripley is not injured, so let's keep our distance. Again, Ripley has his entourage, but I don't want them calling the shots. Make sure I see a press release within thirty minutes for the worldwide wire services. I want the sentiment to be that Ripley is unharmed and that a full investigation is under way involving local and federal authorities. Ripley is not to make a personal appearance until Doug Tillman is in Nashville and by his side. Keep me updated on Simon's condition. Is all that understood?"

"Completely," Carlton Ross said.

"Okay, let's all get to work." Strickland disengaged the conference call.

The three men in London stood up straight and looked at each other.

"You're still our man," MacCabe said to Tillman. "The other issues we were going to discuss will have to wait. We need you with Ripley. He may not have a manager by the time you land. Basically, you will fill that void."

Tillman nodded.

MacCabe punched his intercom. "Gwen, will you get Mr. Tillman on the first available flight back to Nashville?" He didn't wait for her to respond but turned back to Tillman. "Sorry for the quick turnaround. I want you to call Tommy when you reach Ripley."

MacCabe then escorted Tillman toward the same door he had entered only forty-five minutes earlier. As they reached it, he put his hand on Tillman's shoulder. "I'm a student of history. We must remember that history enables us to navigate the future. We all know that history repeats itself, which is why the most effective form of human exploration is the exploring of our past. It would be arrogant to think we are the first to experience all of life's trials and triumphs, naïve to think the past hasn't shaped the present, and ignorant to ignore its effects on the future. The exploration of humankind is not about discovery. The exploration of humankind is about rediscovery."

Tillman had heard for years that MacCabe worked from a historical and philosophical perspective. It was part of his reputation—citing historical references in his decision making. "I would agree with that," Tillman said.

"The world is smaller and more interconnected than ever," MacCabe continued. "An hour ago, shots rang out in Nashville, and thanks to satellite technology we are watching here in London as it plays out. And yet, while we are watching the world from our modern perspective, the truth is that the nature of mankind has never changed."

Tillman had no idea where this was going and remained silent, like a soldier waiting to be dismissed.

"Twenty-five hundred years ago, when Athens was battling Sparta, Pericles gave a famous speech at the gravesite of his lost soldiers. It is known as 'the Funeral Speech of Pericles.'" MacCabe looked at the ceiling, closed his eyes, and began to recite. "He said, 'The whole earth is a grave of famous men; their story is not only written in stone, but on the very lives of other men far away.'" MacCabe paused, then looked back at Tillman and added, "The shots that rang out today in Nashville will reverberate and have a lasting effect on all of us for years to come."

Again, Tillman had no response. He glanced at Strickland, who hadn't moved.

MacCabe took one step back and firmly shook Tillman's hand as if it were a military send-off. "Call when you get to Nashville."

Tillman nodded without speaking, turned, and left.

Part II
Sound Tracks

CHAPTER 18

The Next Afternoon

Nashville
VUMC
Thursday, March 10
1:15 P.M.

There was a knock on the secured waiting-room door. Ripley, still in the same clothes from the day before, was stretched out on the short pull-out couch. "Come on in," he said as he sat up and put on his black cowboy hat.

Nate cracked open the door. "Sorry to wake you, Rip, but the doc is here."

Dr. Specter had a dignified look with early gray around his temples, highlighting his otherwise full, dark head of hair. He stretched out a hand to greet Ripley. "Hello, Mr. Graham. I'm Josh Specter. I performed the surgery on Simon Stills."

"How is he?"

"I'm sure they told you our greatest concern is potential brain damage from the lack of oxygen while he was bleeding. The bullet entered his neck just below his thyroid cartilage notch—what we all know as the Adam's apple. The bullet shattered the shield—the cartilage that protects the vocal cords. His breathing passage filled with blood. He would have suffocated if not for the EMS team on-site. They bypassed the trauma by performing an emergency cricothyroidotomy—some folks call it 'the pen procedure'—to open an airway."

"I've heard of that, but I thought it was called a 'trach,'" Ripley said.

"Technically, no. A formal tracheotomy is more involved. We actually converted his cricothyroidotomy yesterday here on the trauma floor by repositioning the tube lower in his neck, but you've got the right idea. The paramedics got a clear airway and controlled the bleeding. When we got him, we stabilized the fractured framework of his voice box. Fortunately for Simon, the bullet missed his carotid artery leading to his brain. It went through the upper left side of his neck below his jawbone, which is mainly fatty tissue and muscle. He won't be able to speak for a while, and there could be some speech impediment, but all in all he is one fortunate man."

"So he's going to make it?"

"The first twenty-four hours are the most critical, and he's made it past that. He was conscious for a little while this morning, though not very coherent. For the first morning after surgery, that is significant. He has been off his ventilator for several hours and is beginning to wake up from the sedation. So, barring any unexpected complications, he should make it. We'll monitor his brain activity as he is stimulated. But so far, it all looks positive. Would you like to see him?"

"Absolutely," Ripley answered.

"I have rounds to make, but just check in with the nurses, and they'll direct you. Let's keep it short, but stimulus from family and friends is always helpful. I'll be there in a little while."

A few minutes later, Ripley and his entourage approached the nursing station. "I'm Ripley Graham."

The two female nurses were already on their feet, having lost interest in the paperwork and monitors in front of them.

"Hello. I'm . . . I'm Brenda. . . . This is Maryanne. Dr. Specter said you were coming." Brenda walked from behind the nursing station. "Simon Stills is right down here." She gestured to the ICU and started down the hallway past a sign for Rooms 10204 to 10232.

"Ripley, we'll stay here," the man in the suit said.

As Brenda and Ripley stopped at Simon's room, Brenda asked, "Are all those men police officers?"

"Just the one in uniform. Nate and Jerome, the big guys, work for me. The other guy, the one with the bad suit that said he'd stay by your station, was hired by the record company. It's getting a little old." Ripley reached for the door. "Do you think he's awake?"

"He wasn't a minute ago." Brenda extended her arm to cut off his entrance. "I should tell you, he's going to look different. You need to be prepared."

Ripley dropped his hand. His back stiffened. "Okay."

Brenda paused. "Ready?"

Ripley nodded. Brenda pushed the door open, and Ripley entered alone.

The curtains just inside the doorway had a slight opening in the middle that had been pulled shut. He took both hands and slid them open.

Ripley just stood there. It wasn't that Simon simply looked different. He didn't look anything like himself at all. Even his signature mustache had been shaved completely off. Ripley was facing the foot of Simon's bed. There were machines on both sides with tubes and wires running everywhere. He could not stop staring at the central tube protruding directly out of Simon's throat. A bandage completely wrapped Simon from his shoulders to his chin. A humidifier blew air across the open tube from his neck. The moist air engulfed Simon's face, which was black and blue and swollen to the point Ripley was not even sure if his eyes were open. Simon looked like a character in a science-fiction movie, frozen in time, part of some wild experiment. For the moment, Ripley was as frozen as Simon.

"Just because he can't say nothin' don't mean you can't come over here and talk to him."

The voice came from a rather large black female nurse standing on the left side of the bed. Until she spoke, Ripley hadn't noticed anyone else in the room.

"Honey, he just might wake up for you. I sure would." The sunlight coming in the window backlit the nurse. "Come over here on this side." She pulled up a small stool on wheels next to where she was standing.

"Yes, ma'am." Ripley moved past the foot of the bed and around to the far side.

"I'm Shirley Rogers, and I already know who you are. You're the one who's got the whole nursing staff turned upside down. I don't think I've seen anybody take a lunch break all day, just hopin' they'll bump into you somewhere."

Ripley gave a shy smile, sat on the stool, and pulled closer to Simon.

Shirley, completely comfortable, leaned over Simon, put her hand on his arm, and said in a slightly louder voice, "Simon, Simon, you've got company, sweetie. Now, are you gonna wake up only for me, or are you gonna say hi to your famous friend here?" Shirley checked the level of his neck IV, connected under his collarbone, as she talked. "Now, don't be rude. He's been waitin' to see you since you got here." Shirley signaled Ripley to go ahead.

He leaned forward and said, "Simon, it's Ripley. They say you're gonna be fine, buddy. Everybody is asking about you." Ripley's voice was shaky, which surprised him. He stopped to swallow hard and regain his composure.

Shirley noticed his uneasiness. "You're doin' fine, sweetheart. Keep goin'."

Ripley let out a chuckle. "Hell, I think you got more press than I did this week, taking the bullet for me and all. You know it's supposed to be all about me." Ripley reached out and took Simon's hand. "Simon, can you hear me?"

Simon squeezed slightly with his fingers.

"Okay, I felt that."

"Now, come on, Simon," Shirley said. "Let's see those pretty blue eyes. No more sleepin' late."

The door opened, and Dr. Specter walked directly to the bedside. Judd Nix entered behind him, his left arm in a sling. Not wanting to be intrusive, Judd backed around the curtain by the doorway, out of Ripley's view.

"Well, good afternoon, Dr. Specter. Looks like you're just in time to say hello to Simon."

"Hi, Shirley," Dr. Specter said as he started checking the readings on several monitors.

"I think he can hear me," Ripley said.

"I'm sure he can," Dr. Specter replied, lifting the sheet and checking some tubing connected to Simon's chest. "Simon, are you doing okay?" He grasped Simon's other hand, which was lying still atop the sheet. "Squeeze your left hand if you can hear me."

Simon squeezed his hands ever so slightly, but Dr. Specter and Ripley both felt the movement.

"Good," said Dr. Specter. "Now, try to open your eyes."

Simon didn't move.

"Come on, Simon. It's time. Let's try to move those eyelids."

Simon's eyes suddenly opened wide, without any expression. It was as if a corpse had awakened. And because of the tilt of his head, he was staring directly at Ripley.

Ripley stood immediately. It was so unexpected and haunting that it frightened him. "Simon," he said awkwardly.

Simon's eyes were affixed on him. He didn't blink, he had no expression—just a dead man's stare.

"Very good, very good. You're doing great," Dr. Specter said. "You're over the hardest part now, Simon. You're going to get stronger by the day. You're doing fine. It will just take some time. Your body has absorbed a great deal, but you're on your way back."

Ripley couldn't handle the disfigured face, the stare burning a hole in him. He felt dizzy and started to back toward the door, knocking over his stool in the process.

"Are you okay?" Shirley asked. She picked up the stool and helped him sit back down.

"It must be the lack of sleep. It's been a rough twenty-four hours," Ripley said.

"Let me get you a glass of water. You look a little faint."

Seeing that Shirley had things under control, Dr. Specter returned the attention to the patient. "Okay, Simon. If you can hear me, try to move your right hand."

Simon's arm began to rise, almost as if he were pointing at Ripley.

The weight of the eerie, disfigured Simon pointing at him with a dead man's stare came crashing down on Ripley. He stood again, brushed by Dr. Specter, and exited the room.

"I need some fresh air," he muttered under his breath.

In his rush, Ripley never noticed Judd standing behind the curtain with his mouth gaping open.

CHAPTER 19

New York City
Midtown Manhattan
7:15 P.M.

The black Lincoln Town Car with New York plates that read GLXY II navigated slowly north through Midtown up Sixth Avenue, the Avenue of the Americas. It was dark, and the reflection of the red neon lights announcing Radio City Music Hall scrolled across the back right window, behind which Tommy Strickland sat. He didn't look up, as his eyes were fixed on the glow from his iPad. Strickland had departed London on the company jet at 3:00 P.M. Greenwich Mean Time. He slept for two of the eight hours it took to travel four thousand miles across the Atlantic and landed in Teterboro, New Jersey, at 6:15 P.M. local time. It was a twelve-mile ride from the private airfield into Manhattan. Now, weaving through evening traffic, headed toward the office, Strickland read the *Bulletin,* curious to see its take on the events in Nashville.

Billboard.biz Bulletin™

YOUR DAILY ENTERTAINMENT NEWS UPDATE
THURSDAY, MARCH 10, 2011

Assassination Attempt on Country Superstar Ripley Graham

Chip Avery, Nashville

Country-music megastar Ripley Graham is being held voluntarily under tight security today at Vanderbilt University Medical Center in Nashville. Graham was the target of an apparent assassination attempt yesterday while filming a music video on the Grand Ole Opry stage. The Opry was closed to the public during the filming. A gunman, still at large, fired shots, missing Graham but seriously injuring his personal manager, Simon Stills of Elite Management. Stills suffered a gunshot wound to the throat. Paramedics performed an emergency procedure on the site to clear his airway, then flew Stills by helicopter to VUMC, where he underwent immediate surgery.

Reports this morning say the surgery went as well as doctors hoped. However, Stills remains in intensive care, and sources tell the Bulletin that his condition remains critical.

The two other victims did not have life-threatening injuries and did not require surgery. They are reported to be Judd Nix, an intern at Elite Management who was accompanying Stills at the time of the shooting, and Walter Randle, a camera operator. Nix had a bullet graze his left shoulder and was held overnight at the hospital but is expected to be released later today. Randle had a bullet wound to his right leg. Officials believe the same bullet that exited Stills' throat ricocheted and hit Randle. Randle was released from the hospital late last night.

Officials from Galaxy Records, Graham's record company, released an open statement to the press last night from New York: "We are shocked and outraged at the violent attack on Ripley Graham and his manager, Simon Stills, in Nashville

today. We will commit all necessary resources toward helping local and national officials in identifying the perpetrators of this crime and bringing them to justice. Our prayers are with Simon Stills as he undergoes emergency surgery, as well as with the two other victims in the shooting. We spoke with Ripley Graham moments after the incident. He is unharmed, and his only concerns are the treatment and recovery of Simon Stills. Mr. Graham has requested to stay at the hospital, solely for the purpose of monitoring and assuring the greatest of care for Mr. Stills and the two other victims. Mr. Graham will not be speaking with reporters until the condition of Mr. Stills is made clear. Any inquiries in that regard should be directed to the VUMC public-relations staff. We speak for Mr. Graham in thanking the thousands of concerned fans who have reached out and expressed their good wishes."

The music industry has not been historically immune to assassinations and assassination attempts. John Lennon was shot to death in New York City on December 8, 1980. Selena was murdered in a hotel room in Corpus Christi, Texas, on March 31, 1995. One year later, rapper Tupac Shakur was a victim of a drive-by shooting while riding in a car on Flamingo Road in Las Vegas.

The driver drifted to the far right lane between West Fifty-first and West Fifty-second, then slowly came to a stop as Strickland finished reading.

Strickland reached for the door handle. "Thanks Li, appreciate it," he said dryly, almost as an afterthought.

"No problem," Li answered in his thick Korean accent. "Ten o'clock pickup tonight?"

"Unless I call." Strickland, already out of the car, headed toward the lobby entrance.

"You got it, you got it."

The thirty-ninth and fortieth floors of the AXA Financial Center at 1290 Sixth Avenue had been the home office of Galaxy Records

North America since 1989. Until that year, the offices were on the fifty-ninth and sixtieth floors of Carnegie Hall Tower. That's when Warren MacCabe ascended to chairman of the board. MacCabe's first official act was to announce new operation locations for both New York and Los Angeles. In New York, he moved the offices one block east and five blocks south, from 152 West Fifty-seventh Street to the current 1290 Avenue of the Americas. In Los Angeles, the offices stayed in Century City but moved one block south from 10100 Santa Monica Boulevard to 2029 Avenue of the Stars.

MacCabe told the board it was part of a long-term strategy to reduce overhead in both New York and L.A. That was debatable. The move was costly. For one, Galaxy still had a long-term lease remaining at Carnegie Hall Tower. MacCabe wanted to keep the top-floor suite for himself when he was working in New York. His reason for the moves, though he never admitted it, was simple. He wanted the changes of address. In MacCabe's view, it was imperative for Galaxy's address to read Avenue of the Americas on one coast and Avenue of the Stars on the other. That was it, period. The locations in New York and L.A. fit with his corporate vision of conquest and exploration.

Examples like this over the years had led Strickland to see MacCabe as nothing more than a philosophical oddity. In his opinion, Galaxy was in dire need of real leadership based on facts and market trends, not cosmic and theoretical whims. Strickland felt MacCabe's eccentric ego had gotten the best of him.

Before Nashville became a boom town in the nineties, most record companies—including Galaxy Nashville—had modest offices. But then the climate changed as country music became the fastest-growing genre in the industry. Warner Bros. Records Nashville was the first to build an enormous new structure at the end of Sixteenth Avenue. Soon afterward, Capitol Records constructed a building complete with a rotunda. It then turned around and sold the property to Gaylord/Word Entertainment. Next was Reba McEntire's Starstruck complex, consisting of several recording studios, a satellite TV broadcast facility, multipurpose office suites, and a platform on the roof that could be transformed into a heliport. Then the RCA label group, now Sony, spent millions revamping a run-down Catholic nursing home into a mega office facility. It even converted the chapel into a conference facility with state-of-the-art staging for live musical performances.

So, to keep up with the Joneses, MacCabe in 1998 sketched on a napkin his vision of the perfect Galaxy corporate office. It was to be a modern creative workspace with a façade resembling the castle in Edinburgh, Scotland.

MacCabe's new facility—"The Castle," as it began to be called—was approved by the board in 1999. In another show of nonconformity, MacCabe decided to move the offices off Music Row and built his landmark south of town in the rolling hills of Williamson County on Old Hillsboro Road, in an area that reminded him of Scotland. It would be the perfect architectural combination of the Old World and the New World, as befit MacCabe's philosophical motto. He sold the concept to the Galaxy board by forecasting continued exponential growth in country music, as calculated by James Clark.

Clark had been the first to articulate to MacCabe the theory that rap music's rise in America would inadvertently create an explosion in country music—the reason being that rap would alienate baby boomers, the largest buying segment of the population. That audience, who grew up listening to the Eagles and James Taylor in the seventies, would not take to the urban influence in pop and rock music. The "suburban" audience would need a new radio format other than pop/rock to call home. Country music was the logical answer.

Clark later admitted that the colossal growth of country music in the nineties exceeded even his own expectations. He was so accurate in his fortune-telling that MacCabe anointed him president of Galaxy Nashville. Those were golden years in Nashville, when record labels expanded and new buildings went up. MacCabe flew to Nashville every quarter to view The Castle's progress and discuss the building with Clark. Upon its completion in 2000, MacCabe described it as "Galaxy's crown jewel."

Ironically, that year was the beginning of the lost decade in the music business. Nineteen ninety-nine was not only the year the Galaxy board approved construction of The Castle, it was the year Sean Parker and Shawn Fanning launched Napster. With a single click, the next generation of music consumers would come to believe music was free. The business would never be the same.

For the next ten years, Strickland was incensed by how MacCabe, Clark, and other music executives ignored obvious trends. Strickland knew they may never recapture the days of old but believed the digital world could be more dynamic—if music companies would simply use the technology to their advantage. The industry had to embrace the new technology, not fight it. It had to educate the world about legal downloads and find the artists to drive the new model. For ten years now, it had been a struggle. CD sales started to slide in 2000. They hit rock bottom by 2010. Strickland felt like he had been beating his brains against a wall.

And then, finally, one week ago to the day, a breakthrough—Strickland called MacCabe at home and subsequently convinced him in the privy garden that he needed to oust his most loyal comrade, James Clark. Strickland no longer had to worry about Clark and his old-school approach. He had known that if he was patient, a situation would present itself in which MacCabe couldn't save his favorite soldier. And when it did, Strickland struck with lightning speed. Clark didn't know what hit him. When Strickland and Ripley had spoken by phone on opening night in Greenville, Ripley agreed to deal only with Strickland—directly, without going through a manager or an attorney. That alone gave Strickland more power than MacCabe. In a week's time, both James Clark and Simon Stills were out of the picture. But the sweetest part of it all was that Strickland's own appointed soldier, Doug Tillman, would now domesticate MacCabe's Castle.

Strickland felt light in his step as he walked into the AXA Financial Center. He passed the guards in front of the three-paneled collage on the far lobby wall and headed toward the back elevators.

His earpiece was in, and he pushed speed dial on his cell phone.

"I'm in the lobby. Did MacCabe call?"

"Yes, sir," a baritone voice responded.

"When?"

"Fifteen minutes ago," Strickland's executive assistant replied.

"What did he say?"

"He wants you to call him immediately. He did ask me if it looked like Ripley would regain the number-one position this week on all the charts after the shooting."

"Yes, he will. I checked online when I landed."

"I wasn't sure. I told Mr. MacCabe you would have more accurate information."

"Good. I'll call him back in a while. I'm coming up."

Strickland closed his cell and gave a rare half-smile as he thought, *This is perfect. Better than planned.*

CHAPTER 20

Nashville
White Bridge Road

The white-and-blue Music City Taxi turned right off West End Avenue onto White Bridge Road.

"It's about a mile up on the right, just before you get to Charlotte," Judd said.

When Judd had first set out to get an internship, he drove a U-Haul down from La Crosse, Wisconsin, by himself and rented a cramped three-room brick duplex off White Bridge Road, a fifteen-minute drive from Music Row. It was nothing to write home about, so he didn't.

"You're the kid on the news tonight that got shot, ain't ya?" asked the soft-spoken black cabbie.

"Yes," Judd answered, not wanting to get into it.

"You ain't got nobody to drive you home from the hospital?" the cabbie said.

"Everybody's out of town."

The cabbie pulled beside the dark duplex. "Did they catch the guy?"

"Not yet."

"And one guy's hurt real bad, I hear."

"Yep."

"Damn shame. I mean, if you ain't safe at the Grand Ole Opry, then where are you safe? But you're okay?"

"Yeah. It could have been a lot worse." For some reason, Judd offered up more information. "It turns out I tripped right when he was firing, and the bullet just grazed my shoulder. Otherwise, I might not be here at all."

The cabbie turned his head to get a better look at Judd. "You're a fortunate young man."

"I'd have to agree."

"Well, you take care. And be sure to thank Almighty God tonight for looking after you like that."

Judd got out. "I'll do that. I appreciate it."

Judd let himself in his back door, turned on the light, took his cell phone from his pocket for the first time all day, noticed he had unheard messages, and dialed his voicemail. As he sat at the kitchen table, he heard the familiar female voice say, "You have nine new messages. Message one received at 10:53 A.M."

> Hey, sweetheart, this is Mom again. I know you said you were fine, but Dad and I are ready to get on a plane. Please give us a call to discuss details. We love you.

> Judd, hi. This is Megan. I just wanted to make sure you got home. I called the hospital, and they said you were discharged. You should have called me. I would have picked you up. Anyway, I'm just calling to check on you. You have my numbers. Please call if you need anything tonight.

Judd smiled. *Megan calling my cell phone after hours,* he thought. *I never could have imagined that.*

"Message three received at 2:53 P.M.," the automated voice said.

> Judd, it's Derek. Derek Townsend. Dude, you are the talk of La Crosse! You even made the cover of the *Tribune* today.

I called your parents. They said you were okay, doing fine. I know you said you were going to make some noise in Nashville, but this is a little extreme, don't you think? Anyway, a lot of folks back here are asking about you. Call me tonight. It doesn't matter how late.

Hi. Megan again. Mathew saw a picture of you on the news tonight and was worried. I told him you were okay, thank God, but that I would call you again. I also wanted to make sure you have my cell-phone number. Maybe you don't. It's 300-8889. I stepped out for a bit and realized you might not have my cell. Anyway, just call us if you need anything—anything at all.

Judd smiled again. He had no problem playing the sympathy card. "Message five received at 5:43 P.M."

Hey, Judd, this is Brad Holiday at Elite Management. The hospital said you were released this evening. I'm calling to check on you. Would you give me a call when you're feeling up to it? My direct line is 256-6710. If I'm not around, speak with Liz. Depending on how you feel, I'd like you to come by my office. I'll be covering Ripley's press conference tomorrow morning at 11:30, but outside of that, I'll be in the office. Okay, hope you're feeling better.

Judd, good evening. This is Dr. Specter. I'm calling to see if the medication is working. I also wanted to let you know that Simon Stills was heavily medicated today when he woke up. I know it must have been strange for you and Ripley Graham to see him in that state. The good news is that he continues to improve rapidly. This evening, he is much more cognizant. As a matter of fact, he has made it clear that he wants to see you as soon as possible. I would even say he's desperate to see you. Because of that, I'd suggest you come by the hospital first thing in the morning for a short five-minute visit. I'd like the nursing staff to see you as well and check your bandage. Give us a call this evening if you have any discomfort. Good night.

Judd hit the off button on his cell phone without listening to the remaining three messages. The words "desperate to see you" made his gut tighten. The excitement of hearing Megan's voice vanished. He now felt a rush of anxiety. *Simon is lying in an ICU bed in critical condition, and he desperately needs to see me?*

CHAPTER 21

New York City
Midtown Manhattan

Tommy Strickland stepped through the elevator doors onto the fortieth floor of the AXA Financial Building. He took a right opposite the Galaxy lobby entrance, punched a code on the side of an unmarked door at the end of the hall, and entered into his back office suite.

He sat and rolled his executive chair to face his computer console, then double-clicked an open-padlock icon with the words *Secure Galaxy* in red underneath. A status grid then appeared with another logo—that of Cisco Virtual Private Network Systems. Then a *Secure Site* box appeared with an empty grid below.

Strickland reached into his pocket and pulled out what looked like a key fob, which he carried with him at all times. The key had a series of digital numbers that changed every sixty seconds. Those numbers were assigned exclusively to Strickland and had to be entered into the empty grid to further his access.

After he typed in the series of numbers before they changed, a final grid popped up displaying the words *Current Password*. Strickland entered a final password. A blue bar ran across the grid as numbers began to flash rapidly. A moment later, he was connected to the Secure Galaxy Center site. The padlock icon closed and locked at the bottom of his computer screen, indicating a secure connection had been established.

Strickland then began typing.

Secure Galaxy Communiqué
Sent: Thursday, March 10, 2011
To: MacCabe, Warren
From: Strickland, Thomas

Objective: To secure Ripley's project at all costs. To obtain confirmation that delivery will occur prior to fourth quarter and that fourth-quarter release will be made public by March 20—10 days and counting.

Communiqué: My last conversation with Simon regarding Ripley's delivery was Wednesday while I was still in London, just prior to the incident and Tillman's arrival. Now I will deal with Ripley directly. Tillman will be my eyes on the ground. I will put that in motion tomorrow from Nashville.

T. S.

THIS DOCUMENT WILL NOT PRINT.

Strickland clicked the *Send* command, and the page vanished. Then he spoke into the speakerphone on his desk. "Are the pilots ready?"

His executive assistant immediately walked into the office. "They are on call. I've got the meeting confirmed for eight o'clock tomorrow morning in Nashville at the Noshville Deli. Doug Tillman and Ripley's PR agent, Janice Burns, will meet you there. The three of you will discuss the protocol of the press conference at breakfast, then go over to the press conference together. It starts at eleven-thirty. Ripley will be in a holding room, where you and Tillman can brief him directly."

"Did you change the press conference from the hospital to Vandy Plaza?"

"The change is hitting the wire right now. It's going out to all key media."

"Good. Call the car and the pilots. I want to leave in forty-five minutes."

"Will do."

"And get MacCabe on the phone."

Strickland turned back to his computer. A message flashed across the screen: "Secure Galaxy message sent 6:29 P.M. EST. Received and opened 6:32 P.M. EST."

"Mr. MacCabe is on line one."

"Thank you." Strickland took the headset connected to his desk phone and said, "Warren."

"Tommy, did you have a smooth trip back?"

"Yes. I just walked in and sent the communiqué. I see you received it."

"I did, and I have some concerns about the press conference tomorrow," MacCabe said. "Did you hear from Tillman?"

"Yes, right after I landed. He has arrived in Nashville."

"Do you have the press conference under control?"

"Absolutely," Strickland said. "Ripley is going to announce that he is getting back on tour—that's the hook. Back to the fans, back to a place where everyone is asking him daily, 'When is your next record coming out?' That is the good news. I knew he would get stir-crazy hanging around that hospital."

"Will you and Tillman have time to prep him on what he should and should not say?" MacCabe asked. "That is my greatest concern."

"We will see him tomorrow morning. But Ripley is a broken record. He'll do the usual—thank the fans for their letters, thank God for saving Simon's life. He'll cry. Then he'll say, 'As much as I want to stay here and be with my manager, I have an obligation to my fans, and I'm getting back on tour.'"

"Are you sure he's ready to resume touring?"

"Yes, but first we'll coordinate a media blitz."

"What about the major retail accounts?" MacCabe asked. "Have you checked on Ripley's record sales since the shooting?"

"I pulled them up online. In the last twenty-four hours, all national accounts have upped their orders dramatically—not just for the second Ripley release but also for his debut. Ripley's albums are sitting at number one and number two on *Billboard*'s Top 200 Albums chart. Sales should be even stronger after the press conference and hold through the weekend. I don't see this changing for quite some time because the media is so intense."

"The accounts are calling us for orders. We are not soliciting them this week, correct?"

"Correct. It is happening naturally," Strickland said.

"That must remain for the rest of the week. We can't look like we are taking advantage of a tragic situation. It must be organic. That's critical, Tommy."

"I understand," Strickland said.

"So you'll be in Nashville in the morning?"

"Yes. I'm taking the jet tonight."

"Tommy, you realize Ripley has the potential of being the biggest black hole you and I have ever seen in our careers."

Strickland understood what MacCabe meant by "black hole." MacCabe often spoke in such cosmological terms. MacCabe believed that artists, at their core, either gave light or absorbed light. It was one or the other—positive or negative energy. If people got too close to an artist whose ego absorbed light, and if that artist was powerful enough, the artist would suck them in, absorb them completely, and then implode, destroying all.

"Yes, but it is not a concern, now that I have Tillman in place on the ground," Strickland replied.

"It's always a concern," MacCabe said. "If this black hole implodes, our corporate venture will never happen. The merger will be history. We don't need him creating a PR nightmare. We have traveled too far to miss our mark."

"Again, I can now speak with him directly, and Tillman will keep everything in our sights. We are looking good, now that both Simon Stills and James Clark are out of commission."

"E-mail me an update tomorrow on the secure site after the press conference."

"I will," Strickland said.

"And Tommy, I am still predicting a very rough landing."

"Don't worry. I have everything under control."

CHAPTER 22

The Next Morning

Nashville
Friday, March 11

Although Nashville was not known for restaurants with diversified menus, Music Row believed in conducting business while breaking bread. There were only one or two good options for breakfast around the Row. Noshville New York Delicatessen on Broadway was one of them. It was the only place in Music City that had a smoked fish platter as a menu item. True, the authentic New York deli got more kudos than actual orders for its selection of sliced nova, sliced lox, and pickled herring. But it rivaled the Pancake Pantry for music-industry breakfast gatherings.

Janice Burns sat alone at a booth in the back right corner. In keeping with the New York theme, black-and-white photographs of Ethel Merman, Marlon Brando, and Carol Channing were behind her on the wall—not exactly what people expected in the home of country music. On the side wall to her right was a framed county map of the state of

New York. The entire ambiance was captured in a nutshell by Frank Sinatra's big-band version of "Old McDonald Had a Farm" playing on speakers overhead.

Janice was unaware of the cultural clash as she read the morning's *Bulletin*.

Billboard.biz Bulletin™

YOUR DAILY ENTERTAINMENT NEWS UPDATE
FRIDAY, MARCH 11, 2011

Luxor-Galaxy Merger Still Rumored

Edward Weintraub, London

Contrary to a statement made earlier this week by Tommy Strickland, President and CEO of Galaxy North America, an undisclosed top executive at Luxor Entertainment Group told the Bulletin that Luxor has been in quiet contact with Galaxy in recent weeks regarding merger discussions. After several attempts were made to reach Strickland today, a spokesperson contacted the Bulletin late this afternoon to say that Mr. Strickland had been in closed-door meetings with Chairman Warren MacCabe and was not available for comment. The spokesperson went on to say Strickland was in London this week to discuss policies and priorities with MacCabe prior to the company's annual Board of Directors Meeting and Shareholders Meeting, which will take place next Friday and Sunday, respectively.

The Bulletin has also learned from sources that Strickland plans to announce that Doug Tillman will replace James Clark as President of Galaxy Nashville. Clark resigned Tuesday night during a company tribute honoring Ripley Graham, prior to the assassination attempt on Graham's life Wednesday. In a press statement at the time, Galaxy said Clark's replacement would be named in short order. Sources say overtures were made immediately to the New York–based Tillman, Senior Vice President of Sales and Marketing North America. However, due to

the extraordinary events in Nashville, Galaxy decided to hold the Tillman announcement. Tillman was also in London this week and plans to be in Nashville today with Strickland to attend the Ripley Graham press conference—the first since the shooting. When Tillman is named, he will be the first non-country-music executive to hold the post for Galaxy Nashville.

Strickland's executive assistant had phoned yesterday informing Janice that Strickland would attend the press conference and wanted a breakfast briefing with her to go over any details from Ripley's camp. He also said in passing that Tillman would be joining them. *It all adds up,* Janice thought. Strickland invited Tillman—a hotshot, abrasive New Yorker—because he was to become the new president and head the Nashville label. *This will be interesting.*

Janice remembered Simon's telling her once that the Shareholders Meeting was just a dog-and-pony show. It was Galaxy's Board of Directors Meeting where all the business decisions were made and where Warren MacCabe and Tommy Strickland laid out the year-long projections and announced which artists would be named worldwide priorities. It was about budgets, money, and the distribution of power.

Powerful or not, she thought, *they're late for breakfast.* She started to read an article from that morning's *USA Today,* which featured a picture of Ripley front and center.

Ripley Graham Dodges Bullet: Singer Speaks Out About Assassination Attempt

By Brian Mansfield

Nashville—Country superstar Ripley Graham will make his first personal appearance and public statement at a press conference today in Nashville since the apparent assassination attempt on his life earlier this week. . . .

"Janice."

She jerked her head up to see Tommy Strickland standing over her, hand extended. He was wearing his usual black pants, black mock turtleneck, and black leather jacket. Janice reached for his hand while dropping her papers. She tried to stand but got caught by the table.

"Don't get up," Strickland said as he slid into the opposite side of the booth. "This is Doug Tillman. I don't believe the two of you have met."

"Nice to meet you, Janice." Tillman's tone was all business.

"Likewise, and I'm reading that congratulations are soon to be in order," Janice said.

"Yes. For once, the press is actually correct," Strickland said. "We were planning on announcing Doug's acceptance of his new post this week in London, but for obvious reasons that will be delayed. But yes, congratulations are in order. Warren MacCabe and I are pleased that Doug has accepted, and we will move him to Nashville shortly."

"Starting this week must be quite a challenge," Janice said.

"You have to be ready when your number is called," Tillman replied.

Ty, a longtime waitress at Noshville Deli, whizzed by the booth, dropped off coffee cups in front of Strickland and Tillman, and said as she passed, "Hot coffee's in the pitcher, menus are on the side, water is on the way."

Tillman poured his coffee and asked Janice, "So what do you expect at the press conference?"

"You mean as far as attendance?" Janice said.

"Yes."

"We will have a list of attending media when we get there. It will be full coverage."

"Is the hotel suited for full media coverage?" Tillman asked.

"Yes. No offense, but it always surprises me that folks from New York or L.A. don't think Nashville can handle national or international press," Janice said. "It's not like Obama and McCain had any security issues at the Belmont University debate."

"I didn't mean that to insult you," Tillman said.

"Well, Vandy Plaza is where Al Gore made all his major campaign announcements in Nashville when he ran for president. And if you're a big-business Republican, you might like to know Senators Bill Frist and Fred Thompson have used the same room over the years. The security is excellent, and the national media know the setup here very well."

"I don't mean to step on your toes here, Janice, but I wrote out some talking points for Ripley and the play-by-play for the flow of the press conference." Tillman handed pieces of paper to both Janice and Strickland. "Schedule-wise, Janice, I'd like you to welcome the press and then bring me up to the platform. I'll introduce Ripley, so he doesn't go up to the podium cold. He can read the prepared statement here and say his thank-yous. We have both the director of the Tennessee Bureau of Investigation and the doctor that operated on Simon Stills on hand. Ripley should call them up immediately after his statement to field questions together. That way, he can refer any questions he is uncomfortable with to the experts. Basically, I'll tell him to refrain from giving any comments about the ongoing investigation, or any medical information. Ripley needs to stay on point and stick to his thank-yous and the fact that he plans to get back on tour."

"That all feels right," Strickland added.

Janice was stunned. *That didn't take long,* she thought. *I'm supposed to bring you onstage so you can introduce Ripley?* "Well, you two have obviously put some thought into this," she said. "But I'm surprised no one mentioned to you that Ripley runs his own show."

Strickland leaned in toward Janice and said, "That's why we're having this breakfast. We want to make sure you run this show with him, just as Doug has outlined."

"Water," Ty announced as she placed three glasses on the table. "Do you guys know what you're going to get?"

Without taking her eyes off Strickland, Janice answered, "I think these guys know what they want, but they have no idea what they're going to get."

"Excuse me?" Ty said.

Strickland turned to the waitress. "We don't have time to eat."

"Suit yourself." Ty tore off a ticket for the coffee, stuck it under the salt shaker, and quickly moved on.

Janice started gathering her papers.

Tillman ignored the fact that Janice was insulted. "How much national press does Ripley want to do next week around the incident?"

"He said he would do *Leno*, and that's all," Janice snapped.

"That's it?" Tillman asked.

"That's it."

"Our New York office is prepared to coordinate a full media blitz for Ripley," Strickland said. "I was planning on having them integrate with you."

"Obviously, you like to run things your way. Coordinate all you want, but Ripley will do only *Leno*. If you don't believe me, you'll see him in a minute, and he'll tell you himself. If you'll excuse me, the coffee is lukewarm, and the company is even colder."

Janice picked up her things and walked out.

CHAPTER 23

Nashville
VUMC

Judd pushed open the door.

"There you are." Shirley Rogers was washing her hands at the sink.

Judd stopped just inside.

Shirley looked over while reaching for some paper towels. "How's that shoulder of yours feelin' today?"

"Better . . . a little sore. I'm just glad there aren't any major organs in a shoulder."

"Ain't that the truth! Well, Simon is doin' so much better, too. I don't think he even knew you were here yesterday." Shirley walked to the bed. "Simon, he's here—the buddy you've been askin' for." Shirley motioned for Judd to come close.

As Judd approached, Simon opened his eyes. He closed them for a second, then reopened them to focus. He signaled Shirley for a pen.

"Oh, I've got a surprise for you this mornin'." Shirley held up a small white board with markers and an eraser. "Very high-tech."

Simon gave a nod. He took the marker and wrote, "*Thank you.*"

"You're welcome, sweetie. I'm goin' to the nurses' station. You boys buzz me if you need anything."

Simon had already erased his thank-you and was writing something to Judd.

"You look like you're feeling better," Judd said.

Simon did not respond but kept writing, then held up the board: "*I need your help. It is dangerous.*"

Judd was taken aback. "What are you talking about, Simon?"

Simon erased and wrote again: "*Things are not what they seem.*"

Feeling uncomfortable, Judd started to back away, "Look, Simon. I'm glad to help, but there are law-enforcement people that need to handle that kind of stuff. Hey, we're lucky to be alive, that's all. Ripley is the one that could still be in danger. We were innocent bystanders—wrong place, wrong time."

Simon wrote fast, looked up, and waved Judd back over. Then he held up his board. Judd moved closer to read it: "*It all went as planned. Except I'm still alive!*"

Judd was shocked. "Jesus, Simon. You're not well. The medicine is making you delirious. Look, you just need to get some rest and worry about your recovery."

Simon, getting noticeably irritated, scribbled angrily on the board: "*I'm not crazy. Ripley was not the target. I was!*"

"Simon, you're not making any sense at all. Why would you be the target? Come on, now. Let me get the nurse to check your medicine or something. You may not even remember this conversation tomorrow. You should just relax and enjoy the drugs."

As Judd talked, Simon grew so angry he jerked his hand, disengaging the oxygen probe from his finger, which sounded an alarm.

"Oh, God." Judd turned from the bed to get a nurse, but Shirley was already in the room before he made it out the door.

"What on earth?" She silenced the alarm before replacing the probe on Simon's finger. "You are in no condition to get riled up like this."

"He's not making any sense," Judd said.

Nurses Brenda and Maryanne came into the room.

"We're okay," Shirley told them.

"You sure?"

"Yeah, I've got it. But I think that's enough excitement for the mornin'. Your visiting time is up," Shirley said to Judd as she leaned over Simon.

Simon held up a finger and mouthed, "One more minute."

"Simon, you are really pushing it. And I'm definitely not in the mood."

"Please," he mouthed.

"One minute. And I mean one minute only."

Simon closed his eyes and nodded.

"Okay, clock's runnin'." Shirley turned for the door.

Simon felt around for his marker, found it on the left side of the bed, and started writing.

Judd got closer. "Don't do that anymore. Please."

Simon wrote, "*I need you to copy my phone conversations off my computer. Put them on my iPod and bring it to me. Don't tell anyone.*"

"Sure, of course. I'll bring you the entire Willie Nelson boxed set if you'll stop freaking out like that."

Simon wrote, "*Then erase everything off the hard drive.*"

"No problem. Now maybe I should leave before Shirley comes back in and kicks my butt. You get some rest."

Simon was writing frantically again: "*Work from home. Get Elite to give you a laptop with Internet service—you were injured while working. Come see me every day!*"

"Simon, I appreciate that, I really do. But with all due respect, I don't think you need to worry about work-related stuff just yet. If you do, Shirley will definitely kick *your* butt."

Simon's eyelids looked heavy. His head sank into his pillow.

"Sure, I'll come back tomorrow," Judd said.

He turned toward the door as Simon mouthed a thank-you while trying to write one more message. But Judd didn't notice. When Simon finished, he was too exhausted to get Judd's attention. He rapidly descended into sleep as the board slipped out of his hand. By then, no one else was in the room to hear it hit the floor.

It landed face up: "*I know too much.*"

CHAPTER 24

Nashville
Loews Vanderbilt Plaza Hotel

The hired black sedan with Tommy Strickland and Doug Tillman seated in the back moved westward along West End Avenue. Janice Burns drove just in front of them in her red Jaguar XK convertible toward Vanderbilt Plaza Hotel.

Three months ago—in December, right before the Christmas break—Ripley had called an "emergency team meeting" on a Sunday afternoon. Simon, Janice, and Pumpkin met him at Simon's office. Ripley was late. Simon swore to Janice that he had no idea why Ripley seemed so desperate to meet with them.

When Ripley walked in, he was poker faced. As the others sat, Ripley paced and started talking about how important it was for Ripley Graham to "make a statement," to "express himself," to "let the team know where Ripley Graham stands."

When he refers to himself in the third person, it's never good news, Janice thought.

Then Ripley said, "I've been meeting with my accountants, and Ripley Graham has now sold over 25 million downloads. So I called you here to say thank you for believing in me from day one."

Ripley then reached into his pocket, pulled out three key rings, and put them on the table. "Three brand-new Jaguars are in the parking garage downstairs. One is red, one is blue, and one is silver. Other than that, they are identical. You guys decide among yourselves which one gets which color." As Simon, Janice, and Pumpkin exchanged stunned looks, Ripley grinned from ear to ear. "What did you think I was going to do, fire you?"

As Janice approached Vanderbilt University in her salsa-red Jag, half a dozen television news trucks were parked on the street with satellite dishes pointed to the heavens. She turned right off West End Avenue into the horseshoe entrance of Vandy Plaza Hotel. The black sedan pulled up behind. The two cars were quickly met by valet attendants, and Janice, Strickland, and Tillman were then escorted into the crowded lobby.

Immediately inside, a gentleman who was obviously waiting on their arrival advanced. "Good morning. I'm with hotel security. The press conference will be down the hall to the right in the Symphony Ballroom. As you can see, a tight security check is going on now." A large crowd of people was backed up, waiting to go through two metal detectors stationed in the hallway leading to the ballroom. "We have Mr. Graham in a holding room downstairs. If you'll follow me, I'll take you to him."

They all followed him to an elevator across the lobby.

Their security escort punched *LL*. To the right of the illuminated button was a sign that read, "Gold and Platinum Rooms and Ruth's Chris Steakhouse, Lower Level." The elevator door opened to a room where two men in dark suits were standing. Each had a coiled plastic-coated wire protruding from his back collar that connected to an earpiece. Rooms were to the left and right. Directly in front was a hallway that led to the well-known eatery. They were led to the left toward the Gold Room. One of the security guards put his hand over his left ear, obviously monitoring instructions, as he opened the door. Janice, Strickland, and Tillman marched in without slowing their stride.

Strickland expected to find only Ripley, but he was not alone. A stout man and a very attractive woman were talking over coffee at a round table in the center of the room. Strickland also saw two extremely large men in ill-fitting suits that threatened to explode off their bodies. Ripley was at the far end of the room surveying an array of fruit, danishes, croissants, juice, and coffee. He picked up his coffee cup while stirring in his half-and-half and walked over to the new arrivals.

"Good morning, Ripley," Janice said. Then, with less charm, she motioned to Strickland and Tillman. "I think you know these two."

Ripley embraced Janice and then shook the hands of both men. "It has been a long week for all of us." Then he said to Strickland, "I wondered if you would make the trip."

"Of course," Strickland said.

Ripley turned to the table behind him. "This is my tour manager, Pumpkin, and my girlfriend, Cindy." They all exchanged hellos. Ripley pointed to the two men still seated in the back. "Over the years, I'm sure you've met Nate and Jerome at some point. They work personal security for me." He turned and looked around the room. "Where's Megan?"

"She went out to check if we're startin' on time," Pumpkin said.

"Oh, that's right. I know you guys have spoken with Megan by phone. She'll be back in a minute." Ripley turned to Tillman. "Well, you've been jet-setting. How are you holding up?"

Doug Tillman looked a little road worn since Ripley had seen him privately four days ago. "I think I'll remember my first week on the job."

Strickland began the small talk. "I saw you briefly at the Christmas party, but you and Doug spent most of that dinner talking. Before that, it must have been the CMA Music Fest two years ago."

"It's been quite a ride," Ripley said.

Every June, country-music fanatics make the pilgrimage to Nashville to attend the CMA Music Festival, a four-day event during which they go to concerts and seek autographs from country stars. It is a tradition so ingrained in the consciousness of country music that the lines between fan and zealots, between ritual and religion, begin to blur. To some, it is a mecca where year-long savings pour out like water from a baptismal font. The country-music coffers are filled, and the tourists return home lightened of money but renewed in the spirit of country music.

Two years ago when Strickland came down to Music Fest, Ripley had been radiant, focused, and fit. He was the undisputed wonder kid of country music, his legacy already growing. Ripley was quickly becoming the savior of modern country. His appearance at Music Fest that year was now legendary. He went onstage and accepted a plaque acknowledging his then 8 million records sold, presented by James Clark, Tommy Strickland, and Warren MacCabe. Immediately afterward, Ripley went over to the Country Music Hall of Fame and started signing autographs. He told security not to cut the line, meaning that every single person who wanted an autograph would get one. He signed for sixteen hours straight without taking a break.

Strickland remembered watching Ripley all that day and into the night and being amazed by his stamina. But today, he immediately noticed something different. The radiant Ripley had been replaced by a guarded Ripley. The magnetic glow was hidden behind a shield of protection. He could still flick the switch and turn on the charm, but it was not the easy natural radiance that it was before. Strickland knew he was dealing with a different animal.

Tillman began to orchestrate the small group. "I have some talking points to review. Janice will open, and then I'll say a few words to kick off the press conference and bring Ripley up. Then Ripley, you can make your statement and bring up the agent in charge of the investigation and the Vanderbilt doctor that is here to field some questions."

"That's fine," Ripley said.

Tillman started handing out his talking points, which contained Ripley's written statement. "I would like to go over this. There are a few key issues we should look at and a few things we should flag to stay away from."

Ripley put his paper on the table. "Look, it's going to be fine. I don't mean to be rude, Doug, but if you don't mind I'd like to have a few minutes alone with Tommy. As he said, it's been quite some time since we've seen each other."

Janice snickered, then tried to compose herself. "Sorry."

An awkward silence hung in the room at the suggested change of direction.

Tillman said, "Well, I do think it is very important to address a few—"

Ripley cut him off. "I'm sorry, Doug. This is important to me. I don't have much time. Please, if you wouldn't mind, I'd like to speak with Tommy alone."

Tillman hesitated. "Sure, but I . . ."

Strickland held up his hand and motioned all to leave the room. Everyone but he and Ripley filed out.

As the door shut, Ripley went to warm up his coffee. Then he turned to Strickland and said, "You and Simon had a conversation just before he came out to see me Wednesday at the Opry House—just before the shooting. I want to know what was said."

Strickland wasn't flustered. "Are you trying to say there was a connection between our conversation and the shooting?"

"I want to know what was said."

"Simon wanted to talk about renegotiating your record contract. He wanted to discuss a reversion clause. I told him that you and I had already made a side deal—that you waived your right to an attorney and your manager, and that you signed it. Our new deal is binding by law."

"Nothing in this life is binding," Ripley said. "When we were discussing our side agreement, it seems you failed to mention your little merger plans."

"I don't know what you're talking about."

"You're a bad liar, Tommy! You told Simon we struck a deal behind his back, and then you told him Galaxy was about to merge with another major record company. I don't do business with liars!"

Strickland didn't raise his voice. "I did tell Simon I could give you something you wanted and you could give me something I wanted in return. That's all."

"The merger. Why didn't you tell me about the merger?"

"Ripley, we're not having this conversation."

"Damn you!" Ripley exploded. "What were you thinking, that once you get my new CD I'll be worth more to you dead than alive?"

Infuriated now, veins bulging from his neck, Strickland said, "That's insane. I'm not trying to kill you, I'm trying to keep you alive! You and I have a signed agreement. I've delivered on my end, and you are legally bound to deliver on yours. By my account, you're in material breech."

"I don't do business with liars."

"Oh, you'll deliver!" Strickland said.

Just then, Megan walked into the room. Both men's faces were beet-red. From their body language, there was no hiding the fact that they were in the middle of a heated exchange.

"Sorry," Megan said, "but everyone is waiting." Realizing her timing could not have been worse, she added, "Should I tell them you need more time?"

Tillman, Pumpkin, P. C., Nate, and Jerome were all looking in from the hallway.

"No," Strickland said. "We're done." Then he walked directly to Tillman, leaned toward his ear, and said, "Ripley's all yours. I don't want to talk to the son of a bitch again. Don't let him out of your sight. I'll be in New York."

Strickland then walked into the elevator alone, exited the hotel, and was gone before the press conference even began.

CHAPTER 25

Nashville
Music Row
12:15 P.M.

The Elite Management logo was projected in white lights onto the back lobby wall of the office entrance on the ninth floor of the Roundabout Building. Elite's office space had an open, sleek, high-tech design. Recessed in the wall behind the receptionist's desk were three TVs—one tuned to Country Music Television, another tuned to Great American Country, and the third playing continuous videos of Elite clients. To the right were two sage-green sofa chairs with a paisley pattern, a love seat, and a coffee table. Lying on the coffee table was a *Time* magazine with Ripley on the cover. The headline in bold black print under his photograph read, "The Ripley Effect! Can One Artist Save the Music Industry?"

"Judd, I didn't expect to see you today," Ellen said, genuinely surprised. "You look great!" She stood from behind the receptionist's desk to give him a half-hug, maneuvering around his sling. "How are you feeling?"

"I'm doing good, thanks. The bullet grazed my shoulder, but nothing a little needle and thread couldn't fix."

"Thank God. But surely you're not coming in to work."

"Brad called me last night and said he wanted to see me today."

Ellen repositioned herself behind the desk. "He's gone down to Ripley's press conference. I think everybody went."

"Oh," Judd replied, as if he hadn't realized that was the case.

The phones started ringing, and Ellen's attention turned to the switchboard.

"I'm going to get some things on my desk," Judd whispered.

The company's space was very efficient. To the left as Judd walked down the corridor were open stations where the management assistants worked. Their stations faced their individual bosses' offices directly across the hall.

When Judd interviewed for the intern position, Simon had asked why he wanted to be a personal manager in the music business.

Judd had answered, "Honestly, I'm not sure. That's why I'm here, to find out what a manager really does and to see if I have what it takes."

Then Simon asked something Judd didn't expect. "Do you know who is considered the father of modern economics?"

"Excuse me?"

"Trivia question. Who is the father of modern economics?"

"I have no idea, but I don't think it was Colonel Tom Parker."

"Nope," Simon said, almost smiling. "Adam Smith. In 1776, Smith wrote his great work, *The Wealth of Nations,* where he talked about the invisible hand of capitalism and basically said all men are naturally greedy, and our goal is to be wealthy and have more stuff, and you do that by making a profit, which happens exponentially when you make things faster and cheaper, and you can do that only if you specialize, and he used the example of a pin maker to explain all that." Simon finally took a breath. "You didn't study economics?"

"Somehow, I guess I missed the pin maker." Judd thought, *What in the world is this guy talking about?*

"Too bad, because Adam Smith explained why people's jobs are so boring. They do the same thing over and over until they're bored out of their minds. If you want to be a doctor, you can't be just a doctor, you have to be a specialist. Every day, you work in gastroenterology or hematology or oncology—there are no ordinary doctors anymore. Same deal with lawyers. They specialize in tax law or corporate law or divorce law. Same thing over and over until they're bored to the point of heavy drinking. It is also true in the music business. It's a specialized industry. You've got your booking agent, publicist, business manager, record producer, music publisher, all doing the same thing day in and day out. But then you get to artist managers. We are the exception. We are the ones that say, 'Adam Smith is dead!' We don't specialize in any one sector of the music industry. We master it all. We advise and counsel our clients on every aspect of their careers. We build a team of specialists around an artist and direct them all. Artist management as a profession is the only unrestricted, unrestrained, non-boring career in the modern world! That's why you should strive to be an artist manager."

It was vintage Simon Stills. He was energetic, passionate, and smart, all at the same time. Since that first day Judd walked into his office, Simon's energy level and work ethic had been beyond reproach. Judd noticed from the start that every other manager in the company envied Simon. He had the most successful client in the music industry, had all the clout anyone could ask for, and yet never abused his power. He was inspiring. He had a way of extracting the best from people while working relentlessly on Ripley's affairs.

And yet, in retrospect, Judd had noticed a few days prior to the shooting that Simon seemed preoccupied. His demeanor and routine had changed after he returned from Greenville on Saturday. Judd knew Simon had been in the office over the weekend because some work was left in his chair Monday morning. But Simon did not come in or call that morning, which was unusual. Finally, around noon, he visited the office briefly without his usual warm greeting, simply saying, "It was a long weekend, and I need to get some rest before the Mardi Gras party tonight. No need to patch any calls to me unless it's Strickland. That's the only call I'll take." And then he was gone.

Tuesday, Simon didn't say two words to Judd until the gala that evening. But on Wednesday, he was already on the phone with his door closed when Judd came in at seven-thirty, ready to brew some coffee. Simon worked the phone all morning but hardly spoke to anyone in the office. His mood and physical disposition seemed strained. Judd remembered sitting at his work station wondering if Simon was ill. Then Strickland finally called. Simon's door was closed, but because the managers' offices were partially glass brick, Judd could see him pacing while having a heated conversation. As soon as it was over, Simon bolted from his office toward the elevators. But he forgot his keys and came back down the hall. That's when he looked at Judd and asked, "You want to take a ride?" Surprised by the invitation, Judd instinctively said yes. On the way out, Simon asked Ellen to call in Judd's name to the Opry security desk. Moments later, Judd got into Simon's silver Jag and Simon turned onto the I-40 East ramp, accelerated into five lanes of traffic, and headed to the Opry House to see Ripley.

Now, two days later, Judd walked down the empty corridor to Simon's office. No one had touched his desk. There it was, exactly as Simon had left it, yet nothing was the same. The shooting had changed everything. A sudden thought made him uneasy. What had Simon meant by writing, "*Things are not what they seem*"?

As Judd stared at Simon's computer, it dawned on him that something important must be on the hard drive. Why would Simon be so anxious to get his taped conversations unless something incriminating had been recorded? What else would make Simon think he was the target?

For the first time, Judd became frightened. *Something is on his computer that explains all of this,* he thought. He'd bet his life on it.

And maybe Simon had done just that.

CHAPTER 26

Nashville
Vanderbilt Plaza Hotel

After his opening remarks and the introduction of those standing on the riser alongside him, Doug Tillman stood behind the podium and marveled at how articulate and collected Ripley was in answering the questions fired at him by the national media.

"Ripley, so you're planning to resume your tour even with your manager in critical condition?" one reporter asked.

"Look, you can ask anybody on my team, Simon is like a father to me," Ripley said. "But there is nothing I can personally do for him at the moment. He is in the best of hands. And as you have heard, he is making progress, thanks to God and to Dr. Specter standing up here with us. As I said, I've been by his side for the last two days, and now I'm going to do what he wants me to do, and that is to get back on tour."

"Ripley, are you going to do any other media or only live concerts?" another asked.

"I've been asked to do all the national morning shows, the late-night shows—the whole deal. Look, I don't want this to be a media frenzy any more than it is. I've agreed to do one, but that's all. I'm doing the press conference today to let people know I'm fine, and I'm going to do *The Tonight Show* this Monday, and that will be it. I do want to let the fans know what happened, how Simon is, and I want to thank them for their support during this time. But I don't want to do a media blitz. That would be in poor taste, in my judgment."

A few miles away on Music Row, Judd sat at Simon's desk and hit the iTunes icon on his computer. The program opened to Simon's music library. Judd scrolled down and clicked. There they were: Simon's recorded phone conversations, starting on March 4, 2011, the day Simon had called from Greenville and asked Judd to set his computer to record mode and tape his phone conversations onto the hard drive. The playlist showed six daily entries from March 4 to March 9, the day of the shootings. Judd quickly looked around for Simon's iPod nano so he could transfer the information before he deleted it from the computer. The problem with the iPod nano was that it could get lost faster than a set of car keys. He found Simon's TV remote and instinctively picked it up and pointed it toward the television mounted on the wall. As it came to life, the image of Ripley Graham addressing the crowded press conference appeared. Ripley was standing at the podium with Dr. Specter to his right and a gentleman on his left Judd did not recognize.

"Ripley, aren't you worried about your personal safety, about going back on tour while the gunman is still at large?" a reporter asked.

"Actually, I'm glad you brought that up," Ripley said. "Believe me, plenty of people in my camp have advised me not to go out yet. But singing is what I do. The fans have always been there for me, and I'm always going to be there for them. Being a target is an occupational hazard, and I'm not going to run and hide. Now, I do want to say there will be heightened security at all my concerts. But that is for everybody's safety, not just mine. I want people to know that my concerts are as safe as any place on earth."

While listening, Judd kept looking under paperwork on Simon's desk until he finally found a polished blue aluminum nano. He plugged the UBS cable from the nano into Simon's computer. Immediately, it began the process of transferring the recorded phone log from the hard drive onto the iPod. The computer screen read, "Syncing iPod. Do not disconnect." Then a blue rectangular status bar came up:

```
2.2 MB of 25.5 MB
1 minute remaining
```

Judd looked again at the television.

"Ripley, why do you suspect someone would try to kill you? And do you think it was a fan?"

"I have no idea," Ripley answered. "I do know there are some real crazies out there. But I'm not the one to give you an update on the who or the why. Let me bring up Mr. Rod Engels, director of the Tennessee Bureau of Investigation, the man now overseeing this case. Agent Engels?"

Ripley moved back from the podium as the gentleman Judd had not recognized stepped to the microphone.

Judd glanced down at Simon's computer and watched the completion of the transfer. He then moved the mouse to the *delete* symbol and started deleting the recorded phone log from the hard drive. A red alert message appeared on the monitor: "All files will be permanently deleted. Do you wish to continue?" Judd hit *Yes*. A blue rectangular bar came up indicating how rapidly the files were being deleted—5 percent, 20 percent, 60 percent.

Then, out of nowhere, he heard a surprised and irritated voice cut through the air: "Judd, what are you doing in there?"

Judd's whole body jerked as if he had grabbed a live wire. Brad Holiday was staring at him from the doorway.

Engrossed in the news coverage of the press conference, Simon Stills watched Ripley's every nuance.

Shirley Rogers came in but didn't notice that it was Ripley on the TV. "Let me open these curtains for you, Simon." She pulled back the curtains with the long plastic rod. "How are you feelin'?"

Simon broke away from the TV and immediately started writing on his board: "*What did the FBI agents say?*"

"Do you always answer a question with another question? They have a guard posted outside your door 24/7, and he is a very good-looking young black man, I must say. And he said he was with the TBI, not the FBI. So you might not be as important as you think. Although I've never had a patient with his own guard at his door, so that does rank. But I still have to hurt you. Dr. Specter wants more of your blood."

Simon wrote, "*When do I see the head agent?*"

"Since you are the man with a thousand questions, I guess the answer is, 'Yes, Shirley, I'm feelin' much better, thanks to your care and attention.' Mr. TBI is comin' by at four o'clock for fifteen minutes only. Dr. Specter doesn't want you to get as excited as this morning. He doesn't want any alarms soundin' again. Seeing as I let Judd stay in your room too long, I got my little cute butt chewed out. You really need to start appreciating me a little more, Simon. Now, give me that arm."

Shirley sat on the stool on the left side of the bed. She had laid out all the necessary paraphernalia to draw blood when she saw the TV for the first time. "Well, how 'bout that? Speakin' of Mr. TBI, there he is up there. He does get around."

Simon hardly felt the stick, as he was back listening.

"We are considering any and all leads at this time," the TBI man said. "If anyone in the listening audience has information that they think would help in our investigation, I encourage them to call the 800 number we've set up."

"Agent Engels, you say you are considering any and all leads," a reporter said. "But does the agency think this is the work of a lone gunman, or a concerted effort by some group or even by organized crime?"

"I'm not going to say much about the investigation or our leads at the moment. However, I will say it is obvious that the gunman, whether acting on his own or in cooperation with others, was a professional. He also must have had some inside connection to Ripley or his team to have known Ripley's whereabouts and gain access to a closed video taping. That's all I'm going to say at this time."

Simon winced with pain.

"Why are we watching this?" Shirley grabbed the remote and clicked the TV off. She had already filled several vials and marked them. "I'll change your IV bag in a second, and then you can get more rest before your company comes. How is your pain pump? Okay?"

Simon nodded.

"It'll give you the morphine when you need it. Don't be shy. It's there for you. Dr. Specter will be switching you to oral pain meds soon. In the meantime, he ordered a variety of medications in your IV drip to help you relax—you know, to help you adjust to all the tubes and wires. After surgery, while you were still on the ventilator, he had you on a continuous infusion of Propofol. But now that you're more alert, we start to be more careful with the meds. We do have you on Versed because you're still anxious. It will make you a little forgetful, but on the other hand they say it makes you have wild dreams."

She received no answer. Simon had already drifted into unconsciousness.

CHAPTER 27

Nashville
Elite Management

As Brad Holiday stood staring from the doorway, Judd quickly thought, *Don't panic.* "Hey Brad," he said. "I came by to see you, actually. I got your message. Ellen said you weren't back yet, so I came in here because Simon was asking for his iPod, and I started watching the press conference." Judd disconnected the USB cable, looked up at the TV, and saw Engels speaking. "It's still going on."

"I cut out early," Brad said. "You shouldn't be working on Simon's computer. The bureau told us not to touch anything in here. They're coming Monday to pick up his computer and some files."

"Really?" Judd got up from behind the desk. "Like I said, Simon wanted the tunes that he listens to in the office when he works on weekends. They relax him. He said they were on his computer playlist but not on his iPod." Judd flashed the blue nano in his hand.

"Well, you definitely should not be hanging out in here. Come on down to my office."

Judd followed as Brad walked down the hall to his office and sat at his desk. Judd took one of the high-backed chairs positioned in front.

Brad shuffled some papers and said in a matter-of-fact tone, "The reason I called, first and foremost, was to check on you."

"I'm doing okay," Judd said. "The bullet grazed my shoulder—nothing broken, a lot of stitches and pain."

"I'm glad to hear it's not worse. I also wanted to relay to you that Elite will pick up any medical bills and any rehabilitation that might be required."

"Thanks. My folks will be relieved to hear that."

"Also, even though you were not on salary, I'm happy to pay you what would amount to workmen's compensation for the next few weeks. If you want that, I'll just need you to sign some paperwork." Brad handed Judd a folder. "It basically says that you indemnify Elite—big word meaning 'to hold harmless'—of any liability regarding the incident, and accept our compensation without any accusation of blame toward the company. It's just some basic legalese."

"Uh-huh."

"We also want you to know that even though your internship will be cut short since Simon is out of commission, you will be under review for the next hiring internally."

"I see." Judd was a little surprised at how sterile the conversation seemed. He'd never thought Brad would be afraid he might blame Elite for his injury. Then it occurred to him that Brad was only protecting the company's deep pockets from a potential lawsuit.

Judd remembered how Simon wrote, "*I need your help,*" on his white board. He swallowed hard and thought, *Okay, here goes nothing.* He looked up at Brad and said, "I guess Simon didn't tell you that he actually did hire me. We talked about it on the phone when he was in Greenville and then again Wednesday driving out to the Opry House. He hired me as his second assistant."

"No. Actually, I was not aware of that."

"Yes, sir, he did. He hired me. You can ask Megan—or Ripley, for that matter."

Brad hesitated. "Judd, I don't want to be insensitive at a time like this. But the proper protocol for Simon and me as partners is that we must mutually approve such a hiring. I'm sure Simon was not being disingenuous, and he may have mentioned something to you about his intentions, but I assure you, you were not hired. We have to sit down and go over numbers, bring you an offer, get some signatures. And obviously, under the circumstances, none of that happened."

Knowing Simon would approve, Judd said in a quiet, steady voice, "Disingenuous or not, I took Simon at his word. And he said what he said."

That was not what Brad expected to hear. "Well, Judd, if you're taking that position, I need to tell you that the partnership between Simon and me is very explicit. We also have in writing that if one of the partners becomes incapacitated for any reason, then the other partner has executive power to make operational decisions such as this. So let me say this plainly. You are not an employee at Elite. Now, in the meantime, if you want your medical bills covered and two weeks of pay, I'd suggest you sign the paperwork. Again, I'm sorry to sound insensitive at a time like this, because you have impressed us all with your work ethic. And believe me, you are on the top of our list for the next available position. In the meantime, if there is anything we can do until then, just let me know." Brad nodded to close the conversation and reached for some work on his desk.

"I see." Judd stood and started for the door, then thought, *What kind of partner is this guy? Simon is in critical condition, and now he's on some pompous power trip? No way can I can go back to Simon empty handed.* Feeling the blood flowing toward his face, he turned around and said, "I need a laptop computer. Because of the severity of my injury, I'll need to work from home. And to do an efficient job for Simon, I'm going to need a laptop."

"Excuse me?" Brad said.

"First of all, I'm not so sure Simon is incapacitated. And second, I *am* sure he hired me. You just said if there was anything you could do for me to let you know. And there is. I need a laptop to use at my apartment so I can work while I'm recovering—one with wireless Internet service."

"I see," Brad said.

"That would be great." Judd paused at the door as Brad turned his attention back to his desk. "So you'll look into that today?"

"I'm sorry?" Brad thought Judd had exited already.

"Can I count on getting that laptop with Internet service worked out today? Because I'll need to use it this weekend."

"How 'bout I think about it?"

"Sure."

Ten seconds later, Judd was back in the doorframe. "Brad, I thought of something else."

Brad had a "you've got to be kidding" look on his face. "Yes?"

"I also need a BlackBerry. Like everyone in the office uses."

"Judd, I just told you my position on your status with this company. And when I said, 'Let me know if you need anything,' I didn't mean to imply a Christmas list."

"Oh. Well, it sounded sincere to me. I guess we're just getting to know each other."

Brad stood and walked around his desk. "I was sincere. I mean, I am sincere. I'm just a little surprised at the immediacy of your needs outside of the issues we were discussing. We were talking about your status with this company, and our willingness to pay workmen's comp and medical coverage even when you're not officially an employee, and now you've digressed to a Christmas list of laptop computers and smart phones. I'm just not quite sure how this fits into our earlier discussion."

Judd thought of Megan—her drive, her confidence—and just went for it. "Okay. Well, call me naïve. I was just thinking of a few things that could help during this trying situation. There is no doubt in my mind that Simon hired me. And it seemed to me after what you said earlier—the part about wanting me to sign something to indemnify the firm, that big word you used meaning you *are* nervous that I have a legitimate claim because I was with Simon on official business for the company when I was shot—that you were trying to shove some paperwork in front of me to control this potentially devastating situation for Elite. Maybe I'm wrong, but I think you have a fiduciary responsibility to this company—big word meaning 'obligation'—to listen to any requests I may have. But maybe I missed something the first time around."

Brad pushed a button on his desk phone. "Ellen," he said, "do you have the phone number of our IT guy?"

"Yes, sir."

"Will you call and see if he has an office laptop and BlackBerry not being used that we can assign to Judd?"

"Of course."

"And if he does, will you let Judd know this afternoon?"

"Sure, no problem."

"Thank you, Ellen. Judd is on his way out now." Brad turned to Judd with a stoic stare and asked, "Is that all?"

"That's all," Judd said as he gave a polite smile. "This afternoon will be perfect."

CHAPTER 28

THE NEXT MORNING

Midtown Manhattan
Nashville
Saturday, March 12

Tommy Strickland sat as usual on a Saturday morning, not noticing the awe-inspiring vista behind him. He occupied a coveted corner office with large windows on both the east and south sides. From behind his desk, he had a breathtaking view of the East River, Roosevelt Island, and Queens. And the south end of his fortieth-floor office gave a perfect aerial view of the heart of Midtown, the Chrysler Building, and the Empire State Building beyond that. Complete with private bathroom, it was one of the most expensive offices per square foot in America.

But his mind was occupied by corporate events. Strickland typed a message into his PC:

```
Secure Galaxy Communiqué
Sent: Saturday, March 12, 2011
To: MacCabe, Warren
From: Strickland, Thomas

Communiqué: I met with Ripley in Nashville. He now
has my complete trust. I will obtain new recordings
shortly. The press conference went flawlessly. We
```

have agreed the best PR strategy is for Ripley to address the incident only once more, on The Tonight Show Monday night. I've instructed Tillman not to let him out of his sight. Both are headed to L.A. tomorrow (Sunday).

T. S.

THIS DOCUMENT WILL NOT PRINT.

"Good morning, Simon," Shirley said as she entered the room.

Simon didn't move. His eyes were closed.

"You have not turned that iPod off since Judd dropped it off yesterday afternoon. Don't you care at all about me anymore?" He hadn't heard a word she said. "Simon." She poked his shoulder. "I know you're awake because you keep hittin' the controls."

Simon looked up, surprised by the interruption. He pulled out one earbud. Instead of music, Shirley heard speaking voices.

"I thought you were listenin' to music." That sounds like a book on tape or somethin'. Somebody started messin' with you before you had time to finish your Grisham novel? Now, that was rude!"

Simon was writing on his board: *"Did you give Judd my note when he dropped off the iPod?"*

"There you go again. I don't get a 'Good morning, Shirley' or an 'I didn't know you worked weekends, too.' Yes, I gave Judd your note. I thanked him for bringin' your music, even though you didn't tell me to. He called this morning to check on you, as did Megan. I told Judd that you've been listenin' to your iPod nonstop. Now, how are you feelin'? Did you have any wild dreams last night you want to tell me about?"

"I'm not sure," Simon wrote.

"See, that's the only problem with Versed. It manages the pain, helps you sleep, and activates your dream state, but it also affects your short-term memory. So you have crazy dreams and just don't remember them!" Shirley sat on the stool by the bed to take Simon's vital signs. "A couple of years ago, we had this six-year-old blond-headed boy named Jeremy. I'll never forget him—precious. He was fighting leukemia, and because of the pain medication he kept havin' these vivid dreams about his puppy. All he wanted was to see his puppy, Inky. Every night, he'd dream about Inky, and Inky would talk to him. Inky told him to keep fightin', to fight like a dog and not give up. It was the most amazing thing. Well, finally, Brenda and I couldn't stand it, and we helped the parents sneak the puppy up to his room. I'll never forget Jeremy's eyes when that puppy bounced out from under the food cart where we hid him. Inky licked him all over his face like he was a Milk-Bone dog biscuit." Shirley's eyes watered as she smiled wide.

"Course, you know what little puppies do when they get excited. We got the little fella out without anybody seein' him but couldn't clean the sheets fast enough. The attending came in and started askin', 'Why is his bed wet? Who is responsible for his catheter? What is going on around here?' Well, we came clean that it was puppy pee." Shirley laughed so hard she had to let go of Simon's arm. "Let me tell you, that doctor was upset. You know, we did lose our minds for a moment, allowing a puppy into the hospital. But I'd do it again, no doubt about it. I will never forget his little face when he saw his best friend in the whole world." Shirley paused. "I was with Jeremy when he passed away. He said out loud, 'I see Inky. Really, I'm not dreamin'.'" Shirley couldn't talk for a minute. "I'm sorry. I don't know what got into me this mornin'."

Shirley saw a smile creep onto Simon's face—the first one since they met. He wrote on his board, "*Good morning, Shirley. I'm feeling better. Thank you for asking!*"

Across town in his apartment, Judd pressed the *On* button of his newly acquired Dell laptop computer with wireless Internet, courtesy of Elite Management. The computer ran through its internal checks, and a myriad of icons appeared in front of him. Judd pointed the arrow to the AOL icon and double-clicked. He then pulled out Simon's note that Shirley had given him:

```
    Judd,

    There is no one else I can trust. Please follow
the instructions below.

Sign onto AOL from any computer.
Go to Select Screen Name.
Find Guest.
At Sending From, type Ripoff.
Go to Password and type BillyHIll.
Go to Mail.
At Sending To, type in e-mail address warren.maccabe@
galaxymusic.com.

    Then type this message:

    I need to communicate with you and only you. We
have some unfinished business to discuss. If you tell
anyone about this e-mail or forward it, I will deny
it came from me. If you agree to talk to me, it must
be under my terms and my terms only. To confirm, sim-
ply reply. If you are declining to speak with me in
private, do not reply to this message.

Ripley
```

Judd sat and stared at Simon's note. He realized what Simon was doing. He was sending the CEO of Galaxy Records Worldwide a confidential e-mail as if it were coming from Ripley. He was basically forging Ripley's name. *Does Ripley know about this?* Judd thought. *Not likely. Does Simon have the right to do this? Maybe he has power of attorney or something?* Judd did know one thing: This seemed out of character for Simon. Simon was always so levelheaded, and this seemed . . . well, reckless.

After Shirley left the room, Simon continued to listen to the recorded phone messages Judd had retrieved off his hard drive. He kept replaying his last conversation with Strickland—the conversation they had just before he and Judd drove out to see Ripley at the Opry House. Simon hit rewind again and listened to his own voice: "You and MacCabe have made it clear that you want new Ripley music out this year. To make that happen, we have to renegotiate Ripley's agreement. I'm holding fast on this. We have an antiquated deal. We need a modern record agreement. Ripley is the best-selling digital artist in history, and his royalty rate is based on physical CDs. You don't have any manufacturing, shipping, or handling costs when you sell music online. We need an increased royalty rate for all digital goods and ultimately a reversion clause that gives Ripley control of his master recordings. You guys keep saying no, but if you want to see his new music this year, that's what it's going to take."

"Simon, first of all, for reasons I cannot disclose, MacCabe has put a freeze on the signing of new acts and the execution of any new contracts," Strickland said. "So I am not in a position to discuss a new contract with you—not until after the Board of Directors Meeting and Shareholders Meeting next weekend."

"So the merger is on!"

"I didn't say that."

"You might as well have. There is no other reason for a freeze on new contracts and negotiations. You and I both know that would be the only reason for a freeze. MacCabe is waiting for the ratification of the Luxor merger by the Galaxy board and the shareholders."

"That is not something I am prepared to discuss. Secondly, and more importantly, if you intend to continue to use Ripley's new CD as blackmail, it is now a moot point. You need to know that Ripley and I had a conversation directly. We spoke by phone the opening weekend of his tour. He waived his right to an attorney, and we already have an agreement in place."

"In regard to what?"

"The delivery of his next CD. Let's just say I was able to give Ripley something he desperately wanted, and in return he is giving me something I want. The issue is settled."

"Strickland, what are you talking about? You have no legal right to negotiate directly with my client. It will never hold up in court. He didn't have proper representation, and you know it! Even if you did speak to Ripley directly, one telephone conversation isn't a binding agreement."

"It was Ripley's idea. He initiated the call. I covered my bases on this one, Simon. He was willing to sign a document, and I have it all in writing. You should also know that Doug Tillman has accepted the post in Nashville. We'll announce it on Friday. I know you like Tillman. So it's a win-win situation. And Ripley isn't crying foul play. He is content. And if he is content, then you should be, too. Don't turn this into a pissing match. It's done. This issue is settled."

"Believe me, nothing is ever settled with Ripley, and he is *never* content!" After a pause, Simon continued, "James Clark's resignation for Ripley's new music. That was the deal, wasn't it? That was the deal you cut behind my back. This is unbelievable!"

"Simon, why are you surprised Ripley called me directly? MacCabe is right—you're too close to see it. Ripley is today's shooting star, but just like all the rest, he'll burn out. They always do. It's part of the cycle. In the meantime, we must all take care of ourselves. You can't get too close to these artists. They are all black holes. Open your eyes, Simon. You've been sucked in and blindsided."

Simon couldn't stop listening. He had to rewind once more: "You can't get too close to these artists. They are all black holes. Open your eyes, Simon. You've been sucked in and blindsided."

Simon's head tilted back on his pillow and his eyes closed as his medication kicked in. He saw himself in slow motion back on the stage of the Opry House. *Okay, Rip, we're going to be back behind the monitors. Knock this thing out.* Ripley turned and said, *It'll be fast, Simon, I promise.*

Then, in his dream state, he flashed back to the day he and Ripley first spoke. They were sitting in Simon's office in the Roundabout Building. Simon was next to the large window overlooking Music Row on a bright early-spring day in March 2005. But inside, the feeling was dark and heavy as Simon watched Ripley telling him about the tragic event that had recently occurred. Ripley described in great detail how he was thrown from the family car and then watched helplessly as his mom's Chevy Caprice Classic was swallowed up by the raging Cumberland. Simon relived his own surprised reaction when Ripley slowly reached into his pocket, unfolded a letter, and handed it over. It was a letter Simon himself had written. But now, from this new vantage point, he saw for the first time an expression he hadn't noticed in the original encounter. Ripley's head was lowered, his eyes tearful, his brow furrowed. But he was smiling. Simon looked closer at the letter he had written. He focused on the date—March 12, 2005. He had written the letter to Ripley exactly six years ago this very evening.

Then Tommy Strickland appeared in the scene, too, standing in front of Ripley. Ripley was looking directly at Strickland, but Strickland was invisible to him. But not to Simon. Strickland had a chalky complexion, and his eyes were bloodshot. Suddenly, Strickland turned, looked toward Simon, and said, *You're too close to see it. We must all take care of ourselves*. Strickland floated effortlessly across the room. He got right in Simon's face and said, *Simon, you've been blindsided*.

Simon heard the shots ring out, and then everything went black.

CHAPTER 29

Nashville
White Bridge Road

After sending the e-mail for Simon in Ripley's name, Judd called the hospital. He wanted to know a good time to visit Simon. The nurses said Simon was sleeping and that he should check back later. Judd had questions. Why had he sent an e-mail to Warren MacCabe, and what unfinished business needed discussing? Did Ripley know about it? Judd had a strange sense of guilt. It was like he was an accomplice to something wrong, but he was not sure what.

Then the phone jarred him from the couch.

"I've been trying to reach you. Are you okay?" Megan asked.

Pleasantly surprised, Judd said, "I'm fine. Thanks for your messages. I went by Elite yesterday but missed you. You were at the press conference. And you . . . How are you?"

After a pause, Megan said, "I'm not doing so good."

"Really? What's wrong?"

"I'm not sure. That's part of the problem."

"I thought things were looking up. I mean, the doctors seem pleased with Simon's recovery. It looked like Ripley's press conference went well. The authorities are taking control of the investigation. And after speaking with Brad Holiday yesterday, I got a company BlackBerry and a laptop!"

Megan didn't respond.

"Megan?"

"Yeah, I'm here. Sorry."

Because Megan was obviously distressed, Judd decided not to mention Simon's note and the "Ripley" e-mail to MacCabe. Besides, he was trying to convince himself that Simon was overreacting—that it had to be the medication. Simon's paranoid state would pass once the meds were scaled back.

Megan broke the silence. "Judd, I've seen things—some legal documents at the office. Not that I would pry. It just comes with the job."

"What kind of things?" Judd's moment of optimism started to vanish.

"I'm not supposed to talk about it."

"Well, you brought it up."

After another pause, Megan added, "And there is something else."

Judd had a sinking feeling. "What?"

"Ripley called me. He wants to see you."

"Me? Why me?"

"He said he wants to check up on you and asked if I would call to see if you were well enough to go out to his house tonight."

"Tonight? Can't you just call him back and tell him I'm fine?"

"I don't think so. He sounded adamant about seeing you and said he felt personally responsible. Tonight is the only time he has. Tomorrow, he's leaving for L.A. He's on *Leno* Monday. Then he goes back on tour. Can you make it out to his place?"

"I guess."

"Then I'll call and let him know. Just call me afterward, no matter what time, and tell me how it went. And Judd, do you remember what I said about Ripley when you and I were at his house on Monday?"

"The part about him being a little different in person than in public?"

"Yeah, that."

"Believe me, I remember."

"Well, just go with it. Don't let anything throw you. It should be fine."

"Hey, I'm the one that asked why he had an annual Mardi Gras party, and he said to celebrate the death of his estranged father. I mean, how much more different could it get?"

"Just call me afterward."

"Okay, but what about the things you've seen at the office?"

"Just call me as soon as you leave Ripley's house."

CHAPTER 30

Brentwood
The Governors Club
9:05 P.M.

After getting cleared by the guards, Judd drove up to Ripley's palatial home and walked to the front door. He thought, *Megan was right, as usual—no party, no valets.*

Inside, a housekeeper welcomed him into the grand foyer. "Please, make yourself at home. Some drinks are over on the wet bar. Ripley will be right down."

Judd walked toward the fireplace, passing the rustic da Vinci dining-room set and life-sized wooden cross. *How can I make myself at home when I'm afraid to touch anything?* Judd thought. The standing candelabras and wall lanterns were lit, and the fire was roaring. Judd sat in one of two French bergère chairs facing the hearth.

"Judd!" Ripley made a grand entrance. "I'm so glad you could come."

"Thank you." Judd stood, and they shook hands.

"Please, have a seat. Do you care for something to drink?"

"I'm good, thanks."

"I have Coke, beer, whatever."

"Maybe just some water."

"By all means. Let me get it for you."

Okay, so far so good, Judd thought. *Maybe tonight he'll be the polite Ripley, not the different Ripley.*

Ripley walked over to the wet bar. "Megan said you were feeling better. How's your shoulder?"

"It'll be fine. I was lucky."

"Well, thanks again for coming. I wanted to see you. I had heard you were doing well and would make a full recovery, but I wanted to see for myself."

"That's very kind."

"Judd, you and I don't know each other well, but I'm a God-fearing man."

Judd looked around the room. "I gathered that."

Ripley reached for a Bud Light and screwed off the top after handing Judd a bottled water. "This has been a trying time for me—and for you, I know. God tests each of us. This is nothing more than a test." He lifted his beer toward Judd and added, "And to be honest, I could use some company as well. It can get lonely inside these walls."

Judd didn't quite know how to respond. He broke eye contact and took a sip of water.

Ripley looked toward the cross. "Who do you think is the most influential person in history?"

Judd thought about Megan's advice: *Don't let anything throw you.* "In music?" he asked.

"No, no, in all of history."

Judd responded with an answer he never would have thought of in a different setting: "Jesus Christ?"

Ripley beamed. "That's correct! It would have to be the Lord Jesus Christ. Are you a believer?"

Judd felt a bit of panic. "I did not grow up in a religious family. We didn't go to church, but I believe in God."

"I grew up with a man that was all sin. He was hell on earth. That's why my life has been a test."

Trying to avoid discussion of Ripley's father, Judd asked, "Is your mother still living?"

"No. I've been orphaned since I was eighteen. My mother, my old man, and my twin brother have all passed."

Twin brother? Judd thought. He couldn't let that slip by. "I never knew you had a twin brother."

"Not many people do. I tend not to talk about my family. It's a sad history. Both my mother and brother died before I got into the music business. But the truth is, my brother *is* the reason I got into the business. I've been thinking about them today. I guess what happened this week—the shooting, Simon's condition—brought some things to the surface."

Ripley sat and stared into the fire while finishing his beer. "We were a military family."

Judd could tell he was about to hear Ripley's family history.

"My old man fought in Vietnam. When he came back, he was deranged. I'm not sure if he was 100 percent sin before Vietnam, but he was all sin by the time he came home. I was raised just north of here around Fort Campbell, Kentucky. My old man was in and out of the VA hospital. He couldn't hold a steady job. He drank all of his earnings. Then he'd come home and beat us to make him feel strong. When he did work, it was at a local funeral home digging graves. He became obsessed with the dead. The drinking got worse. My mother worked long hours at a beauty parlor and tried to keep away from the drunk. We basically raised ourselves. When we were eleven or twelve, my brother got a guitar. And while Mom worked, we'd entertain ourselves playing and writing songs. We both wanted to be country-music stars. Mom thought my brother had the better voice. That was all we wanted, to be rich and famous and get the hell away from our old man."

Ripley paused. "One night when we were sixteen, the drunk came home and started in on Mom and us. He got my brother's guitar and broke it over my back. But my brother and I were finally big enough to handle him—two against one, anyway. We turned on him and tore him up—broke his nose and some ribs, threw him out of the trailer, and told him if he ever put a hand on us again, we'd kill him. And we would have."

"And I guess he never did?" Judd asked.

"Nope. He moved out. Started living in an old rural hunting cabin in Williamson County, not too far from here. We stayed and lived in the trailer park with Mom in Clarksville near Fort Campbell. I didn't see him again until two years later, the day after my mom and brother died."

After another pause, Judd asked, "When was that?"

"We had just turned eighteen. Mom came home carrying on about a talent contest in Nashville that one of the ladies at work told her about. The grand prize was a recording session paid for by a well-known country-music manager. I'd never seen her so excited. But there were a couple of problems. One was that she couldn't get off work. And the only car we had was a piece of junk, a Chevy Caprice Classic that always broke down. And Mom said she had enough money for only one entry fee."

"So, obviously, she entered you into the contest."

"No, like I said, she thought my brother was the better singer. She also did something she said she'd never do. She called her low-rent, alcoholic, wife-beating husband and begged him to let us borrow his truck and some money so their boy could hit it big in Nashville. Of course, he wouldn't do it. So she called in sick to make the trip. I went along for the ride. And lo and behold, it turned out my brother won. They told him that night that he'd get all the details on the recording session in the mail. I noticed how the main judge never took his eyes off my brother. Afterward, Mom kept saying, 'This is it. This is what I've been dreaming about.' She just kept going on about how amazing my brother was, that he was destined for greatness, that he was a superstar in the making. And then the nightmare began."

That's when the nightmare began? Judd thought. *What part of your childhood wasn't a nightmare?* "You've really been tested," he said. "But we can change the subject. It's fine, really. Or maybe I should go."

"Honestly, I think it would help me tonight to talk about it."

Great, Judd thought. *Where is Megan when I need her?*

Ripley got up, walked over to the fire, put his hand on the hearth, and looked down at the flames. "It was about midnight when we were driving back from Nashville to Clarksville. Mom headed right into a heavy rainstorm. The Chevy wasn't interstate worthy and couldn't handle the storm. She couldn't see. The windows were fogged, the tires were bad, the brakes didn't work. We came over a hill to a bridge. She lost control. The car slid off an embankment and went through a guardrail and into the Cumberland River. I was in the backseat. I remember being thrown from the car and hitting mud and sliding for what seemed like eternity. I've played it over and over in my mind. I was caked in mud, but otherwise not a scratch. I scrambled up the embankment just in time to see the headlights burning under the water. And then they were gone. I watched helplessly, knowing my mother and brother were trapped inside. They were both killed."

"I'm sorry," Judd mumbled.

"Three days later, there was a letter in the mail giving the details about my brother's recording session. They wanted him in Nashville to record one of his songs and to take a meeting with a manager." Ripley paused. "That's how I got my record deal."

Judd knew he hadn't misheard. "But I thought Simon discovered you."

"He did. Simon was the judge who kept looking at my brother. He was the one that wrote the letter."

Judd was stunned. *What? Simon wanted to sign Ripley's brother, but he was killed the same night of the talent contest, so he signed Ripley instead?*

"It's all true. Now there are three people that know the entire back story—Simon, Megan, and you. But enough of all that. I have one important question for you. Why do you think Jesus Christ is the most influential person of all time?"

Judd had no idea. Nor could he grasp the transition from Ripley's tragic childhood and the disclosure of how he got his twin brother's record deal to this game of Christian Trivial Pursuit. "Because of His teachings?"

"No. Jesus Christ is the most influential figure of all time because of His resurrection. They never found the body!"

Judd swallowed some water and thought, *Okay, now we've officially gone way past his being a little different.*

"I told Simon at our first meeting that I wanted to do this—to live out the dream my family was denied. It would be our personal resurrection."

Judd was struggling to follow the conversation. "Sorry. You wanted to do what?"

"Become famous. Become a country-music star. I did it so my brother could live his dream. I couldn't let his dream die. He is living in me, like Jesus Christ. And just as Jesus was betrayed, there are those who will betray us and wish us dead, and they must be held accountable."

Judd was beyond uncomfortable. *Can I please leave now?*

"Have you ever felt trapped?" Ripley asked.

"Yes, I have!"

"I feel it every day. I never thought it would happen, but now I'm trapped inside this fame. It's a tricky thing. With fame, everything becomes amplified. You can't sleep because you know that somewhere, someone is listening to you, thinking about you, trying to get close, trying to expose your secrets."

Judd could no longer make eye contact with Ripley. He just kept staring into the fire.

Ripley walked over to the long wooden table and sat in the center seat. He put his beer down and bowed his head. Judd wondered if he was remembering his past or praying.

Ripley finally asked, "Did you notice my supper table?"

"I did. It's very unique."

"It's an exact replica of the table in the painting of *The Last Supper*. Jesus knew He was about to transcend this world and go into the spirit world. In the painting, da Vinci depicts the very moment Jesus declared, 'One of you shall betray me.' It was one of God's tests! The wrath of God is so powerful."

Judd dared not say a word.

"Just like the resurrected Christ, they never found the body of my twin brother. He, too, just disappeared."

"What?"

"It's true. The search team recovered my mother's body trapped in the car." Ripley looked up and extended his arms as if to depict Christ on the cross. "But not my twin brother. He vanished. Just like Jesus."

CHAPTER 31

THE NEXT AFTERNOON

Forty-two thousand feet over Colorado
Sunday, March 13

The eight-passenger private Cessna Citation 10 took off from Nashville International Airport at 1:12 P.M. Central. The flight to Burbank, California, would take three hours and forty-eight minutes, according to Brentyn Sanders, the plane's chief pilot.

Ripley was wearing sweatpants, a House of Blues sweatshirt, a Tennessee Titans baseball cap turned backward, and sunglasses. The plane had eight tan leather captain's chairs, each facing another seat. Ripley was in his usual far back left seat. He looked at the small screen positioned beside him. The screen controls allowed the passengers to watch movies or view the in-flight readout that tracked the plane's route. Ripley clicked the flight information. A map of the United States appeared with a line graph showing Nashville as the origination point. The line went northwest over the southwestern tip of Kentucky, passed just south of Springfield, Missouri, and traveled directly over Wichita, Kansas. The current position was west of Pueblo, Colorado. The screen automatically changed and gave a more detailed look at the plane's exact global positioning. It zoomed in to show the Rocky Mountains and located the plane directly over Windom Peak just south of Red Mountain Pass. The screen changed again, giving flight information:

```
Speed: 591 mph
Altitude: 41,800 feet
Temperature: -76 degrees
Time remaining: 1 hour, 54 minutes
```

There was plenty of separation between the front four seats and the back four—enough that it was difficult for those in the back to hear the conversations of those in the front and vice versa. Pumpkin, Jerome, and Nate were leaning toward each other in the front seats talking.

Cindy—a.k.a. P.C.—faced Ripley, her long legs stretched out and her bare feet resting in his lap. Janice sat across the aisle from Ripley and P.C., with Doug Tillman directly in front of her. Janice had her nose buried in Kathryn Stockett's novel *The Help* while Tillman worked off his iPad. Normally, Janice would have taken advantage of a new travel mate with one of her famed one-way conversations, but she had no interest in engaging Tillman. Ripley stared out the window, lost in his thoughts. He must have felt the gaze of his trophy girlfriend, who was now taking a break from the latest issue of *Vogue* to scrutinize him. She was stunning enough to grace the pages she was reading. He looked over and gave a halfhearted smile. She blew him a kiss and then returned to her magazine. Ripley looked toward the front of the plane but couldn't decipher what Pumpkin, Jerome, and Nate were saying.

"Jerome, when we get down to Monterrey this year, you've got to come with us. It will blow your mind," Nate said, then looked over to Pumpkin. "We are playing there, right?"

"Oh, yeah. Ripley wouldn't miss it," Pumpkin said.

"Jerome, you don't know what you've been missing, man. It is actually a very classy place. The girls are unbelievable. You'd never know they were hookers, I swear. They are grade-A, top drawer, *el primo fantastico!*"

"Naw, man, that just ain't my bag. I don't need to get it like that," Jerome said.

"I know you don't. I'm not saying that, man. But this is different.

When you're in a foreign land, it's important to check out the country's natural resources. These ladies are *fine*. And you don't have to pay a penny. It's a company expense. Right, Pumpkin?"

"Yup. The bean counters write it off as a food and entertainment expense."

"I don't know, man," Jerome said. "What if Ripley finds out?"

"It's his good friend that takes us there!" Nate said. "A rich promoter guy who owns a ton of nightclubs in northern Mexico."

"We'll see. What's the name of the place again?"

"La Casa Blanca—The White House," Pumpkin said. "It's the most famous casa in Monterrey. Man, we spent so much money there last trip, I bet they've got themselves a new West Wing!" All three busted out laughing. Pumpkin saw Ripley looking at them but could tell Ripley had no idea what they were talking about.

Captain Sanders stepped out of cockpit and past the guys in the first four seats. "Ripley, is everything to your liking?"

"Everything is fine, captain," Ripley said. "I think you know everybody on board except Doug Tillman." He pointed. "Doug is the new president of my record company in Nashville."

"Glad to have you," Captain Sanders said.

"Nice to be here. This is quite a plane," Tillman said. "Is this the newest in the fleet?"

"Actually, Cessna came out with the Sovereign in 2004, but the Cessna 10 is still the fastest commercial plane in the sky. Only the Concorde was faster. But unlike the Concorde, we are not allowed to break the sound barrier, though she is capable. We keep her just under Mach 1. We can take her up to fifty-one thousand feet. We can travel cross-country without stopping—New York to Heathrow, for that matter."

"Nice. So what's the price tag, if you don't mind my asking?"

"Just under $20 million," the captain said.

"That's why they told me to lease, not own," Ripley said.

"True. Most people just pay a leasing fee, and we're on call. They don't have to worry about maintenance issues, logs, pilots' schedules. We do all that. But a few buy. Arnold Palmer purchased the first Citation 10 that was made."

"Really? I'm in the wrong business," Tillman said.

The captain turned to Ripley and asked in a serious tone, "What is the update on Simon?"

"He's hanging in there."

"Thank God. Just like everybody else, we were on pins and needles when we heard the news—first, that someone tried to get to you, and then that Simon was hurt."

"It's been difficult. But we're heading right back to work. You guys should be getting the updated tour schedule, but we're basically back where we left off after we do *The Tonight Show* tomorrow night."

"Got it. Pumpkin told me earlier. So Simon's going to recover?"

"They're taking it day by day, but he's in the best of care."

"Please tell him we were all asking about him. I better get back to flying this plane—not that she isn't capable of flying herself." The captain looked over to Tillman, "Nice to meet you."

As Captain Sanders turned and headed back to the cockpit, Tillman looked over to Janice. "Since you guys fly private, and the show isn't until tomorrow night, why not go out tomorrow morning?"

Janice pulled herself away from her novel and replied, "*Tonight Show* rules. It is mandatory for all entertainers to be in L.A. the evening prior to the taping, due to potential travel delays, bad weather, or whatever. They can't risk it. Besides, call time for Ripley is eleven in the morning, and then we're there all day."

Janice reached into her bag, pulled out a sheet of paper, and handed it to Tillman. It was a memo on *The Tonight Show* letterhead. It read,

> **This is to confirm Ripley Graham will be our musical guest on The Tonight Show with Jay Leno on MONDAY, MARCH 14, 2011. PLEASE NOTE THAT IF GUEST(S) ARE FLYING IN FROM OUT OF TOWN, THEY MUST ARRIVE THE DAY BEFORE THE SHOW, NOT THE DAY OF TAPING. The taping will take place in Studio 11 at NBC STUDIOS, 3000 West Alameda Avenue, Burbank. The schedule is as follows:**
>
> **8:00 A.M.** **Equipment load-in/technician(s)**
> **10:30 A.M.** **Musicians' & Background Singers' call time**
> **11:00 A.M.** **Ripley Graham's call time**

```
10:45 A.M.–12:00 P.M.   Sound check/rehearsal
12:00 P.M.–1:00 P.M.   Lunch (Will not provide—
commissary is available)
1:00 P.M.–1:30 P.M.   On-camera rehearsal
2:30 P.M.–3:30 P.M.   Makeup & Hair
4:00 P.M.–5:00 P.M.   Tape
```

"Are we doing only one song?" Ripley asked.

"We need to talk about that," Janice said. "The show's producers want you to have as much couch time as you need. It's really your call. They weren't sure how comfortable you were going to be. But in the meantime, they're doing a promotional blitz around the show."

Tillman leaned toward Ripley. "When we first talked about national media after the shooting and you said you would do only *Leno*, I've got to tell you, everyone at the label wondered why. But this *Leno* exclusive is getting more hype than I would have ever expected. It worked."

Ripley leaned back in his seat, eyes shut, and said, "I did my homework. Before all the drama last year with Jay Leno taking *The Tonight Show* back from Conan O'Brien, there were years and years of ratings wars between Leno and David Letterman. Letterman wanted *The Tonight Show* when Johnny Carson retired, but Leno got it. We all know that. Letterman's ratings were better in the early years, but Leno hung in there. Eventually, Leno surpassed Letterman. TV trivia question: Who did Leno book on his show to finally turn it around in his favor?"

No one answered.

"Janice?" Ripley opened his eyes and looked at her.

"I don't know. Obviously, it's my job to know, but I don't."

"Come on, guys. These are the important things to notice. Leno can't win, and then suddenly he makes one big booking, and—bam!—he starts taking the lead."

Everyone looked a bit meek.

"Hugh Grant. Leno was the first to talk to Hugh Grant after he picked up the Hollywood hooker Divine Brown when he had Elizabeth Hurley at home. Remember? The first words out of Jay's mouth were, 'What were you thinking?' It was about sex. About the insanity of a guy with everyone's fantasy woman, and he still goes after a whore. But the truth is, that was not what gave Leno one of his biggest ratings in history. It was because he had the *exclusive* on that story. One time! Tune in or miss out! And tomorrow, I want to beat that rating. Come on, guys, how can you not know that?"

There was an awkward silence as the experts realized they had been beaten at their own game.

"I got another one," Ripley said. "Anybody know what the average viewing audience of Jay Leno or David Letterman is at the moment?"

"Leno averages over 4 million households a night, and Letterman is less," Janice said.

"That's right. And both are declining," Ripley said. "Next question: What was the single biggest musical event in the history of television?"

"Last month's Super Bowl with the Black Eyed Peas," Tillman said. "All-time record with 111 million viewers."

"Yes and no. It was the most-watched show in history, but it was all about the Packers and the Steelers, not Fergie and will.i.am. What was the biggest single musical event on TV?"

"The Beatles on *The Ed Sullivan Show*," Tillman said.

"Bingo." Then Ripley upped the ante. "Do you know how many people watched?"

No one did.

"Seventy-three million Americans, and it happened forty-one years ago! Come on, guys, I'm supposed to be just the singer here."

"Okay. Speaking in terms of television marketing, since you will have America's undivided attention tomorrow, let's talk about the segment," Tillman said. "How are you going to address the shooting without looking like we're taking advantage of this situation commercially?"

Ripley leaned his head back and closed his eyes again.

Tillman looked at Janice. "What would you suggest?"

"Well, that's the beauty of an exclusive. It will look like we're talking about this only once, as Ripley said in the press conference. That will make him look like we're not taking advantage."

"What are the topics of conversation?"

"You can guess what Leno will ask," Janice said. "'What happened? How close was it? Who do you think would do this? And why?'"

"I'm fine with 'What happened?' " Tillman said. "Ripley can talk about that. He can refer the *who* question to the authorities heading up the investigation. It's the *why* we need to be careful with."

Ripley spoke without opening his eyes. "A lot of crazy people out there want their own fifteen minutes of fame and don't care how they get it. Look at John Hinckley, shooting Reagan to impress Jodie Foster, or Mark Chapman gunning down John Lennon the same day he got his autograph. It's an occupational hazard."

"There's still a problem," Tillman said. "Those crazies got caught immediately and got their faces plastered all over the world. They wanted fifteen minutes, and they got their fifteen minutes. Our guy seems to be less interested in publicity and more interested in not getting caught."

Ripley opened his eyes and looked at Tillman. "Okay, so I'll tell Jay I have no idea why someone would do this, period."

"Bad idea," Tillman said. "America is watching, remember, and when the public watches, they want answers. Saying 'I don't know' won't cut it. We need an answer that makes you look smart and brave, not stupid."

Ripley leaned forward. "What about Yolanda Saldivar, the fan-club president that shot Selena? She killed her because she was jealous, not for fame. I don't know what makes crazy people crazy."

"You better be careful," Tillman fired back. "If you don't give America an answer, people will start conjuring up their own."

Janice said, "As much as I hate to agree with him, he's got a point."

"Look, Ripley," Tillman said. "I'm just telling you the truth. Mass marketing and the manipulation of the media can be your greatest asset or your worst nightmare. There is no in-between. Average Americans don't tune in to watch the rich and powerful succeed. They tune in to watch them fail. That's the real reason Jay Leno got his ratings from Hugh Grant."

Janice said, "That's why the tabloids are so lucrative. And they're calling, by the way—asking about old girlfriends, love triangles, the works. Nothing we haven't dealt with before. It's just a new angle for them."

"What did you tell them?" Ripley asked Janice.

"The same as always: 'If you're running a story, call me. And legally, you better cover your butt and call me for a comment. Otherwise, don't waste my time.' They're fishing. They don't have anything. Not yet, anyway."

"I'm telling you, Ripley, we have to be careful," Tillman said. "*Why* could become a big, big problem."

Ripley raised his voice in frustration. "I'll tell you why, damn it! Because some freak doesn't have any balls, that's why. Somebody put a contract out on me. Why? For one of two reasons—either because Ripley Graham is worth more to someone dead than alive or because I have a gift and I live in the USA, where we're free to use our gifts for personal profit. I'm living the dream—that's why I'm the target. Ripley Graham is doing what he was put on this earth to do, using his God-given talent. And if someone tries to stop Ripley Graham from living his dream, then they are going to feel the wrath of the Almighty. The psycho who tried to kill Ripley Graham tried to kill the American dream. And guess what? He missed. The atheist communist bastard missed! Those are the only two logical reasons." Ripley, red-faced, tilted his head back into his seat and closed his eyes once more.

"Okay, that answers the *why*," Tillman said. "We're going patriotic, without the profanity."

Janice got up and excused herself to the restroom. When she came out, Jerome was standing near the door waiting his turn. Janice squeezed by him and walked to the front of the plane for a change of scenery. She sat beside Pumpkin.

"You guys were raising the roof up here earlier," Janice said. "What were you howling about?"

"Politics," Nate said. "Trips to the . . . ah, The White House."

Pumpkin's eyebrows rose.

"Oh," Janice said, ready to tell a story. "It's been a few years, but I'll never forget my first trip with Ripley. His first invitation to the White House, and President Bush invites him to a black-tie state dinner. Of course, Ripley didn't have a tux. I told him not to worry, that I'd have the label rent him a killer designer tux. He said fine but refused to wear the black patent-leather shoes that came with it. I said, 'No problem.

Just wear the most expensive boots you own. President Bush is from Texas, and he'll totally appreciate it.' What I didn't know was that Ripley's most expensive boots were light brown ostrich skins. His first visit to the White House, and he gets out of the limo violating rule number one—never, ever wear brown shoes with black pants, much less brown boots with a black tux. I was totally humiliated, but it was too late. We entered the East Gate, walked down the red carpet to see President and Mrs. Bush standing shoulder to shoulder, greeting every guest as they walked in. Ripley was in front of me and shook the president's hand and then Mrs. Bush's. Then the president turned to Ripley, grabbed him by the shoulder, and pulled him back. He pointed to Ripley's boots and yelled out so everyone could hear, 'I've got a pair just like those! Ostrich, the real McCoy.' Ripley beamed while cameras started flashing everywhere. I just stood there with my mouth gaping."

Pumpkin and Nate were laughing as Jerome returned from the restroom.

"What did I miss?" he asked.

"We're just laughing about Ripley's first trip to the White House," Janice said.

"Good Lord, I don't think we should be talkin' 'bout that place!" Jerome said. "I didn't think Ripley's visits were common knowledge."

"Of course they're common knowledge," Janice said. "It's a pretty famous place."

Nate quickly added, "Yeah, well, that's probably all we need to say on that subject."

Agitated, Jerome said, "Hey, you guys brought it up, not me. Personally, I've never been, and I'm not going. It's a den of thieves with nothing but whores!"

"Well, everybody's entitled to their own opinion, I guess," Janice said.

Jerome turned away. "Too kinky for me, man," he mumbled. "Bunch of rich freaks."

CHAPTER 32

Nashville
White Bridge Road
1:45 P.M.

Judd checked the inbox again for new messages on his computer. It was empty. His head was spinning—too many thoughts, too many questions.

Last night with Ripley couldn't have been more bizarre. Judd had wanted to call Megan as soon as he left, but it was late. And to be honest, he needed a little time to process the meeting before he could explain it. He had called her first thing this morning but got her voicemail. He then called the hospital. The nurses said Simon was awake and alert.

Judd had gotten to the hospital about nine o'clock, eager to tell Simon about his visit with Ripley. But Simon wanted only to know about the e-mail. Judd told him that he had sent it to MacCabe as instructed but that so far there had been no reply. He also asked Simon why the message was sent from Ripley. That was when Simon signaled Shirley to leave the room. She did so, but not without commenting, "Like you boys think I give a hill of beans about country music. Now, if you were offerin' up some scoop on Will Smith, I might actually care!"

Once Shirley left, Simon wrote, "*Confidential—you don't need to know too much, for your own safety. Let me know if MacCabe replies.*"

"That's all you're going to tell me? Simon, I'm already way deep in this thing. I was shot, too, remember. I think I deserve to know more."

"*Check it every hour,*" Simon wrote. "*Rip doesn't use that e-mail account.*"

"Can you do that?" Judd asked. "I don't want to break any laws here. This doesn't seem right."

"*Someone's trying to kill me. Does that seem right?*"

"Okay, okay. I said I'd help, but you've got to help me, too. You can't expect me to go flying out of here like Robin the Boy Wonder without a clue."

"*You've done good.*"

"Come on, Simon. Take my blindfold off. Let me help."

Simon shook his head as pain shot across his face. He grimaced and hit the button for his PCA pump to get some morphine. He wrote, "*Galaxy needs Rip's record now. Trying to merge with Luxor. They need Rip on board. Listen.*"

Simon handed Judd the iPod with his phone conversations on it. Judd put in the earphones and pushed play. "Simon, first of all, for reasons I cannot disclose, MacCabe has put a freeze—" That was all Judd heard before Simon flinched with pain so violently that he bolted up out of bed. All the alarms went off. Shirley and the crew rushed in and pushed Judd out of the way. They got Simon sedated and his vital signs back to normal. Simon had then slipped into an unconscious state. He never knew Judd departed.

Now, it was almost two in the afternoon. He had left Simon hours ago. Sitting in his apartment alone, he kept thinking about the bizarre night with Ripley. And now he was also more worried than ever about Simon. He wondered if Simon was right or just too heavily medicated to think straight. He looked down at the iPod in his hand. *I'll listen later,* he thought. Then his train of thought was interrupted by the new computer as it announced, "You've got mail."

Sure enough, the inbox flag was raised. He clicked it open. It was from MacCabe's office.

Sent: Monday, March 14, 2011, 1:51 P.M.
To: Ripoff@aol.com
Subject: (Auto Reply)

Please note that your e-mail was received. It is impossible for Mr. MacCabe to respond to every e-mail personally. Because of this, if you have an urgent need to contact him directly, we ask that you first communicate with Derrick Andrews, VP of Special Services and Security at Galaxy Records. We apologize in advance for any inconvenience.

Office of Warren MacCabe
Chairman & CEO, Galaxy Records Worldwide

CHAPTER 33

Nashville
VUMC

Shirley kept a careful watch on Simon all day. Once Judd left, visibly upset from seeing Simon in pain, Shirley had continued to medicate him and stabilize his vitals. He woke intermittently and was uncomfortable most of the afternoon. But by late evening, before she left for the day, she administered the last round of Versed. It finally calmed his restless movements but definitely not his dream state.

He was standing in a large, empty ballroom. The floor was made up of sixty-four squares—eight rows of eight squares, alternating black and white. There was no furniture. Down one side of the floor were the numbers 1 through 8. On the adjacent side were the letters A through H. Simon stood tall and erect in the middle of the room on one of the white squares.

Hearing his name called, he turned and saw a woman approach wearing an ornate gown, as if she were a member of a royal court. She held a decorative peacock-feathered mask over her face. "Welcome, Simon. We are so glad you got our invitation and were able to come. I am in charge of the games tonight. We are about to begin Who's Who. Do you know how to play?"

"Yes," Simon replied.

"Excellent. Whoever wins the match will be coronated this year's king, and the ball will commence. Are you ready?"

"Yes."

"Who else is on the board with you?"

"No one."

"Look again."

From out of nowhere, a man appeared on the black square to his right. He, too, wore a royal costume with a mask. Without speaking, the man turned his back so Simon could see the name pinned on his costume. It read, "Assassin."

The woman spoke. "Simon, you have read the name on his back, and now you have to guess who this person really is. But we've added a twist to make it more exciting. Once you make your guess, the man will remove his mask. If you have guessed correctly, you will be crowned king, and our other guests will join you in a grand celebration. However, if the man removes his mask and you are wrong, then you must die."

Suddenly, the man pulled a gun from underneath his costume. As he pushed the barrel into the bridge of Simon's nose, he grinned.

The woman began to float effortlessly across the ballroom—first away from Simon, then back toward him. "You've been blindsided, Simon, but by whom?" she asked. "You're running out of time. Who is the assassin? Tell us the truth. Your life depends on it."

Simon's whole upper body violently jerked, disconnecting his neck IV. The alarm went off. The blood in his IV started backing up. Two night nurses rushed through the door. One tried to reconnect his IV while the other checked his pulse.

"He's in a cold sweat. His O_2 is dropping. Call the crash team. *Now!*"

One of the nurses got a suction device and placed it down the tube in Simon's throat to clear the airway. "There's blockage. He's not getting any oxygen."

"His O_2 is still dropping."

"He's going into shock."

"This should clear it. Come on!"

"There must be bleeding inside. We're losing him!"

A machine alarm went off.

"It's causing arrhythmia. Get the crash cart!"

Medical personnel rushed into the room.

"He's in V-tach," one of the nurses said.

"Give him two ccs of epi and get the paddles," a doctor said.

"Are we clear?" the doctor asked a moment later.

"No!"

"Let's go. We're out of time!"

"Okay, clear!"

The doctor shocked Simon's chest.

"Nothing."

The alarm continued. They watched the monitor flat-line.

"We're losing him. Try it again. Are we clear?"

"Clear!"

With the next blast of current, the alarm stopped. The line on the monitor showed movement.

"We got him!"

"Okay, okay. Nice work, everybody. Let's stabilize him. Put him on the ventilator. We've got him back."

CHAPTER 34

Nashville
White Bridge Road

The e-mail makes sense, Judd thought. *MacCabe wouldn't respond like any normal Galaxy employee. And really, how would they confirm the authenticity of an e-mail from someone as famous as Ripley? How would MacCabe know if it was really him?* Judd assumed that without some type of secured e-mail system, any crazed hacker could make it look like Ripley sent a message to the label head. Some security specialist probably filtered every e-mail before MacCabe read them. He needed to talk to Simon.

In the meantime, he was engrossed in the recorded conversations on Simon's iPod. He had started listening from the beginning. The recordings ran from Friday, March 4, to Wednesday, March 9. Judd figured something on the iPod would shed light on who was behind the shootings and why, but he didn't know if it would be obvious to *him* or not.

He was listening to Pumpkin talk about production problems on opening weekend. During a pause between Simon and Pumpkin, Judd heard someone knocking at his door. He took out the earbuds and peered through the security hole. Immediately, he felt his stomach lurch. It was the investigative agent he had seen with Ripley on TV.

Oh, God, he thought. *How long has he been here?* He took a deep breath and cracked the door.

"Judd Nix?" the agent asked.

"Yes, sir."

"I'm Agent Rod Engels with TBI, the Tennessee Bureau of Investigation." He pulled his badge from his jacket. "Can I come in and ask you some questions?"

"Ah, all right." Judd opened the door fully, and the agent walked in. Judd felt lightheaded.

"This will take just a few minutes," Engels said. "How are you feeling?"

"Better." After an awkward pause, Judd added, "Sorry I was slow getting to the door. I was listening to some music with my earphones. How can I help you?"

"Can I ask you some questions, on the record?" Engels took a handheld recorder out of his pocket.

"Of course," Judd said. He knew he looked nervous. But he thought, *Why should I be? I was one of the people shot. He's here to get my take on what happened. Stay cool. This is normal.*

Engels held up the recorder. "Do you understand we are on the record?"

"Yes, sure."

"Good." Engels sat in a chair next to the only table in the room. "I know you answered some general questions for the metro police officer while you were at the hospital. I have that information. But just to review, you said you didn't notice anyone suspicious around the shooting or see anything that seemed unusual at the Opry House. Have you remembered anything new since then?"

Judd began to relax a little and also took a seat. "No, sir."

"So you basically didn't see anything at all?"

"Well, like I told the police officer, I thought one of those large overhead studio lights exploded. I looked back over my shoulder and was blinded by all the spotlights hanging from the ceiling. I fell or tripped, and I remember seeing Simon Stills already on the floor. That's when I felt a pain rip through my shoulder. I must have hit my head when I fell because that's all I remember."

"You said you had been working for Simon for only six months as an intern."

"That's right."

"In that short amount of time, would you say he had more friends or more enemies in his business?"

Judd was starting to feel uncomfortable again. "Simon is a great guy. People really seem to like him. I mean, it's a tough job, but it seems like he has a lot of friends in the business."

"Is there anybody you can think of who sticks out as someone he hates or who hates him?"

Jesus, Judd thought, *maybe they also think Simon was a target.* "Not really. Not that I can think of."

"If you do think of someone, give me a call. Or if you remember anything you feel I should know, call me." Engels got up and opened his wallet. He handed Judd his card and then nonchalantly said, "Brad Holiday told us he found you in Simon's office on Friday, working from his computer."

Oh, Lord, Judd thought. *This is like a bad* Columbo *rerun. The lieutenant waits until the end of the conversation, then messes with your mind.* "That's true, but just for a few minutes."

"What were you doing?"

"Uh, Simon had his iPod at the office that he wanted, so I went over and picked it up for him. He wanted me to sync it first with his computer. So I did."

"Did you give it to him?"

Not wanting to elaborate, Judd kept it simple: "I did."

"Are you sure Simon asked you to do this?"

Judd felt a sense of anger rising. "Of course. Ask him yourself."

"I can't. He's in a coma."

"What?"

"Sorry to be the one to tell you. Apparently, Simon took a turn for the worse this evening. You should also know we brought Simon's computer to our crime lab. The computer specialists tell me that someone was actually erasing files on Friday, March 11, at 12:32 P.M. That was during Ripley's press conference. That would have been exactly the same time you were in Simon's office. Judd, didn't the metro officer make it clear not to tamper with anything that could be used in the investigation?"

Still in a daze from the news on Simon, Judd said, "Maybe. I guess so. But I was just getting something for Simon. It didn't seem like a big deal. I was just trying to be helpful."

"Well, for the record, obstruction of justice and lying to a bureau agent are very serious offenses in the state of Tennessee, Judd. I'm sure I'm going to need to speak with you again soon. Don't leave the city or state without letting me know. You have my numbers."

Engels turned and left.

Judd fell back onto his sofa while the agent's words rang in his ears: *Obstruction of justice and lying to a bureau agent are very serious offenses.* Feeling nauseous, he called Megan's cell but again got voicemail. "Megan, where are you? I'm sorry I didn't call after seeing Ripley last night. Did you get my message this morning? Call me back. It's about Simon . . . and a visitor I just had. We need to talk!"

CHAPTER 35

The Next Morning

London
Kensington
Monday, March 14

Warren MacCabe sat at his desk on the third floor at Galaxy earlier than usual, ready for what would prove to be another turbulent week. He was usually in his office by seven-thirty. This morning, he had arrived at seven. Gwen, also in early, already had a fresh cup of coffee poured and a tall silver coffeepot on a serving cart next to his desk. In front of him were current copies of the *London Times* and the *Bulletin*. MacCabe noticed the lead article in the *Bulletin*:

Billboard.biz Bulletin™

YOUR DAILY ENTERTAINMENT NEWS UPDATE
MONDAY, MARCH 14, 2011

Ripley Graham to Make TV Appearance "Tonight"

Chip Avery, Nashville

Country-music megastar Ripley Graham will give an exclusive television interview and performance on *The Tonight*

***Show* with Jay Leno tonight in Los Angeles. Graham says it is the only show on which he will discuss the assassination attempt on his life last week.**

In a press conference Friday, Graham said, "I'm going to do *The Tonight Show* this Monday, and that will be it. I do want to let the fans know what happened, how Simon (Stills) is, and I want to thank them for their support during this time. But I don't want to do a media blitz. That would be in poor taste, in my judgment."

MacCabe had worked off his secure e-mail service at home several times over the weekend but had not seen the e-mail from Ripoff@aol.com. A "clearance system" was in place by which approved e-mails sent from the company's server were forwarded to his office computer, laptop, and BlackBerry. However, any incoming e-mail that didn't have such clearance—like junk e-mail—didn't get through, and all were automatically reviewed by the company's Internet security guru, Derrick Andrews. MacCabe received an auto response from him on any correspondence that wasn't secure.

Through the years, most top executives in the music business had learned to be careful with e-mail and not to put too much in writing in order to protect themselves and their companies. Because it was such a high-profile industry, music executives every year saw more and more nuisance lawsuits—people suing entertainment businesses for anything under the sun. The top brass had become very guarded. E-mail had actually worsened the problem. In the old days, people couldn't get through to the top decision makers. Then, almost overnight, commercial e-mail made it possible for anybody to send messages, pictures, and even music to anyone around the world. For a moment, everyone had access to the top brass. But soon afterward, new mechanisms like secure e-mail were put in place to keep the top executives inaccessible.

MacCabe's computer indicated he had an unsecured e-mail, forwarded by Derrick Andrews. Prior to opening it, he clicked the daily organizer on his computer. Gwen made the entries. He had several key meetings and conference calls on tap: the daily preparation for the

Board of Directors Meeting this Friday and the Shareholders Meeting on Sunday; a meeting with the accountants regarding the year-end numbers, a situation that was worsening; a current employment-contract renewal meeting with the in-house attorneys; and a highly confidential phone conversation about the ongoing merger negotiations with Luxor.

"Good morning, Mr. MacCabe," Gwen said. "Here are the files you asked me to pull, as well as your call sheet."

"Thank you. Are you initiating the call with Mr. Schultz at Luxor this morning, or is his office doing it?" MacCabe asked.

"I am."

"Good. Just give me a good ten-minute warning before you set the call, please."

"Absolutely."

"Thank you, dear."

As Gwen left, MacCabe took his first sip of coffee and clicked open the unsecured e-mail.

Sent: Saturday, March 12, 2011, 8:55 P.M.
To: Warren, MacCabe
From: Andrews, Derrick
Subject: E-mail from "Ripley"

The authenticity of the "Ripley" e-mail cannot be confirmed. Our automated system sent the standard response. We will continue to monitor.

Derrick Andrews
VP of Special Services & Security

---Original Message---
Sent: Saturday, March 12, 2011, 8:47 P.M.
To: MacCabe, Warren <warren.maccabe@galaxymusic.com>
From: Ripoff@aol.com
Subject:

I need to communicate with you and only you. We have some unfinished business to discuss. If you tell any-

one about this e-mail or forward it, I will deny it came from me. If you agree to talk to me, it must be under my terms and my terms only. To confirm, simply reply. If you are declining to speak with me in private, do not reply to this message.

Ripley

MacCabe sat staring at the screen. His first thought was, *What an idiot, to e-mail me a confidential message on an unsecured server*. His second thought was, *Ripley probably thought it was secure with his password*. Then he pondered the all-important question: *Is there a way to know if it is from Ripley or not?*

"Gwen." MacCabe buzzed her from his desk. "Is Derrick in?"

"Not yet."

"See if you can get him on his cell phone before my conference call."

As he waited, MacCabe thought about what Strickland had written in his secure e-mail on Saturday. Instinctively, he knew Strickland did not have Ripley's complete trust. He wondered if Ripley knew of the merger discussions. It crossed MacCabe's mind that Ripley might be going around Tillman and Strickland, wanting him to disclose the status of the merger.

Gwen's voice came over the intercom. "Derrick Andrews is on one."

"Thank you." MacCabe picked up his handset. "Derrick."

"Good morning, Mr. MacCabe. Is there a problem?"

"Good morning, Derrick. No, sorry to bother you before you get to the office, but I'm going to be on a dead run all day, and I have some e-mail security questions I want to ask. Is now a good time?"

"Sure."

"Over the years, you've told me that the commercial Internet is like a card being delivered by the post. And that it is unsecured—that anyone can read it. Could you briefly explain that to me again?"

"Well, sir, unsecured e-mail goes to a server and is held there until the one receiving the mail logs onto their Internet server to read it. While the mail is sitting and traveling between these Internet servers, it is not secure. Even though there are passwords, it is possible that someone working at any of the server companies could tap into the mail. It is a criminal offense, just like mail fraud, but it is easy to do. However, the more dangerous reality is that hackers can get to your mail on the commercial Internet quite easily. In any event, commercial servers are unsecured."

"We spend a great deal of money making our e-mail secure. In your opinion, how secure are we?" MacCabe asked.

"Our Cisco Virtual Privacy Network computer system is the most sophisticated system on the market today, sir. We've set it up so that when you send and receive e-mail through one of our secure VPN computers, it encrypts and scrambles your message as it travels. No one can decode it until it gets to your intended recipient. Your message can be read only by someone on the other end that has the same code pre-programmed on their computer and access to that site to decrypt your message upon receipt. Obviously, there are very sophisticated hackers—just ask WikiLeaks. Nothing is 100 percent protected, not even the government's top secrets. But again, we are state of the art."

"Good. I have another question about this Ripley e-mail you forwarded from AOL, an unsecured server. How can I tell if it is real or not?"

"By *real*, do you mean how do you know whether it actually came from the person who it says it came from?"

"Precisely."

"You can't." Derrick paused. "We are secure only when we stay within our system. Once we send or receive e-mails from a commercial server, all bets are off. Technically, the *From* portion of a commercial e-mail is totally forgeable. It is not authenticated at all. All anyone needs is that person's password. That is why we monitor the e-mails you receive that are not cleared through our system. So there is really no way of knowing for sure who sent an unsecured e-mail. Is that what you mean?"

"Yes, exactly."

Anything else, sir?"

"No, I think that's it, Derrick. You've been very helpful. You have a good day."

"Thank you, sir."

Gwen was back on the intercom. "You have about ten minutes until I place the call to Luxor. I wanted to let you know, sir, that I have been informed that Lukas Schultz and Hans Bergen will have only thirty minutes on the phone this morning, as they are traveling to the U.S. today." Sounding surprised, Gwen added, "Their message also indicated that they are planning to meet with *you* in New York tomorrow."

"I see," MacCabe said. "It would be nice to have more than twenty-four hours' notice on a transatlantic meeting like that, now, wouldn't it?"

"Yes, sir, it would. Should I make arrangements?"

"I'll let you know after the call."

MacCabe looked back at his computer. He pondered for a moment, then started typing an unsecured e-mail of his own.

Sent: Monday, March 14, 2011, 7:31 A.M.
To: Ripoff@aol.com
From: MacCabe, Warren
Subject:

The only way to talk in total confidence is to meet in private. If you are really R., tell J. L. tonight on the air that you have business in New York this week. That will be your signal to me that this is really R. e-mailing me. Then meet me Wednesday at 8:00 P.M. at the AquaGrill in NYC. The restaurant will say "Closed" on the door. Come alone.

If you don't say the signal tonight to J. L., I will know one of two things—either this is not you, or if it is, you have passed on the opportunity to communicate with me privately. Do not e-mail me again on this site.

W. M.

CHAPTER 36

Nashville
VUMC

Judd had received the unsecured e-mail from MacCabe at one-thirty in the morning Nashville time. He hadn't been able to sleep and now was a complete wreck. He knew Ripley could never confirm a private meeting with MacCabe in New York by telling J. L., Jay Leno, that he planned to be in New York because, one, Ripley never checked his e-mail and, two, Ripley was headed back on tour, not to New York. Judd kept thinking, *This has gotten totally out of control.* When Ripley didn't say anything on *Leno* this evening, MacCabe would figure the e-mail was forged, or he'd think Ripley blew him off. Judd was starting to panic—first the auto e-mail from MacCabe's office to "Ripley," then the questioning by Engels and the news that Simon was in a coma, and now a real e-mail from W. M. himself directing Ripley to confirm a private meeting with an RSVP in code via national television.

Judd rushed to the hospital at daybreak, hoping Simon's comatose state was just a temporary setback, that Simon would be awake and tell him what to do. He stood beside Shirley in disbelief as Dr. Specter tried to explain what had happened the previous evening.

"His vital signs are now stabilized. We have him back on a ventilator. The mucus plug caused an anoxic brain injury. He is in a coma."

"When will he come out of it?" Judd asked.

"Honestly, we don't know the answer to that. But Judd, the human body can be amazingly durable. Even without medical attention, the body naturally starts a healing process. We can help to a certain degree, but part of this is a waiting game—watching to see if the brain will slowly return to its normal state. In the meantime, we'll keep him on the ventilator, monitor all brain activity, and wait."

"I know what the worst case is. What's the best case?"

"Hopefully, we will see some signs within a few days when the brain functions begin to return. However, it could be a week, maybe two. The truth is, we don't know."

Judd turned to Shirley. "I need you to write down all my numbers so you can call me as soon as Simon wakes up."

"Sure, sweetheart." She reached over the nursing station counter to get a pen.

"Does Ripley Graham know?" Judd asked Dr. Specter.

"We did not alert anyone last night. I wanted our in-house PR people to be in the office before we gave an update. They will get in touch with Ripley's people this morning."

"Okay, what are your numbers?" Shirley asked.

Judd told her. "You've *got* to call me as soon as he wakes up."

"You know I will."

"What about you?" Dr. Specter said. "How's your shoulder feeling?"

"It's fine." At the moment, it was the least of his concerns.

"Good. Have the nurses check your stitches while you're here, and we'll keep you posted on Simon's condition." Dr. Specter gave Judd a confident nod and walked away.

CHAPTER 37

Beverly Hills, California

The driver of a black stretch limo crossed Third Street on Doheny Drive and put on his left turn signal as he pulled to the front of the Four Seasons Hotel. Jerome was standing at the corner. Nate was just inside the lobby corridor.

"Are you from *The Tonight Show?*" Jerome asked the driver.

"Yes, sir. I'm here to pick up Ripley Graham and his party."

"That's us. The rest will be right down." Jerome brought his wrist to his mouth. He was wired with a miniature microphone on his inside right sleeve, so it looked like he was talking to his thumb. "Pumpkin, over."

"Pumpkin here," a voice replied in his earpiece.

"The limo is here."

"Good, we're close."

Hearing the conversation, Nate exited the lobby and walked past a bronze statue of two people sitting on a bench reading the morning paper. He stopped for a second to observe the art until he heard familiar voices behind him.

Ripley went directly to the driver, who was standing by the limo holding the back door open. "Can you drive us up Sunset Boulevard on the way to NBC? I always love looking at the overgrown billboards." Before the man could answer, Ripley slid a fifty-dollar bill in his hand and climbed into the back.

"That will not be a problem."

Janice, Tillman, Pumpkin, Nate, and P. C. all entered the back. Being six foot four, Jerome decided to skip the contortions necessary for him to join them and jumped into the front shotgun seat instead. The closed electric window behind the front seat kept him and the driver from hearing the conversation in the back.

"Did you see the *Today* show this morning?" Janice asked Tillman. "Matt Lauer and Meredith Vieira were talking about Ripley's exclusive on *The Tonight Show*."

"That's good."

"Did you watch any of the TV magazine shows last night?"

"No."

"Wow," Janice said. "Nothing like keeping your finger on the media pulse. Anyway, all of *ET* and *Inside Edition* was commentary about tonight's appearance. You can't buy that kind of coverage."

The driver pulled onto Doheny and drove due north, as instructed.

"I love Sunset Boulevard," Ripley said to no one in particular. "No other single road in the world screams entertainment marketing like Sunset Strip. The billboards as big as buildings on every block. The Viper Room, the Roxy, the House of Blues—it just seems like the heart of Hollywood to me." Ripley looked at Tillman. "Why doesn't Galaxy move its L.A. offices to Sunset?"

Tillman smiled. "I think Warren MacCabe likes the office being over in Century City, where he can keep an eye on all his stuffy lawyers."

The limo took a right turn onto Sunset.

"That makes no sense."

There was a long silence. The fact that the limo had two rows of seats facing each other made it worse. Everyone started checking their BlackBerrys and iPhones—the ultimate save in awkward moments. Tillman gave a forced smile. Pumpkin tried to ease the tension by saying softly, "Cricket . . . cricket." P. C. chuckled.

They passed the huge Hustler Hollywood, which had an enormous sign out front that read, "America's Largest Erotica Store!"

"George Strait and I once watched an X-rated movie on his bus together," Ripley said.

Janice's mouth dropped. "Excuse me?"

It was not Ripley's nature to small-talk. He was usually too focused on his own career to discuss other artists. Nate was the first to encourage this rare lighthearted conversational track. "Do tell," he said.

"I thought that would get your attention," Ripley said.

Janice jumped in. "I *don't* want to know about it. Not if you're going to ruin it for me. I *love* George Strait!"

Hearing *don't* was enough to egg Ripley on. "Well, it's true. After my second CD came out, Simon called and said we got a slot on the George Strait concert to open the new Dallas Cowboys billion-dollar stadium."

"June 2009," Pumpkin said.

"Exactly. Simon knew I wanted to meet George Strait. I mean, to me, there is no one more successful in country than George Strait. So Simon worked it out for me to play. We got there the day before. They had been setting up for days. First thing I noticed was all the artists' tour buses were parked in a fenced-in secured area behind the stadium—except for Strait's. They actually assembled a huge tent backstage and drove his bus inside. No one ever saw him. We went through sound check—no sign of George. The festival started in the afternoon. I did my set, and then the other acts started filing in—Blake Shelton, Reba McEntire. Once they finished and before George came out, security cleared the entire backstage area of all the workers and artists, too. Then Strait walked off his bus, through the tent, and directly onto the stage in front of a hundred thousand screaming fans. But none of us ever saw the man. Well, we saw him on the largest video screen ever built, but not in person."

"I never knew that," Janice said. "I figured the crews weren't supposed to see him, but I always figured the other artists on tour hung out with him."

"Nope. So I told Simon emphatically that I was not leaving without at least shaking the man's hand. I mean, come on—it's George

Strait. All evening, Simon kept saying, 'Hey, don't be offended, but he keeps to himself. He's really nice but kind of shy.' Finally, an hour after the show, I saw Simon talking with George's manager, Erv Woolsey. When I walked over, Erv said, 'George wants to thank you for being out here with him.' I was, like, 'Finally!' So they escorted me back to the inner sanctum."

"Decoy bus, right?" Janice said. "He's not there. You guys watch a dirty movie without George, and that's that."

"Nope. So George's bus is laid out like ours. You walk up the front steps past the driver's seat into the front lounge. On the left side is a long couch. There's the aisle in the middle and a table on the right with two seats on either side. Simon and Erv were standing at the bus door talking, so I just went on up. George and his wife were sitting in the front lounge. He got up—couldn't have been nicer—introduced me to his wife, Norma, who was very sweet, and asked me to sit on the couch across from them, so I did."

"If there were dirty movies, I really don't want to know about it," Janice said.

"True story. So they were both looking at me sitting on the couch. George faced the front of the bus, and Norma was facing him, and directly behind Norma was this large inlaid TV with a satellite system—five hundred channels, the works. The TV was on, but the sound was off."

"I don't like where this is going," Janice said.

Ripley grinned. "So *Entertainment Tonight* was on, and as I got seated I could hear some guys talking in the back of the bus. I glanced back, and George read my mind and said, 'Some of my crew guys are working on the satellite feed. I missed the running of the Belmont Stakes today, and they're re-airing the race.'"

"Good. He's a horseman and loves his Triple Crown," Janice said. "I like that."

"So George went on to say some very nice things to me, like my career was on fire, and how they were lucky to have gotten me on the show early. But while he was talking, I noticed the TV went blank, and a screen came up that read, 'One moment, please. Satellite searching for service.' I told George that I wanted to thank him for having me out, that he was the ultimate icon in our industry. While I was talking, the TV came back on, but now it was on a different channel and kind of fuzzy. So we started talking about sports. He said he never had tried horse racing but loved to rope and ride. He started talking about the San Antonio Rodeo. And then, all of a sudden, the TV went haywire and started flipping channels really fast. Then it stopped accidentally on a channel it wasn't supposed to land on."

"No way!" Janice said.

Just then, the driver turned right on Bob Hope Drive and into the back NBC lot. The guard stopped the limo to check credentials. The driver lowered the window that separated Jerome and himself from the others. Jerome interrupted Ripley. "Sorry, just wanted you to know we're on the NBC lot. It will take a minute to clear the limo."

"Thanks. You're missing a really good road story," Nate said. "Ripley's telling us about watching X-rated movies with George Strait and his wife on their bus." Nate didn't give any clarification, and Ripley just jumped back in where he left off.

"So it stopped on the channel, and I looked up, and it says, '*Girls Gone Wild—Totally Uncensored*,' and these girls were on the party boat, and they were—"

Janice screamed, "Oversharing!"

Everyone laughed except for Jerome, who looked at Nate in disbelief and said, "Are you kidding me?"

"No," Nate said. "True story!"

"What did George do?" Tillman asked.

"He was totally cool," Ripley said, smiling now for the first time in days. "He looked over his shoulder and said to the guys in the back, 'Can somebody please hit the remote?' Of course, I forgot everything I was saying. I just stopped talking in midsentence, completely frozen. Norma had no idea what I was looking at behind her or why I had turned into a wax figure. She asked, 'Are you okay?'—thinking I might be having a heart attack or something. Finally, a crew guy came flying up from the back of the bus with the remote. George took it and calmly changed the channel to the horse race. And without missing a beat, he looked at me and said, 'Let's get back to those thoroughbreds, shall we?' And smiled. That was it."

"Okay, I'm still in love with him," Janice said. "*Love* him!"

"Yep, definitely a bonding moment."

Jerome shook his head and rolled the window back up.

They all took deep breaths to regain their composure while the limo got waved through and stopped in front of the Studio 11 Artist Entrance. Leno was already on campus, his orange 1966 Dodge Coronet Hemi in the first parking space, where his name was clearly marked.

A representative from *The Tonight Show* was standing outside the limo to usher them in. As they climbed out single file, Pumpkin's cell phone rang.

"This is Pumpkin." He paused. "Yeah, we're just gettin' out of the car at *The Tonight Show*. . . . Yep, he's right here." Pumpkin covered the mouthpiece and whispered to Ripley, "It's Brad Holiday from Elite. He says it's urgent."

Ripley put his arms in the air and stretched, then gave Pumpkin an "I wonder what he wants?" look. "Hey Brad, what's up? . . . No, it's fine." As Ripley listened, the humor dissipated from his face. "Oh, God." Ripley turned his back to the others, lowered his head, and stared at the pavement. "No, it's okay. I needed to know. Call me as soon as you have more." He hung up without saying goodbye and addressed the team in a monotone. "Simon had some kind of major blockage in his airway last night. He went into cardiac arrest and coded. The doctors on call were able to revive him, but he's in a coma. It's bad."

CHAPTER 38

Nashville
Burbank

Back from the hospital, Judd had just entered his apartment when his cell phone rang.

"Judd, it's Megan."

"Megan, I've been calling you since yesterday. I was getting worried."

"We need to get some shepherd's pie."

Judd snapped back, "Simon's had a setback. Things are totally out of control. I've been leaving you messages. And all you're thinking about is an early dinner?"

"We shouldn't be using cell phones. Let's go, shepherd's pie."

"Excuse me? Why exactly shouldn't we be using the phone?"

"Judd, are you coming or not?"

Judd heard the nervous tension in her voice. "Of course," he said.

"Okay. And hurry!"

A *Tonight Show* aide escorted Ripley and the others through the Artist Entrance. This had been the studio of *The Ellen DeGeneres Show* from 2003 to 2008 until she moved to Stage 1 on the Warner Bros. lot, right down the road. Studio 11 was actually larger than the old

Tonight Show set in Studio 3, on the other side of the famed NBC commissary. The escort led Ripley's entourage down the maze of hallways to the assigned dressing room. Attached to the door at eye level was a small navy-blue cardboard sign that read, "Ripley Graham," and then in smaller type below it, "*The Tonight Show with Jay Leno.*"

"This is your room. Some catering and drinks are in the back. One of our producers will be here in a few minutes to talk with you. Please let me know if you need anything."

"What was your name again?" Ripley asked.

"Suzie."

"Nice to meet you, Suzie. Thanks for your help."

P. C. spoke up as Suzie turned to exit. "Are there any current fashion magazines around?"

"I can send a runner to go out and pick some up for you."

"That would be great."

"Any particular magazines?"

"Whatever is on the stand—*Cosmo, InStyle, Glamour*, that sort of thing."

"No problem."

Ripley added, "A healthy diet of fashion magazines and water—that's all the sustenance we need."

"You guys are easy," said Suzie, smiling as she left.

The entourage settled into the dressing room. Ripley and Tillman headed back toward the small catering table. Janice hit the bathroom. P. C. stood in front of the full-length mirror tucking her highlighted blond hair behind her ears and checking her makeup.

A thin, stylishly dressed brunette knocked, pushed the already half-cracked door open, and stepped into the room. "Ripley?"

Ripley turned around.

"I'm Barbera Libis, the show's talent booker. Nice to see you again."

Ripley walked across the room to shake her hand. "Of course, Barbera. Nice to see you, too." He turned to the group. "This is Cindy, and Doug Tillman, head of Galaxy Nashville. And of course, you know Janice, my publicist."

"Absolutely. Well, thanks for being here. If we could, I'd like to go over some things before you head down for sound check and camera blocking."

"Sure."

"Our writers need to get a feel for what you want to say. They'll write some dialogue for you and Jay to look over. And you know Jay—he'll be down here in a little while to say hello."

"Great." Then, in a more serious tone, Ripley added, "I should tell you, we just got some bad news. Simon Stills, my manager who was shot, took a turn for the worse this afternoon. He's in a coma."

"Oh, my God. We had heard he was doing better. I know Jay wanted to ask you about his current condition. Are you still okay with that?" Barbera asked.

"Yeah, but that will be the toughest part for me. Jay needs to know that."

"Sure, sure. Now, are you okay with talking about exactly what happened?"

"Yeah. It all happened so fast, but we can go over that."

"He will want to ask about how you're holding up, and to confirm you're on the road. I'm sure people will want to know why you're going back on tour so soon."

"Sure, that's easy. No problem."

"And then Jay will want to touch on why you think someone would do this."

"Yeah. Obviously, we don't know who or why, but I'll take a stab at it."

"Okay. Then we'll end the show with your song. We know you want to dedicate the song to Simon, and we won't go to commercial until after you sing. So Jay will ask you about the song, and you'll set up the dedication. As you'll remember, your band will be to the right of the couch. So after you talk, just get up and walk over to the band—there will be no commercial break. Jay will come over when you finish and sign off. You won't go back to the couch."

"Gotcha."

There was another knock on the door. "They're ready for Ripley on the set for his first run-through," a young man wearing a headset said.

"Okay," said Barbera. "I'll have the writers work some of this up for Jay, and he'll drop by after lunch. Oh, one more thing. Jay will want to mention your first tour stop. Where do you go from here?"

"Austin, Texas," Ripley said. "The tour starts back at the Frank Erwin Center at the University of Texas on Thursday night. We'll get some rest here tomorrow, then fly to Austin on Wednesday. My team knows that when we play Texas, they have to build an extra day into the schedule just so I can go to my favorite barbecue joint."

"Really?"

"Absolutely. The City Market. It's in this little one-horse town an hour south of Austin—in Luling, Texas. I promise, there is no better barbecue anywhere!"

"I'll have to remember the name. I love Austin."

"If you're close, you've got to go." Ripley pointed toward his entourage. "Ask these guys. If I'm playing a hundred miles from Luling, come hell or high water, we're eating barbecue at the City Market. I'll be there Wednesday."

CHAPTER 39

Nashville
McGuinness Irish Pub

Megan had made the short walk from Elite and was sitting alone in a far back booth drinking water with lemon when Judd arrived.

He slid into the seat opposite her and began where he left off. "When you didn't call back, I was worried something was wrong."

Megan looked nervous. "Sorry, but I don't know if our phones are safe. First thing this morning, Brad called me in and assigned me to a new manager. I started working with Marc Matheson today."

"Why?"

"Brad said his assistant would handle Ripley's day-to-day management duties."

"And Ripley is okay with that?"

"I guess so. There's nothing I can do until Simon gets back."

"I see." Judd paused, then said, "Did you hear Simon is in a coma?"

"Yes. Everyone was talking about it at the office. It's very scary."

"I know. I saw Dr. Specter at six o'clock this morning. He said the best case would be to see some signs of normal brain function in a couple of days. We're just going to have to wait and see."

The waiter approached the table. "Are you both ready?"

Megan looked up. "If it's okay, I'm just going to sip this water."

"Sure." Then he looked at Judd.

"Just a cup of coffee—black."

The waiter put his mini notepad away and took the menus. "No problem. If you change your mind, let me know."

Judd looked at Megan. "Why do you think our phones aren't safe?"

Megan didn't answer the question. She just started talking. "This weekend, I decided to go into the office, figuring no one would be around, especially after the week we had. I pulled some files. I told you there are some things I've seen."

"Like what?"

Megan took a sip of water. "At the Mardi Gras party, Ripley gave me two envelopes containing confidential documents that came to his house, and he needed me to send them back overnight the next morning. Sending overnight packages for Ripley is not unusual. But for some reason, Ripley told me this time not to mention it to Simon."

"So?"

"Well, it struck me as odd when he said it. He'd never mentioned anything like that before. Simon and Ripley talk about everything—always. And why were documents sent to his house, not to the office? I overnighted one envelope back to his attorney in New York and the other to Strickland's office. I didn't mention anything to Simon. But I did make copies of the documents—without reading them—and put them in a confidential correspondence file. Then, after the shooting, I started thinking. Did Ripley ask me not to mention it to Simon because he wanted to tell Simon himself or because he didn't want Simon to know at all? So, this weekend, I pulled them. I was planning to show Simon today. But now, with his condition, I'm not sure what to do. I don't trust Brad Holiday."

"So you read them?"

Megan was for a moment lost in her own thoughts.

"The documents—you read them this weekend?"

"Yes."

"And?"

Megan was slow to answer. "I signed a confidentially agreement when I took the job at Elite. I'm sure I'm crossing the line if I tell you."

"Well, I'm sure someone crossed the line when their bullet grazed my shoulder."

Megan nodded, then said softly, "The first was a side agreement Ripley signed with Galaxy. I feel sure Simon never knew about it. And if Ripley signed it without Simon's knowledge, then he broke the cardinal rule in an artist/manager relationship."

"And you made a copy of the agreement?"

"Yes."

Judd was getting uncomfortable. "If Simon didn't know about it, who else did?"

"I don't think anybody but Ripley and Strickland."

"What did it say?"

"It laid out the terms and conditions under which Ripley agreed to deliver his new record to Galaxy this year."

"And Simon didn't know about that?"

"I don't know . . . I don't think so."

That news took a minute to process.

"What's the other thing?" Judd asked.

Megan began to whisper. "Ripley had me FedEx some signed papers to his lawyers in New York. They were financial documents. He was having his attorneys move his entire personal estate and financial portfolio—basically, his net worth—from SunTrust to a bank in Mexico."

Judd was totally surprised. "And this happened?"

"I guess so. He loves Mexico. He vacations there twice a year. My first thought was maybe this is some kind of tax loophole, like in the Cayman Islands, and he's discussed it with his financial team. But I'm not sure. That's what I was also going to ask Simon."

They sat in silence for a minute until Judd's curiosity got the best of him. "How much . . . What is Ripley worth?"

"I'm not privy to that kind of information, but Ripley put a handwritten note on top of the signed documents that read, 'Move the entire twenty.'"

"Twenty what?"

Exasperated, Megan whispered, "Twenty million, I would assume. It certainly isn't twenty thousand."

"You're saying Ripley told his lawyers to move $20 million?"

"I think so, yes. But that was what I planned on asking Simon. I don't know for sure, but now I'm thinking Simon never knew about the transfer of funds or the Galaxy agreement."

"Let's get out of here," Judd said.

"Where are we going?"

"To my apartment. I need to show you some e-mails, and we've got some recorded conversations we have to listen to."

CHAPTER 40

Midtown Manhattan
Nashville

Tommy Strickland's computer notified him that he had just received a secure message from Warren MacCabe. *It's getting late in London,* he thought.

Strickland logged in, and the secure site immediately decrypted the communiqué from London. It was an update regarding the ongoing Luxor merger negotiations. MacCabe was making a swift unannounced trip to New York tonight to keep the negotiations on a fast track. Luxor's two top executives were calling the shots. They had decided to travel from Germany to New York on a moment's notice and wanted MacCabe to jump as well. With what was at stake, MacCabe was certainly willing to accommodate them.

```
Secure Galaxy Communiqué
Sent: Monday, March 14, 2011
To: Strickland, Thomas
From: MacCabe, Warren

Communiqué: Successful call with Lux. Tête-à-tête
set for tomorrow afternoon. Schultz, Bergen, you,
```

and I in NYC. I will call tomorrow morning upon arrival.
W. M.

THIS DOCUMENT WILL NOT PRINT.

After reading the "Ripley" e-mails between Judd and MacCabe, Megan was even more on edge. She called her newly assigned Elite manager, Marc Matheson, after hours and told him that today's news regarding Simon had hit her hard. She asked if she could take an immediate leave of absence. She needed a little breathing room before she started working with a new artist. Matheson agreed without hesitation.

The rest of the evening, Judd and Megan kept asking questions that neither knew the answers to.

Mentally exhausted, they decided to take a break and order some takeout. Megan asked if she could stay and watch Ripley on *The Tonight Show*. Judd was more than happy to oblige. She called Mathew and told him she was with Judd and would be home late and added that he could watch ESPN's *SportsCenter* before going to bed. Mathew immediately asked if she and Judd were now boyfriend and girlfriend. She assured him the late night was purely work related. Judd could tell from Megan's repeated response that Mathew was unconvinced. In a day with very little to celebrate, that was Judd's one bright spot.

While waiting for the late local news to finish, Judd read the documents Megan had copied and Megan listened to the recorded phone conversations on Simon's iPod.

"The document is signed and dated Monday, March 7, 2011. Ripley signed it the day of his Mardi Gras party."

Megan nodded without taking out her earphones.

"Can you hear me?"

"Yes," she said, pulling out one white earbud. "I just don't want to miss anything."

Suddenly, Judd heard Jay Leno's voice booming in the background. "Here we go," he said.

Megan stopped listening to the recording. "Can you turn it up?"

Jay Leno stood on his stage rubbing his hands together. "Well, the most talked-about man in entertainment is here. Ripley Graham is in the house." The crowd went crazy. "I just saw him backstage a moment ago. He looks great." Young girls screamed. "We didn't get to talk, really. It was more of a sighting, mainly because of all the mounted policemen in the dressing room. But that's okay. We're excited just to get him here."

"This is weird," Judd said.

Leno continued, "You know, our people called his people and asked Ripley to come on the show tonight and talk about the events in Nashville last week. They called back and said Ripley was happy to come on, but he needed some changes in his dressing room from the last time he was here. We were like, 'Sure, no problem. What does he need?' His handlers said, 'Well, Ripley wants a lot of Pepsi because of his new endorsement deal.' 'Fine,' we told them. 'And a treadmill in the room because he likes to work out.'" The girls screamed again. "'And a forty-foot moat stocked with South American piranha around the studio.' Needless to say, security is tight tonight. But first, give a big welcome to Rickey Minor and the Tonight Show Band!"

"Leno's going to commercial," Megan said. "Judd, I was thinking. Maybe you're right. We might not recognize any incriminating evidence on these recordings. Maybe you should hand them over to the agent that came to visit you. Tell him you didn't listen, that Simon asked you to record them."

"The problem is, Agent Engels is already treating me more like a suspect than a victim," Judd said. "He would say, 'Why didn't you tell me you copied the recordings from Simon's computer when I brought the subject up in your apartment?' Or better yet, 'Why didn't you tell me you had Simon's iPod with you?' Isn't that obstruction of justice?"

"Easy answer—because he scared the bejesus out of you. Just tell him the truth."

"I don't know, Megan. I'd rather have Simon just wake up so I can hand it back to him with nothing said."

"I don't think Agent Engels would throw the book at you. You shouldn't be in any trouble. Just tell him you had the iPod because

Simon asked you to sync the recorded conversations from his computer and listen to them, and you were simply obeying your boss. But now he's in a coma. So, no harm done."

A huge crowd noise came from the TV. Judd looked up to see Ripley give Jay a handshake and a guy hug, then sit on the camel-colored couch. "There he is."

"Yep, here we go."

Leno turned to Ripley. "I made a few jokes before you came out. But on a serious note, this has been a very scary week and is still a very serious situation. I certainly don't want to make light of that. And I know I speak for everyone when I say, 'Thank God you're okay!' "

At the eruption of applause, the cameras panned back to show a standing ovation from the studio audience.

"Thank you . . . Please." Ripley gestured for everyone to sit. "Please. Really, I appreciate that, Jay, but I've got to tell you, I'm not the hero here. Several guys were shot. As you know, my manager is hanging on to his life in Nashville." Ripley paused to clear his throat. "And there were some very talented and courageous people that jumped in to protect us."

"This is odd, hearing him talk about it on national television," Megan said.

"Extremely," Judd said.

Leno spoke softly to Ripley. "I heard we got some bad news today regarding your manager, Simon Stills."

"Yes, and that's going to be tough for me to talk about tonight."

"I'm sure. Let me tell the audience that we got news just before the show started that Simon Stills slipped into a coma at a local hospital in Nashville. And we are all praying that this is just a temporary setback and he's going to pull through. He's a good man. I've had the pleasure of meeting him." The crowd applauded. "So, Ripley, let me ask you. Why you? Why do you think you were a target?"

"Good question!" Judd said.

"You know, Jay, I'm just living the American Dream," Ripley replied. "That's the only thing I can think of. There are a lot of unstable people out there, and I guess one of them is pissed off that an average guy like me can pick up a guitar, write songs, sing them in the land of the free, and make money. Hell, I'd do this even if I didn't get paid. But that's what makes America great. And guess what? He missed!"

The crowd stood and applauded again as Leno smiled and nodded.

"It's not that simple," Megan said.

"If I turn the iPod in now, they'll say I was tampering with evidence and withholding information," Judd said. "The best bet is to get it back to Simon. He's the only one who'll know if there's something incriminating on this. Until he wakes up, nobody needs to get their hands on it. And nobody needs to know I have it."

Megan didn't respond.

Ripley looked into the camera. "There's nothing I can do for Simon at the moment. And he would be the first to say, 'Get back on the road. Don't stop touring because I'm in the hospital.' He's the one that taught me to take care of the fans first." Ripley teared up as the crowd applauded.

"You're getting back on tour, and your next concert is in Austin this week at the Frank Erwin Center," Leno said. "They tell me you've already sold out two nights, this Thursday and Friday. So, will you go straight to Austin from here, or will you go back home to Nashville to see Simon first?"

"Neither, actually," Ripley said. "I would go to Austin, but I just made plans to be in New York City. I have some business there I need to attend to. So I'm actually flying to New York tonight and then from there to Austin and back on tour."

"Busy man," Leno said. "Before you go, I know you have a special song you'd like to dedicate to Simon."

Judd yelled, "Did he just say he's going to New York City?"

"Oh, my God!" Megan said.

"He just answered the e-mail!"

"Judd, what the hell is going on?"

"I'm in way over my head without Simon. I have to get out of here, Megan. I have to get out of here tonight!"

CHAPTER 41

THE NEXT DAY

New York City
Midtown Manhattan
Tuesday, March 15

Warren MacCabe and Tommy Strickland were not noticed by anyone while walking east on West Fifty-seventh Street around noon. They were deep in conversation as they passed the world-renowned Carnegie Hall.

"Warren, how can you be certain the timing is right with the merger? Do you think we could be rushing this?" Strickland said.

"Rushing? Tommy, twelve days ago, you were the one that woke me up in the middle of the night telling me we had a crisis. We plotted a strategy to secure the operation, one that would buy us two weeks. I believe your exact words were, 'We don't have the luxury to consider long-term implications.' We fed the beast—Clark is gone, Tillman is in—and now you have cold feet? Why?"

"It's a gut check—a simple question worth asking. How can you be certain this is the right time?"

"How can we be certain of anything? The world was flat until Columbus. Everyone was certain Sir Isaac Newton uncovered the laws of the physical universe until Einstein. Newton claimed that time was an absolute. And then, in 1905, Einstein proved him wrong."

"I've heard of the theory of relativity. I was questioning the timing of this merger proposal."

"Einstein's views changed the universe. He said that time was relative to space. It was not an absolute."

"We're not talking about the speed of light here. We're talking about the speed of a merger in the music business."

"We are talking about what is *absolute* and what is *relative*. Perception is reality in our business. There is no certitude whatsoever. The only constant force in the music business is the force of change. And there are two types of people—those who fear change and therefore remain stagnant, and those who seize the day. It is not in me to remain idle. Tommy, this is Galaxy's time. If we don't act, we go down in history as leaders of a remarkable company that failed to make a mark. I refuse to die a victim of trepidation."

"And in time, what if this merger proves to be a mistake? What if these are the wrong partners?"

"It will not prove to be a mistake on my watch."

"How can you be so sure? You just said we cannot be certain of anything," Strickland said.

"Tommy, I cannot tell you with certitude how to succeed. But I can tell you with certitude how to fail. There is no glory without risk. We both know that."

"Okay, let me be frank. I don't trust the Germans. I never have. I think most of the time they are lying. As a matter of fact, I'm not sure these guys have ever told us the whole truth."

"What is the whole truth? I like to think of the truth as a prism, always changing colors depending upon the angle from which you view it. Our challenge is to view this merger as if *we* were the Germans. Ultimately, what do the Germans want out of this merger, and how far will they go to get it? How is that relative to us? Those are the questions, not whether or not they're telling the whole truth."

Just prior to reaching the Russian Tea Room, they turned right into the lobby entrance of Carnegie Hall Tower, where MacCabe kept his workplace while in New York. The long, straight corridor with green marble flooring stretched all the way to West Fifty-sixth Street. In the middle of the corridor was a semicircular guard desk. To the left were three elevators with the numbers *45–60,* indicating the floors they served. MacCabe and Strickland stepped into the opening elevator. MacCabe pushed *60.* They were the only two inside.

"What about the price? The Germans aren't there yet," Strickland said.

"We're closer than you think. I've continued to say 1.56 billion pounds or 2.5 billion U.S. They are at 2 billion U.S. I would close at 2.3 billion. That could be today. Luxor will secure the line of credit through Deutsche Bank before Friday. Once that happens, we'll be home free. The board of directors will give it unanimous approval. And Sunday, we'll take it to the shareholders for a final vote." MacCabe finished just as the elevator door opened on the sixtieth floor.

A man in a butler's tuxedo was awaiting their arrival. "Hello, Mr. MacCabe, Mr. Strickland. Your party is already in the suite."

"Thank you."

"We have begun serving cocktails and light hors d'oeuvres."

"Very good."

MacCabe stopped Strickland before they walked into the suite and looked at him sternly. "We fed the beast, and you assured me that one offering would be enough. I warned you that beasts have insatiable appetites. It wasn't enough, was it, Tommy? That's why you have cold feet."

"Believe me, the feeding was more than enough."

"Even after Clark's firing, Ripley still won't deliver his record to you, will he? That's why you want to stall, because the beast needs another feeding!"

Strickland stood in silence.

CHAPTER 42

American Airlines Flight 639

The nonstop American Airlines flight from Nashville to LaGuardia Airport departed on time at 12:15 P.M. Judd had a window seat. Looking at cloud formations at twenty-nine thousand feet calmed his nerves. He kept thinking, *Is it a good idea for both of us to fly to New York?* All he knew was that he needed to get out of Nashville. He felt like he was in a fishbowl but couldn't tell who was looking in. It was Megan's idea to take separate flights, in case they were being watched.

Last night, after they heard Ripley say he had business in New York, Judd and Megan had jumped in Judd's old Honda Accord, gotten on I-440, and headed south on I-65 for no particular reason. Getting out of the apartment and speeding through the night air somehow helped. After a long silence, Judd finally said, "Simon asked for my help because I'm so new. He could trust me because I don't know anybody important and nobody important knows me. No one could have gotten to me yet."

"That's probably true," Megan said. "But don't think for a minute that you're alone. We're all in this together—you, me, and Simon."

They passed the Spring Hill exit, home of the former GM Saturn automotive plant.

"So who else besides me was reading MacCabe's e-mail?" Judd asked. "And who told Ripley to go to New York this week?"

"Figure that out and you've probably got yourself an attempted assassin," Megan said.

"God, I never thought of that."

A few minutes later, Judd saw a billboard for a Steak 'n Shake. "I need coffee," he said.

He got his usual—no cream, no sugar. Megan stayed with water.

Feeling the need to change the subject, Judd asked, "How did you end up in Nashville, anyway?"

"I think I mentioned we grew up in the Bronx. After college, I moved to the Village and worked in the city. We had a family friend that was an attorney in this big law firm in New York. My plan was to work my way through law school. That changed when our mother died. With just Mathew and me, law school was out of the question. The job was okay, but it became more and more difficult for the two of us to manage. We'd still be in that situation if it wasn't for Simon."

"How did you and Simon meet?"

"The firm had a large intellectual property practice, and I was one of the assistants to a lawyer in that division. One day, Simon walked in to take a meeting with my boss, who had done some legal work for a few of Simon's clients in the past. This time, Simon brought with him this new, young, unknown singer that he wanted my boss to meet. His name was—"

"Ripley Graham."

"Exactly," Megan said. "Within a year, Ripley exploded. And one day, out of the blue, Simon called me up and asked if I'd consider working in the artist management side of the music business. He said he needed someone like me who was really organized to help with Ripley's day-to-day management. Simon went on and on about how great Nashville was—that the cost of living was so much cheaper, and the people were so friendly. To be honest, Mathew was beginning to withdraw. I thought a new start would be good for both of us. Besides, Ripley was already making so much noise. How could I say no?"

"You've done great." After a pause, Judd pulled them back to the present. "You think someone has tapped our phones?"

"Yes . . . Maybe. I definitely think we're being watched. We need to hide—go under the radar and buy some time."

"Yeah, but how? And where?"

"New York City," Megan said.

"New York! Why New York?"

"Well, that's where Ripley's going. There's no better place to be under the radar than in the city. And besides, I know it like the back of my hand."

"For how long?"

"Long enough to figure this whole thing out, or until Simon wakes up."

"But what about Mathew?"

"He can stay with Courtney for a few days. He'll love it."

Judd had a rush of adrenaline. He had never been to New York. He would go to Afghanistan if she asked him.

A flight attendant's voice came over the intercom. "The pilot has put on the Fasten Seatbelt sign due to some turbulence. We ask that everyone remain in their seats at this time with their seatbelts securely fastened. Thank you."

For a moment, Judd questioned if going to New York was really a good idea. It was too late to change his mind now. He turned on his laptop to open the *Bulletin* that had been zapped to his computer. Someone at Elite had programmed it to receive all the industry news updates and e-mail blasts.

Billboard.biz Bulletin™

YOUR DAILY ENTERTAINMENT NEWS UPDATE
TUESDAY, MARCH 15, 2011

Ripley Graham Grabs Late-Night Ratings; Landmark Night for Leno

Chip Avery, Nashville

Country-music star Ripley Graham gave The Tonight Show with Jay Leno the highest-rated show in its history last night.

Nielsen Media Research reported an 11.7 rating. The Leno camp landed a coup by garnering an exclusive interview with Graham to discuss the assassination attempt on his life last Wednesday. Graham has been quoted as saying a media blitz would be in poor taste and has declined all other requests to discuss the incident, including hard news coverage.

Graham's appearance crushed previous Nielsen ratings records, including the one held by Hugh Grant's appearance on the show July 11, 1995, which yielded a 10.2 rating. Since 1995, both Leno and David Letterman have seen their audiences steadily "gray" and decline. The Tonight Show currently averages 4 million households to Letterman's average of 3.3 million. Prior to Graham's appearance, Leno's best night of late was his return to The Tonight Show at the 11:30 hour nearly a year ago on March 1, 2010, a show that garnered 6.6 million viewers.

On a separate but related note, Simon Stills, Graham's personal manager who was seriously injured in the shooting, took a turn for the worse Sunday night, according to officials at Vanderbilt University Medical Center in Nashville. Stills is now in a coma. Graham was made aware of Stills' worsening condition just hours prior to last night's taping.

Judd felt the plane tilt slightly downward. The pilot's voice came over the intercom. "We are starting our descent into LaGuardia. We should be down in twenty minutes. Flight attendants, please prepare for landing."

Judd wondered if Megan would be at the gate. She had insisted on taking an earlier flight, saying she had to get up with Mathew anyway, and that if they were being watched they definitely should not travel together. She planned to have a car rented by the time he landed.

He felt nervous and noticed his palms were sweaty. But this time, it was not because of the mess he was in but because he was thinking of Megan. In the midst of this nightmare, she was the one standing beside him and trying to help bail him out. And she was the one he had fallen for—and fallen hard.

CHAPTER 43

New York City
Carnegie Hall Tower

MacCabe entered the suite and walked directly toward Lukas Schultz, CEO of the Luxor Group for the past twelve years, and his in-house chief legal counsel, Hans Bergen. The German guests had been talking quietly while looking over the top of the Essex House Hotel and north to a breathtaking aerial view of Central Park.

"Lukas, Hans, welcome."

"Thank you," Lukas Schultz replied in his thick German accent.

"I think you both know Tommy Strickland."

"Of course."

"Please, sit down, sit down."

"I've never seen such a magnificent view of Central Park," Hans Bergen said.

"It is amazing. Most people, even those who live here, can't appreciate how large an area it is unless they see it from sixty stories high," MacCabe said.

A female bartender approached. "Can I get you something from the bar, Mr. MacCabe?"

"Yes, I'd like a fine French claret. How about a glass of Château La Violette?"

"Certainly. And you, Mr. Strickland?"

"Water with lemon, thanks."

MacCabe turned back to his guests. "From the last correspondence, it looks like we are getting closer."

Lukas Schultz was far less verbose than MacCabe. Hans Bergen nearly always spoke first for the Germans. "Yes. We continue to have strong interest on our side. Your latest proposal was well received."

"I'm very pleased to hear that," MacCabe said.

Bergen added, "Regarding integration, we are in agreement on all issues. In regard to price, your number continues to be 2.5 billion U.S. We will move to 2.3 but no further. But for us to get comfortable with 2.3, we need further clarity on your current projections for this fiscal year and next. Your projections must hold. There is no room for error here. We want to review these and go over the assumptions in detail again. We also need to discuss our plan to approach both U.S. and European regulators once we have approval from your shareholders." Bergen was always thorough and to the point.

"Fine, let's continue," MacCabe said.

"Good. But first, may I ask, how is Ripley Graham?" Bergen said. "Obviously, we were all greatly concerned for him personally and professionally. Mr. Graham's continued success greatly affects your projections and all of our plans."

MacCabe wasn't surprised by the inquiry. "First and foremost, Ripley is fine on both accounts. He is an extraordinary young man. Not that anyone would ever have wished these events, but between us, because of the media, we believe this incident will actually increase our projected income 2 to 3 percent from where we were on our last round of discussions. We will gladly show you the new numbers. No one could have predicted this turn of events. However, they are in our favor. It is now time to act. It is now time to move!"

Lukas Schultz stood, walked toward the window facing Central Park, then turned in the direction of MacCabe and said, "We understand he is in New York today."

"Apparently, he said on television last night that he was coming here. But we do not have a meeting scheduled. Why do you ask?"

As usual, Schultz was slow to answer. But when he did, it carried weight. "I would like to meet him while he's here."

Surprised, MacCabe said, "Why do you feel the need to meet with him in person?"

Before Schultz could answer, Strickland took over. "I've not heard from Ripley today, and I certainly can't confirm if he is in New York or not. He was not scheduled to meet with us this week. Why would you find a personal meeting important? And if we have all agreed that this matter should not be discussed in public, why on earth would any of us wish to disclose information to an artist on our respective rosters? It could prove careless."

"No, you misunderstand," Bergen said. "We do not wish to disclose anything to him. We'd simply like to meet him in a casual way, perhaps a dinner."

"Maybe I'm missing something, but again I ask why," MacCabe said.

"Ripley Graham symbolizes the future of the music business," Schultz said. "Besides that, he is the bedrock of your current sales success and the force behind your economic forecast. When the merger is announced, the worldwide news outlets will focus on the top-earning artists on our rosters. With our announcement, combined with the recent events in Nashville, it is clear Ripley will be the media's prime focus. He will be interviewed and asked his opinion about Luxor/Galaxy. Because of that, I'd like to get a feel of his character and his commitment to his artistry by speaking with him in person. We need our lead Luxor/Galaxy artist to put a positive face on this merger. That is critical. We certainly don't need any PR problems—not after we announce and start seeking U.S. and European regulatory approval."

After a pause, MacCabe said, "I understand. But a meeting in person at this late stage may prove to be more difficult than you think. However, Tommy and I will discuss it this evening and see if it is possible. Hopefully, we will have something for you to consider tomorrow. What time shall we gather in the morning?"

"Ten o'clock," Bergen suggested.

"That will work fine."

All four men shook hands as the help stepped forward with the Germans' overcoats and showed them out the door.

Strickland was still holding his glass of water with lemon. He turned to MacCabe and said, "You can't possibly arrange a meeting between Ripley and the Germans. How do you know he's even in town?"

MacCabe looked blankly out the window. "I don't."

CHAPTER 44

Queens, New York
LaGuardia Airport

Megan waited at baggage claim on D concourse, central terminal. She had checked the monitor twice for the arrivals. It showed American Airlines Flight 639 from Nashville coming into gate D2 at 2:55 P.M. She checked her watch. It was 3:15, and she saw no sign of Judd. She was more nervous than she had anticipated.

How strange, she thought. *I never imagined coming back to New York under circumstances like this*. She looked around to make sure no one suspicious was watching her. It was becoming a habit. She wanted Judd to come down the escalator so they could jump in the rental car and start to blend in with the 8 million New Yorkers.

"Hi," a familiar voice said in her left ear.

Megan flinched and turned quickly. It was Judd. He was right behind her. He gave her a warm smile. Without saying anything, she instinctively lifted up on her tiptoes and hugged him. Her arms crossed slightly as they extended behind his neck. Their cheeks touched. She closed her eyes, held on tight, and then just as quickly released him.

"Where did you come from?" she said.

"I took the elevator."

"You look great. I mean, for a guy with no sleep."

"You, too. Thanks for getting up here early. Was Mathew okay with your leaving?"

"He was fine. Thanks for asking."

Realizing they had never embraced before, they needed a moment to collect themselves.

"Okay," Judd said. "Well, not to be paranoid or anything, but let's get out of here."

"Yeah, follow me."

They walked briskly through a line of limousine chauffeurs holding signs with the names of expected passengers. *It starts right here—the separation of the powerful and the not-so-powerful,* Judd thought. Being two of the not-so-powerful, Judd and Megan exited outside to the street level. The low, heavy clouds looked ominous. The sky made it seem even colder. Crossing the median into the parking lot, they headed toward Megan's rental—a grey Ford Taurus with New York plates and a small blue-and-white Thrifty rental sticker on the corner of the windshield. Judd threw his backpack in the rear seat. Megan started the car, exited the airport, turned onto Grand Central Parkway West, and headed toward I-278.

"So you know your way around the expressways?" Judd asked.

"Oh, yeah."

Megan changed lanes and drove under a sign that read, "Bklyn-Qns Express." Construction was everywhere. The barricades all along the freeway were covered in graffiti.

"This doesn't feel like Middle Tennessee," Judd said, looking out the window. "Where did you live when you were here?"

"Mathew and I shared a small apartment with a friend in the Village."

"Is that anywhere close to the AquaGrill in SoHo?"

"Not far. By the way, I was able to get two hotel rooms. A friend of mine from the law firm has connections at the SoHo Grand. She hooked us up." Megan got in the left lane and followed the sign that read, "Williamsburg Bridge Manhattan."

"You do know this place!" Judd was impressed with her navigation.

"Yeah, but I had forgotten how bad the traffic is. This is going to take awhile."

After a lull, Megan said, "Now that we know Ripley cut a deal with Strickland behind Simon's back and moved all his assets to Mexico, do you still think Ripley was the assassin's target?"

"Honestly, now I'm thinking someone was after both Simon and Ripley. There were two shots. One got Simon, and the other missed Ripley and grazed me—that's what I think. Ripley's secret side agreement with Strickland and moving his money just show he thought someone was out to get him. Hey, I'll be the first to admit he's one serious Psycho-Billy, a paranoid megastar that talks about himself in the third person and says he's fulfilling the dream of his late twin brother. But still, hearing *Leno* last night, and knowing MacCabe's message was sent to me and somehow Ripley replied, it looks to me like someone is setting Ripley up big time. And that someone has already put Simon in the hospital and plans on finishing the job with Ripley right here tomorrow night in New York."

Megan felt a cold shiver.

The traffic came to a complete stop as they approached the Williamsburg Bridge. On the buildings to the left and right were signs for Peter Luger Steak House and Bangkok Market. Farther to the left was a huge, abandoned, completely gutted warehouse. Etched in the brick was "GRETSCH BUILDING No. 4." Judd thought, *This place is just one big junkyard with a mass of humanity piled on top.*

"So here is what you do," Megan said. "Call Agent Engels and tell him about the meeting at the restaurant tomorrow. He'll contact the FBI or the U.S. Marshals or somebody. They'll contact Ripley and tell him it's a setup and not to go. Then the FBI can go in and bust the thugs. Ripley will be safe, and you'll be the hero!"

"I can't call Agent Engels from up here. He told me at my apartment not to leave town without telling him."

Megan was shocked. "You didn't tell me that."

"Sorry, I forgot. But I did tell you he was treating me like a suspect. Besides, how am I supposed to know about this secret meeting between Ripley and MacCabe unless it was me that tampered with Simon's computer, erased information, and e-mailed top record executives under false pretenses? No thanks. I don't think I'm going to make that call." Judd paused, then added, "If I could just get to Ripley before he goes to the restaurant, I'd tell him I was the one e-mailing MacCabe—that Simon asked me to do it—and let him know he's walking into a trap. Then he could call Engels or the FBI and tell them. He wouldn't need to bring me into it. He could just say he got an anonymous tip."

"How in the world are you going to get Ripley alone by tomorrow? And with all due respect, even if you did, why would he believe the intern?"

"I don't know yet," Judd said under his breath.

"I'm sorry. I didn't mean that the way it sounded."

"No, you're right."

Traffic started moving slowly over the bridge. Judd looked out his window. All the way to the bank of the river were nothing but housing projects and fire escapes. "This place is depressing."

"It gets better, I promise."

On the other side, Judd noticed hordes of Asian people. "Where are we now?"

"Delancey Street—Chinatown."

"This is unbelievable." Judd gazed at what looked like a mini Beijing.

Megan crossed Bowery and took a left on Lafayette Street. "I don't know exactly where the AquaGrill is, but the concierge will. I'm sure it's close." She turned right on Canal and then onto West Broadway into the heart of SoHo.

As they neared the hotel, Judd said, "Megan, you've been unbelievable, really—checking in on me after the shooting, talking things over, flying up here early today. But you don't need to get sucked into this any further. I don't want you to get in trouble as some kind of accomplice or anything. Engels is watching me, not you. Tomorrow, I'll track down Ripley on my own and tell him what I know. He'll call the authorities, and then it'll all be over."

Megan pulled in front of the SoHo Grand Hotel and put the car in park. She sat for a second, then looked over and smiled. "That's very noble, Judd. There's only one problem. You're never going to get to Ripley without me."

CHAPTER 45

New York City
Carnegie Hall Tower

Immediately after the Germans exited, Strickland returned to his office on Avenue of the Americas. MacCabe, now alone with only the suite staff, worked on his opening remarks for the Shareholders Meeting in five days.

> Fellow shareholders, board of directors, Galaxy presidents, and members of the press. This is the most important day in the history of Galaxy Records. I think you all know the state of the company to date. The reason you are here is not to be told what you already know but to be inspired by a vision of things to come. The laws of the universe and the laws of the arts are parallel. These laws are cyclical. Just as in life, there is birth, there is death, and there is rebirth. Today is our day to experience a rebirth.
>
> From 2000 to 2010, we had a lost decade in the music industry. We went from selling physical product at a price point of £8 or $14 to *free* with the emergence of Napster. We had a four-year gap before iTunes impacted our world. By that time, 60 million Napster users had begun to believe music was a free commodity. We lost that generation of consumers and started a downward cycle that we still feel ten

> years later. During that time, in the United States alone, the music business plummeted from $14.6 billion in 1999 to $6.3 billion in 2009. We lost half our industry in ten years.
>
> What we know now is that the same technology that nearly destroyed us will also be our salvation. Digital technology—download services, ad-supported services—is the future. Already, iTunes has 97 percent awareness as a brand. It sold more than 5 billion songs from June 2008 to February 2010. The Beatles catalog alone sold 5 million songs via iTunes in the last two months. Our future is in digital licensing revenues from e-commerce sites, the licensing of content onto mobile units, and licensing to Internet radio. Those avenues reached $85 million in sales in 2009, and we are closing in on $100 million today. The British Phonographic Industry, BPI, reports that 98 percent of the singles bought now are purchased via downloads. Even larger growth is in legal streaming and Cloud services. When we add all the legal digital services and sites into the overall mix, the total consumption of music in the world is at an all-time high. By embracing the digital age, the music industry will have a complete rebirth by 2015.
>
> My sole agenda today is to discuss how we will lead that rebirth with a Luxor/Galaxy merger, an opportunity that I will outline and we will openly debate. But make no mistake. A Luxor/Galaxy merger would create the largest record company in the world as our industry embarks on the greatest resurgence in its history.

The phone rang in the suite. "Sir, it's the London office," the in-house staffer said. "Gwen would like to speak with you."

MacCabe took the phone. "Gwen, are you still in the office?"

"Yes, but I'm trying to get out of here, actually. The after-hours service will handle the next call. This will be the last for me tonight."

"Very good. Sorry if I kept you."

"Not a problem, sir. Derrick Andrews came up and asked to speak with you. He did not realize you were out of the country. It seems to be of some importance. Are you free?"

"Yes. Please put him on."

"Mr. MacCabe?"

"Hello, Derrick."

"Sir, do you remember the conversation we had early yesterday morning about secured and unsecured e-mails?"

"Of course."

"Well, I said that if you received a message from an unsecured server like AOL, and if someone had gained access to a password, then it was virtually impossible to know who actually wrote the message."

"Yes, I understand. That is what you said."

"Although that is correct, I failed to mention that even though we can't determine who actually wrote the message, we can find out whose computer the message originated from."

"Go on."

"Well, it's simple, really. Every e-mail has a *To* header and a *From* header. Each e-mail header file gives the address of the server. From the server, we can obtain the address of its origination. Every server has a log. AOL has tools to track e-mails by using the headers. I'm not sure if it matters to you or not, but what I'm trying to say is this: From an unsecured e-mail, we can never tell conclusively who was operating the computer when an e-mail was sent, but we can certainly tell conclusively from whose computer an e-mail came."

"I see," said MacCabe.

"I just thought I'd clarify that for you."

"That may be more useful than you realize. How long would it take to track that information?"

"It depends on the server and the type of connection. But usually, it can be obtained in a day or so."

"It doesn't matter if the sender was in the U.S. and I was in London?"

"Not at all. That's the beauty of the World Wide Web."

"Then I need you to work on something for me."

"Absolutely."

"Can you find out whose computer sent the 'Ripley' e-mail?"

"That should not be a problem."

"Derrick, this is confidential and is not to be discussed with anyone but me."

"I understand completely, sir."

"Good. And it would be extremely helpful if you were able to find out something before my eight o'clock dinner tomorrow night."

"You'll hear from me by then, sir."

"Very well. Thank you, Derrick."

MacCabe hung up the phone and thought, *If Ripley didn't send the e-mail, then how did he know to say he had business in New York? Chances are, he won't be alone tomorrow night.*

CHAPTER 46

THE NEXT MORNING

New York City
SoHo Grand Hotel
Wednesday, March 16

Room 421 was the nicest hotel room Judd had ever stayed in and surely the most expensive, though he never saw the rate when they checked in. Megan continued to pick up all the bills for their little excursion. All Judd could say was, "I owe you." And her standard reply was, "And someday, I'll make you pay!"

The room had an oriental feel. It was functional, stylish, comfortable, and very feng shui. The queen-sized bed was firm but low to the ground like a futon. The glass desktop, illuminated by a thin brass light fixture, supported a matching notepad holder, a portable alarm clock with an iPod docking station, and an organizer for the room-service menu and a spiral-bound SoHo Grand Hotel directory. The closet had no door but rather metal beads that hung down to create some separation. The mini bar had wine, beer, sparkling water, snacks, and a disposable camera. Judd stood in the middle of the room and thought, *I should be a complete nervous wreck. I'm in New York for the first time, staying at a place I never could afford, and trying to somehow get a message to a superstar before the authorities—or worse, the thugs—get to me. Yet I've never felt better.*

Megan had suggested they get some rest and meet in the Grand Bar on the second floor for an early lunch. But he couldn't sleep, so he exited his room, turned to the right, and went two doors down to the service pantry. The hotels he had stayed in before simply had an Ice or Vending sign. Not here. The "door" to the pantry was beads again. Inside was the most modern coffeemaker he'd ever seen. The clear plastic window in the center displayed the inner workings of the machine. What looked like a hydraulic arm pushed the water through the cylinder holding the coffee grounds and blended the brew. The coffee was then channeled through a tubing system and exited at the bottom into Judd's waiting SoHo Grand–engraved mug. It was art, it was entertaining, and—unlike the mini bar—it was complimentary.

It dawned on Judd why he felt so good even though his life was in turmoil. For the first time since he had laid eyes on Megan five months ago, he actually thought she might have feelings for him. Being thrown into an insane situation would be worth it if it meant getting close to her. The warm sensations from last night—her laugh, her glance—still lingered.

After they had arrived yesterday and gotten their bags to their rooms, Megan's friend recommended Felix's Bar—one block north at the corner of West Broadway and Grand Street—for dinner. But first, Megan wanted to show Judd around.

Maybe it was the fact that no one noticed them in a city of 8 million, or maybe it was the experience of being together outside Music Row, but for whatever reason, it was the first time since the calamity in Nashville that they put the shooting on the back burner and enjoyed life—for a few hours, anyway. They walked through SoHo, known for its vintage shops, bars, restaurants, and galleries, a universe within a universe, a culturally rich neighborhood between high-powered Midtown and Wall Street. Megan told Judd how in the nineteenth century it was an industrial section known for its ironworks and textile wholesalers. When those industries moved out, they left behind their iron-fronted buildings and all their warehouse space—a perfect combination for an artistic community to cultivate. Young, creative people, artists of all types, and entrepreneurs renovated the area to create an upscale neighborhood full of spirit and vitality.

They found Felix's Bar and sat at a small window table with candles beside a framed poster of Monaco.

"I think I'm ready for a drink," Megan said. "Do you like red wine?"

"Sure."

Megan looked over the wine list. "What about a Château Beau Soleil, Pomerol Red, 2009?"

"I've never had the 2009," Judd replied with a grin.

"I'll take that as a yes."

The waiter brought the French red, and the wine and conversation flowed. They both knew it was a momentary but needed escape from their tangled situation. They talked about Megan's childhood in the Bronx and her life in New York. She got glassy eyed when she mentioned the gaping hole in her heart since her mother's passing, but how Mathew helped fill the void. She laughed about having no time for any other man in her life. Then her chin quivered when she said Simon had been like a father to them both. Judd listened well. He wanted to know every detail. Then she stopped herself and said she couldn't remember when she had rambled on so.

"Enough about me. What about you? Is there someone in your life?"

Judd laughed. "No, not anymore. I mean, I have some great friends back home in La Crosse, and there was a girl." He paused. "I just had to chase the dream, I guess."

"Do you still communicate with her?"

"No," Judd said. "We're done. We went to high school together and then to the University of Wisconsin in Madison. We dated on and off the whole time. She's a wonderful person, but she just never could understand why I wanted to leave Wisconsin and move to Nashville. We broke up our senior year. The long-distance-relationship thing was never an option for her."

"What's her name?"

Judd laughed again. "Why do you want to know?"

"Just curious, I guess. Curious to know the name of the girl whose heart you broke while chasing your dream."

"Ah, well . . . Her name is Mindy. Mindy Holmes. But I assure you she's not brokenhearted. My friends tell me she's been seeing another guy since we broke up."

"So you do keep tabs on her."

"No, not really. It's just a small circle of friends."

"Well, you know what they say—good things come to those who wait."

That's what I keep hoping, Judd thought. He took a sip of wine and looked up to catch Megan smiling at him in a way he hadn't seen before. It was *the glance*—the look that confirmed she was starting to see him in a different light, too.

This could all be worth it, he thought as he cradled his complimentary coffee and walked back from the service pantry to his room. He checked his watch. His early lunch with Megan couldn't begin fast enough.

CHAPTER 47

The Next Day

New York City
Carnegie Hall Tower
10:15 A.M.

Back in MacCabe's Carnegie suite, Lukas Schultz sat in front of the window overlooking the morning sun in Central Park while holding a coffee cup in one hand and the *New York Times* in the other. Tommy Strickland and Hans Bergen were discussing strategy in regard to the American and European Union regulatory commissions.

MacCabe walked in and interrupted. "Gentlemen, can we gather over here, please?"

Strickland and Bergen discontinued their conversation and joined Schultz and MacCabe for their closing discussion.

"I have been reading our lawyers' notes on the most recently drafted merger agreement," MacCabe said. "It was delivered to me last night. Our lawyers have a few minor issues, as I'm sure yours do, but as far as having a deal in place on price and integration, all major points are agreeable to us. We are ready to present this to our board of directors on Friday for its endorsement and then take it to our shareholders for a vote Sunday in London."

Hans Bergen smiled and said, "As we expected. But first, what about our meeting with Ripley Graham?"

"I have what I think will be a suitable solution to your request to meet Ripley in a casual environment," MacCabe said. "Here is how I suggest we proceed. This inner circle of four will produce a letter of intent that outlines all the major deal points agreed to in the merger negotiation. Lukas, you and I will sign the document. At the same time, all four here will sign a confidentiality agreement. Any breach of the contents of our letter of intent prior to the shareholders' vote will be punishable to the full extent of the law."

MacCabe took a sip of water and continued. "Even before the shooting, Ripley was far too visible to attend a casual dinner with the CEO of Luxor Entertainment. Rumors already surround our merger proposal." He looked at Schultz. "Neither you nor I can afford any leaks in the agreed-to deal points. It could undermine the process. And it would cast a negative light prior to our shareholders' vote."

"How, then, do you suggest we proceed?" Schultz asked. "As I said yesterday, a meeting with Ripley will give me the opportunity to evaluate his demeanor and speak with him candidly about the new project he plans to release this year. This is not a minor issue. This *is* a deal breaker."

"It is not that I have any concern personally about you and Ripley Graham meeting prior to the vote," MacCabe said. "The problem is the confidentiality of our agreement. As well intended as it may seem, and as necessary as it is from your perspective, it is very problematic at this juncture. I cannot simply introduce you to Ripley Graham and say, 'Ripley, please meet Lukas Schultz, CEO of Luxor Entertainment. He would like to ask you some questions regarding your album and your intentions thereof.' Ripley, or those around him, would begin to ask questions, and the risk of exposing our deal prior to our shareholders' vote would be too great."

"Again, what are you suggesting?"

"Here is what I propose. We will afford you an opportunity prior to the shareholders' vote to hear Ripley Graham talk in person about his absolute commitment to delivering a new studio record for worldwide release this year. We will write this into our letter of intent. If it does not happen, then you can declare the agreement null and void, and the merger will be off."

"You say it will be prior to the vote. Where and how?" Bergen asked.

"I will ask Ripley to come to London for the Shareholders Meeting this weekend. The merger will be on the table. At that time, we'll take a break to honor Ripley as the best-selling artist in the Galaxy system. Ripley will then be invited to say a few words about his new project and its upcoming release. That will happen before the vote. If you don't like what you hear and you want out, you will have time prior to the vote to exercise your contractual option and take the merger off the table. You will get to see and hear Ripley, it just will not be one on one. That way, we can keep our agreement strictly confidential until the Shareholders Meeting."

Bergen glanced at Schultz, who remained silent for a moment while staring out over Central Park. Then Schultz looked directly at MacCabe and said, "You create the letter of intent in such a manner, and I will sign it before we fly out this evening." Schultz then put down his coffee cup and stood. "This has been a very productive trip. Thank you for your hospitality."

"You are welcome. I am pleased to continue this historic journey with you." MacCabe walked them across the room to the door. "The letter of intent will be delivered to you by three o'clock this afternoon."

Before MacCabe even turned around following the Germans' exit, Strickland asked, "How do you think you'll pull that off? There is no way Ripley will go to London for the Shareholders Meeting."

"I'll tell him he is going to be awarded the highest honor ever given to a Galaxy artist in the history of our company, and that we'd like to do it at the most visible ceremony—our Shareholders Meeting."

"He'll never go. And even if he does, what in God's name makes you think *you* can get Ripley to commit to a new release this year?"

MacCabe responded sharply. "Obviously, you miscalculated what it would take to make good on Ripley's promise. So it is now my turn. And I plan to start work on that this very evening."

CHAPTER 48

New York City
SoHo Grand Hotel

It was Judd's detection of Megan's meaningful glance that made him feel so confident and energized. Or maybe it was the ample cups of complimentary caffeine he'd been drinking all morning that had him buzzing. Either way, it was five minutes past noon, and he had now been sitting anxiously for thirty minutes at a corner booth in the Grand Bar on the second floor waiting for Megan. Last night while walking back to the hotel from dinner, Megan had mentioned that she would call Pumpkin first thing in the morning and find out where Ripley was staying. They had agreed to meet at eleven-thirty to figure out their plan for tonight. Judd glanced at his watch again.

Megan suddenly appeared. She looked distraught, pale, and shaky. Judd's first thought was, *Oh, God, she's got food poisoning.*

She said, "I didn't sleep at all!"

"Did you get sick?"

"No, I listened to the recorded conversations. It's all right here on Simon's iPod." Megan looked at Judd, and he saw fear in her eyes. "Simon is right. Ripley was not the target. Simon was! And I think Ripley was involved."

"What? Wait, settle down. Your nerves are getting the best of you."

"Judd, it's all right here. Did you listen to the whole thing?" She held up the iPod.

Judd passed her the glass of water with lemon he had ordered for her. "To be honest, I didn't know what I was supposed to be listening for."

"I can't believe it! It's all right here."

"Okay, just calm down. Let's go through it together. Take a breath."

Megan sipped her water. "Ripley and Strickland had a private phone conversation the day the tour opened, when Ripley was in Greenville and Strickland was in London."

"How do you know that?"

"Well, remember when Strickland called the office and you forwarded it to me because you couldn't reach Simon on his cell in Greenville? That was the first time Strickland ever made a call to put something on Ripley's calendar. For reasons I don't know, he wanted me to put a two-hour block on Ripley's schedule for that next Monday, before the Mardi Gras party. Then he said Ripley was already aware of the details because they had spoken by phone the afternoon of opening night. I asked Strickland if Simon was aware of this, and Strickland said there was no need to bother him. So I put a block on Ripley's schedule and didn't think any more about it."

"So?"

"So when Simon traveled back to Nashville after Ripley's show in South Carolina, Ripley called him from the road. At that point, Simon didn't know Ripley and Strickland spoke earlier that week. And you're not going to believe this. It's the conversation on Saturday between Ripley and Simon you've got to hear. Ripley's definitely behind all this!"

"What did Ripley say?"

"He asked Simon if he had any news. Simon said Strickland was in London, that they had traded calls, and that Ripley should be patient. Obviously, Simon was totally out of the loop on the secret side agreement. And you know what Ripley did?"

"I'm afraid to ask."

"Ripley blasted Simon over the phone. The dark side came flying out. Listen." Megan handed over the iPod and pushed the button.

Judd heard Ripley's voice, noticeably angry: "If you really were trying to protect me, you would have had James Clark fired by now! You never stand up for me. You're soft. You never fight fire with fire. You never do! So now I have to deal with those who keep stealing from me. I'll be damned if I let you get soft and not protect the dream!"

Judd stopped the iPod. "What in the world?"

"That's not all," Megan said.

Judd hit the button and continued to listen to Ripley rant: "It's time to call it quits, Simon. I always knew this would come. I know you were always disappointed that I wasn't my brother. You still think he was more talented, just like my own mother did."

Judd turned it off. "Can you believe it?" he asked. "And Ripley is saying all this after he cut his own deal with Strickland to have Clark ousted."

"Keep listening," Megan said. "Simon tells Ripley to relax, almost like they had this conversation before."

Judd heard Simon's calm and collected voice: "Ripley, that's just not true. I know you're upset, and I know how you get when you're upset—what happens to you. Just try to calm down, like the doctors tell you. When you settle down, you'll see this is a better way to get what you really want. There is no need to take things into your own hands. In the end, it's about winning, not about making sure somebody else loses. It's about your success, your payoff, not about making other people pay. This is a very delicate chess game. From your vantage point, you can't see the entire chessboard. That's why you have me. Many things are at play here. Don't try and maneuver on your own."

"You never help me!" Ripley said. "You're no better than they are! Truth be told, there is no greater enemy than the enemy in your own camp. Why do you think Jesus Christ staged the Last Supper? To reveal there was an enemy eating at his table!"

Simon raised his voice. "Are you calling *me* the enemy? I took you in. I'm the only one that has protected you. You came to me after the wreck."

"Don't *ever* mention the accident again," Ripley said. "It's over, Simon. You've got to go—disappear. It's over."

For a moment, both Megan and Judd stared at the iPod. Then Megan said, "It was Ripley. He's deranged. He cut a deal on his own, and now he sees Simon as his greatest enemy. It all adds up."

"He's definitely a clinical, certifiable, schizoid Jesus freak."

"Simon is Ripley's Judas. And a betrayal in Ripley's mind means he's 'got to go'—Simon must die."

Judd said, "Wait a second, he didn't go all the way there. I mean, Ripley is firing him. He said, 'You've got to go.' He didn't say, 'Simon, you must die.'"

"He might as well have. Think about it, Judd. What day was the shooting?"

"Wednesday, March 9."

"Ash Wednesday!" Megan said. "The day of repentance. *Carne vale*—'farewell to the flesh.' Meet your maker. It's got Ripley written all over it."

Judd sat in disbelief.

Finally, Megan asked, "Then what does Ripley mean by *disappear*?"

"Ripley is firing Simon," Judd said.

"That's not what you say when you fire somebody."

"Oh, God." Judd was white as a ghost.

"What?"

"Remember when I went to Ripley's house alone? The night you called and said he wanted to see me? One of the last things he said was something like, 'Just like Jesus Christ, they never found the body of my twin brother. He disappeared.'"

CHAPTER 49

Carnegie Hall Tower
SoHo

After dismissing the Germans and Strickland, MacCabe went back to working on his opening remarks to the shareholders. Prior to the vote, he would explain the many advantages of the merger:

> So why are we a match for Luxor and they for us? The most impressive component of this merger is the way we complement each other. In territories where we are weak, Luxor maintains high market share. And that trend is reciprocal in respect to us. Some of their weaker territories are our strongest. It is true in the U.S. It is true in Asia. It is true in Germany and Brazil. With our output increasing, our shared services will actually cut overhead and costs. Both companies have worked hard to create a comprehensive merger analysis for your review.

MacCabe's phone rang. It was Strickland.

"Tommy, what is the status?"

"Schultz signed the letter of intent with no changes," Strickland said. "It is being couriered over to you now. Once you cosign, it will be fully executed. Also, both Schultz and Bergen signed the confidentiality agreement."

"Good. Call Hans Bergen and let him know that I will forward fully executed copies tomorrow, that everything is on schedule. Confirm with him that your office will coordinate the details for their attendance at our Shareholders Meeting in London on Sunday. Also, Tommy, I need you to sign the confidentiality agreement as well."

"You're in over your head, Warren. You will never be able to get Ripley to London, not without me."

"Tommy, I don't have time to elaborate at the moment. However, when we're back in London, you and I will discuss your tremendous error regarding Ripley's behavior. Your ego has blurred your better judgment. It is a grave miscalculation for someone in your position. That's all I have to say at this time."

And with that, MacCabe hung up the phone and turned his attention back to his speech.

Still seated in the Grand Bar, Judd and Megan ordered drinks. Judd also suggested Megan eat something.

"Okay, even if Simon was the sole target and Ripley was involved, what's got me stumped is why MacCabe would agree to meet with him secretly tonight," Judd said. "What 'unfinished business' was the e-mail I sent to MacCabe referring to? If Ripley tried to kill Simon because he believed Simon was his greatest enemy, then maybe the record company had reason to help. Maybe Ripley and Galaxy were working in tandem. I don't know."

Megan didn't respond.

"Did you try and call Pumpkin this morning to see where Ripley is staying?"

"Are you crazy?" Megan said. "Not after listening to the recordings. It's not like I can call now and say, 'Hey, we figured out Ripley tried to kill Simon. So where are you guys staying?' "

"I'm just wondering if he's actually here in New York."

They paused to ponder that thought. Then Megan added, "Maybe you're right. Maybe they *were* working together. Two different motivations, one objective."

"But why would Galaxy want to get rid of Simon?" Judd asked.

"I'm not sure. But when Strickland called me to set that two-hour block of time for Ripley, he definitely did not want Simon to know about it."

"I think I've got it!" Judd said. "It must have something to do with the merger rumors."

"What makes you think that?"

"Okay. Simon called me back from Greenville after he missed the call from Strickland. When he did, I asked him how it was possible that Galaxy's stock could be at an all-time low with Ripley selling more records than anyone in the music business."

"And?"

"And Simon said something like, 'Galaxy's problem is it has only one giant egg in its worldwide basket. So it either needs to hatch more eggs or get a *bigger basket*.' He was talking about the merger."

"But still . . . So?"

"So maybe Ripley cut his own deal with Galaxy without Simon to pave the way for the Luxor/Galaxy merger. Look, we know Galaxy has been desperate for Ripley's CD—that its stock price is at rock bottom, that Ripley and Strickland cut a deal behind Simon's back, that there are merger rumors. Ripley holds all the cards. And maybe Simon and Ripley didn't agree on how to play those cards. So, in the two-hour secret block of time, Ripley decided to play without Simon. And maybe the record company decided it would rather Simon not find out about it—ever!"

Megan was starting to buy into the theory. "Well, the only way to find out if Ripley and MacCabe actually are working in tandem is to see if they *both* show up tonight at the AquaGrill."

CHAPTER 50

New York City
SoHo

Evening had come, and the city was lit in all its glory. Warren MacCabe sat in the back of the black Lincoln with *GLXY I* plates heading south down his favorite street in New York, Avenue of the Americas. His cell phone rang.

"Good evening, Mr. MacCabe. I have Derrick Andrews on the phone. He said you were expecting his call."

"Yes, please patch him through."

Derrick came on the phone. "Mr. MacCabe?"

"Derrick, it's after midnight in London. You've been working late."

"Yes, sir, and I have a name for you."

"Excellent."

"The e-mail you received on your unsecured AOL server on Saturday, February 12, at 8:47 P.M. from 'Ripoff' signed 'Ripley' went over a wireless system, and we've been able to identify its designee. It belongs to Judson Nix."

"Who is he?"

"Judd Nix, sir. He is the young intern who was shot in the shoulder in Nashville, the one that worked for Simon Stills."

"I see." MacCabe paused. "Derrick, that is very helpful. Again, this is strictly confidential."

"Don't worry, Mr. MacCabe."

"Okay, thank you."

The car slowed, turned left on Spring Street, and stopped in front of the AquaGrill. He was ten minutes early.

The Galaxy security man riding shotgun in the front turned and said, "Mr. MacCabe, I'm going in first to make sure everything is secure. I'll be right back."

"Thank you."

MacCabe watched his bodyguard walk into the restaurant. Although the sidewalk wasn't busy at the moment, some people walking by noticed the restaurant was closed. No one could have known MacCabe's office had bought it out for the evening. Only the chef and one waiter were to be on hand. No limos were parked in view. MacCabe saw no sign of Ripley.

The bodyguard made his way back to the car and opened the door for MacCabe. "It's all clear. Only the two hired hands are inside. We'll be parked across the street. I have my ears on, if you need anything. We'll be monitoring from here."

"Very good."

MacCabe got out of the car and briskly walked inside.

CHAPTER 51

New York City
SoHo

After being up all night, Megan had promised Judd she would try to sleep some that afternoon before they met in the lobby at 7:15. When she arrived, Judd was asking about the AquaGrill.

The concierge knew everything about the eateries in the hotel's little corner of New York. "It has a highly acclaimed raw oyster and clam bar." He bent down to retrieve something from under his desk. "I should have a menu here. Yes." He placed it in front of them. "Here you are. Look at these wonderful appetizers—Spicy Tuna Tartare with Cucumbers, Ruby Flying Fish Roe, and Crispy Taro Chips in a Thai Vinaigrette. How fabulous is that?" The concierge seemed genuinely delighted. "The weather is mild tonight. You can walk from here. Just go out our door and turn left on West Broadway. You will cross Grand and then Broome, and then you will get to Spring Street. Take a left and walk to Sixth Avenue. It is on the corner of Sixth and Spring."

"And you're sure it's open?" Judd asked.

"Let me check the hours for today. Oh, absolutely. It says here dinner is served on Wednesday from 6:00 until 10:45."

Ten minutes later, Megan and Judd stood on the opposite side of Spring Street looking across at the bright blue AquaGrill Oyster Bar. Megan felt numb. The small, inviting local classic was one of the thousands of neighborhood restaurants taking advantage of the amalgamation of cultures to carve out a niche. And yet all Megan could see was the red sign in the front door: Closed.

Judd, standing just behind her, looked at his watch and said, "We're a little early."

Then they saw a black Lincoln pull up in front of the establishment and a large man in a dark suit get out and go inside. "Look at the license plate," Judd said. "*GLXY I*—it's Warren MacCabe. Just keep talking to me and stay close."

The man in the suit returned to the car, and MacCabe walked inside.

Fifteen minutes later, a sedan with two men inside pulled up to the curb a block away. They didn't get out. Both Judd and Megan noticed.

"What's taking Ripley so long? Maybe he's not coming," Megan said.

"Do you think the two guys in MacCabe's car are watching us?" Judd asked.

"Seems like it."

"What about the other car? Can you make out those two people? I wonder if it's Nate and Jerome."

"I can't tell, but they're scaring the crap out of me."

"Megan, check out the front of the restaurant."

Megan turned and looked. "Yeah, what?"

"What do you see, exactly?"

"A brick restaurant painted bright blue."

"Close. Half of the front is brick, but the other half isn't."

"Yes, it is. But the other half has painted ripples, like aqua blue water."

"No, it's not ripples. It's a garage door. A one-car garage is connected to the restaurant."

Megan squinted. "You're right. Which means a car could be inside the garage. Ripley could already be here."

"Exactly."

"I don't know. Maybe he parked in the garage, or maybe that car down the street dropped him off before we got here. Or maybe Ripley isn't here at all, and the two guys in that second car are thugs waiting for us with their guns cocked."

"Look, this isn't good. We've been here too long, and there's no sign of Ripley. I'm not sure who is who, but it feels like they're all staring at us. If we stand here any longer, we're going to get busted by somebody," Judd said.

"I've got an idea," Megan said, grabbing his hand. "Let's act like we're saying goodbye. I'll give you a hug. You turn around to Sixth Avenue and act like you're trying to hail a cab. I'll walk past the restaurant and look in the window to see if I spot MacCabe and Ripley, or at least two people talking alone. If I don't see anyone, I'll shake my head and keep walking toward the second car. If the guys in the car are Nate and Jerome, I'll turn around and come back."

"What if they see you?"

"This is New York. They're not expecting to see me. I'll be discreet."

"But what if they're real thugs instead?"

"I'll run my hands through my hair. That's your sign to forget this and get out of here. We'll meet back at the SoHo Grand."

"Okay, that should work. But one other thing. What if a cab stops to pick me up before you get back?"

"Just lean in and tell him you've decided to walk. He'll drive off. Anybody watching will think you're asking to ride somewhere he doesn't want to go. It happens. Then stick your hand out again and wait for me."

"Perfect. Let's do it."

"Judd, wait." Megan looked at him as if she wanted to say something. She glanced down at the sidewalk, then back up at him. "Judd, be careful." She reached up and tenderly kissed him on the lips, then gave a nervous smile.

Judd smiled broadly and said, "Now, that's my kind of goodbye!"

Megan turned and walked down Spring Street in the direction of the restaurant. Judd moved toward Sixth Avenue. He stuck out his left hand and turned his back toward oncoming traffic. That was exactly the opposite of what a New Yorker would do to hail a cab, but he wanted to keep an eye on Megan. She approached the restaurant, looked at the Closed sign on the door, took a long stare in the front window, and kept walking while she shook her head. To anyone else, it looked as if she was disappointed that the restaurant was closed for the evening. Judd knew she hadn't seen anyone inside.

As Megan headed toward the suspicious car, a cab stopped. Judd waved it off as if he had changed his mind, then turned away. A man got out of the rear seat, walked up behind Judd, and pointed a blunt object in his lower back. Judd knew instantly it was a gun. He jerked.

The man grabbed his arm as the cab drove off. "Don't move and you won't get hurt."

"Jesus," Judd said.

The man flashed a badge in Judd's face. "U.S. marshal. Just walk slowly toward the restaurant. Mr. MacCabe has asked that you join him inside. Don't do anything stupid or your girlfriend will get to meet the men in the car she's walking toward."

Judd felt weak. He started walking. The man remained right behind him, jamming the gun into his ribs. Judd saw Megan walking away from them. She had not reached the car yet. Without saying a word, he turned and walked into the restaurant. A heavy red velvet curtain hung just inside the door. "Go on through, all the way to the back," the man told him.

As Megan approached the car, she took a quick glance to her left. Two beefy men dressed in black were staring straight at her. *Oh, my God,* she thought. Her heart started racing. She ran her hands through her hair to signal Judd without looking back, then picked up her step until she was half running. When she got to the cross street, she turned and looked behind her. Judd was gone. *Thank God,* she thought.

Judd walked through the opening in the curtain. The bar, on the left, featured a display of exotic oysters. The restaurant was small. In the back, he saw three men talking at a table. The one facing him was Warren MacCabe. Judd knew his face from the trade magazines. But he never expected to meet him like this. The other two had their backs to Judd as he approached. *Who are they? Is that Ripley?* He couldn't tell.

Just as he reached the table, one of the men stood and turned. Judd stopped in his tracks. It was Agent Engels.

"Hello, Judd." Engels then addressed the man with the gun. "Thank you. I'll take it from here." The man behind Judd walked back toward the front door. "Judd, I don't believe you've ever met Mr. Warren MacCabe, although we know you've been e-mailing each other. And this is Agent Jacowski with the FBI."

Agent Jacowski stood. "Mr. Nix, we're here to conduct a formal interrogation, and my hope is that you will cooperate with us fully. Believe me when I tell you it is in your best interest."

MacCabe cradled a coffee cup in his hands and looked at Judd without getting up.

Judd stood motionless.

"Sit down, Judd," Engels said. "You've been a very busy young man. I'm disappointed that you didn't call to tell me you were leaving Nashville."

CHAPTER 52

THE NEXT MORNING

Austin, Texas
Four Seasons Hotel
Thursday, March 17

The morning bellman at the Four Seasons couldn't help noticing the name *Mr. Ripley Graham* on the front of the two-page fax as he slid it under the door of the Congressional Suite. Having prompt business service was a trademark at the five-star hotel. The fax arrived in the hotel's business center at 6:42 A.M. and was delivered to the megastar's room at 6:50. Ripley retrieved it immediately. He stepped out onto the wraparound terrace overlooking Austin's Town Lake and read it without delay.

Billboard.biz Bulletin™

YOUR DAILY ENTERTAINMENT NEWS UPDATE
THURSDAY, MARCH 17, 2011

Authorities Detain Former Management Intern in Connection with Graham Shooting

Chip Avery, Nashville

The Tennessee Bureau of Investigation and the FBI released a joint statement early this morning stating that Judd

Nix of Nashville was detained last night outside a restaurant in the SoHo district of New York City and taken in for questioning in connection with the apparent assassination attempt on the life of country superstar Ripley Graham last Wednesday, March 9, in Nashville.

The authorities did not elaborate on the reason for Nix's detention.

Nix, 23, was one of those injured in the Graham shooting, but his wound was not life threatening. At the time, he was working as an intern for Simon Stills, Graham's personal manager. Stills was also shot and is currently in critical condition at Vanderbilt University Medical Center in Nashville.

The TBI said it would have a news briefing today at 8:30 A.M. Eastern at the FBI offices in New York to address this latest development.

Still in her nightgown, P. C. rang room service. Janice had awakened both Ripley and P. C. with a call at 6:20 A.M. to tell them some dramatic news was breaking regarding the shooting. The FBI planned to release the new information at 7:30. CNN would cover it live. A fax was on the way to the room with details. Janice said she had been fielding phone calls from national media since 5:00 A.M. asking to be the first to get Ripley's response as soon as the news was released. Ripley told her to have everybody gather in his suite at 7:00. He wanted to watch the news together.

"We'd like enough coffee for five people," P. C. said. "Cream and sugar, some bagels and cream cheese, orange juice, and some ice water, please."

"Certainly, we'll have it right up."

Ripley, Janice, Pumpkin, and Tillman gathered in the spacious living quarters of the suite around the large TV.

"Here it comes, here it comes," Janice said, turning the volume up.

"I'm Kiran Chetry with *American Morning* in Atlanta," the anchor said. "CNN has obtained information regarding a detention made in conjunction with the apparent assassination attempt on the life of country-music superstar Ripley Graham." A picture of Ripley appeared in a shadow box behind the announcer's head. "According to a report released early this morning, the FBI detained Judd Nix for questioning late last night in New York City. Nix was one of the men wounded, though not seriously, in the Nashville shooting a week ago." A picture of Judd appeared on the screen. "CNN correspondent Jim Nestle is at the FBI's New York City bureau at Federal Plaza, where he is awaiting a press briefing. Jim?"

The picture moved to a reporter standing in the back of a crowded conference room in New York.

"That's right, Kiran. We know that Judd Nix was detained here in New York by authorities and taken in for questioning. Apparently, he was apprehended at a popular restaurant in SoHo last night. As you said, Nix was shot in the incident in Nashville. He was working at the time as an intern for Simon Stills, Ripley Graham's personal manager. We are waiting to find out why he was in New York and why the FBI has detained him. This certainly brings into play more questions than answers. Was Judd Nix directly involved, and if so, how? Does this have any connection to Simon Stills, who after being shot had emergency surgery, looked to be improving, and suddenly suffered a setback? Stills is currently in a coma at Vanderbilt University Medical Center in Nashville."

The reporter looked over his shoulder toward a podium. "It looks like the briefing is about to begin."

Agent Engels reached the podium, opened a thin notebook, and looked at the cameras.

"Good morning. I'm Agent Rod Engels of the Tennessee Bureau of Investigation. I'm the lead agent assigned to investigate the shootings that took place at the Grand Ole Opry House in Nashville on March 9 while country-music singer Ripley Graham was filming a video. From the beginning, the TBI has had jurisdiction over this case, but it has been assisted by a concerted effort involving local police in Nashville and the Federal Bureau of Investigation. Because the investigation is ongoing, I will have to limit my remarks to some degree but will confirm that Mr. Judd Nix of Nashville was detained for questioning by agents here in New York City at approximately ten o'clock last night outside the AquaGrill restaurant at 206 Spring Street in SoHo. Mr. Nix was detained by federal agents without incident or resistance. After a subsequent interrogation, Mr. Nix has been formally charged with several counts in connection with the shootings—charges of obstruction of justice, mail fraud, conspiracy, and lying to state and federal agents."

There was a collective gasp in Ripley's suite.

Janice said, "Oh, my God!"

Agent Engels continued, "He is currently being held in New York without bail and awaiting extradition back to Nashville, Tennessee."

The media clamored for attention.

"Agent Engels!"

"Agent Engels!"

"Agent Engels!"

"Over there." Engels pointed to a reporter.

"Agent Engels, was Ripley Graham at the restaurant last night, and did this abort a second assassination attempt?"

"Ripley Graham was not in New York. Because of the ongoing investigation, I cannot comment in regard to the second part of your question. Over there."

"Were you or has someone in the agency been in contact with Ripley Graham in the last forty-eight hours? He said on national TV Monday night that he was coming to New York. Did you ask him not to come, and was he aware that the bureau was tracking Judd Nix?"

"I'll answer the first part of your question. I have personally been in close contact with Ripley Graham within the last twenty-four hours. I can't comment on Mr. Graham's itinerary other than to say he did not travel to New York this week. If he was planning to do business in New York City, then he obviously changed his plans. Yes, right down in front."

"Can you be more specific on Judd Nix's charges and the evidence the TBI and FBI have against him?"

"The charges against Mr. Nix were brought after he was observed in suspicious activities we had been monitoring. Specifically, Mr. Nix was seen after the shooting in the office of Simon Stills, tampering with his personal computer. We now know that someone illegally erased documents from that computer, which contained sensitive and potentially incriminating evidence. We believe that person to be Mr. Nix. Also, Mr. Nix has apparently been e-mailing top record-company officials and fraudulently claiming that these e-mails were coming from Ripley Graham. When Mr. Nix was initially questioned by agents regarding these activities, we believe his answers were untruthful and intentionally made to mislead the investigation. We believe that Mr. Nix thought Mr. Graham had business in New York last night, as mentioned on national television, and was attempting to gain access to him. Mr. Nix traveled to New York from Nashville on Tuesday afternoon and was detained here yesterday outside the restaurant where he believed Mr. Graham would be dining. That is all I can say at this time."

"As a follow-up, are you suggesting there was another planned attempt on Ripley Graham's life last night, an attempt you believe involved Judd Nix?"

"I didn't say that. You said that. All I said was that we have evidence that Mr. Nix believed Mr. Graham was going to be at the restaurant last night, when in reality he wasn't. However, Mr. Nix was. We watched Mr. Nix survey the restaurant prior to taking him into custody and subsequently charging him with the counts that I have just listed. That's all I can say at this time. Thank you."

Agent Engels then turned and walked away from the podium.

Janice hit the mute button on the TV. Everyone in the suite stood stunned.

"It's the day of repentance, you little bastard," Ripley said.

CHAPTER 53

Austin
Four Seasons Hotel

"Room service."

P. C. pulled the door open to a young man with a silver pushcart holding two pitchers of coffee, juice, water, a half-dozen coffee cups, and bagels.

"Just put it over here," Ripley said, clearing the hotel brochures off the coffee table. The young man placed the coffee on the table and smiled when Ripley handed him a twenty-dollar bill as he exited.

"Okay, I'm really confused," Janice said. "Obviously, I hadn't heard anyone mention New York anytime recently. Of course, I would have noticed. It is only the media capital of the world. And then, Ripley, you talked on *Leno* about having business in New York. I was, like, 'Really?' I mean, not that you have any obligation to tell me everything, but still, why wouldn't you tell me you were going to New York? And then after the show, nothing else was mentioned. Pumpkin gave us the updated itinerary, and nothing had changed. We were flying from L.A. to Austin—nothing about New York. So I thought, 'Well, maybe it's a record-company thing. Maybe they don't want me to know.'"

No one said anything.

Janice continued, "Shouldn't we talk about this? I mean, from the PR angle, I need some direction here. What am I to say to the press?

They've been calling me since five this morning. They ask, 'Who told Ripley not to go to New York?' What do I say, 'I don't know. No one bothered telling me he was planning a trip to New York in the first place'?"

"It wasn't a record-company thing," Tillman said, glancing at Ripley.

Without looking up, Ripley spoke quietly and deliberately. "Agent Engels called me while we were at *The Tonight Show*. He said they were closing in on someone. He also said he believed it was a conspiracy, and if they got this one guy it would crack the case." Ripley took a sip of coffee. Everyone in the room stood motionless. "He said they were setting a trap and needed my help. They needed me to say on *The Tonight Show* that I was going to New York before Austin. So I did. It was a setup."

Ripley walked to the fireplace in the corner of the room. He stood there for a moment, then yelled at the top of his lungs, "Damn it!" and shattered his coffee cup against the mantelpiece.

Everyone jumped.

"Hey, hey." Tillman rushed over. "Take it easy."

"Don't you patronize me!" Ripley pushed him away and sent Tillman crashing into the silver cart. Coffee flew everywhere. Ripley's voice was now traveling all over the top floor of the hotel. "No intern could do this all by himself!"

Jerome and Nate came busting into the room.

"It's okay. Calm down, everybody," Tillman said when he was back on his feet, holding out his arm to stop Jerome and Nate's advance.

"The hell it is. You know damn well it's not okay!" Ripley roared. "I want to know who else is behind this, and you're telling me to calm down!"

"Ripley, come on." Tillman held out his hands in Ripley's direction, trying to calm him. "Don't jump to conclusions. Let the FBI do its job."

Ripley covered his face. He crouched and began to rock back and forth, hands braced on his knees, eyes fixed on the floor. "I can't trust anyone." Then he stood, walked over to Jerome, and said, "I want security so tight on these shows coming up that you know the blood type of everyone within fifty feet of me. Do you understand?"

"Yes, sir," Jerome replied.

Ripley leaned into Jerome's face and yelled, "I'm not kidding! I don't want to walk by one person that you haven't gotten your nose so far up their ass that you can't tell me what they had for breakfast. Is that clear?"

"Perfectly."

"Good. Then go on to the venue and start beefing up the security. I want to see uniformed officers everywhere I go. I want a police escort when we drive—one in front and one in back. I want you to plan alternate travel routes. Get a stunt double to throw off the fans if you need to. I don't give a damn what you have to do."

"We're on it." Jerome and Nate left the room.

Ripley walked to the mini bar and poured some Jack Daniel's in an empty coffee cup. Everyone was quiet. The phone rang.

"Hello," P. C. said. "Yes, who is this? . . . Oh, it may not be a good time. Just a moment." She looked at Ripley, who was sipping his whiskey. "It's Warren MacCabe calling from New York City."

Ripley hesitated for a second, then took the phone. "This is Ripley."

"Ripley, this is Warren MacCabe. I'm sure you've heard about the arrest here in New York."

"Yes, we were watching the news. I thought you worked in London."

"Normally, I do, yes, but I'm here at the moment doing business with Tommy Strickland. I've been told by Agent Rod Engels that the two of you are in close contact and he is briefing you almost on a daily basis."

"Yes."

"Well, I wanted to call for a couple of reasons. One, to check in with you and again assure you that as the CEO of the label I will continue to do whatever is in my power to help catch and prosecute any and all who were behind this."

Ripley didn't say anything.

"Are you still there?"

"Yes, I heard you."

"Very well. I just wanted you to hear that from me. Now, as you know, I've asked Doug Tillman to stay with you for another few weeks. Use him if you need to. He knows how to get hold of me at all times, just in case."

Again, Ripley didn't respond.

"The other reason for my call was to invite you to attend our Shareholders Meeting in London this weekend. I'm aware you have some concert dates, but if you were to juggle your schedule, I'd make it worth your while. I'd like to have you as our surprise guest. It may seem odd timing, but I'd like to give you a very special award—the highest honor our record company has ever bestowed upon an artist—and I'd like to do it in front of our shareholders."

"It's not a good time."

"Maybe not, but maybe so. Just hear me out. It would be a very meaningful moment for all of us, especially in light of all you've been through this week. The company would like to honor you not only for your success but for your character in these most difficult times. In light of the young intern's arrest, a few days away could be good. It might help stabilize the situation—for all of us. I'll give Doug all the details for your consideration."

"There's a lot going on at the moment, and a fast trip to London is the last thing on my mind. I don't think so."

"I understand. However, don't answer now. Think it over. We would make it an extremely easy trip for you. I will send a private plane for you and your people. I do hope you give it some serious consideration. Doug Tillman wouldn't by chance be watching the news with you, would he?"

"Yes, he's right here."

"Splendid. If you don't mind, I'd like to have a word with him. And I look forward to hearing from you in a day or so."

"He wants you," Ripley said.

"Mr. MacCabe?" Tillman said into the phone.

"I've invited Ripley to our Shareholders Meeting. We'd like to give him a special presentation Sunday in London."

"I see."

"I'd like you to escort him over. I'll take care of any and all costs and clear any security issues he may have. I'll send our jet over to pick all of you up."

"That's nice, but I did hear him say the timing isn't good."

"If Ripley doesn't come, then the timing is not good for *you*. Let me be clear. You get him over here to our Shareholders Meeting or you and I have no further Galaxy business to discuss." And without saying goodbye, MacCabe hung up.

CHAPTER 54

THE NEXT MORNING

New York City
SoHo Grand Hotel

Judd, wearing a baseball cap, heavy coat, and sunglasses, got off the elevator on the fifth floor, found Megan's room, and knocked on the door. He waited and knocked again.

"Who is it?"

Judd loved her warm, familiar voice even when she sounded fearful. He said, "My first encounter with a New York taxi didn't go so well."

The door swung open. "Oh, my God!" Megan stood in the doorframe, hand over her mouth, tears welling in her eyes. She hugged him tightly, then broke the embrace and began rambling without taking a breath. "I got to the hotel and you weren't here. I knew something was wrong. I waited up all night. I started to call in a missing person report. Then I saw you all over the news this morning. I didn't know who to call about—"

Judd kissed her in midsentence.

The elevator door chimed and then opened. A man wearing black stepped into the hallway.

Megan broke off the kiss and pulled Judd into her room. "They're here!"

"It's okay. I'll explain. A car is waiting for us outside. You need to get your things."

"Waiting for us? Judd, what's going on?"

"You were right all along. It's Ripley! Agent Engels figured it out."

"Agent Engels! I'm not going anywhere until you tell me what's going on."

"Okay. I was taken into the restaurant by a man with a gun while you were walking toward the second car."

"Oh, God."

"Yeah, well, it turns out he was a United States marshal. Inside were Agent Engels, an FBI agent, and MacCabe. That's when Engels confirmed what you thought. He believes Ripley was behind everything. The only glitch was that whoever he hired to make the hit actually missed and didn't finish the job. Simon is still alive. Now, Engels is convinced Ripley is planning to disappear—go underground, maybe even fake his own death—and continue to go after people he perceives to be the enemy."

Megan sat on the bed and stared into space. Then she asked, "So how does Engels know all this?"

"He's been monitoring all of our unsecured e-mails and cell-phone calls. He also has a copy of Simon's recorded phone conversations—the ones on his iPod."

"I thought you deleted those and we had the only copy."

"So did I, but apparently when someone erases information from a computer, it's still obtainable if you know how to access it. The FBI computer forensics lab recovered it."

Megan was still trying to absorb all the information. "I see."

"Engels was nervous that the recordings would get into the wrong hands and Ripley would find out about them—or worse, actually hear them. He also secured a copy of the side agreement from your files. He didn't want Ripley to find out we have a copy. That's why he was following us. He was protecting us, in a way—although I'm in a bit of trouble."

"What kind of trouble?"

"Well, at the restaurant, Engels actually read me my rights and informed me I had committed several crimes. That's the bad news. The good news is, if I agree to fully cooperate, they'll keep me in protective custody and, best case, perhaps drop the charges."

Megan nodded. "Are you in protective custody now?"

"Yes." Judd nodded toward the door. "My friend's in the hallway."

"Okay, here's my question. Did Simon know Ripley was behind the shooting? And if he did, why did he have you e-mail MacCabe?"

"According to Engels, Simon knew Ripley was behind it, but he didn't think Ripley could have pulled it off alone. Simon was trying to figure out if Ripley had turned the record company against him, too. He asked me to e-mail MacCabe about 'unfinished business' because he was trying to see if Galaxy was working in tandem with Ripley, like I was thinking. But they weren't. Galaxy had nothing to do with the shooting. It was all Ripley."

"You know that for sure?"

"Yes. MacCabe was in the restaurant, too. He's trying to get Ripley to London to save the company. He got the forged e-mail I sent. But before he arrived at the AquaGrill, his people told him that Ripley didn't send it—that I did. He had no idea how Ripley knew to say on *Leno* that he was going to New York, so he went to the restaurant to see who showed up. He said he wouldn't have been surprised if it was Strickland with some thugs. It was rather brave of MacCabe, actually. As it turns out, Strickland is on the outs with Ripley, like everyone else."

"So Ripley never was here in New York?"

"No. Engels captured our e-mail exchange. After he read MacCabe's e-mail setting up the AquaGrill meeting, he played us all like a fiddle. He called Ripley and told him to say on *The Tonight Show* that he was traveling to New York. He tracked us as we flew here. He convinced MacCabe he was going to meet the culprit behind all this. Engels is pretty smart. After he read me my rights, he explained that he needed Ripley to think the TBI and the FBI had a primary suspect—me—so he would let his guard down. He said that if I fully cooperated, I might get off the hook." Judd paused to let Megan grasp all that, then added, "The guys in the car that we thought were thugs were FBI agents."

"This is unbelievable."

"Even though I'm in his custody, Engels has kind of been protecting both of us. He's had guys in a car on the street outside the hotel watching you all night."

"Where?" Megan went to the window.

"They're out there. Engels and MacCabe talked for over an hour in front of me last night. MacCabe didn't know about the side agreement. That's all Strickland. Strickland has been trying to coordinate a hostile takeover, but Ripley reneged on his deal by not turning in his finished album. Ripley still hasn't given it to him."

"That's no surprise," Megan said.

"By the way, do you know Ripley Graham isn't Ripley's real name?" Judd asked.

"Yeah, it's a stage name. His real name is Jeff Williams. It's on his passport. So?"

"Do you know what his mother's maiden name was?"

"No."

"It was Graham. Now, can you guess his dead brother's name?"

Megan said hesitantly, "Ripley?"

"You got it. His stage name is his brother's first name and his mother's maiden name."

"This is freaking me out." After a pause, Megan asked, "How does Engels think Ripley could ever just disappear?"

"He said he doesn't know for sure what Ripley's next move will be, but he's aware of the money transfer to Mexico. And you were right—it was $20 million. The transfer is in his legal name. So Jeff Williams could take his legitimate passport, cross the border into Mexico, and do whatever he wants with his $20 million, and it's not even illegal."

"But he'd still be recognized. He's too famous."

"Really? You said yourself you're surprised more people don't recognize him in public without his cowboy hat and jeans. Think about it, Megan. He takes off his hat, grows an out-of-control beard like Brad Pitt did a few years ago, and puts on some sunglasses, sweatpants, and maybe a hoodie. It could happen. The day Jeff Williams goes underground and slips down to Mexico with $20 million is the day superstar Ripley Graham gets away with having Simon shot."

"Now you're starting to really freak me out."

"Engels and MacCabe said a mysterious disappearance would become an American obsession. It would rival the age-old question of whether Elvis is still alive. There would be books, movies, even sightings. In Ripley's case, some of them might actually be real. That's what Engels is trying to prevent."

"Are you in danger?" Megan said.

"Maybe. Ripley knows I was helping Simon. Engels says I'm in more danger if Ripley disappears. And to stop him, Engels needs me to look like I was the perpetrator. He doesn't have enough hard evidence to prove Ripley hired the hit on Simon. But he needs to nail Ripley before he vanishes, and the clock is ticking. What Engels has to get is a confession. So, if I'm the fall guy, he's hoping Ripley will let down his guard and get sloppy."

"So, while he tries to keep you safe, Engels lets the world think you're the one who tried to kill Simon?"

"The deal is, if I cooperate, Engels will drop the charges against me. So we'll go back with him to Nashville today—"

"*We'll* go?" Megan said.

"I told him I wasn't leaving the city without you."

Megan smiled slightly.

"I can post bail immediately and be able to go home. But I'll still be under his watch, which may not be a bad thing. In the meantime, Engels has devised a plan to stop Ripley before he crosses the border. He said he's going to use *me* to get the confession."

"How?"

"I don't know yet. But I'm not in a position to negotiate."

Part III
Sound Proof

CHAPTER 55

The Next Afternoon

Austin
Friday, March 18

The motorcycle cop pulled out of the Four Seasons Hotel and into the intersection of San Jacinto Boulevard and Cesar Chaves Street. He slowed his bike, stopped traffic, and motioned to Ripley's limo driver to pass him. The stretch limo bearing the usual Ripley Graham entourage turned left onto Cesar Chaves and headed west toward Brazos Street on its quick trip to the University of Texas and the Frank Erwin Center. A second police motorcycle suddenly zipped passed Ripley's limo and put itself into position to stop traffic at the intersection of Cesar Chaves and Congress Avenue. Once the limo made the right turn onto Congress, the first motorcycle took a position bringing up the rear.

"It's cool how they trade places like that," P. C. said, looking up momentarily from her daily nourishment of *Self* and *Harper's Bazaar*.

"Who?" Janice asked from her seat across from P. C. and Ripley.

"Those motorcycle cops. They have this escort thing down to a science."

As they made the turn, Ripley looked out his window toward the Texas State Capitol at the north end of the street. It was nearly an exact replica of the United States Capitol except that it was mud gray, rather than pearly white. Without looking at anyone in particular, he said, "Texas, just like everywhere else in the South, is obsessed with three things—history, religion, and music."

"They do take their music seriously in Texas," Tillman said.

Ripley continued, "Texas gave us Western swing. New Orleans gave us jazz. The birth of the blues came from the Mississippi Delta. Rock-'n'-roll came from Memphis thanks to Elvis—a white guy singing black music. And then Southern gospel and hillbilly music converged in Nashville to create country."

"I've always wondered why the South is such a fertile breeding ground for music," Tillman said.

"Because the South is a complicated culture full of guilt and sin, yet always looking for redemption. There are more strip clubs and churches in Dallas than anywhere else in the country. In the South, you sin Saturday night and repent Sunday morning. And every Sunday morning, everyone in the South gathers—sometimes together but mostly still apart—to pay homage to our history, confess our sins, and ask for repentance. Repentance that can be given only by the Almighty. And how do we worship Him in the Bible Belt? White, black, or brown, we sing. And when we sing, we honor our history and our religion. That's why I'm here. I was put on this earth to sing. And no one will stand in my way. I am washed in the blood, and I was put on this stage to collect my inheritance."

Everyone in the limo sat staring at Ripley except for P. C., who looked over her magazine and said, "He's just a walking Trivial Pursuit."

Ripley stared out the window as the others pretended to check new messages on their BlackBerrys. The circular arena was now in sight, just on the edge of campus. People were walking toward it from all directions. The huge, scrolling marquee read, "Ripley Graham—Sold Out." All the corporate sponsors had positioned themselves around the outside of the complex. Local country radio stations KASE 101 and KVET 98 were there with their branded, custom-made vans, broadcasting live remotes and talking to crowd members as they passed. Country Music Television's promotional truck played Ripley videos while employees tossed out *CMT* Frisbees. Ford had two new Excursions parked at the entrance under a banner reading, "Ford presents Ripley Graham's Rip It Up Tour."

The limo pulled past the loading dock and into a yellow roped-off area in front of the backstage Artist Entrance. Jerome directed a dozen uniformed police officers to form two lines—a human barricade to protect Ripley as he exited the car and headed in.

Ripley turned to Tillman and said, "I need to talk to you privately inside."

Pumpkin brought his hand to his mouth and said, "Jerome, he's coming out." He then turned to the others as they exited the limo. "Everybody, please make sure you have your 'All Access' laminates from this point on. Tonight, we're making no exceptions."

Ripley and Tillman walked across a large "Welcome to the Frank Erwin Center" mat and entered the back of the arena. Pumpkin headed to the production office. Janice and P. C. went in search of catering. As usual, the road crew had placed large signs with arrows around the backstage area to help everyone navigate the concrete maze. The first set of signs—Dressing Rooms, Production, Stage, and Catering—all pointed in different directions.

Without breaking stride, Ripley said to Tillman, "Let's go to the floor."

Ripley took the lead and headed toward the center of the arena, where a black curtain draped the entrance. A crew sign next to the curtain read, "Arena Floor." Standing just in front of the curtain were two uniformed police officers. Sitting close to them in metal folding chairs were two men in yellow T-shirts that read, "Rock Solid Security." All eyes were on Ripley, but the guards had obviously been told not to speak to him.

Ripley approached them and stuck out his hand. "How are you guys doing?"

"Good," the first officer said, obviously pleased. "Nice to meet you."

"Good to see you guys. Thanks for taking care of us tonight." Ripley shook hands with the others.

"No problem," the first officer said. "Let us know if you need anything."

"I'll do that."

"Have a good show."

The two security guards pulled open the curtain so Ripley and Tillman could walk into the enormous circular-shaped concert hall.

They stood there for a second looking out onto 16,755 empty seats and twenty-eight upper-level luxury suites surrounding the stage in the center of the arena. Above them were stacks of speakers and an entire lighting system flown from the ceiling by a gigantic silver truss. A mass of speaker cables and electrical wiring was drawn together on the left corner of the lighting rig and dropped down to the staging area to connect with generators on the ground. Ripley's crew was still on the stage and climbing the rigging to work on last-minute adjustments.

Ripley and Tillman were now in a place where no one could hear them. Ripley looked at Tillman and said, "They know there is no merger without me, and they know I'm not going to play their game anymore. That's why they tried to kill me."

"What? We just found out Judd Nix is in custody."

"The intern couldn't do this by himself. Galaxy is behind this and is going to pin it on him. Now they want me in London to bless the merger to make it happen!"

"They never said that."

"Of course not! They haven't told you anything at all. They're just whoring you out, too. Don't be a complete idiot! They're not actually going to tell you that they're using you. I could make out the gist of what MacCabe said to you on the phone. What was it? 'Get Ripley to London or don't bother showing up for work.' Wake up! Think about it. If I don't show up in London tomorrow, you're history. But if I do and the merger goes through, guess what? You're still history! After the merger, they won't need you anymore. It's all about Strickland and MacCabe, not you and me. And I'm the workhorse that is making the merger possible. And if it happens, who gets the billions in cash benefits and stock options? Me? Hell, no! MacCabe, Strickland, and the other corporate raiders, that's who!"

Ripley had Tillman's undivided attention.

"But I've got a plan. I handpicked you to be the number-three guy at Galaxy, and now I'm going to make you the number-one guy."

"What are you talking about?"

"Do you know why James Clark was ousted?" Ripley asked.

"No. I thought he resigned."

"No. He was forced out because Strickland loathed Clark—because Clark was becoming too powerful. Then Strickland offered me a side agreement and said I could handpick the next head of Nashville if I'd agree to turn in my new music directly to him. And I wanted you because of your marketing savvy, so I agreed. But in my gut, I knew Strickland was up to something. And then I found out about the merger proposal, so I didn't give the recordings to him. That's why he plotted to have me killed before the shareholders' vote. I was going to be more valuable dead than alive. That's what we were yelling about in the holding room at Vandy Plaza just before the press conference. I called Strickland out and told him that I was on to him. If I had finished the CD and given it to him, Strickland's plan was to walk into the London boardroom and stand in front of the shareholders and say, 'Ripley Graham has agreed to turn in his new music, but only to me, and I have that in writing.' And that would pave the way for Strickland to oust MacCabe and become the new CEO while finalizing the merger."

"That's hard to believe. How can you possibly know all this?"

"If someone was trying to kill you, wouldn't you be interested in why? Why else would Strickland cut a deal with me directly, without telling my manager and without his own boss knowing about it? He was trying to take over the company. And I was his whore."

"Do you think that's still his plan?"

"Well, his problem is that he's not getting my finished music. And I can prove I signed the side agreement under duress." Ripley reached in his back packet, took out a letter, and put it in Tillman's hand.

"What is this?" Tillman asked.

"It's a notarized letter written and signed by me, to your attention. I like to think of it as a living will."

Tillman unfolded the letter and read.

Ripley waited until he finished and looked up in astonishment. "I'm going to entrust that power to you, if you swear on the grave of my family that you will honor Ripley Graham in all that you do. By this document, I promise to deliver my finished master recordings and all the power that comes with them to you and only you. I will finish my vocals and deliver the recordings in the next two weeks. Once you receive them, you and Galaxy will have my full support of this merger. But as you can see, I have one stipulation—that this music will be released only when MacCabe *and* Strickland are ousted. I'm not going to London tomorrow. You're going to London. You're going to be my official representative and accept the Galaxy award on my behalf. Then I want you to tell the audience that I personally gave you a letter to read to the shareholders as my acceptance speech. That's when you read this letter and deliver the message. My only regret is that I won't be there to see the reaction on Strickland's and MacCabe's faces."

CHAPTER 56

Austin
Frank Erwin Center
10:15 P.M.

Alone in the bathroom of his dressing room, he could hear the chanting: "*Rip-ley, Rip-ley, Rip-ley, Rip-ley . . .*"

The crowd in the Erwin Center was deafening. Pumpkin stood outside the closed bathroom door with Jerome, Nate, and two uniformed police officers. According to Pumpkin's stopwatch, the electrified crowd had now been stomping and chanting for over three minutes in hopes of a third encore.

Ripley was dripping wet. He stood half naked, hands on the sink, water running, staring into the mirror. He took a deep breath and said to himself, "It's almost over." For a moment, he was at peace. He began to relax. He heard and saw nothing. Then, without warning, it appeared. It wasn't his imagination. There it was, right there! In that one millisecond, he was no longer looking at his own face. But rather, the reflection in the mirror was now staring back at him! The all-too-familiar haunting eyes penetrated his soul.

"*Stop!*" Ripley yelled.

The others heard him. Pumpkin leaned in close to the door and asked, "Ripley, did you say to stop the show? You're done? You don't want one more encore?"

Ripley didn't reply. Instead, there came a knock on the dressing-room door from the hallway. One of the uniformed officers opened it, and Janice stepped inside.

"What is it?" Nate asked.

"I need to talk to Ripley," Janice said coldly.

"He's still in the bathroom cooling down," Pumpkin said. "I think he's done for the night."

Janice didn't even acknowledge Pumpkin's response but knocked on the bathroom door herself. "Ripley, I need to talk to you. It's Janice, and it's urgent."

Again, Ripley didn't answer.

"Ripley, I'm sorry but I need—"

The door opened. Ripley was still half dressed and had a towel around his neck. He looked white as a ghost.

"Maybe we should clear the room," Janice said, looking at the others.

"No, tell me now," Ripley said.

Janice paused, then motioned for the two uniformed police escorts to leave. They hesitated.

"We'll be all right," Pumpkin said, nearly pushing the officers into the hallway.

"We got a call from the hospital tonight while you were onstage." Janice cleared her throat as she teared up. "Simon had a turn for the worse tonight. He has no brain activity. The doctors said it's just a matter of hours." Janice put her hand over her month and dropped into a chair.

Ripley didn't move for several seconds. Then he turned to Pumpkin. "Light my mic stand. I'm going back onstage. I'm not done yet."

"What?"

"Light it!" Ripley screamed.

Pumpkin said into his two-way radio, "It's not over. Don't bring up the house lights. Hit Ripley's mic with the spot. He's coming back."

From inside the dressing room, the entourage heard the crowd erupt as the spotlight lit Ripley's microphone stand at center stage. The decibel level peaked when, moments later, he walked into the blinding light with just his guitar. He motioned with his hands for the crowd members to quiet down. They didn't at first, but Ripley was patient. He motioned again and said, "Thanks for staying." The crowd roared. "Thanks." Ripley waited as the crowd started to settle. "This has been a rough few weeks for me, and I just wanted to come back and thank you guys for your prayers and your good wishes."

Someone screamed, "We love you, Ripley!" and the crowd cheered in support.

"I love you, too. And sometimes, I feel like you're the only family I have, and the only ones I can turn to in times like these. And . . . well, while I was backstage just now, I got some bad news. I don't think I'm going to be able to talk about it. So let me just leave it at that for now. But I do want to say we are all put on this earth for a purpose, and we will all leave this place when our Maker calls us home." The crowd cheered again. "And I, uh . . . I was placed on this earth to sing for those who have no voice of their own. And before I walk off this stage tonight, I just need to tell you that I have a date with destiny. So here is my last song."

The crowd settled as Ripley started playing his acoustic guitar underneath the spotlight.

"I've never sung this song for anyone until tonight. You guys are the first." The crowd erupted again. "I'm going to ask my record company to release it as my first single from the new album." The response was deafening. "It's called 'I Lived My Life for You.'"

Ripley started singing:

You laid down your life
You paid the price—sacrificed
I watched, what else could I do?
You overcame the dream, reclaimed
And whispered to me inside, insane
It's all on the line, it's destiny's time
Take a stand, stake your family name
And when you do, I'll know it's true
I lived my life for you . . .

The crowd erupted in a state of utter frenzy.

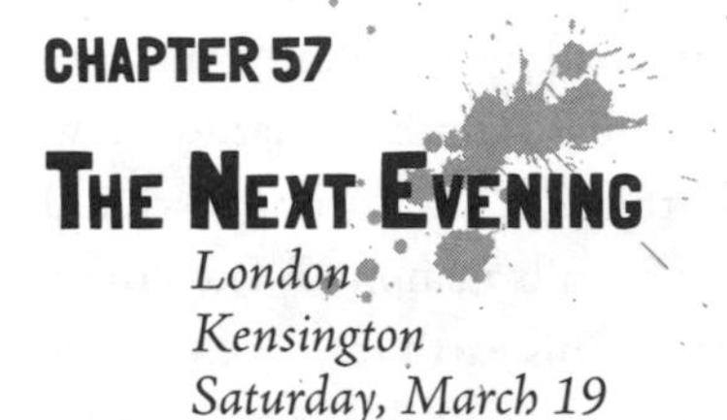

CHAPTER 57

The Next Evening

London
Kensington
Saturday, March 19

The Galaxy Records home office was deserted on Saturday evening except for Warren MacCabe, who was pacing his office on the top floor. Yesterday's Board of Directors Meeting had gone off without interruption, the directors agreeing unanimously to take the merger vote to the shareholders tomorrow. However, MacCabe knew that the only way the vote would even take place was if Ripley made the trip to London. Strickland and the Germans had all checked into the Royal Garden Hotel. Immediately after the board meeting, MacCabe had called Tillman to see if Ripley was making the trip, but Tillman had not yet returned his call. MacCabe had already sent the private jet to Austin to pick them up.

He opened the leather binder on his desk to look again at tomorrow's opening remarks. MacCabe then closed it without reading the speech. He knew it by heart. He sat and picked up yesterday's *Bulletin* from the side of his desk and read it one more time.

Billboard.biz Bulletin™

YOUR DAILY ENTERTAINMENT NEWS UPDATE
FRIDAY, MARCH 18, 2011

More Details Made Available in Nashville Shooting; Graham Back on Tour

Chip Avery, Nashville

Following the first arrest made in connection with the apparent assassination attempt on the life of Ripley Graham nine days ago, more details were released by the FBI yesterday regarding the shooting.

According to the latest report, ballistic tests confirmed that rounds from an FX-05 Mexican-made assault rifle were found. The report also confirmed the shootings were the work of a lone gunman stationed in Section 37, Row H, the first row in the balcony of the Grand Ole Opry House. That portion of the theater was dark and not in use at the time of the incident.

The Opry security staff has confirmed that an unidentified man carrying a guitar case came earlier in the day claiming to be Graham's guitar technician. Graham's people have stated that they were unaware of any such person on the premises.

Agents believe since the Opry House was not open to the public at the time, the gunman hid in the balcony until his attack, concealing the weapon in the guitar case. Agents speculate that immediately after the shots were fired, the gunman simply walked out the front of the theater into the Opry Mills complex.

Judd Nix, an intern at Graham's personal management company, was taken into custody late Wednesday night. The FBI believes he holds key information regarding the assassination attempt on Graham's life. Nix was arrested in New York City and transported back to Nashville yesterday afternoon. He is being held on charges of obstruction of justice,

conspiracy and lying to state and federal agents.

Ripley Graham's people have not commented on the latest developments. Graham is currently back on tour and will play his first date since the incident tonight for a sold-out crowd at the Frank Erwin Center in Austin, Texas.

MacCabe put down the article and walked out into the atrium. His whole career seemed to be in the balance. All his life, he had dreamed of creating the largest record company in the world. Hands folded, he pondered the words of English mathematician turned cosmologist turned philosopher Alfred Whitehead: "Nature is a structure of evolving processes. The reality is the process." Meaning that everything in existence has an evolutionary relationship to everything else, that we are all moving toward our own sense of self-determination, striving to reach our greatest potential. For MacCabe at this moment in time, that was the creation of Luxor/Galaxy. And yet by his understanding of the laws of human nature, he knew everything was interrelated. Today, it was Ripley Graham's actions that would determine the fate of MacCabe's own life's ambition.

As he did from time to time, MacCabe found himself standing in the center of the atrium next to the armillary sphere, the symbol he had chosen years ago to represent his business philosophy. He looked upon the inscription etched at the bottom of the sphere—the Galaxy Creed, an article of faith he had written in a moment of inspiration and had adopted as his life's compass: "Never fear the exploration of the galaxy or the human spirit, for they are one and the same. Fear only those who see the human condition as a galaxy too vast to explore. Those who are afraid to succeed, or worse, afraid of the truth, will assuredly fail. Exploration is the father of courage and creativity. Therein lies our humanness."

MacCabe's cell phone interrupted his train of thought.

"Mr. MacCabe, this is Agent Engels."

"Yes, Agent Engels. I have not heard back from Doug Tillman. Do you have an update?"

"I do. Your company jet arrived in Austin this morning and has just departed this afternoon carrying only one passenger."

"So Ripley is acting as you predicted?"

"I'm afraid so."

"I see." After a pause, MacCabe added, "Well, then, I guess that is all I need to know. It seems I have a communiqué to send. Good luck to you and your people as you see this thing through."

"Thank you for your help."

After they disengaged, MacCabe walked back to his office and logged onto his secure e-mail.

Secure Galaxy Communiqué
Sent: Saturday, March 19, 2011
To: Strickland, Thomas
From: MacCabe, Warren

Urgent: Meet me in the privy garden tonight at midnight.

W. M.

THIS DOCUMENT WILL NOT PRINT.

CHAPTER 58

Nashville
VUMC

After a brief acknowledgment, Megan walked by the guard standing in the hall. Opening the door, she stepped into the room and pushed away the privacy curtain just inside. Shirley was seated by Simon's bedside. Megan paused, surveying all the wires. This visit felt different, as Simon lay completely motionless.

Shirley stood and signaled for Megan to approach.

As she drew close, she whispered, "Can he hear me?"

"No," Shirley said.

Megan sat on the stool beside the bed and stared at Simon for several minutes. The only noise was that of the ventilator. Simon's eyes were closed, and his face held no expression.

Without touching Simon, Megan leaned close to his ear and whispered her goodbye: "Thank you for everything you did for me and Mathew. You were more than a mentor. You were truly our father figure. The one we never . . ." She choked up and put her hand to her mouth.

Shirley took Megan by the arm and said, "Come on, sweetie. Let's go outside for a minute."

They walked down the corridor to get away from the guard at Simon's door.

"Megan, even though Simon never came out of his coma, he did say some things in his unconscious state," Shirley said. "To be honest, he said only one thing, but he said it several times when I was in the room. And it was about you."

Megan tried to regain her composure. "Really?"

"Yes, really. And I personally believe that there are messages in the dream state."

"What did he say?"

"Well, I'm not sure what it means, but he kept saying, 'Megan, look in the car.' "

"What car?"

"I have no idea," Shirley said. "He was heavily medicated. It may not make any sense, but you never know. Maybe he was tryin' to tell you something. One time, he might have said, 'Check the car.' I just thought you should know."

Megan shook her head. "I don't know what that means."

"Well, there is one other thing. Before he went into a coma, when he was doin' better, he kept listenin' to his iPod, writin' notes, writin' to me on his white board. And at some point, he insisted that Agent Engels look up some information for him. Then the day before his seizure, he wrote on his board to me, 'If anything happens to me, give Megan the Engels info.' I didn't know what he was talkin' about, and at the time he was improvin' rapidly. But it was the very next day he had the attack and went unconscious. The next morning, one of Engels's agents brought in this letter from the bureau addressed to Simon. I don't know what it is, but I know Simon wanted you to read it if he wasn't able. Simon was definitely clear about that." Shirley reached into her pocket, pulled out a TBI envelope addressed to Simon, and handed it to Megan. "Maybe it'll connect the dots." Shirley gave Megan a hug and walked back toward Simon's room.

Megan held the envelope for a few seconds, then opened it. It contained a pink copy of a police report. It took her a minute before she realized what she was looking at—part of the official police summary from the scene of Ripley's family's car crash into the Cumberland River in 2005. The report was only two pages. The first gave standard police-report information:

```
Date—3/13/2005
Time—12:30 A.M.
Vehicle Information—1991 blue four-door Chevy
Caprice Classic
```

However, at the bottom of the second page were several lines labeled, "Narrative—Statement of Facts":

```
    The vehicle drove over a steep embankment outside
Clarksville, TN, on US 41 Alt. Bypass, Mile Marker
105, and crashed in the Cumberland River. It was
removed the next day approximately 200 yards down-
stream. I, C. J. Crowley, officer on the scene, noted
there was only one survivor (male, 18 years old,
Jeff Williams), who told officials on hand that both
his brother and mother had been in the car with him
at impact. Upon removal, however, only one body was
located in the vehicle, an adult female with severe
lacerations from the crash. She was still strapped
into the rear left seatbelt. No other body was found
in the vehicle.

Sgt. C. J. Crowley, Mon., 3/13/2005
```

Megan read the last part again: "She was still strapped into the rear left seatbelt. No other body was found in the vehicle." Suddenly feeling ill, she rushed into the women's restroom fifty feet down the hall, threw open the stall door, dropped to her knees, and vomited.

CHAPTER 59

The Next Morning

London
99 Kensington High Street
Sunday, March 20

Five minutes past the stroke of midnight, MacCabe walked onto the rooftop and into the private outdoor Garden of Eden. Making his way across the multicolored tiled walkways, past the live flamingos, and underneath the grapevine trellis, he saw Strickland standing next to the stone statue alone and, as usual, dressed completely in black.

"Tommy," MacCabe said, "I must get straight to the point. I know you cut a deal with Ripley Graham directly—a deal you never discussed with Simon Stills, a deal you never discussed with me, a deal that Ripley doesn't plan on honoring. I warned you right here in this very place that beasts have insatiable appetites, but you forged ahead and now have made a fool of me."

"What are you talking about?" Strickland said.

"Don't play games with me, Tommy! You wanted James Clark gone as much as Ripley did. But one feeding is not nearly enough for the likes of Ripley Graham. He wants you and me ousted as well."

"That is absolutely not true."

"Isn't it? Tommy, I have heard the phone conversations between you and Simon prior to the shootings. I also have a copy of the side agreement you and Ripley Graham executed. That is corporate insubordination at its highest level. You were withholding this information from me. Once the board recommended the merger, your plan was to go to the shareholders tomorrow with our German cohorts watching, to tell them that Ripley Graham had given you full control of his project, but only if I was ousted. Isn't that right, Tommy? You were planning to organize a takeover with the merger intact. But what you miscalculated was the fact that Ripley despises you as much as he loathes me. What a foolish attempt!"

"You're the fool, Warren."

"Am I? Then show me Ripley's finished CD. You can't—because you don't have it, do you? And you will have nothing to say tomorrow when your protégé, Doug Tillman, shows up without Ripley but with Ripley's blessing to undermine *you* just as you have tried to undermine *me*! Apparently, you trained him well. Backstabbing must be an acquired attribute."

"You have no idea what you're talking about."

"Don't I? Tillman is planning on stealing your thunder tomorrow, Tommy. Ripley has a new disciple. Tillman has been commissioned to gain control of the merger discussions and oust both of us."

"That is ludicrous!"

"No, it's not. This beast has a fantastic appetite. Clark was only the appetizer. I am his dessert. You, in fact, are the main course."

Strickland was silent.

"As I was leaving the office this evening, I got a voicemail message from Tillman, who called from the corporate jet. He made a formal request to address the shareholders tomorrow to state that Ripley Graham, who will not be able to attend, has asked him to deliver his acceptance speech. Think of it! We are actually paying for Tillman to fly back alone on our company jet so he can commit a corporate coup d'état."

MacCabe turned his back on Strickland and started up the tiled pathway. Then he stopped and, without turning his head, said, "It is by no means what I envisioned, but tomorrow will no doubt be a day Galaxy Records will long remember. And by the way, your presence there is no longer needed."

CHAPTER 60

Nashville
VUMC Parking Garage
8:15 A.M.

The weather was windy, cold, and rainy. Judd parked his Honda and joined Megan in her Audi coupe to watch the rain come down outside the five-story garage across the street from the medical center.

"You're not going to believe it." Judd was telling her about the plan Engels had discussed with him yesterday to get Ripley's confession. "The Feds have this white van with Jake's Plumbing printed on the side, but inside is all this surveillance equipment—more gear than you could ever imagine. It looks like a miniature version of Mission Control. Two technicians with headsets sit in bucket seats staring at a wall of video monitors and recording devices."

Megan was barely listening.

"One of the technicians gave me this new cell phone. It works like a normal cell but has some special features. When you hit *star 1*, it automatically connects you to the van so the technicians can listen and record. It also has a GPS tracking device so they know where you are at all times—or at least where the phone is. It's like the ones they advertise for parents with teenage kids."

Megan sat looking out the window.

"They're going to arrange for me to have a surprise encounter with Ripley one on one. They want me to confront him and hopefully record a confession using the phone. Engels thinks Ripley will come to the hospital today to say his goodbye. It will be emotional, and that's when I should walk in and confront him. Engels hopes I'll hit some kind of trigger while we're in the same room with Simon lying there on life support."

Again, Megan didn't respond.

"Megan, this is kind of important. Have you heard anything I said?"

"You're not close enough to Ripley. He's not going to disclose any secrets to you."

Judd was slightly irritated. "Well, we're running out of time. Engels thinks Ripley is about to make his move. Ripley plans to get out of the U.S. and start his life in hiding. There's a man the FBI has been watching for years that runs a drug-trafficking operation—a cartel that has outfits in Mexico and South America. They launder their money through several entertainment enterprises—mainly nightclubs and concert promotion companies. In the U.S., they operate as Starbound Entertainment. Ripley knows the owner and visits him periodically in his establishment in Monterrey, Mexico—a place called La Casa Blanca, The White House. Engels has no evidence that Ripley is involved in the cartel's illegal business, but he believes that's the connection he used to hire the hit on Simon."

Megan let that information sink in, then finally turned to face Judd. "Ripley is capable of much more than just hiring a hit."

"What are you saying? Do you know something I don't?"

Megan took a breath. "Ripley killed his family."

Judd looked at her to see what she meant, but she didn't elaborate. "Megan, Ripley survived a car crash that killed his mother and twin brother. You know that. Simon knows that. Ripley even told me at his house."

"Exactly what did he tell you?"

"You know the story."

"Can you remember what he said word for word?"

Judd paused. "Okay, well . . . He said they were driving back from

Nashville to Clarksville after his brother auditioned for Simon and the others. It was midnight. His mom had a dilapidated car with bad tires and brakes. She drove into a heavy rainstorm and lost control. The car went off the road and into the Cumberland River."

"What else?"

"Well, he was thrown from the backseat and landed without so much as a scratch. He watched as the car was engulfed by the river with his mother and brother inside."

Megan said, "Yes. Then Ripley showed up at Simon's office a few weeks later, told him the story, and showed him he had the letter Simon wrote his brother outlining the details of his contest winnings. Ripley asked if Simon would sign him instead and help him live out his brother's dream."

"Exactly."

"But that's not what happened," Megan said.

"How do *you* know what happened?"

"Why did Simon keep listening to the iPod conversations? He was on those calls. He knew what was said."

Judd shook his head, not knowing the answer.

"Something was obviously bothering him, but he couldn't put his finger on it. Well, he finally did. It was the heated conversation between him and Ripley, when Ripley yelled at him for being soft and not protecting him and then said, and I quote, 'Don't *ever* mention the accident again. It's over, Simon. You've got to go—disappear. It's over.'"

Judd didn't follow. "Okay, so what? I'm not surprised Ripley told Simon to never mention the accident."

"No. It was the *way* he said it. Simon heard something different in Ripley's voice. That was why he kept playing it over. Simon realized Ripley was hiding something."

"Okay, what?"

"Shirley gave this to me yesterday." Megan unfolded the police report and passed it to Judd. "Right before he went into a coma, Simon asked Engels to get this. Simon was checking to see if Ripley's mother was actually driving." She paused to let Judd read, then said, "She wasn't. Her body was found in the backseat. And you can't drive a car into the

Cumberland River when you're in the backseat."

"Well, it's possible she ended up in the backseat from the impact of the crash."

"Not with her seatbelt fastened."

Judd was starting to get the picture. "So who was driving?"

"Ripley."

"Or his brother."

"No, it was Ripley," Megan said. "That's the only reason he would lie to all three of us—because it wasn't an accident. Ripley drove the car into the river and jumped before it hit the water. Why else would he lie? He hated his brother for winning and hated his mother more for not believing in him. He went along for the ride, and after his brother won he drove them into the river that night. He killed them and stole his brother's dream. And six years later, that's why he hired the hit on Simon. Ripley saw Simon as the enemy. He realized Simon was the only one that had the ability to figure out his deepest, darkest secret, and he could never risk it. That's why he said, 'Don't *ever* mention the accident again.'"

"Megan, even if that's true, there's no way to prove it. And besides, no one would ever believe it."

They sat in silence, knowing the truth of that realization. Just then, Megan's phone rang. They both jumped. She reached into her purse and stared at the name on her cell: *Ripley Graham*.

CHAPTER 61

London
Kensington
Royal Garden Hotel

Galaxy Records' Annual Shareholders Meeting was always held in the Palace Suite Banquet Hall on the hotel's lower level. The large, beautifully decorated room could easily hold five hundred people in theater-style seating. Although the Shareholders Meeting was not for another four hours, the room was already perfectly set. At the far end was a carpeted platform, draped at the bottom, with four chairs on either side of the podium. Behind the podium was a large video screen that displayed the Galaxy Records armillary sphere. The room had state-of-the-art built-in audio services, multimedia technology, and programmable lighting.

Just outside the hall was a spacious lobby with a bar on one side and a hallway leading to several smaller conference rooms. They all had fittingly English names: the Chelsea Suite, the Westminster Suite, the St. James Suite, the Buckingham Room.

MacCabe was in the Chelsea Suite holding an emergency Board of Directors Meeting prior to the Shareholders Meeting. Although the board had met on Friday and given its approval for the merger vote to go in front of the shareholders, MacCabe had called an emergency executive session, citing "a potentially damaging set of circumstances that urgently requires the board's attention." It was two in the afternoon, and MacCabe had already been addressing the twenty-member board for over an hour.

He articulated in great detail the questionable activities of the past weeks, days, and hours. He disclosed that Strickland had usurped his authority by secretly asking Ripley Graham to sign a side agreement. He also disclosed that although the Germans had signed a letter of intent, they could exercise a clause taking the merger off the table prior to the shareholders' vote if Ripley did not appear in front of them in person. Since Doug Tillman was now traveling alone from Austin, Texas, the board had to assume the Germans would exercise that option, MacCabe said.

The board members riddled him with questions.

Was a Ripley release this year absolutely necessary for the merger to be viable?

Did he know what Doug Tillman planned to say if he were allowed to address the shareholders?

When would he tell the Germans that Ripley would not be present to accept his award?

Should the board bury the merger discussions for now and not bring up the vote until the Ripley, Strickland, and Tillman issues were all settled?

Because none of those questions could be answered immediately, the board voted to postpone the Shareholders Meeting for at least twenty-four hours. It was now clear that MacCabe needed to pay a visit to his German colleagues.

CHAPTER 62

Nashville
VUMC Parking Garage

Judd nodded for Megan to go ahead and answer the call from Ripley.

She sat up straight behind the driver's seat. "Hello?"

"I know it's early on a Sunday morning. Thank you for picking up. It's Ripley."

"No problem."

"This is hard. I feel like an orphan once again. I have no one."

Megan didn't respond.

"Simon was my rock."

Megan was appalled. She tried to answer with no emotion in her voice. "He means the world to all of us."

"I'm going to talk to Brad Holiday about getting you assigned back to me. I'm not sure why that happened, and I want you to understand it was not at my request."

Megan, knowing he was lying, said, "Well, I'm taking a little time off."

"I heard that." After a pause, Ripley said, "I assume you got the news about the intern."

"Yes. You mean Judd."

"You're not still hanging out with him, are you? He's a very dangerous guy."

"I thought they arrested him," Megan said.

"He's out on bail. You need to be careful. You should definitely call the authorities if he tries to contact you."

"I will."

"Megan, I hate to even bring this up, especially knowing you're taking some time off, but I'm in a bit of a bind. Would you mind helping me out with something this morning? It won't take long."

The request hit Megan like a blow to the gut. She tried to stay calm, but she knew Ripley had sensed her hesitation. Not wanting to immediately commit, she asked, "What do you need?"

"Help with some personal business. I told the team to take the weekend off, and I know Brad's assistant would do it, but honestly, with Simon in this condition, I just don't feel like dealing with anyone else."

Wanting to end the conversation quickly, and knowing Ripley would be suspicious if she declined, Megan said, "Sure."

"I really appreciate it. Again, I'm sure it won't take long. Can you meet me at my house in thirty minutes—say, around nine o'clock?"

"Okay," Megan said. "I'll head that way."

"Great. I'll see you in a few." And with that, Ripley hung up.

"What does he want?" Judd asked.

"He said he needs my help with some personal business and asked if I'd meet him at his house in thirty minutes."

"And you said yes? We've got to call Engels."

"No!" Megan said. "Ripley is much more in tune to things than you both realize. It's a gated community. If I roll up with you and the NASA van behind me, we'll never get the confession. This is our only chance. I've got to go alone."

"No way! Megan, I can't let you do that. You just told me he killed his family. Are you crazy?"

"Give me the cell phone from Engels, and I'll get that bastard on tape."

"Megan, listen to me. This is a bad idea. I'm going to call Engels, and he'll walk us through it. This is way too dangerous."

"Judd, there isn't enough time. I could hear it in his voice. He's about to make his move. Somehow, he knows we've been seeing a lot of each other. The man has people that watch out for him 24/7. I'm telling you, I've got to go alone. It's our only shot."

"Damn it." Judd reached into his pocket. "Okay, you take the phone. Hit *star 1* as you walk up to the house. That way, the agents will be listening. I'll follow you out to The Governors Club and park on the other side of the street and watch the gate. I have my own cell phone. If you feel like this could even remotely start to go south, just bolt. Don't try to be a hero, just leave and call me. I'll call Engels, the TBI, the FBI, the freakin' National Guard. I'll be there in two seconds flat."

Megan took a deep breath. "Okay." She reached over and gave him a long embrace. Judd felt her arms trembling. Then she sat back and said, "Let's get this over with."

CHAPTER 63

Brentwood
The Governors Club

Judd drove close behind Megan's Audi in the cold rain until she reached Ripley's highly secured community. As she turned right toward the guardhouse, Judd veered left off Concord onto Liberty Church Road and parked so he could watch the gate from across the street. After recognizing Megan, the guard waved her through. Judd had a clear view of her red taillights cresting the hill and disappearing on the other side of Governors Way.

When she entered Ripley's manicured drive, it was obvious she was alone. Before she got out, she hit *star 1* and put the cell back in the pocket of her jean jacket. She knew Engels and the other agents in the van would be surprised to hear her voice live over Judd's device.

Megan was hurrying up the walkway under a small umbrella when Ripley bolted out of his house toward her. He looked rough. He was wearing jeans, a flannel shirt, a black rain jacket, and a baseball cap instead of his signature cowboy hat. She noticed his hollow, bloodshot eyes.

He didn't say good morning. "You can help me with an errand. Let's take my car."

Ripley gunned his black 2011 Cadillac Escalade out of the drive. But instead of turning left on Governors Way, back toward the entrance, he went right. He raced through the winding streets and reached a residents-only exit that Megan hadn't known existed. The unmanned gate opened upon his approach.

Ripley turned left and sped out onto Crockett Road. Two miles later, he turned left onto Wilson Pike, then west on Moores Lane, the windshield wipers on high, whipping the rain. Within minutes, he accelerated onto I-65 South and raced away from town. Everything around them—the road, the sky, the day—was turning grayer and more threatening by the minute.

"Where are we going?" Megan asked, knowing she needed to give everyone listening a heads-up that she was traveling alone with Ripley.

"My hunting cabin, to take care of some unfinished business."

Megan's gut tightened. "Where is it, exactly?" *Please give detailed directions,* she thought, not knowing if the GPS on Engels's phone was working.

"Back in the hills of Williamson County. My old man lived there until he died, and then I turned it into my hunting cabin."

The mention of Ripley's dad made Megan flinch.

Judd watched the light Sunday traffic on Concord Road, keeping his eye on the entrance.

His cell phone rang. "Hello?"

"What the hell is going on?" Agent Engels roared.

Startled, Judd said, "Well, long story short, Ripley called Megan less than an hour ago and wanted to see her alone. She insisted on going. I agreed to it only if she would take your cell phone, so your agents could listen. I'm watching the gate outside The Governors Club. Are your guys picking her up yet?"

"Judd, she's already in trouble. Ripley has her in his vehicle, and they took the west gate out of Governors. He went down Crockett Road and just turned south onto I-65. This is a disaster!"

"Oh, Jesus!" Judd started his car and peeled out onto Concord. "Where is Crockett Road?" he yelled into his cell.

Ripley turned and looked at Megan in a way she had never seen before. "So you heard that the intern hacked into my computer, stole my password, and e-mailed the record company using my name?"

Okay, Megan thought. *Engels and the agents are listening. Stay calm. Let's see where this goes. Maybe I'll hit a trigger and get a confession.* "Yes, I did. I heard that on the news. Unbelievable."

"He e-mailed MacCabe saying I wanted to meet with him one on one. Then MacCabe responded and said he'd meet me in New York, and to confirm, I needed to say on *Leno* that I was going to New York."

"How did you find out? Did you read it?"

"No, Engels called me. He told me every detail—what happened, where and when the rendezvous was. He told me to say I was going to New York, but to travel on to Austin, that he would go to New York and catch whoever was behind all this."

"So that's why you said that on the show. I noticed. Before I left the office, you hadn't mentioned anything about New York to me. But then again, it was a horrible week for all of us, and communication was bad."

Ripley didn't answer at first. "It *was* bad. After Engels called, I kept wondering who could be behind that e-mail—who had access to my passwords, my computer. Obviously, you and Simon did, but Simon was in the hospital in a coma."

Megan held her breath.

"Megan, I'm not stupid. After his call, I decided to hire a private investigator to see who showed up at the AquaGrill—to find out for myself who was behind all this." Then Ripley dropped the bomb. "The intern wasn't the only one at the restaurant in New York last Wednesday night, was he? Just like the intern wasn't the only one behind MacCabe's e-mail, or the only one digging into my personal unfinished business. The intern's just not that smart, now, is he, Megan?"

Judd made the turn onto I-65 South more than five miles behind Ripley and Megan. The white Jake's Plumbing van carrying Engels and the other agents peeled out of the Vanderbilt medical complex and was at least fifteen miles in back of Judd. The engineers working the surveillance gear tracked Megan on the cell phone's GPS while listening in on the conversation. One of them gave directions to Judd via his cell phone. After Ripley revealed that he knew Megan was in New York, Engels said out loud, "Keep your cool. Just hold it together. Don't freeze up. Keep asking questions. Keep Ripley talking."

Megan looked over at Ripley. "Believe it or not, Judd tricked me, too. He used me to gain access to you. But at the time, he told me we needed to get to you to protect you—to keep you from walking into a trap."

"Good girl!" Engels said.

Ripley fired back, "Don't try and spin this. I'm on to you, Megan. I gave you and only you the paperwork to FedEx to Strickland. You were the only one that had access to that information. So how the hell did some intern get my password to e-mail MacCabe and then write, 'We have some unfinished business'? The intern knew about *my* unfinished business? About the side agreement with Strickland? I don't think so. It was you. Why did you read it, Megan? I told you it was confidential. Who else did you show it to? What about the transfer of funds? Did you tell anybody about that?"

"Ripley, I swear I did not hack into your computer. I did not e-mail MacCabe. I just sent the FedEx out. I don't know what you're talking about."

"You're lying! You should never have gone against Ripley Graham. You were the one pulling the strings and using the intern. He didn't trick you. Do you really think I'm that stupid?"

Megan tried to regain some composure but couldn't keep her hands from trembling. Ripley was driving dangerously fast in the bad weather.

She prayed Judd and the van were close. She knew Engels was listening and tried to think of something to say. "What about Strickland? He must have told somebody, and they hacked into your computer."

Back in the van, Engels said, "Good! Keep talking."

"That's insane," Ripley said. "Strickland had too much to lose. It was you. You just couldn't let it go, could you?"

"Ripley, you've got it wrong."

From I-65, Ripley unpredictably took Exit 59-B onto a short stretch of State Highway 840 West. Construction on the massive highway had been put on hold when local environmentalists filed a suit citing irreparable damage to the hill country's ecosystem and the disruption of Indian burial grounds. Soon afterward, the state had stopped the roadwork. The combination of a legal battle and shrinking state and federal funds had caused the project to be all but abandoned.

"What road is this?" Megan asked.

Ripley didn't answer. She could tell he thought it was a suspicious question. He seemed to be shutting down. Megan knew she needed to hit a trigger, but she was starting to panic. She had to believe Engels was listening and that Judd had called every law enforcement agency by now. She didn't want to think what might happen if they had lost contact.

Coming into view on both sides of the highway were bright yellow electronic warning signs. Megan read the message out loud: "S.R. 840 now closed—1 mile ahead."

Ripley turned his head and looked at her. *Oh, God, he knows what I'm doing,* Megan thought.

Tracking her, the van told Judd to look for the 840 West exit. Judd was so nervous he could hardly breathe. Engels said out loud, "Come on, Megan, ask a question. Keep talking."

"Did your dad live out here by himself?" Megan asked.

"Good girl!" Engels said again.

Ahead of them were several orange-and-white-striped concrete barriers across the highway. Ripley followed the yellow arrows marking the mandatory exit, which led onto Columbia Pike.

Then he began to speak as if he were in a trance. "My old man was the devil. All he wanted was to beat the crap out of me. But I finally got strong enough to retaliate, and so he moved out here. Today, it's time to put all that ancient history to rest. Ripley Graham will finally complete his unfinished business."

Megan was lost. She didn't know where they were or how they had gotten there. After several turns, they were now speeding down a badly paved, unmarked county road. As the rain ran down her side window, all she saw were metal fence posts, barbed wire, cattle crossings, and endless acres of hillside farmland. She didn't know what Ripley was talking about or where he was taking her.

Without explanation, Ripley slowed the SUV and pulled onto the shoulder, where he drove slowly until he found a narrow open gate in the overgrown fence line. He gunned the engine and drove the truck through the opening, going completely off-road up a muddy incline into an overgrown pasture. Ripley blazed a trail, mud churning behind them. Without letting off the gas, he drove across the pasture, then through a tree line and into another clearing in the rolling hill country. Megan saw a decaying wooden shack with an old Ford pickup truck parked next to it. Ripley headed for the side of the cabin, where he stopped the Escalade next to the old Ford and cut the engine. Before he took the keys out of the ignition, Megan opened the door and started to make a run for it. Ripley lunged across the seat, grabbed her by the arm, and pulled hard.

"What are you doing?" Megan screamed.

"Megan, you never should have lied. You never should have turned against Ripley Graham."

Shaken and distraught, Megan asked the first question that popped into her head. "Why do you do that? When you get upset, why do you refer to yourself as Ripley Graham?"

Ripley opened his door and pulled her out of the truck. Megan jerked her arm away, but Ripley grabbed her again, put both her arms behind her back, and pushed her toward the cabin.

"Ripley, what are you doing?" she screamed again.

At first, he didn't respond. Then he said coldly, "I'm not Ripley. Ripley is inside."

CHAPTER 64

Southwest Williamson County, Tennessee

Judd exited the abandoned Highway 840, took Columbia Pike South, then turned right onto Thompsons Station Road heading west, per the van's instructions. He had already passed Evergreen Road and sensed he had gone too far. He stopped the car on the shoulder and spoke into his cell phone. "There's nothing out here. What should I do?"

One of the engineers watching the monitors said, "Hold tight. We're checking. It seems her GPS signal is weakening."

"This is not good. Judd missed a turn somehow," Engels said.

The engineer heard the SUV's door slam. He said out loud to Engels, "That was Megan. Why did she scream?"

Engels turned to the second engineer. "Refresh her signal. Judd may have driven too far."

"Did someone say Megan screamed?" Judd said.

"Please stay calm," Engels said.

Judd fired back, "Stay calm? This is now a hostage situation!"

The second engineer said, "Judd, you need to turn around. They've gone off-road and are rapidly moving out of range. They definitely took a turn that you missed."

The other engineer said, "GPS shows we didn't miss a paved county road, so they've definitely gone off-road. We still have a slight signal."

"With all your gear, how the hell do you lose a six-thousand-pound truck, for Christ's sake?" Judd said.

"Judd, turn your car around and look for a dirt road or a private gate," Agent Engels replied. "Her signal is now going due north. Look to your left."

Everyone got quiet. Judd did as instructed and looked out the driver's-side window through the rain for an unmarked side road. "There's no road to my left—just a huge mountainside with patches of farmland squared off by tree lines."

"They've turned off-road up into that hillside. Keep looking for a dirt road or a cattle crossing—a gate, a break in the fence, anything. They are exactly due north of you."

"I'm looking! It's just a mountain with farmland—nothing else."

Engels broke the silence that followed. "Okay, Megan, say something. Keep the conversation going. Don't stop now."

The old, run-down, one-room hunting cabin had a dilapidated front porch and two side windows. Inside, the décor consisted of nothing more than two deer heads—bucks with full racks—mounted on the wall alongside a small, square mirror. The furnishings were sparse—a natural-gas stove and oven, a wooden table with two chairs, and a military-style green foldable cot. The place was littered with hunting gear—camouflage hats, vests, and several hunting magazines. Other than the cigarette butts on the floor, the only other object in the cabin was a six-foot black metal gun safe pushed against one of the side windows.

Standing just inside the door, Megan was too frightened to think about what she was supposed to ask next. The cell phone was still in the pocket of her jean jacket, but now she doubted if anyone was picking up the signal this far out in the country.

Ripley picked up one of the chairs and moved it over by the stove.

He looked at Megan and said, "Sit down." Megan moved to the chair as Ripley sat in the other, leaned back, and put his boots on the table. He stared at Megan without saying a thing.

"What are we doing here?" Megan asked.

Ripley didn't answer immediately. "I first came to this place six years ago—the night my brother and mother went down in the river. The cops brought me here to stay with my old man. The next day, I took him back to the site of the accident. They had pulled my mom's body out of the river early that morning, but they didn't find my brother. My old man and I watched from the riverbank while they dragged the car out of the water. After a while, he said, 'Let's walk.' We walked downstream. Then he said, 'We'll come back after dark.'"

Megan stared at the floor, avoiding eye contact. Her heart was racing.

"So we did. My old man had figured out that the highway patrol was looking for my brother's body in the wrong place. We walked with flashlights downriver to a beaver dam he had seen that afternoon. He stripped down and jumped in. The water was cold. I honestly didn't care if he got hypothermia and drowned. He'd come up and then go back down again. After about ten minutes, he finally came up pulling what at first looked like a log, but it wasn't. It was Ripley."

Megan felt faint.

"My old man got out, put his clothes on, and said, 'Come on.' We carried my brother out of the woods, put him in the truck, and brought him back here. We laid him out right here on this table." Ripley kicked the table with the heel of his boot.

"Oh, God," Megan said.

"My old man dug graves for a living to where he was sick of it. He'd say, 'A dead body six feet under is a waste of space. The dead should be turned to ashes. It's the proper way.'"

Megan was sure she didn't want to know more. *Where is Engels?* she thought. *What does Ripley have to say for Engels to get me out of here? Where is Judd?*

"A few days later, he drove me home to Clarksville to collect my things. He looked through our mail hoping there would be some money. That's when he found the letter from Simon about the recording session. My old man didn't care about Simon's letter. He was looking for a check. I told him the winner didn't get a check but a chance to record some songs. He grew furious and started yelling, 'Where's the damn check?' I took the letter with Simon's information and hitchhiked to Nashville. I left my old man there looking for spare change in the sofa. I never saw him again. He died of alcohol poisoning the next year. That was when I claimed my inheritance. I got my old man's cabin and my brother's recording career."

Forget about the confession. Just get me out of here! Megan thought.

Ripley took his feet off the table, walked over to the gun safe, and started working the combination lock. "I told you I had some unfinished Ripley Graham business to take care of. It's in here."

He pulled the handle of the safe and opened the door wide. Megan noticed several hunting rifles inside. Then she heard a thud. A body bag rolled onto the floor.

"All that's left is to give him a proper burial. Ashes to ashes, dust to dust."

"What just happened?" one of the engineers asked, responding to Megan's scream.

"I think we found the dead brother," Engels said dryly.

Judd pulled to a stop on the shoulder and said into his phone, "Got it. Right in front of me is a metal gate with fresh tire marks. It has to be where they turned off. But the mud is thick, and the incline may be too steep for my Honda."

"That's got to be it," Engels said. "Can you tell where it goes?"

"Just straight into the pasture."

"Go for it. Follow the tire marks."

Ripley took one rifle and a duffel bag from the gun safe and put them on the table. He opened the bag and removed a pistol. Megan saw it and instinctively made a run for the door, but Ripley turned and grabbed her from behind. She screamed until he put a hand over her mouth and the butt of the pistol on her right temple and said, "Oh, no, no, no."

Ripley pushed her back into the chair with the gun still pointed at her head, got the duffel bag, and dropped it on the floor next to her. He grabbed some rope and duct tape from the bag, taped her mouth, and tied her hands and feet. Megan started slipping into a state of shock as Ripley opened the body bag. She slumped over and fell off the chair, roped and tied like a rodeo calf.

Ripley carefully laid the skeleton onto the table. "It's time for you to finally leave me alone," he said. He moved his index finger around the circumference of a bullet hole in the skull. Then he turned to Megan and shouted, "You and Simon and that intern should never have started digging into my personal business! You shouldn't have turned against me!"

Judd gunned the gas and was halfway up the incline when the Honda started to fishtail, then got bogged in the mud and slid backward. He pressed the accelerator to the floorboard, only to hear his tires spinning helplessly as the car started to settle in the mud. "I'm stuck," he said into his cell. "I'm not waiting for you guys. I'm going to find the cabin on foot. This is insane! Confession or no confession, Ripley is dangerous."

"No, wait for us," Engels said. "You're not equipped, Judd. We've called in for backup."

But it was too late. Judd jumped out of the Honda and started running. He cleared the incline and could tell exactly where the SUV had recently passed. He ran through the hillside pasture toward the thicket and the shack on the other side.

Engels was reaching for his radio for more backup when everyone in the van heard Ripley start talking to Megan. "Here's the deal. I'm going to cremate my brother when I set this cabin on fire. This is his final resting place. We were twins, and everyone will assume these are my bones—that Ripley Graham died in a fire. Then they'll discover he has a bullet hole in his skull, so there must have been foul play before the fire. They'll also find your bones and assume you shot me before you set this place ablaze and killed yourself. The public always turns assumptions into fact. They'll create the story that works for them. They don't want to know that I shot my brother before sending him and my mother into the river. They don't want to know that I had Simon shot. They won't want to know that I killed you."

Engels shouted, "There it is! We got it."

Ripley walked over to Megan, knelt beside her so he could see her face, and said, "You will make this story even more interesting for the fans. They'll start asking, 'Why was Megan Olsen with Ripley Graham in the cabin?' They'll assume you were an insanely jealous assistant that was getting too personal, so Ripley had to fire you. But you could never live with that humiliation of being fired by your idol. So you schemed your way up here to my cabin. And you know what the fans will think—that Ripley was so nice he probably invited you so he could let you down easy. And all the while, you were thinking, *If I can't have Ripley Graham all to myself, then no one is going to have him. We'll die together and be eternally connected.*"

Megan gave a muffled sob from behind the duct tape.

"After you shoot me in the head, do you want to know how you kill yourself? With the gas stove." Ripley stood, walked over to the oven, opened the door, and cranked the gas on high. "There'll be questions—an official investigation. But it won't turn up anything. The fans' story always becomes fact. For years to come, people will travel to this spot and place bouquets on the hallowed ground. They'll write love letters and leave stuffed animals and plastic flowers. This is a fitting place for you and Ripley Graham to rest together eternally. And you'll both be cremated. It's the proper way."

CHAPTER 65

The Cabin

Totally soaked and caked in mud, Judd sprinted a quarter-mile through the thicket and up and down a steep, wooded ravine, slipping several times as he followed the broken branches and tire tracks. He finally came to the clearing, where he spotted the cabin, the black Escalade, and an old red pickup he'd never seen before. The window on the side where the vehicles were parked was blocked by a large piece of furniture pushed against it from inside. Judd figured it must be for privacy. Even though the window on the far side was partly covered by small trees and bushes, it allowed a view inside. Nearly crawling, he made his way to it.

When he peered into the cabin, his heart nearly stopped. Megan was lying on the floor face down, her mouth taped and her hands and feet tied. A dark skeleton lay on top of a wooden table. There was an oven with its door wide open. The piece of furniture pushed against the far wall was actually a metal gun safe. Its door was open, and Judd saw several weapons inside. Ripley was walking around with a pistol in his hand. He reached into a duffel bag on the floor next to Megan, took out a long rope, and tied one end to the gun safe and the other to Megan's feet. There was no way she could escape on her own, even by crawling.

Ripley walked to the skeleton. "It's over." He looked directly into the empty eye sockets. "I don't want to see you ever again. Don't follow me."

Then Ripley reached into the duffel bag, pulled out a pair of brown-and-green camouflaged rain pants with suspenders, and slipped it on over his boots and jeans. He took out a matching hunting parka with a three-piece hood, put it on, and checked himself in the mirror. After he adjusted the hood, only his eyes and the upper part of his nose were visible. He could be anybody. He stood there looking for a long time but saw no other face staring back. He then turned and stepped over Megan, grabbed his hunting rifle and duffel bag, walked out the door, slammed it shut, and gave it a hard tug behind him.

As Ripley walked onto the porch, Judd remained crouched beneath the side window. He didn't move until he heard Ripley slam the truck door on the opposite side of the cabin. Judd stood and, with his back to the outside wall, inched toward the porch and peered around the corner. Ripley was in the old Ford pickup. He tried to start the engine. It was cold. He tried again. Finally, it roared to life. He revved the motor and peeled out, taking a hard left turn away from Judd's side of the cabin toward the clearing.

Judd had one foot on the porch and was about to hoist himself up when the truck skidded to a stop. Ripley stuck the rifle barrel out of the truck and aimed at the cabin's obstructed window thirty yards away. Judd lunged toward the porch. He heard the shot but didn't see the bullet crack the side window or hit the back of the gun safe on the other side. Nor did he see the spark created by the bullet's impact ignite the gas trapped inside the cabin. He did, however, feel the power of the explosion as the ignited air hit him like a derailed freight train, carrying him off the porch and dropping him fifteen feet away.

For a moment, it felt like everything was moving in slow motion. The blast first caused a painful ringing in his ears. Then Judd heard nothing. The detonation had thrown him backward and headfirst into a small ravine. The rain-soaked brush and soft soil had probably saved his life as he slid down the embankment until coming to a rest on his back with his feet slightly elevated. His hearing came back. For a peaceful moment, he heard nothing but the rain hitting his clothing and saw nothing but gray sky above him. He was numb but okay.

"Jesus." Judd took stock of his condition. Nothing was broken or bleeding. He rolled onto his side, got to his knees, and took a couple of deep breaths. He was alive. Then he remembered Megan.

When he ran back to the top of the ridge, his heart sank. The cabin was ablaze. Smoke billowed into the downpour.

"Megan!" Judd rushed to the cabin as the front wall collapsed. He felt the intense heat balloon out toward him. He hurried to the near side, where the Escalade was parked. "Megan! Megan!" The heat was extreme. He couldn't get close enough to the cabin to see inside. The roof collapsed, providing more fuel. Sparks, flames, and smoke soared skyward. Judd watched helplessly. "Oh, God," he said.

Judd looked away from the cabin and peered toward the top of the hillside, staring aimlessly at nothing. And then his eyes caught something. In the distance, just below the crest in the final pasture, he spotted Ripley driving due north across the field in the old red truck. Blind rage filling him, Judd spun around to the Escalade and opened the driver's door. The keys were in the ignition. He jumped in, brought the engine to life, stomped the accelerator, and spun out toward the tree-line opening, hellbent on revenge.

CHAPTER 66

Williamson County

The Jake's Plumbing van parked by the narrow gate on the shoulder of Thompsons Station Road near the muddy incline where Judd had abandoned his car. To passersby, it looked like a vehicle making a neighborly stop to see if someone was in need. However, within five minutes, the area had the appearance of a military outpost.

Inside the van, the two technicians talked over each other on separate headsets, fielding a barrage of incoming calls and switching them over to Agent Engels. He, in turn, spat out assignments and directed a brigade of first responders, federal and state agents, a SWAT team, Tennessee Highway Patrol officers, county sheriff personnel, and city police.

On the phone with the TBI and the FBI, Engels relayed the breaking news: "Ripley Graham is now a fugitive of the state. We released an all-points bulletin notifying all federal and state authorities that he is to be considered armed and dangerous. We believe he is traveling in a 2011 black Cadillac Escalade near his hunting cabin in southwest Williamson County, in the vicinity of Thompsons Station. We've set up roadblocks for five square miles around his property, including northbound on Seaberry Lane, westbound on Cayce Springs Road, eastbound on Columbia Pike, and southbound on both Dean Road and Evergreen Road. We also have air patrol close to I-65 looking for the Escalade."

One of the technicians called to Engels, "I've got Governor Haslam on the line for you."

"Patch him through. . . . Yes, governor."

"Agent Engels, I just read the bulletin. I don't have to tell you the media frenzy that is about to hit. It will be like nothing this state has ever seen. What do you have on Ripley, and where is he?"

"I have a recorded confession for the murder of his brother and the attempted murder of his manager. It is also possible that we have one or two more fatalities this morning at his hunting cabin, and Ripley was involved with both."

"And you are sure it is Ripley Graham's confession on these recordings?"

"Positive, sir."

"I see. And do we know his whereabouts?"

"We believe he is traveling in his SUV. We have roadblocks in place, but no SUV matching the description has been spotted." Engels followed the sound of the sirens as the first responders approached the cabin.

"Who are the possible fatalities this morning?" the governor said.

"Again, they are not confirmed, but neither Megan Olsen nor Judd Nix is accounted for at the moment."

"The young man that worked for Ripley's manager—that we arrested and released on bond?"

"Yes, sir. We have a plea bargain in place. He was helping us get information from Mr. Graham. Ms. Olsen was acting independently but was a third-party informant for us through Mr. Nix."

"Okay, carry on. Please contact me immediately with any pertinent updates. I will coordinate with the agency to set a press conference within the next hour."

"Yes, sir. Thank you, sir."

The second engineer turned to Engels. "We have the first responders at the cabin. It's in flames. There are no signs of either Megan or Judd."

"Damn it," Engels said. "Get me Sergeant Harris with the Tennessee Highway Patrol."

"I'll patch you through now."

Engels waited a moment. "Sergeant Harris?"

"Yes, Agent Engels."

"Any news from the roadblocks?"

"No, sir. Traffic is light on Sunday morning. We've seen and stopped only one Escalade. It was a female headed to church. I've got nothing."

"What about I-65 South and the 840 interchange?"

"We have helicopters patrolling. Nothing yet. And again, it's not because of heavy congestion. We've just not spotted a vehicle fitting that description on the road this morning."

"Okay, keep me posted."

"Agent Engels, I've got Deputy County Sheriff Masters on the line," one of the technicians said. "He's at the cabin."

"Patch him through. . . . This is Engels."

"Agent Engels, I hear you're our central coordinator."

"Yes. How can I help you, deputy?"

"I'm at the cabin. The fire department has the blaze under control. We were able to cut the gas line. The rain is helping now. But there isn't much left to speak of."

"Any sign of Megan Olsen or Judd Nix?"

"No, sir. No one is accounted for."

"Okay. Keep me posted."

As he hung up the phone, another call was waiting. "Agent Engels, this is Sheriff Blackstock of Williamson County. I've got television trucks and other news outlets arriving and asking to get through the roadblocks."

"No media for five square miles around the cabin," Engels said. "We need to find Ripley. We don't need TV trucks blocking the roads."

"Yes, sir. My guys will handle."

"It's the governor's office," one of the technicians said.

"This is Engels."

"Agent Engels, this is Ben Herron in the governor's office. The governor will be holding a press conference in approximately thirty-five minutes to discuss the situation. Any new information by then would be greatly appreciated."

"You'll be the first to know."

"Thank you, sir."

"Agent Engels, you've got to see this." Both engineers were watching the same GPS tracking screen.

"What is it?" Engels got up to look at the monitor.

"It's the GPS from the cell phone."

"Whose?"

"The one we gave Judd—our cell phone, the one Megan had with her in the cabin. We lost the signal after the blast, but it's up now, and the GPS tracking system is working clear as day."

"Where is it?"

"It seems to be on the site, sir, sitting in the middle of the cabin."

"How the hell did it remain intact? Have somebody go check it out."

"Yes, sir. I'm on it."

"Agent Engels," the other engineer said, "I have Deputy Sheriff Masters calling in."

"Deputy, what do you have for me?"

"We got the fire out pretty quick, but there ain't nothing left. This thing was a matchbox. Now, here's the thing. We were checking the perimeter when we noticed fresh tire tracks all around."

"So?"

"Well, there's way too many tracks for just one vehicle. And when you look close, it's obvious there are at least two sets of tracks that don't match. I'm getting photos of them now. What I'm saying is, there's been some off-road mud racing going on here in the last hour or so."

After a pause, Engels said, "You're telling me you've found at least two sets of fresh tracks up there, and no vehicles are in sight?"

"Yes, sir."

"So if Ripley had a getaway vehicle parked at the cabin, and he used it, then someone else drove the Escalade."

"That sounds about right, sir. And they were both in a real hurry. They gunned it out of here real good—dug some deep tracks, and not very long ago."

"It's Judd," Engels said. "He's still going rogue. If Ripley had a getaway vehicle, then Judd must have taken the Escalade. He's not missing. He's chasing Ripley!" Engels immediately went into action. "Okay, everyone with ears on, listen up. Ripley Graham is most likely *not* driving the black Escalade. I repeat, Ripley Graham is not in the black Escalade. I have reason to believe the Escalade is being driven by Judd Nix. We are looking for Ripley in the wrong vehicle. However, it is possible that Judd is in pursuit of Ripley while driving the Escalade. Remember, Ripley is still a fugitive of the state and should be considered armed and dangerous. We now, however, believe Judd Nix is driving the black Escalade. Again, Judd Nix is driving the Escalade, and he is working for us."

CHAPTER 67

Williamson County

Judd drove the Escalade straight up the hillside. He felt the rain was now to his advantage. He knew he must be closing in on Ripley, since he had the far superior machine.

As he came over the hilltop, he slammed on the brakes and tried to process the startling sight directly below him. At first glance, it looked like a UFO landing strip. Slicing through the mountain to his right, and for at least ten miles as far as he could see down the hill to his left, was a four-lane, unfinished gravel highway, totally abandoned. Absolutely no one was around for miles. After a minute, he realized this was the backside of the postponed Highway 840. And as soon as he figured that out, he saw Ripley and his old Ford truck rumbling onto the abandoned freeway and heading west. It was the perfect escape route.

"No, you don't!" Judd said out loud. He threw the SUV into gear and headed down the embankment. He had no time to figure out a plan of attack. *I'll just run him down,* he thought.

The Escalade easily handled several drainage crossings to gain access to the highway. Once on the road, Judd took off at high speed after Ripley. In the distance, he saw a completed overpass, also abandoned. Just beyond it was Ripley.

Judd was gaining quickly. Ripley must have noticed him in the rearview mirror because he started to pick up speed. Judd's plan was to hit him from behind and simply drive him into the rocky embankment.

The back of Ripley's head was now in clear view, and Judd noticed he was starting to look over his shoulder. *Two hundred yards.* Ripley cut the wheel of the old Ford to the left. *A hundred fifty yards.* Judd realized he had to slow his speed, since Ripley was beginning to swerve back and forth to make the angle of impact more difficult. *One hundred yards and closing.* Ripley looked over his shoulder again. There was no doubt that he now knew it was Judd gunning for him. *Fifty yards.*

Judd accelerated, anticipating Ripley's next swerve, but Ripley turned in the opposite direction. The Escalade barely scraped Ripley's left bumper. Ripley slammed on the brakes, did a three-quarter turn in the middle of the road, and came to a stop. Judd hit his brakes and turned around. A hundred yards away, Ripley sat motionless, staring at him through the passenger window.

Round two, Judd thought. He floored the gas and headed directly for Ripley, who didn't move or change his expression. *Seventy-five yards.* Judd thought, *This vehicle will smash that piece of junk into a thousand pieces.* Ripley remained stationary, willing to test his fate. *Twenty-five yards.* Judd wanted to see the whites of Ripley's eyes

Instead, he saw something he didn't expect. Ripley raised the barrel of his rifle into view. Judd ducked, cutting the wheel hard to the right at the same time. He heard the windshield of the Escalade explode, felt the sting of flying glass, and instinctively knew the speed and tilt of the SUV would cause it to roll. Judd felt the impact and heard gravel scraping the side of the vehicle. There was a sudden pain in his shoulder. He was upside down, then back up. Rainwater was pouring in on him, an airbag was in his face, and he smelled gasoline. Then everything went black.

Agent Engels was growing more frustrated by the minute. "Sergeant Harris, I think Ripley slipped our roadblocks. Get me a helicopter directly on top of I-65 and give me a feed. If Ripley got through, he could be south of Lewisburg. I also think we need a second bird looking west."

"Yes, sir. We can handle that."

Engels shouted orders to everyone in the van. "Let me know when we have the live aerial feeds. Put them through to monitors three and four. Let Herron in the governor's office know we currently have no new information. Tell both the TBI and the FBI that too much time has passed. Ripley has slipped our net, and we need to widen the search. Stop any suspicious-looking vehicles. And we're still looking for the black Escalade that Judd is hopefully now driving. If we find him, Ripley will be close. I need some leads, people!"

Both technicians responded.

"Sir, I'm sending the highway patrol helicopter feed to monitor three now."

"I'll notify law enforcement to report any and all leads."

"Sergeant Harris is standing by."

"The governor's office is standing by."

"You should see the feed on monitor three in thirty seconds."

Agent Engels looked at monitor three. The screen showed a live aerial shot of I-65. The highway patrol helicopter was traveling above the southbound traffic. Everyone in the Jake's Plumbing van watched for anything suspicious.

Judd came to as he felt the butt of a rifle in his chest and heard Ripley yell, "Get out!" Judd stayed still a moment longer, letting the fog lift. "I said get out!"

Judd opened his eyes. The Escalade was upright but badly crushed, wedged against a rock wall beside the abandoned highway. Ripley had opened his door and had his gun pointed at Judd's chest. Judd felt blood dripping down the side of his head.

"Get out or I'll just shoot you right here."

Ripley looked like he didn't have a scratch on him. Judd assumed he had missed the Ford completely when he cut the wheel to dodge the bullet. He reached down to unbuckle his seatbelt, and a bolt of pain hit his shoulder and traveled down his right arm. He winced. *Something is broken,* he thought.

"Get out of the damn truck."

Judd used his left hand and inched himself down. His head was pounding. He could take only shallow breaths. He must have bruised some ribs.

Still holding the gun to Judd's chest, Ripley said, "Stand in front of the Escalade."

Judd did as he was told. Standing in the rain, he had no idea how he was going to get out of this situation. But instead of fear, all he felt was rage as he watched Ripley. He thought, *How could any human do what he did to his family, to Simon, and especially to Megan?*

"Why are you here, trying to run me down in my own truck?" Ripley said.

Judd answered coldly, "Megan called me this morning and said you wanted to see her. She was scared, so I've been following you. My car got stuck in the mud. When you left in the red truck, I took the Escalade."

"Who else did Megan tell about my unfinished business?"

The rage built further when Ripley mentioned Megan's name without showing any sign of remorse. "She told just me."

"And what exactly did she tell you?"

Judd was starting to get dizzy. The rain washed blood across his face. "She told me about your secret deal with Strickland and about the transfer of money to Mexico. She told me what you were capable of doing."

"And she told you how to hack into my e-mail and send messages to MacCabe. How to put your nose in places it should never be."

"No."

"No? Then who did?"

"Simon."

"Simon?" Ripley seemed genuinely surprised.

"Simon told me to e-mail MacCabe. I don't know why. All I know is that it got me arrested."

Ripley lowered his eyes. "Simon turned on Ripley Graham. He became a liar and couldn't be trusted. Megan turned on Ripley Graham. She became a liar and couldn't be trusted. Judd, you're a liar, too, aren't you?"

"No."

Ripley opened his eyes wide. "Really? So let me ask you one question. And you should know your life depends on whether or not you tell me the truth."

Judd was lightheaded. Feeling a sharp pain in his abdomen, he leaned back against the front of the truck to keep himself from falling over.

"Who did *you* tell my personal business to?"

"No one," Judd said without hesitation.

"You're lying!"

Judd didn't move.

Ripley pressed the rifle underneath Judd's chin and lifted his head. "Did you tell anybody else you were following me today?"

"No."

"Liar! Give me your cell phone."

Judd realized this was the end. Ripley was going to check his outgoing calls and see that he had been talking to Agent Engels all day. And then Ripley would kill him.

"Give me your cell phone!"

Judd reached into his pocket and handed over his cell.

But Ripley didn't check his calls. "You're just like Simon and Megan. You can't be trusted. So here's what I'm going to do. Before I shoot you and disappear, I'm going to text Engels from your phone and tell him that you posted bail so you could go to the cabin and kill Megan and me. It will be your confession and suicide note."

Judd watched as Ripley opened his phone. Ripley studied it for a moment, then started to text.

"Wait!" Judd said. "If you want to keep everything a secret, there's only one way."

Ripley looked up from the cell.

"You and I both know a text isn't going to hold up. Anyone can pick up another person's phone and text from it. What you need is for *me* to leave you a voicemail message on your cell saying I'm going to kill you and Megan. A recorded confession will hold up in court."

Judd had gotten Ripley's attention. "And why would you do that?"

"Because I'd rather end up alive in jail than dead out here."

Ripley paused for a moment. "Okay." He dialed his cell-phone number from Judd's cell. A moment later, Ripley's cell started to buzz in his pocket. He handed Judd his cell back and said, "Go ahead. Leave me the message."

Judd took his phone from Ripley, cradled it with both hands close to his mouth, and then hit the off button. "No, not right here. You'll just kill me as soon as I finish."

"Don't you play games with me, you liar!"

Judd gestured with his head to the nearby underpass. "I'll take a little walk there—out of range of your target practice. Then I'll turn around and leave a confession on your phone, telling you I posted bail so I could kill you and Megan. Once you hear it, you can leave your phone here in the Escalade for Engels to find, then get in your Ford and drive away. I will gladly walk away from this wreck and live my life in prison. And if I don't leave that message, you can get in your truck and come gun me down."

Ripley stood silently for a moment, then said, "Okay. But if you go one step beyond the underpass, you're dead." *And guess what?* Ripley thought. *After you leave the message, you're dead anyway.*

Judd didn't dare look back. He just walked toward the underpass with his hands cradling his cell phone. When he got halfway there, he inauspiciously dialed Engels.

"Judd?"

Without explanation, Judd said in a low voice, "Ripley's standing in the middle of the unfinished Highway 840, directly over the hill behind the cabin. I'm under the overpass. You've got about thirty seconds to get here or I'm a dead man." Then he hung up.

When he reached the underpass, he turned around. Ripley was standing in the middle of the road next to his Ford. Judd redialed Ripley's cell. It went straight to voicemail.

"Ripley, this is Judd Nix," he said. "I know you killed your mother and brother. I know you hired a hit on Simon. I just witnessed you torture and murder Megan Olsen. And now you intend to kill me. But instead, you're going to start a global media frenzy. *Everyone* is about to know your business. You're finished!"

Judd hung up and stood motionless. Ripley looked like he had his phone to his ear. A second later, Ripley lunged into the driver's seat and headed directly toward him. Judd stood facing the oncoming vehicle. Fifteen seconds seemed like an eternity. And then he heard the roar of a police helicopter behind him. The powerful wind from its rotor started to blow rain and gravel across the highway. Ripley stopped the truck.

Directly above him, Judd heard what sounded like an army of police cars, SWAT personnel, and first responders lining the overpass, lights shining and sirens going. A second police helicopter headed in low from the west.

Then he heard a booming voice from a megaphone on the overpass. It was Agent Engels. "Ripley Graham, you are under arrest. Leave the vehicle with your hands up. I repeat, you are under arrest. You are surrounded. Come out and no one will get hurt."

Ripley opened his door and slowly walked into the middle of the abandoned highway in the pouring rain. Two aerial cameras filmed the arrest from the police helicopters. Without question, the world would soon be watching.

Judd walked behind one of the underpass pylons—out of Ripley's view, out of view of the cameras—and immediately collapsed.

CHAPTER 68

THE NEXT DAY

London
Kensington
Royal Garden Hotel
Monday, March 21

The image had been playing around the world continuously for twenty-four hours. Every domestic and international outlet, from CNN to the BBC—major networks, cable channels, satellite, Internet—was showing the same footage from an unfinished highway near the rural hillside community of Thompsons Station, Tennessee. A dozen or more police and emergency vehicles, all with lights flashing and sirens blaring, were above and around an old red Ford pickup truck. SWAT team members and sharpshooters were positioned in the rain on an overpass, while other heavily armed law-enforcement personnel were stationed behind their vehicles on the wet gravel highway. Then, as the aerial camera zoomed in close, there was Ripley Graham opening the door and slowly stepping out, dressed in camouflaged hunting gear, hands straight up in the air. Officers rushed him from behind, drove him hard onto the wet gravel, and secured his arms behind him.

The overhead lights in the Palace Suite Banquet Hall were dimmed. Several spotlights were positioned on Warren MacCabe as he stood at the podium addressing the shareholders. His image was magnified behind him on the giant video screen. It was standing room only. Cameras and press lined the back wall. MacCabe was poised and articulate:

> Fellow shareholders, board of directors, Galaxy presidents, and members of the press. The music industry sold more than $25 billion worth of recorded music last year. Today, Galaxy Records is the third-largest record company in the world. Three years ago, I had marked this day on my calendar as the most important in the history of Galaxy. It would be the day the world heard of a corporate merger making us the largest record company on the planet.
>
> Never in my wildest dreams could I have predicted the events of the last two weeks. Today, no one is talking about a successful merger. This morning, every news outlet is running images of the arrest of Ripley Graham, the most successful artist at this time. As that scene is played over and over around the globe, I realize Galaxy's turbulence in the last weeks has been created by its own form of corporate violence. James Clark, a loyal servant of this corporation, was pressured into an early resignation. Tommy Strickland, who many of you see as the one who epitomizes company loyalty, is guilty of gross negligence by usurping his authority and undermining his office. Doug Tillman, who recently was considered one of our corporate elite, groomed for greatness, is also guilty of horrendous corporate misjudgment.
>
> My lifelong goal to create the largest, most successful record company in the world is no more. Today, I stand before you a humbled servant and admit that the company's philosophy of winning at *any* cost has caused us to lose at *all* costs. To reach new heights and discover new horizons, an expedition must have great leadership and great courage. Otherwise, the exploration will assuredly falter if the leader is afraid to take a stand or falls asleep at his post.
>
> And it is with that realization that I know there is no one to blame but me for our corporate miscalculations and misdirection. I was ultimately the one that this body entrusted to guide this ship. To say I'm sorry to all of you gathered here is simply not enough. You had greater expectations of me than this deplorable last performance. Therefore, I con-

cluded moments ago with much regret that the only honorable act left for me is to hand over my letter of resignation to the Board of Directors.

CHAPTER 69

THE NEXT DAY

Nashville
VUMC
Tuesday, March 22

Judd lay motionless and heavily medicated in intensive care at VUMC. For the past two days, he had been in and out of consciousness. The impact from the Escalade's roll had ruptured his spleen, dislocated his shoulder, and fractured three ribs. However, his vitals were strong and improving.

The privacy curtain opened. "It's time, Judd Nix. You know it's time to wake up and enjoy this bright spring day the Lord hath made. Drivin' in, I saw red buds and white blossoms poppin' everywhere." Shirley leaned over and checked the level of his neck IV, connected under his collarbone. "I don't think you remember, but Agent Engels came by last night and said all of the charges against you have been dropped. And this morning, I know you're goin' to want to see who is comin' up the elevator." Judd remained immobile under the sheets. "You're just not goin' to believe it!"

As Shirley checked the monitors, Megan walked in the door with Mathew right behind her.

"There you are. I've been thinkin' about you all morning," Shirley said. Seeing Mathew, she added, "Hi, sweetheart. I'm glad you're here, too."

Mathew smiled. "Megan wanted to surprise Judd."

"Well, he's not going to believe his eyes."

Megan asked in a quiet voice, "How's he doing today?"

"Better. He opened his eyes for me twice yesterday, then just closed them right back. He didn't care for one minute that I was here. And I know he doesn't remember any of the kind and wonderful things I did for him."

Megan forced a smile. "Is it okay if we sit here awhile?"

"Of course, sweetheart. This is right where you need to be." Shirley checked the flow of meds dripping through the plastic tubing. "I'll be in and out. They usually limit visits in the ICU. But don't worry, I'm not going to say a thing. You two just sit here as long as you want." She came over and gave Megan a much-needed embrace. "Judd's gonna be fine. Don't worry. We won't lose this one."

As Shirley walked out, Megan unfolded her copy of the morning's *USA Today*. Although she was prepared to read about Simon, she didn't expect it to be on the front page above the fold—with a large color photo.

Simon Stills Dies One Day after Ripley Graham's Dramatic Arrest; Music City Mourns Loss of Respected Artist Manager

By Brian Mansfield

Nashville—Artist manager Simon Stills died yesterday, only one day after the world watched an extraordinary sequence of events unfold in the ongoing saga of famed country singer turned fugitive Ripley Graham. Stills, Graham's personal manager and alleged target in the March 9 Opry House shootings, died Monday evening at Vanderbilt University Medical Center in Nashville of complications from a gunshot wound.

Music Row colleagues, industry executives and artists alike mourn the loss of one of their own. Stills was highly respected as a manager and music-industry leader. A common theme from those closest to him was his unwavering desire to share his knowledge and passion about the music business.

Megan dropped her head, closed her eyes, and cried—again. She was overwhelmed by the loss, the endless questioning, and now the deepening concern that Judd could also take a turn for the worse. The unexplainable had already happened once.

Judd's head turned slightly toward Megan. Then his leg moved from under his sheet. Megan noticed and quickly stood. "Judd, are you awake?" She reached for his hand.

Judd felt a tingling in his hands and feet. The fog was starting to lift. Trying to gather his senses, he thought he heard Megan. But how was that possible?

"Judd," Megan said. "How are you feeling?"

The voice came from right beside him. Again, Judd stayed still. Then she appeared like an angel at the side of his bed.

"Hello," Megan said, smiling.

Judd blinked. He couldn't believe his eyes. She was radiant, more beautiful than ever. Was he dreaming? "You're here? How are you here?" He squeezed her hand. "You look perfect."

"I'm fine," she replied, squeezing back. "I'm perfectly fine now."

"I don't understand. I was at the cabin. You were lying on the floor. I was trying to get to the door when the whole thing exploded. I remember the blast."

"I know, I know. We can talk about it later. You need your rest."

Judd kept remembering. "Ripley left in the truck, and I saw him take out his rifle. Then I felt the heat from the explosion. I saw the cabin burn."

"It's okay, Judd. We're both okay. That's all that matters."

"But how?" Judd tried to sit up and get closer but was leveled by a jolt of pain.

"Okay. Just lie still and I'll tell you everything." Megan pulled her chair closer to the bed and sat back down. "When Ripley left the cabin, I knew he was going to blow it up. He told me everything he was doing. He tied me to the gun safe so I couldn't escape. But lucky for me, he tied the rope to a shelf inside. As soon as he left the cabin, I pulled myself across the floor, crawled into the safe, and closed it—just before the explosion. I prayed to God it was fireproof. They had to cut the safe open when they finally tracked the phone signal."

"She is one smart chickadee," Shirley crowed, coming in and seeing Judd awake. "While you were nappin', everybody's been talkin' about what a quick thinker she is. But I told Megan you didn't have any reason to wake up until she arrived."

Judd smiled sleepily at Shirley and nodded.

"Now, let me check your vitals."

Judd couldn't take his eyes off Megan. "I can't believe you kept your head together in a situation like that."

"Girl, I'd give you a Purple Heart for courage!" Shirley said.

"Me? How about Judd? He's the one who came after me and then chased down Ripley. Ripley would have gotten away otherwise."

Judd wanted to hear more about Megan. "And the gun safe was fireproof. The safe worked."

"I'm living proof. I got lucky and found a safe place just in time."

As soon as she said those words—*a safe place*—she felt an inner peace flow through her. That was it—*a safe place*. That was what Simon had taught her, to find her safe place. Simon's words in some way had helped save her. Megan sat motionless as the realization grew. Then she looked at Judd with a sense of joy and wonder.

Judd's vital signs jumped. He had seen that glance before.

ACKNOWLEDGMENTS

This book would have never been written or published without the unwavering encouragement of my wife, Maral Missirian-Dill, the ultimate in-house editor and PR agent. We spent countless hours reading aloud, discussing plot lines, editing, and reediting long before I contacted a publisher. Over time, our little project expanded into a family affair. I love the fact that our son, Ohan, has become an avid reader of thrillers over the years and read this manuscript several times before its completion. His stamp of approval was mandatory. Our daughter, Ani, has become the true poet of our family, and I predict she will one day create meaningful works that far exceed any ability I may possess.

With that said, my deep appreciation also goes to my extended family, starting with my parents. The Reverend Dr. Stephen F. Dill has written something every week of his life, an amazing pursuit to witness. My mother, Ruth, is dedicated not only to the art of teaching but to teaching all things good by example. Then there are my highly accomplished siblings, Dr. Reeves Dill, Dr. Laurie Dill, and Chris Tesch. Each in their own way has contributed to my desire to make them proud. I always feel fortunate for my "genetic lotto win" as the little brother born into their lives. And I am so grateful to be in the lives of Larry, Susan, Stephen, Rebecca, Andrew, Edward, and Martin.

And then there are the Armenians. I didn't just marry an incredible woman, I married her amazing family. I am at a loss to describe what it feels like to be "taken in" and "claimed" by a culture with a history as old as the creation story. The family members opened up a world I never knew existed and now cannot imagine living without. They shared their abiding love with an *odarr*—a stranger—and I will never forget that. Thank you, Raphael A. and Anahid Missirian, Mania, Sonia, Vahe, Sevan, Talar, Nina, Shaunt, Haiig, Raffi K., Keri, and Raf Saraf.

I also owe a debt of gratitude to several non-family "family members."

I thank Derek Crownover, Allen Blevins, Marilyn Blevins, and Danni O'Neill—my career guardians.

I thank my new family at John F. Blair, Publisher—Carolyn Sakowski, Angela Harwood, Brooke Csuka, Margaret Couch, Steve Kirk, Debbie Hampton, Artie Sparrow, Jaci Gentile, and Heath Simpson, and also Frye and Nancy Gaillard for making the connection.

I thank my early readers and encouragers—Marc Gerald, Carolyn Greeven, Bob Weber, Dr. Brian Spector, Alex Kronomer, Rev. Cameron Randle, Sen. Roy Herron, Julie Colbert, Greg Oswald, Doug and Pat Ralls, Darrilyn and Jeff Cameron, Frank Weimann, Mel Berger, Jay Mandel, Grace Carlson, Jo Dee Messina, Marshall Chapman, Rodney Crowell, Nancy Russell, Bob Kinkead, Greg Janese, Sandy Friedman, and Lori Lousararian.

Finally, all my gifted clients over the past twenty-six years have in some way contributed not only to this fictional story but also to my real-life story. As someone once said, "A manager is a midwife of dreams." And there is nothing more beautiful than witnessing the birth of one's own dream. For that, I thank you.

A NOTE ON THE TYPE

Adobe Jenson is an old style serif typeface drawn for Adobe Systems by type designer Robert Slimbach. Its Roman styles are based on a Venetian oldstyle text face cut by Nicolas Jenson in 1470, and its italics are based on those by Ludovico Vicentino degli Arrighi. The result is a highly readable typeface appropriate for large amounts of text.